MARKED

THE ELITE SERIES: BOOK TWO
CHARLEY BLACK

C.BLACK PUBLISHING

Digital ISBN: 979-8-9923095-1-5

Print ISBN: 979-8-9923095-5-3

CONTENTS

T/C WARNINGS

Content Warning: This is a dark paranormal romance with explicit sexual content, graphic violence, and mature themes. The story includes a child in serious medical danger, power dynamics in romantic relationships, captivity, coercion, systemic oppression, and morally complex choices. Characters engage in deception, espionage, and psychological manipulation. The book contains detailed descriptions of combat, injury, and blood. While containing moments of tenderness, this is NOT a light read.

Recommended for adult readers (18+) comfortable with dark romance, morally gray characters, and emotionally intense situations.

WHO SHOULD AVOID THIS BOOK:

Definitely skip if you're triggered by:
- Children in serious danger/medical crisis
- Leverage/coercion using family members
- Power imbalance in romantic relationships

- Captivity/imprisonment scenarios
- Graphic violence and blood
- Systemic oppression themes

Proceed with caution if sensitive to:
- Morally gray protagonists
- Betrayal in romantic relationships
- War/terrorism themes
- Class warfare/revolution
- Dubious consent elements
- Psychological manipulation

This book is NOT suitable for:
- Readers under 18 (explicit sexual content, violence)
- Anyone seeking "fluffy" romance
- Readers needing clear heroes/villains
- Those triggered by child endangerment
- Anyone avoiding dark themes

For complete content warnings, please visit my website.
Please read responsibly and prioritize your mental health.

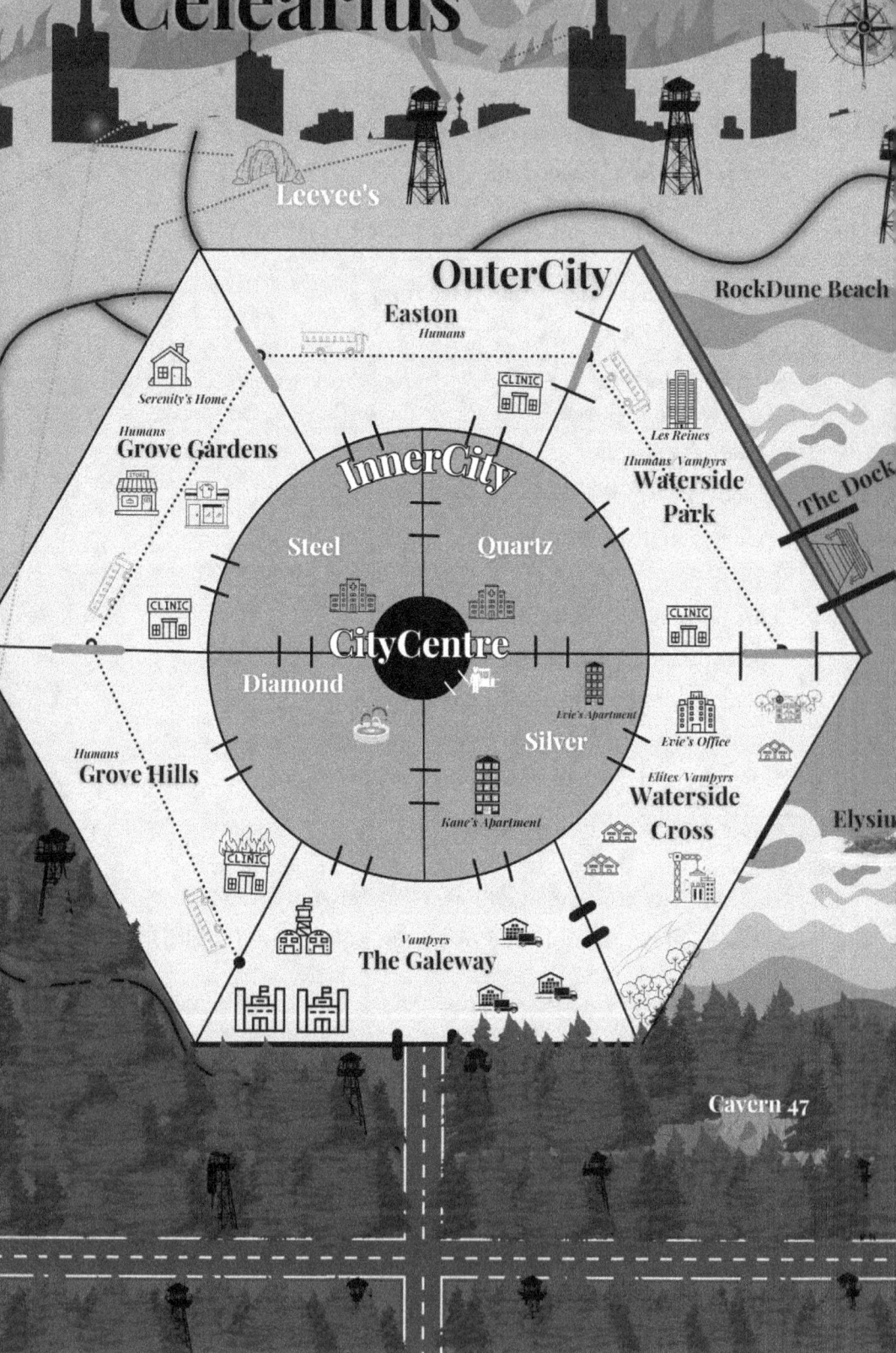

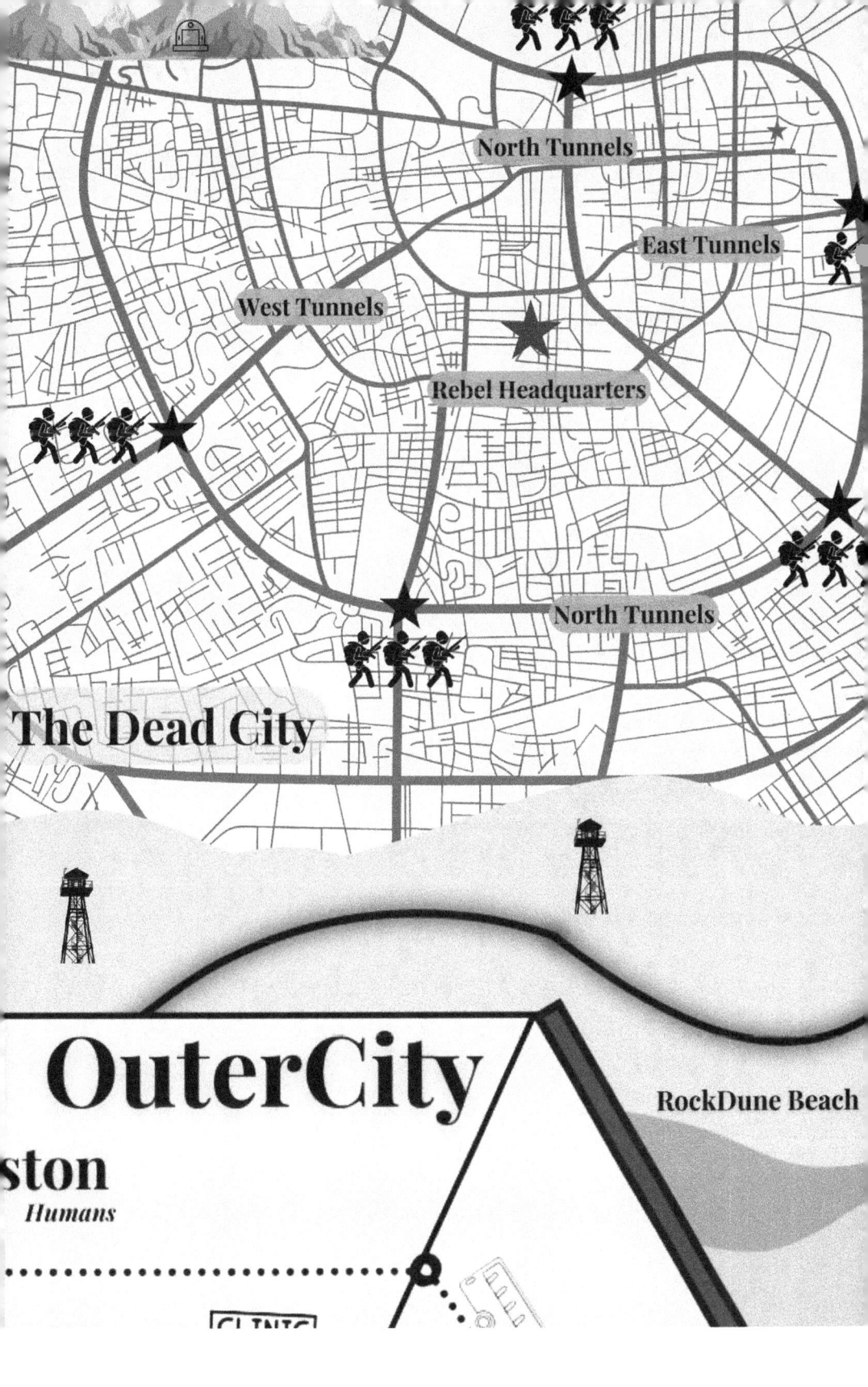

For anyone who would burn the world down to save the ones they love.

CHAPTER ONE

SERENITY

Guilt woke her before the sun did.

She opened her eyes to soft morning light filtering through pastel curtains, and for one blissful second, she didn't remember. Then it all crashed back—Kane's hands on her skin, his mouth against hers, the way he'd looked at her like she was precious beyond measure.

And then, hours later, still feeling the ghost of his touch, she'd opened an encrypted message and agreed to keep spying on him.

Serenity pressed her face into the pillow. What kind of person would betray someone they'd just slept with?

The kind of person who had a twelve-year-old sister who needed medicine to breathe, apparently. The kind who couldn't afford morality when survival was the cost.

The sunlight seemed too bright now, mocking her with its cheerfulness as it spilled across the bed. She squeezed her eyes shut against it, but the light persisted, as did the knowledge of what she'd done.

She said yes to Starr. After everything had changed.

The weight of her decision pressed down on her, making it hard to breathe. It was one thing to spy on a stranger, a vampyr she barely knew. But now? Now she'd felt his skin against hers, tasted his kiss, heard the way his breath caught when she touched him.

Her eyes flicked to the digital clock on the nightstand: 8:47 A.M. Much later than she usually woke. She'd stayed in bed deliberately, ears straining for any sound from downstairs—voices, footsteps, the distinctive hum of the elevator. Nothing.

I'm just making sure he's gone before I go downstairs, she told herself. But the lie tasted bitter. The truth was simpler: she was a coward. She couldn't bear to look into those ancient silver-blue eyes and pretend nothing had changed when everything had.

A flash of memory struck her—Kane's fingertips tracing her collarbone, his lips brushing her ear as he whispered her name like a prayer. The phantom caress lingered on her skin, making her shiver despite the warmth of the covers.

And then, with his taste still on her lips, she'd said yes to Starr. Yes to treachery.

Her stomach clenched violently. Serenity bolted upright, hand pressed to her mouth, bile rising in her throat. For a moment, she thought she might actually vomit. She swallowed hard, forcing the nausea down, and fell back against the pillows, staring blankly at the ceiling.

What have I done?

Kane's resources had transformed her family's life. The specialized medicine for Beth, which had been impossibly expensive before, arrived without question. The nurse came to check on her mother almost daily to ensure she was taking her medicine properly. The fully stocked kitchen, the security of knowing they wouldn't starve before winter.

All of it came from him.

Serenity traced her finger along the silk sheets. She could still smell him—that intoxicating blend of cedar and night air that clung to her skin, her hair, the sheets tangled around her. His scent wrapped around her like a tangible reminder of her duplicity.

"It's for Beth," she whispered to the empty room. "For my father's legacy."

But even as the words left her lips, they rang hollow. Yes, she'd agreed to spy because she couldn't bear the thought of Beth being forced into contracts like hers—becoming an Elite, bound to vampyrs, her blood and body no longer her own. Because her father had died for the rebellion's cause, and she owed him this much.

But Kane had never threatened her family. Had never even hinted at it. He'd only ever offered protection.

The sheets felt suddenly suffocating. Serenity threw them off and forced herself to stand, avoiding her reflection in the mirror as she dressed mechanically in a simple shirt and pants.

Each step down the staircase felt heavier than the last. The apartment was quiet, sunlight streaming through the tall windows, illuminating dust motes that danced in the still air. She paused at the bottom, listening. Nothing but the soft hum of the climate system.

Relief washed through her as she entered the empty kitchen, bathed in amber morning light. Kane must have already left for the day.

Then her eyes caught on an object at the center of the island—a sleek black folder emblazoned with the Elite Program insignia and her name. Her contract. Her heart stuttered as she approached, fingers hesitant as they traced the embossed silver symbol.

A note in Kane's elegant script lay atop it: *"For your consideration. No rush."*

Serenity sank into a chair, the cool marble beneath her fingertips a stark contrast to the heat rising in her cheeks. She flipped open the folder, scanning through familiar clauses about blood donation schedules and compensation, until her eyes landed on a section highlighted in yellow.

"Addendum: Sexual Conduct Agreement Between Parties."

Her breath caught. The legalese was impersonal, clinical even, but the implications were anything but. Kane had drafted terms for ongoing physical intimacy between them—consent parameters, privacy assurances, exclusivity clauses. One line in particular made her heart stutter: *"This agree-*

ment acknowledges the evolving nature of the relationship between patron, K. Draccus, and donor, S. Wright, and establishes mutually agreed boundaries for physical intimacy with respect to both parties' autonomy and dignity."

He'd formalized it. Made it real. Official.

Serenity's fingers trembled as she turned the page, scanning detailed clauses that spoke of mutual pleasure, protection, and—most surprisingly—her right to refuse at any time without repercussion to her Elite status or financial arrangements. The final clause stated that either party could terminate the sexual aspect of their agreement without affecting the primary blood contract.

Protection. Consideration. Respect.

The papers blurred as tears filled her eyes. Kane hadn't just wanted her body for a night. He was building a foundation—establishing trust, creating permanence. Carefully outlining her rights, ensuring her comfort and agency.

While she'd been agreeing to betray him. To dig for secrets that could destroy him. What kind of monster was she?

The folder slipped from her numb fingers. Serenity pressed both hands against the cool marble countertop, head bowed, trying to breathe through the crushing sensation in her chest. She shut the folder, unable to look at it anymore, and staggered further into the kitchen.

Her hands moved automatically, pulling ingredients from the fridge. Eggs. Butter. Vegetables. The mechanical process of cooking might dull the roaring in her head. She chopped peppers with methodical precision, the knife's rhythmic tapping against the cutting board almost hypnotic.

The sizzle of butter hitting the hot pan provided momentary relief—

The elevator hummed.

Serenity froze, pan in hand. It was Kane. The doors slid open with a soft pneumatic hiss, and Kane's unmistakable presence filled the apartment—that particular combination of power and restraint that made the air feel charged.

"Good morning." His voice carried from the entryway, casual yet somehow strained.

"You're home," she managed, keeping her back to him as she plated the eggs, grateful he couldn't see her face. "I'm making breakfast."

"My meeting concluded sooner than expected." His footsteps approached, each one making her heartbeat faster. "That smells excellent."

She forced herself to turn and place a plate on the island counter, careful to avoid direct eye contact. "Would you like some? I made more than enough."

Kane moved into the kitchen space with that fluid grace that seemed effortless despite his imposing frame. "Yes, I would be pleased to join you."

He settled onto one of the barstools, his presence making the spacious kitchen feel suddenly intimate. Serenity felt his gaze on her as she placed silverware in front of him with hands that trembled ever so slightly.

"You've seen the contract," he observed, nodding toward the closed folder.

Serenity swallowed hard. "I glanced at it."

A heavy silence settled between them as she took the seat across from him. The marble island stretched between them like a chasm—close enough to touch, too far to bridge with words alone. She watched him take a measured bite of the eggs, his movements precise and controlled.

"It's well made," he said after a moment. "You have a talent for this."

Heat crept up her neck. "Thank you."

Kane set down his fork and leaned back slightly, studying her with those penetrating eyes. A muscle flickered in his jaw—so brief she might have imagined it. "I have a proposition for you, Serenity."

Her chest tightened. "A proposition?"

"Tomorrow," he continued, his expression unreadable. That same muscle twitched again, as though he were carefully choosing each word. "I'd like to arrange transportation for you to Grove Gardens. To visit your family."

The words hit her like a physical blow. She stared at him, unable to process what he'd just said. "What?"

"Your mother, your sister." Kane's voice softened marginally. "I imagine you miss them. And I suspect Beth misses you as well."

His thoughtfulness struck her like a blade between her ribs. The genuine consideration in his voice made her guilt swell until she could barely breathe. He'd remembered Beth's name. Remembered how much she missed her family. While she'd been plotting against him, he'd been planning this kindness.

"That's..." She swallowed hard. "That would be wonderful. Thank you."

Kane nodded, a ghost of a smile touching his lips before vanishing. "I've already made arrangements. The car will be ready at ten tomorrow morning."

Serenity stared at her plate, unable to meet his gaze. The eggs congealed, untouched. He had planned this for her. After she had conspired against him.

"About the contract," Kane continued, his tone shifting subtly. "I need to know where you stand on it."

Her fingers tightened around her fork. "I haven't had time to review it properly."

"The addendum specifically." His voice dropped lower. "After last night, I thought it prudent to formalize certain... aspects of our arrangement."

Heat bloomed across her cheeks. "I understand."

Kane slid the contract closer to her, the leather folder making a soft sound against the marble countertop. "We cannot proceed further without your signature on these terms, Serenity." His voice dropped an octave, sending an involuntary shiver down her spine. "No matter how much I might..." He paused, as if the admission surprised even him. "Want to."

The double meaning hung between them. Her fingers shook slightly as she traced the edge of the folder without opening it.

"I just need time," she whispered. "Last night was new for me."

Kane moved around the island in one fluid motion, closing the distance between them with predatory grace. Suddenly, he was beside her, not touching, but close enough that she could feel the calm aura that always surrounded him—a testament to his vampyr nature, the chill that marked the boundary between life and undeath.

Their connection flared to life between them. A pulse of heat that made her breath catch. For a moment, she could have sworn she felt more through that connection—not just his desire, which wrapped around her like smoke, but a deeper emotion that felt almost like... conflict. A war being waged beneath that controlled exterior. But the sensation vanished so quickly she dismissed it as her own guilty conscience projecting.

Her body responded instantly, remembering his touch from the night before, their connection thrumming beneath her skin like a second heartbeat.

"Time," he repeated, the word a caress. "Of course. But I find myself..." He leaned closer, and she caught another flicker of that internal struggle through their connection before it disappeared. "Impatient."

Serenity turned her head, their faces now inches apart. His eyes had darkened to a stormy blue-gray, pupils dilating as they dropped to her lips. The kitchen seemed to shrink around them, the air crackling with electricity. The pull between them was magnetic, almost painful—amplified by the blood they'd already shared, the connection forged in crimson and sealed with pleasure.

"Kane," she breathed.

"Serenity," he whispered, her name like a prayer on his lips. His hand came up, hovering near her cheek without touching. "I need your signature." His voice dropped to a husky timbre. "Your explicit consent. Your..." his lips hovered a breath away from hers, "...surrender."

Her body betrayed her, leaning toward him instinctively, craving his touch. For one suspended moment, the world narrowed to just this—his silver-blue eyes, the slight part of his lips, the electric current humming between them.

The scent of him—cedar and night air with an undercurrent of iron and ancient earth—enveloped her, making her thoughts blur at the edges. His proximity was intoxicating, his restraint evident in the slight tremor of his hand still suspended near her face. That tremor spoke volumes—restraint fighting desire, control battling an emotion far more primal.

"I understand the nature of what happened between us requires formality," he continued, his eyes tracking every minute change in her expression. "But make no mistake—my desire for you hasn't diminished with the morning light."

His lips were so close now that she could feel his breath against her skin.

"I can't," she whispered, jerking backward so suddenly her stool teetered. The spell between them shattered like crystal hitting marble. Serenity scrambled to her feet, nearly knocking over her untouched plate. "I'm sorry—I need... I need air."

Kane's expression shifted—something genuine flickered across his features, too raw to be performance, before his mask slipped back into place. He straightened, creating distance between them with a single fluid step.

"Of course," he said, his voice perfectly controlled once more—perhaps too controlled, each word carefully measured. "Take all the time you need."

But the damage was done. Serenity could barely look at him, her breath coming in shallow gasps. The walls of the kitchen seemed to close in around her, the contract on the counter a silent accusation.

"Excuse me," she managed, her voice strangled.

She fled before he could respond, her feet carrying her swiftly across the apartment and up the stairs. Each step felt like an escape, yet the distance did nothing to diminish the crushing weight of her duplicity.

Back in her room, she closed the door and leaned against it, heart hammering. Her guilt and her desire were tearing her apart. She wanted him. She wanted him so badly it hurt. But once he discovered her treachery—and he would discover it eventually—he would destroy her.

She couldn't live in this fantasy. Couldn't pretend this was real when it was built on lies and encrypted messages.

Serenity moved to her bed and sank onto the edge, forcing herself to think practically. She needed a plan. She needed to find out exactly what the rebellion wanted from Kane—specific information, specific intelligence—so she could get it and be done with this nightmare. Or figure out how to walk away entirely before the ground beneath her feet opened up and swallowed her whole.

She pulled out her comm device, shaking, and stared at the dark screen. Sebastian had promised to contact her with more details. She needed those details. Needed to know what she was looking for, what secrets she was supposed to steal from a man who'd shown her nothing but kindness.

A man who'd just offered to take her home to see her family.

A man who'd drafted a contract to protect her rights even as he pursued her.

A man she was systematically undermining.

The device buzzed in her palm, making her jump. A message from Sebastian:

Today. I will meet you downstairs at 1PM. Going to Diamond District.

Serenity stared at the words, her palms growing damp. Today. She would find out what they wanted her to steal. The Diamond District—the exclusive shopping area where only vampyrs and their Elites were permitted entry. She couldn't go there alone. She would need permission. An escort.

She typed back: _I will have to ask permission._

The response came immediately: _Ask. Bring Nox._

Of course. Nox would be easier to deceive than Kane. Nox, with his kind eyes and gentle manner, wouldn't suspect her of anything more sinister than wanting to shop. She just had to hope she ran into him first, before Kane asked any questions she couldn't answer.

Putting the device on her nightstand, she lay back on the bed, staring at the ceiling as tears slipped down her temples. Tomorrow, Kane would take her home. Tomorrow, she would see Beth and her mother. Tomorrow, she would smile and thank him for his generosity while pretending her heart wasn't breaking.

But today—today she would meet with Sebastian and learn exactly what information the rebellion needed. Today, she would take the next step deeper into the maze she'd wandered into, where every turn led further from the light.

The certainty settled over her like a shroud: there was no way out of this that didn't end in ruins. The only question was whose.

But maybe that was fitting. Maybe that was exactly what she deserved for thinking she could have both—her family's safety and Kane's trust. For believing she could play both sides without losing herself entirely in the between.

The guilt would destroy her long before Kane ever discovered the truth.

But at least her family would be safe.

At least there was that

CHAPTER TWO

KANE

Kane stood at the kitchen window long after Serenity disappeared upstairs, watching the morning sun paint Celearius in shades of gold. The reflection showed a man who looked thirty-five and carried five centuries like stones in his pockets, playing at seduction while mapping her destruction.

He'd meant some of it—that was the most dangerous part. The desire had been real, the protectiveness genuine, the careful attention to her rights in that damned contract reflecting his actual values even as he wielded them as weapons. But he'd known, every moment since Rhyzan showed him the surveillance footage, that every touch would serve a dual purpose and every kindness would draw her deeper into the web.

His comm device vibrated in his pocket: Sebastian had sent her the meeting details. The Diamond District at 1 PM. Of course.

Kane allowed himself one moment of genuine emotion—a tightening around his eyes, a heaviness in his chest that felt remarkably like grief—before smoothing his expression back into careful neutrality. There would be time for real feelings later, assuming there was anything left of either of them once this particular game played out.

He recognized Nox's footfall before he entered—a deliberate heaviness that could have been intimidation or simple disinterest in stealth. Kane didn't turn, just spoke to the window. "He has already contacted her."

Nox exhaled, the closest he came to a sigh. "Have you seen her?"

"She's upstairs." He watched the mirrored city, its busy arteries, its little dramas. His own reflection flickered amid the high-rises. "You'll be taking her to the Diamond District. You'll be watching to see if he gives her anything, but they will try to go places where you will most likely wait outside. Give her the space."

Nox's mouth twitched, almost humor. "Rhy is going to love hearing that." He hesitated, his gaze darting past Kane toward the kitchen, as though Serenity might materialize, bare feet on the cold tile, eyes still clouded with regret and resolve. "I see he managed to hack her device."

"All Elite devices are monitored to a degree, so it was easy to extend it beyond."

Nox sighed. Kane knew he still didn't like the idea of using Serenity as bait, but she was the closest lead they had to finding the rebellion and stopping them from causing more damage.

Nox shifted his weight, folding his arms across his chest like a fortress. "Let me guess—Rhy is monitoring comms, there's a scrub team standing by in case they decide to take her."

Kane's voice fell to a chill, precise timbre. "No scrub team. Rhy is at the academy getting recruits ready. If they decide she's compromised and they're foolish enough to take her, you follow. Have Sullivan within the vicinity with eyes on her the whole time. She goes nowhere our eyes can't reach her."

"Understood."

"I'm leaving. I've put off seeing the new recruits for too long. If anything happens, call me immediately." Kane turned from the window, silver-blue eyes catching the light as he moved. "And Nox?"

"Yes?"

"She is not to know you're watching her this closely. She believes she has freedom. Let her keep that illusion."

A muscle tightened in Nox's jaw, but he nodded once, understanding clearly.

Grabbing his coat, he moved toward the elevator. He glanced up the stairs at the bedroom door, hoping she would come out so he could catch a glimpse of her before he left, but the door remained closed. The wanting irritated him—he should be focused on strategy, not yearning for one more look at a woman who'd betrayed him.

The elevator carried him down in silence, and he welcomed the descent—away from her scent, away from the kitchen where he'd offered genuine vulnerability wrapped in calculated intent, away from the upstairs room where she was no doubt agonizing over her choices.

Good. Let her agonize. Let her guilt consume her while he maintained control.

The drive to the training facility passed in a blur of city streets and security checkpoints. Kane forced his mind to shift gears, compartmentalizing with practiced efficiency. Serenity and her betrayal belonged in one locked box. The rebellion and its threat belonged in another. The recruits waiting for him required a different version of himself entirely—the demanding instructor, the warrior, the symbol of vampyr strength and discipline.

By the time he reached the arena, his expression had hardened into command.

Kane's steely gaze swept across the training arena, taking in each initiate. They had all passed their tests with flying colors, and now they stood before him, ready to put those skills to the ultimate test—facing him in the arena.

His silver-blue eyes studied each recruit in turn, assessing their strengths and weaknesses with a single glance. He could sense their nervousness, the way their hearts raced, and the scent of adrenaline in the air. The room crackled with tension as each stood at attention, barely daring to breathe under the weight of his gaze.

It was a familiar scene, one he had witnessed countless times over the centuries.

"You have all proven yourselves worthy of this opportunity," Kane began, his deep voice resonating through the chamber. "But do not mistake your success thus far for true readiness. The challenges that lie ahead will test not only your physical prowess but the very limits of your resolve."

He stepped forward, his movements precise and measured. "There are many outside these walls... and within them, who seek to destroy everything we stand for. It is my duty to ensure that you are prepared to meet those threats head-on. To protect our people. To protect Celearius."

Kane's eyes flickered to the weapons rack along the wall, an array of gleaming blades and firearms. "Each of you will face me in single combat. You may choose any weapon you desire, but know that I will not hold back. This is your final test, and failure is not an option."

With measured steps, he descended to the training room floor, circling the assembled recruits before moving into the center of the arena. Kane stood still as a statue, his hands clasped behind his back as he waited for the first initiate to be announced.

The first initiate stepped forward, a young man with dark curls. Kane caught himself noting the resemblance—soft curls like hers—before shutting down the observation with brutal efficiency. The recruit selected a sleek katana from the weapons wall, the blade singing as it sliced through the air. Kane nodded with approval, appreciating the boldness.

They faced each other in the center of the arena, the initiate's heartbeat thundering in Kane's ears. In a flash of movement, the recruit lunged forward, his sword a blur of silver. Kane sidestepped the attack with ease, his own weapon materializing in his hand as if conjured from thin air.

Their blades clashed in a shower of sparks, the force of the impact reverberating through Kane's arm. The initiate was skilled, with movements refined, but he lacked the experience that made true mastery possible—speed without wisdom, precision without anticipation. With a deft twist of his wrist, Kane disarmed his opponent, sending the katana clattering across the stone floor.

"Do not confuse speed with precision," Kane admonished, his voice echoing in the hushed silence of the chamber. "True mastery lies in the balance between the two."

As the initiate retrieved his weapon and placed it back on the wall, Kane nodded to Rhyzan, giving his opponent the pass.

The next initiate stepped forward, a shapely figure with raven hair pulled back into a tight braid and fiery brown eyes. She selected a pair of daggers, their curved blades gleaming under the arena lights. Kane watched as she twirled them in her hands, a dance of deadly precision.

They circled each other, eyes locked in a silent challenge. When the recruit finally struck, it was with blind speed, her daggers flashing in a deadly arc toward Kane's throat.

He parried the blow with ease, his weapon singing through the air as he countered with a series of rapid strikes. The recruit held her own, her daggers a blur of silver as she deflected his attacks.

The woman moved with fluid grace—and for one unguarded moment, muscle memory betrayed him. His body remembered holding someone else, all soft curves and surprising strength. The dagger aimed at his ribs nearly connected before he caught himself.

With a sharp movement, Kane disarmed the recruit, her daggers clattering to the ground. He couldn't allow distraction. Not now, not ever. He had a responsibility to his people, to the future of both humans and vampyrs alike.

Even if honoring that responsibility was tearing him apart.

As the recruit retrieved her daggers, Kane turned to face the rest of the group, his expression an unreadable mask. "Remember, the key to victory lies not in brute strength, but in focus and control. Emotions can be a powerful weapon, but they can also be your greatest weakness. In the heat of battle, you must learn to master your emotions, to channel them into purpose. Anger, fear, love..." He paused, the word catching in his throat. "These things will only cloud your judgment and dull your reflexes."

He didn't acknowledge the irony. Didn't need to. The lecture was as much for himself as for them.

Kane gave a curt nod to Rhy, who was eyeing him with concern. Then he thought better of it, not wanting to linger here where every face threatened to trigger another unwanted memory. He raised two fingers to Rhy, signaling that Rhy should send two. He would finish this faster, defeating them in pairs.

Rhy's brow furrowed, but he complied with Kane's silent command, gesturing for two recruits to step forward. They were both young men, their faces set with determination as they faced their imposing instructor.

Kane studied them, taking in their stances, the way they held their weapons. They were skilled, no doubt, but he could see the flickers of uncertainty in their eyes, the slight hesitation in their movements.

He moved swiftly, his body a blur of motion as he engaged them both at once. The clash of metal echoed through the arena as they exchanged blows, Kane's weapon flashing in the light.

The recruits fought valiantly, their movements precise and calculated, but they were no match for Kane's centuries of experience. He danced around them, his body moving with a grace that belied his size, finding every opening, every weakness in their defenses.

In a matter of moments, it was over. Both recruits lay on the ground, their weapons scattered around them, their chests heaving with exertion. Kane stood over them, his expression impassive, his weapon held loosely at his side.

"You fought well," Kane said, his voice low and even. "But you still have much to learn."

He sheathed his weapon and extended his hand to each fallen recruit, helping them to their feet. They stood before him, their eyes downcast, their faces flushed with shame and exhaustion.

"Look at me," Kane commanded, his tone brooking no argument. Slowly, they raised their gazes to meet his, and he could see the fear and uncertainty that still lingered there.

"You are soldiers of Celearius," he said, his voice ringing out across the arena. "You have been chosen for a sacred duty, to protect and serve both our kind and the humans we share this world with. But you cannot do so if you allow your fears and doubts to control you. Learn to master them and channel them into strength and purpose."

The recruits nodded, their expressions hardening with resolve as they left the arena. Kane could see the change in them, the way they stood a little taller, their eyes burning with newfound determination.

He continued through the remaining pairs with mechanical efficiency. Each victory was swift, each lesson delivered with precision. By the time the last two recruits collected their weapons and filed out, Kane felt the familiar emptiness that came from compartmentalizing too effectively—victory without satisfaction, duty without purpose.

Kane turned to Rhy, who came to stand by his side, handing him his sheathed weapon. His dark eyes glinted with approval.

"They all passed," Rhyzan remarked, his voice smooth and low. "And surprisingly, you managed to keep your temper in check."

Kane nodded and grimaced at his comment, his gaze distant as he watched the last of the recruits file out of the arena. "They must be ready for what lies ahead. The balance we've fought so hard to maintain will soon shatter, and I want them ready."

Rhy's expression grew somber. "They grow bolder each day. I believe they will try to go for the cavern, but we are not sure when yet. And Chloe is still working on buttering up our prisoner, who seems to be nursing a broken heart. He hasn't shared the details with her, but she guessed someone in his life was either killed by a vampyr or left him for one. We're still digging into his background."

A flicker of unease passed over Kane's face, but he quickly schooled his features into a mask of calm determination. "We cannot allow them to undo years of progress and plunge us back into chaos and bloodshed."

"I stand with you always, my friend. We will be prepared, and we will defeat them," Rhyzan said, placing his hand on Kane's shoulder, his touch a silent offer of support and solidarity.

Kane nodded, his jaw tightening with resolve. "We must be vigilant and stay one step ahead. Have Chloe continue her work with the prisoner, use his vulnerability to her advantage. Any information she can glean could prove vital."

As he exited the arena, Kane's mind raced with the implications of the rebel threat. The delicate balance between humans and vampyrs hung by a thread, and he knew that if the rebels succeeded, it could mean the end of everything.

Including the fragile connection between him and Serenity—one he couldn't decide whether he wanted to preserve or sever before it destroyed them both.

CHAPTER THREE

RHYZAN

Rhyzan had been watching them for the past week. Watching Chloe, their 'human' liaison, weave her spell around the prisoner, Jax. She literally had him eating out of the palm of her hand.

On the monitor before him, Chloe fed Jax some fruit as he ran his hands through her silky, deep red hair. They lay naked on the cot when she placed the fruit aside and turned back to glance at the camera—a brief acknowledgment that this performance was for Rhyzan's benefit as much as Jax's. Then she straddled him and began to ride him. Rhyzan ensured the camera's indicator light was off and that they were recording.

"You know how to get in contact with the rebels?" Chloe said, grabbing a berry and trailing it down his chest.

"My friend, Clyde, may have a contact. I get my first phone call tomorrow," he said, catching the berry from her hand with his mouth.

So far, Jax had given them little of value, but they were banking on his contacts and his hatred for their kind. They'd been able to sentence him to a month in prison for assault against an officer, which meant they only had a matter of weeks to extract what they needed.

They suspected he had ties to the rebels, but they didn't know it. They'd already been looking into his associates—this Clyde and Clyde's girlfriend, Victoria. They'd both been in custody earlier, but, thinking them innocent, he had released them. They knew Clyde worked at the Syn bottling factory, but they hadn't been able to find much on the girl except that she worked at a clinic. Since the Blood Clinic workers fell under Evelyn's jurisdiction, not his, he'd sent the information over to her. He was hoping to hear back soon.

For now, he'd been keeping tabs on them, but he was hoping this staged escape would yield more substantial intelligence.

"I have a plan to escape, but it will only work if I know you can get in touch with the rebels. I need to get my daughter," she stressed.

Jax sat up on his forearm, turning to look at her. "Clyde will help us." He glanced up at the camera. "He has a contact, and we'll convince them to get your daughter."

She nodded before he took her head in his hands and kissed her.

"Then you'll have to be ready and follow my lead when the time comes, because we'll only have one chance at this. And if we're caught, we're dead." She grabbed his face and stared into his eyes, ensuring she had his full attention. "Do you understand? I can't fail. She needs me."

"I understand, Chloe. We'll get her back. I promise."

Rhyzan almost wanted to laugh. If 175-year-old Alexandra could see her mother now, she would laugh along with him. Chloe had told him that human males have an instinct to save their mothers and children. It was an act, a ploy she always used, and surprisingly, it always worked—except for one time. Chloe didn't like to talk about that particular failure, because six months later her son Eric was born, and two months after that, they found his father's body torn to pieces a few miles from Celearius.

Rhyzan had always been tempted to get her drunk one day and pry the whole story from her, but only Kane knew the truth, and he would never be able to extract it from his damn lips.

Switching off the record button, he turned off the screen, giving them a sense of privacy while she screwed the human's brains out.

Rhyzan leaned back in his chair, analyzing next steps. The space was deliberately austere—banks of monitors casting blue-white light across his pale features, the faint hum of electronics the only sound besides his measured footsteps. This Clyde character remained an unknown variable. The girl, Victoria, and her clinic connection could prove valuable if handled correctly.

With a sigh, he reached for his comm device, his fingers hovering over the keys as he debated whether to check in with Nox about Kane and Serenity. Kane had worked the recruits harder than usual at the academy—whether from anger at the betrayal or general fury toward the rebellion, Rhyzan couldn't determine. He'd meant to check in this morning, but preparing the recruits had gotten in the way.

Just as he was about to dial, a knock sounded at the door.

A guard walked in and handed him a file.

"We were able to trace the call, but couldn't get an exact location."

He opened it. They'd retrieved the text messages from Serenity's comm device, but unfortunately, they couldn't record the call itself. They'd traced it to the Silver District, which didn't surprise him. There was one place he suspected they might be using, though he didn't think it was their headquarters, possibly a haven of some sort. It could be where the Elite had found herself that night after the incident with Kane.

His device vibrated. It was Evie.

"Please tell me you have something useful for me?"

"I don't know about useful, but I can tell you what I found. I'm sending over her file now. Her name is Victoria Fruster. She's an entry-level nurse at the Grove Gardens clinic. She passed the background checks, and you approved her with no problems."

Rhyzan turned to his computer and opened the file she'd just sent, scrolling straight to the bottom to find his signature. He noted the date. He'd approved it three years ago. Though something seemed off about it—he'd been approving staff three years ago, but he couldn't recall personally approving entry-level positions. He would have to look further into it. He continued scrolling through the file.

"Nothing stands out. I can see why she would be approved. The only thing that gives me pause is the date."

"Do you think she's part of the rebellion? Wait. Look at page three."

Rhyzan scrolled back until he reached page three, scanning until he found what she was referring to. His verdant eyes narrowed as he stared at the name on the reference letter.

R. Wright. Serenity's father.

The pieces were starting to fall into place, a sinister puzzle taking shape before him.

"Evie, this can't be a coincidence," he said, his voice low and tense. "She has to be linked to the rebellion."

"Let's not get ahead of ourselves. He was a respected doctor from what I could dig up, and if you actually read the letter, you'd see he makes valid points about her skills—observations only a physician would note."

"But it could be—"

Evie continued, interrupting him. "She's a competent nurse with only a handful of complaints, mostly from older nurses who don't like the way she tries new approaches."

"Fine. I hear you, Evelyn. Let's find out everything we can and see if she has any direct ties to Serenity beyond a reference letter."

Evie sighed on the other end of the line. "Alright. I'll keep digging. But Rhyzan, we can't let paranoia cloud our judgment. The rebellion is real, but not everyone is part of it."

Rhyzan's jaw clenched, a flicker of irritation sparking within him at her words. Paranoia? No, this was vigilance. The very thing that had kept their kind alive for centuries, thriving in the shadows while humanity tore itself apart.

"I'm not being paranoid, Evie. I'm being thorough. We can't afford to overlook any detail, no matter how insignificant it seems."

"I know that," she replied, her tone softening. "But we also can't treat every human as a potential enemy. It's a delicate balance."

Rhyzan closed his eyes, taking a breath to center himself.

"You're right," he conceded. "We'll tread carefully. Let me know when you have something concrete."

"I will. Now, I know Kane showed you the plans last night and discussed using Sebastian."

A moment of silence before she answered. "Yes. I've been working on them. I should have them finished by tomorrow."

"Good. Then we need to get them into their hands."

"Sebastian." She stated it flatly, knowing where he was going with this. "You want me to leak them to Sebastian."

"He knows I wouldn't just leave something like this lying around—"

"But you know where I can leave it so that he will check."

Again, another moment of silence before she answered. "Yes."

"I know this can't be easy, Evie. I know how fond of Sebastian you are."

"I know how I feel, but this is more important," Evie's voice hardened. "If Sebastian is involved with the rebels, if he's been working against us all this time…" She trailed off, the pain evident even through the transmission.

Rhyzan's fingers tightened around the device. "We don't know that for certain. Not yet."

"Don't we? The evidence is mounting, Rhy. I just…" A soft exhale. "I understand what needs to be done. I'll finish the plans and have them for you tomorrow."

"Evie, I'm sorry. For both you and Kane."

"Unfortunately, for me, this isn't the first or the last heartbreak. Kane, on the other hand, only opens himself to so few. We have to keep a close watch on him through all of this."

"I know. Just let me know when it's done, and I'll devise a contingency plan."

"Okay."

The call ended, leaving Rhyzan alone with his thoughts in the dim glow of the monitors. He rolled his shoulders, trying to ease the tension that had settled there like a physical weight. The muscles in his neck protested, stiff from hours of surveillance.

He pulled up the footage of Chloe and Jax again, watching their bodies entwined on the bed with clinical detachment. Chloe was a master at her craft—every moan, every whispered endearment calculated to draw Jax deeper into her web. The human didn't stand a chance.

His phone buzzed. The caller ID read: Nox.

"I was just about to call you."

"Were you now?" Nox's tone carried a hint of amusement.

"Yeah, how's Kane? He seemed tense at the academy. Has he seen her?"

"Whoa, slow down, Mr. Million Questions," Nox replied. "If he was that intense at the academy, then you know he saw her."

"True." Rhyzan sighed, leaning back in his chair as his thoughts turned to Kane. "Do you think he's going to be able to maintain this charade?"

"I bloody well hope so," Nox said, though his voice carried doubt. "It's only day one, and he's already like a coiled spring about to snap. Her betrayal may hurt him, but he still wants her."

"I could definitely tell he's wound tight." Rhyzan rubbed his temples. "For now, we need to help him maintain this façade. She's the key to ending this, and hopefully there will be a resolution that doesn't destroy them both."

"I'll make damn sure of it. He deserves it," Nox said firmly. "Look, I've got to go. Serenity and Sebastian just came out of Izzy's."

Rhyzan straightened in his chair. "You're with Serenity and Sebastian right now?"

"Yes, he made contact with her today," Nox confirmed, his voice dropping lower. "So far, I haven't seen him give her anything physical, but he's been whispering to her any time I'm out of earshot. He must be giving her details for her next mission."

"Try to catch what you can," Rhyzan instructed.

"No worries. Sullivan's been listening. He'll call you with what he learns."

"Good. Nox—" Rhyzan paused, his tone becoming more serious. "Stay safe."

"I will," Nox promised before ending the call.

Rhyzan set his device down on the desk, his mind already racing through the implications. Sebastian's quick contact with Serenity meant things were accelerating faster than anticipated. If the rebellion was moving up their timeline, they needed to be ready.

He pulled up the security feeds for Cavern 47 on his secondary monitor, studying the facility's layout with fresh eyes. Sullivan had better pick up something useful from Sebastian's whispered instructions—the vampyr had hearing sharp enough to catch a heartbeat from three blocks away, and Rhyzan was counting on that enhanced perception now.

Given this new development, they needed to accelerate their own strategy. The Cavern had to be prepared for Chloe's staged breakout, which meant coordinating with the security teams, planting the falsified blueprints where Chloe would find them, and ensuring every contingency was covered.

Rhyzan opened a secure message to Kane, his fingers hovering over the keys. His friend needed to know that the game was officially in motion, that Serenity had taken the bait and met with Sebastian. But he also knew Kane was barely holding himself together.

Still, duty demanded honesty between them. It always had.

He typed quickly: *Sebastian made contact. Sullivan monitoring. Will report findings within the hour. Prepare to accelerate the Cavern timeline. —R*

After hitting send, Rhyzan stood and moved to the window overlooking the prison complex. Chloe was weaving her web around Jax. Nox was shadowing Serenity and Sebastian. Sullivan was gathering intelligence. And Kane was trying not to let his heart interfere with his duty.

They were all pieces on the board now, moving in a deadly dance where one misstep could cost them everything.

Rhyzan's reflection stared back at him from the darkened glass—ancient eyes that had seen empires rise and fall, wars won and lost, friends betrayed and avenged. This rebellion would be no different. They would crush it, as they had crushed every threat before.

But this time, he found himself hoping the cost wouldn't include his best friend's heart.

His device buzzed with Kane's response: *Understood. Meet me in my office tonight at midnight. We'll finalize the details then.*

Short, clipped, controlled. Classic Kane when he was holding on by a thread.

Rhyzan sighed and returned to his desk, pulling up the Cavern schematics once more. They had work to do, and the night was still young.

For better or worse, the endgame had begun.

CHAPTER FOUR

SERENITY

Serenity stared at Sebastian, not fully able to process what he'd just asked her to do.

"You want me to what?"

"Seduce him." Sebastian leaned in closer, his voice dropping to a conspiratorial whisper. "Listen, I know it sounds extreme, but this is how the game works. Think about it—Kane Draccus doesn't let anyone close. Not in centuries, at least according to Evie."

"And you think I should be the exception?" Serenity's pulse quickened with indignation. "Are you out of your mind?"

They stood in the back corner of Izzy's Boutique, surrounded by racks of designer clothing that cost more than her monthly stipend. Sebastian had insisted on stopping here after their shopping trip for his new wardrobe. Now she understood why.

He dangled the crimson silk garment before her, its plunging neckline and open back leaving little to the imagination. "This would be perfect. The color alone would drive him wild."

"You're insane." She pushed the dress away, her fingers tingling from even that brief contact with the luxurious fabric. "I can't just... seduce the Head of the Vampyr and Human Council for information."

A saleswoman glanced their way, and Serenity lowered her voice.

"Besides, he'd know exactly what I was doing. He's not stupid."

Sebastian's green eyes gleamed with mischief. "Not if you do it right. Look, Kane needs to trust you. Really trust you in order for you to get out of this alive." He leaned closer. "Getting Kane to trust you is the fastest way to learn what we need. And the quickest path to trust is through intimacy."

Serenity felt her cheeks flush. Her mind flashed to Kane's bedroom, the weight of his body against hers, the cool brush of his lips on her neck. That strange awareness between them had flared to life, making it impossible to tell where her pleasure ended, and his began. The memory made her stomach twist with both guilt and desire.

"I..." She nearly confessed, the truth hovering on her lips. That she'd already crossed that line. That she'd already felt the exquisite pain of his fangs piercing her skin while his hands explored her body.

But caution stilled her tongue. The rebellion didn't need to know everything.

Instead, she deflected. "Is that how you got close to Evie? Your patron?" The words came out sharper than she intended.

Sebastian's perpetual smirk faltered. His fingers tightened around the hanger, knuckles whitening. "Yes," he admitted, his voice suddenly stripped of its usual playfulness. For a brief moment, pain flickered behind his eyes—raw and wounded.

Then he added with a smirk, "Doesn't hurt that she's not a bad lay."

"Was it worth it?" Serenity whispered.

Sebastian met her gaze. "Yes," he said, but the word seemed to cost him. His eyes held a depth of emotion that startled her—regret, determination, and something that looked almost like grief swirling together.

"Why," she pressed, emboldened by his honesty. "Why do you need me to get Kane to trust me so badly? What exactly are you hoping I'll find out?" She clutched her bag tighter, suddenly aware of how little she actually knew about the rebellion's true aims. "What information are we really after here?"

The boutique's bell chimed, cutting her off. Serenity's heart lurched as she spotted Nox's impeccable figure gliding through the entrance, his dark hair perfectly styled, his suit immaculate as always. Sebastian stiffened beside her, then recovered with practiced ease.

"Nox," Sebastian called out. "Perfect timing."

Nox's gaze swept over them both, calculating and cool as he approached, lingering on the red dress in Sebastian's hand before moving to Serenity's flushed face.

"Let me guess. She's saying no," he said.

Sebastian's face brightened. "Correct. I'm trying to convince her that men love seeing their women in red." He held up the crimson silk. "Don't you think Kane would appreciate seeing her in this?"

Nox tilted his head, studying the garment with unexpected seriousness. His gaze flicked to Serenity, assessing her with that unnerving vampyr intensity.

"He would love to see you in something like that," he said after a moment. "Kane appreciates beauty, though he rarely admits it."

Serenity's jaw nearly dropped. She'd expected Nox, of all people, to dismiss such frivolity.

"See?" Sebastian grinned triumphantly. "Even Nox agrees."

Serenity felt heat crawl up her neck. "I'm not wearing that," she insisted, pushing the crimson fabric away. Her eyes caught on a different rack—a soft grey silk that shimmered like moonlight on water. She moved toward it, fingers tracing the delicate material.

"This one," she said, lifting it from the rack. The cut was still daring—a slit up the side, a modest but alluring neckline—but the color... "It matches his eyes."

The moment she said it, awareness bloomed within her—that connection again. She could almost feel him, a ghost of presence at the edge of her consciousness.

"He will love you in it," Sebastian agreed, his smile genuine for once.

Nox nodded, a hint of approval warming his typically impassive features. The grey dress felt right in Serenity's hands, the fabric cool against her skin. Unlike the red one that seemed designed to announce her presence like a siren, this gown whispered secrets.

Sebastian sighed dramatically. "Fine. The grey is... acceptable. Not what I would have chosen, but it suits you." He plucked the dress from her grasp and strode toward the register, pulling out a sleek black card before she could protest.

The saleswoman's eyes widened at the sight of Sebastian's platinum Elite card. Her fingers trembled slightly as she processed the transaction, wrapping the dress in tissue paper with reverent care.

As they stepped outside the boutique into the bustling square, the afternoon sun cast long shadows across the cobblestones. Serenity's stomach growled audibly, reminding her she hadn't eaten since morning.

Sebastian's eyes lit up. "Nox, I have a favor to ask." His voice took on a cajoling tone. "Would you mind grabbing some pretzel bites from that little place down the block? The place with the red awning."

Nox's frown deepened, his dark eyes narrowing with suspicion. "You're perfectly capable of getting food yourself, Sebastian."

"Please? She's never had them before, and you can get them faster than we can." Sebastian gestured toward Serenity with an exaggerated pout. "Listen to her stomach, the poor thing is famished. Would you really make an Elite suffer when you could prevent it?"

Serenity's cheeks burned at being discussed like a neglected pet, but her traitorous stomach chose that moment to growl again, louder this time.

"Imagine what Evie would say if she found out you let her precious Elite go hungry," Sebastian pressed.

Nox's gaze drifted toward the ornate fountain in the center of the square, water cascading over carved marble nymphs. His expression remained impassive, but Serenity noticed the slight relaxation in his shoulders.

"Fine," he relented after a long pause. "Stay right here by the fountain. Don't wander off. I'll be back in five minutes."

The moment Nox disappeared into the crowd, Sebastian's playful demeanor evaporated. His fingers closed around Serenity's wrist, grip firm but not painful as he guided her toward a stone bench partially obscured by a flowering jacaranda tree. The purple blossoms released a sweet, heady fragrance.

"Sit," he commanded, his voice low and urgent. "We don't have much time."

Serenity sat, placing her bag on the floor between her legs as Sebastian settled next to her.

"Now tell me what they want from me, Sebastian. What exactly are your people after?"

"We want freedom." Sebastian's eyes burned with unexpected intensity. "We want to end vampyr dominance over humanity once and for all."

Serenity glanced around nervously, making sure no one could overhear them. "I don't know how much longer I can keep this up. Kane is... perceptive."

Sebastian leaned forward, his fingers tightening around her wrist. "Everything you're doing is helping us gain our freedom. Just hold on a little longer." His voice softened, taking on an almost hypnotic quality. "There are plans in motion that will change everything. Bigger than you can imagine."

The fervor in his expression sent a chill through her. What exactly was the rebellion planning? She opened her mouth, nearly confessing that Kane wasn't the monster they painted him to be—that he'd shown her kindness, vulnerability even. The words hovered on her tongue, but then the memory of that night flashed through her mind. She knew now that it was his hunger driving him to take her blood without asking, but the pain still lingered in her memory even though he'd healed her.

She closed her eyes briefly, conflicted. Whatever kindness Kane had shown her afterward didn't erase that violation.

"What exactly do you need from me?" she asked instead. "What information am I supposed to be looking for?"

Sebastian's expression sharpened. "Cavern 47," he said, the words heavy with significance. "We need to know everything about it—where it is, what's inside, who has access, security protocols, everything."

"Cavern 47?" The name from the file. The one they'd had her download from Kane's computer. "I thought you got all the information you needed on it when I—"

"Unfortunately, we didn't get what we needed." Sebastian's expression hardened. "What we got was encrypted. Useless. We need actual details about what's happening there—locations, security measures, prisoner manifests."

"Prisoners?" Serenity's throat tightened. "People are being held there?"

"That's what we need to confirm." Sebastian leaned closer. "We believe Cavern 47 is a detention facility where the HVC is holding human dissidents—people who've spoken out against vampyr rule. Some have been missing for months, others for years."

The implication settled over Serenity like a shroud. If true, it would mean Kane was directly involved in the disappearance of humans who opposed the vampyr regime. But then again—she thought of the contract he'd drafted protecting her rights, the way he'd arranged for her to visit her family. Could the same man who'd shown her such consideration be running a prison for dissidents?

"So you want me to..." Serenity let the question hang in the air.

"Find anything you can about Cavern 47. Documents, conversations, access points—anything." Sebastian's fingers drummed against his thigh. "People are suffering there, Serenity. Even small details could help us piece together the full picture. They will contact you in two days to see if you've found anything, and they should have more information on what they specifically need you to find."

"Two days?" Serenity's voice pitched higher than she intended. "That's not much—"

"It has to be enough." His grip tightened momentarily. "Your family's future depends on it."

The mention of her family struck like a physical blow. Her mother's pale face, her sister's medication—expensive treatments they could never afford without an Elite's stipend. The reminder was calculated, and Serenity knew it, but that didn't make it any less effective.

Before she could respond, movement caught her eye. Nox approached, carrying a small paper bag that released the tantalizing aroma of buttery, salted pretzels.

"See, that was fast," Sebastian remarked, his tone shifting seamlessly back to casual charm. He straightened, putting appropriate distance between himself and Serenity.

Nox extended the bag toward Serenity. "Fresh from the oven."

She accepted it, the warmth seeping through the paper. "Thank you," she murmured, unable to meet his gaze. Her mind still reeled from Sebastian's revelations about Cavern 47. Prisoners. Dissidents. Disappearances.

"We're finished shopping," Sebastian announced, rising from the bench. He gathered the shopping bags at their feet. "I found everything I needed, and we even managed to find her something nice."

"I need to get going," Sebastian announced, checking his watch with exaggerated concern. "Evie's returning from the office soon, and she always likes me willing and ready when she gets home." His lips curved into a suggestive smirk. "It's the least I can do for my patron."

Serenity shifted uncomfortably, the pretzel suddenly less appetizing as she imagined Sebastian preparing himself for Evie's return. The casual way he spoke of it—as though being sexually available was simply part of the transaction between Elite and patron—made her stomach knot. Is that how it will soon be between her and Kane?

"We should do this again," Sebastian added, his tone lightening as he handed Nox the shopping bags. "Perhaps next week? She'll need a suitable dress for the Elite Ball, after all."

The words hit Serenity like a splash of cold water. Elite Ball? Another event she knew nothing about.

"I'm sure Kane will ensure she's properly attired," Nox replied, his voice cool and measured as he accepted the bags.

Sebastian's eyes gleamed with an unreadable expression—amusement, perhaps, or calculation. "Of course he will. But women should have options."

"Indeed," Nox said, grabbing Serenity's bag. "Though Kane will likely provide whatever is necessary."

Sebastian winked at Serenity. "I'm sure he will." He gave a theatrical bow. "Until next time. Remember what we discussed."

With that, he melted into the afternoon crowd, the sunlight catching his golden hair before he disappeared entirely. Serenity stared after him, the half-eaten pretzel bite forgotten in her hand. Her mind buzzed with everything he'd told her. Cavern 47. Prisoners. Dissidents. And now some Elite Ball she knew nothing about.

"We should return," Nox said, interrupting her thoughts.

The walk to the sleek black car parked at the edge of the square passed in silence. Serenity's thoughts tumbled over each other like stones in a riverbed. Once they reached the car, she finally gathered the courage to ask.

"What exactly is the Elite Ball?"

Nox unlocked the car with a soft click. "It's the annual showcase of the Elite Program—an elaborate affair where vampyr patrons display their chosen companions." His voice carried a hint of distaste. "The Council hosts it to demonstrate the supposed success of human-vampyr cooperation to outside allies and visiting dignitaries—how harmoniously humans and vampyrs co-exist."

Serenity clutched her shopping bag closer. "And Elites... we're just paraded around like prizes?"

"Some view it that way," Nox admitted, sliding into the driver's seat. "Others see it as an opportunity to network, to strengthen alliances. Each Elite receives a formal introduction, presented as evidence of the program's refinement."

"Sounds horrifying," Serenity muttered, sliding into the passenger seat. The leather upholstery felt cool against her skin.

Nox settled behind the wheel. "Kane has never had the opportunity to bring an Elite," Nox said, starting the car with a quiet purr of the engine.

The revelation surprised Serenity. "Never? But he's—"

"The Head of the Council, yes." Nox pulled away from the curb. "Nevertheless, Kane hasn't participated in the Elite Ball as a patron since its inception."

Serenity watched the city blur past her window, processing this information. The idea of Kane—powerful, ancient Kane—never having an Elite to present seemed impossible.

"Why not?" she asked, unable to contain her curiosity.

Nox's gaze remained fixed on the road. His hesitation was brief but noticeable. "That is not my story to tell. If you wish to know, you should ask him directly."

The car fell into silence as they navigated through the city's winding streets. Serenity fidgeted with the shopping bag on her lap, fingers tracing the outline of the tissue-wrapped dress inside.

Eyes still on the grey silk, her thoughts drifted to the Elite Ball. She imagined herself walking into an opulent ballroom on Kane's arm, the dress flowing around her legs like liquid moonlight. Would he be proud to present her, or merely tolerant of the obligation?

The awareness between them flickered at the edge of her consciousness—always there now, like a second heartbeat. This morning in the kitchen, she'd sensed conflict, as though he were fighting himself about something.

She let her imagination take her away, thought of all the possibilities as they drove back to Kane's apartment. Then the moment they reached the garage, she squashed her dreams and came back to reality, steeling herself for what came next.

That awareness hummed beneath her skin, telling her he was thinking of her as well.

CHAPTER FIVE

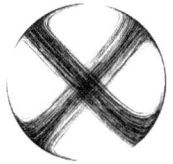

KANE

His thoughts were still consumed by the recruits, the rebels, and the security detail until he stepped off the elevator and was instantly hit by her scent—jasmine and rose, with an undertone of honeysuckle.

It was intoxicating.

Kane paused, gathering himself. Her scent was everywhere, luring him in. He inhaled deeply, savoring it despite himself, before continuing down the hallway.

The light from the kitchen spilled into the corridor, accompanied by the mouthwatering aroma of garlic, tomato, and herbs. Kane found Nox standing by the stove, stirring a pot of what appeared to be pasta sauce. Steam rose in lazy spirals toward the ceiling.

"Where is she?" Kane asked, his voice rougher than intended.

Nox glanced up, his movements precise as he lowered the heat. "She ate earlier. She's in her room now." He gestured toward a covered plate on the counter. "She saved some for you, though."

Kane nodded, his gaze lingering on the covered dish. Such a simple gesture, yet it stirred longing in him—a hunger that had nothing to do with food. "How did the shopping excursion go?"

Nox's expression shifted subtly as he wiped his hands on a kitchen towel. "Productive, but concerning. Sullivan indicates the rebels are still actively seeking information about Cavern 47."

Kane's muscles tensed. "What specifically did Sullivan overhear?"

"I left them near the fountain to grab food for her." Nox's voice dropped lower. "Sebastian wants her to find out anything about the cavern. I believe they'll attempt another system breach when you're not here so she can re-access your office."

Kane crossed the living room to the window and stared out at the city lights shimmering against the night sky. The rebels' focus on the cavern troubled him more than he cared to admit. "Did Sullivan hear anything else?"

"Sebastian informed her they'll provide detailed instructions in two days."

A muscle worked in Kane's jaw. "Has Rhy been informed?"

"Yes, Sullivan briefed us simultaneously. Rhy believes they may be planning an extraction. A prisoner, perhaps. Though he can't yet determine who the target might be."

If Rhyzan suspected an extraction, the situation demanded immediate attention. Then there would be no need to stage a breakout. The rebels would be doing the work for them.

"Sullivan also mentioned she didn't seem particularly eager to receive the information," Nox added, his expression softening slightly. "She seemed... troubled by it."

Kane ignored the comment—and the slight flare of hope it ignited. Nox had always been soft toward humans, especially Serenity. His friend's empathy was both his strength and weakness. Kane couldn't afford such sentiment.

"Is everything prepared for tomorrow?" Kane asked, changing the subject. "The visit to her family needs to go smoothly."

Nox nodded, returning to the stove to turn it off. "The location will be thoroughly searched hours before your arrival. I've arranged for additional security to sweep the surrounding block." He stirred the sauce methodically before grabbing a plate. "The car will be ready at one o'clock. I've scheduled a three-hour window for the visit, though it can be extended if necessary."

"Good." Kane strode back into the kitchen, his gaze automatically falling to the table where Serenity had left the contract that morning—the stack of papers now conspicuously absent. Kane's jaw tightened. Had she taken it to her room? Or possibly slipped it under his office door?

He moved toward his office, intending to check. But with each step, his thoughts drifted further from the contract and closer to her—the way her scent lingered in the hallway, how she'd saved him dinner. The contradiction gnawed at him. Was she that skilled an actress, or was there genuine care beneath the deception?

Halfway to his office, Kane stopped. The weight of the day's revelations pressed against his chest. The lingering trace of her scent pulled him in a different direction.

Before he fully registered his decision, Kane found himself standing before her door. His knuckles hovered against the polished wood. What would he even say?

He lowered his hand. This was madness. She was working against him, possibly endangering everything he'd built. Yet the blood bond between them pulsed with awareness—he could feel her on the other side of the door, awake, restless, conflicted.

His fist connected with the door in three sharp raps before he could reconsider. Immediately, regret flooded him. Kane pivoted, prepared to disappear back down the stairs, when the door swung open.

Serenity stood before him, wrapped in a slate-grey silk dress that clung to her curves like water. Her hair fell in loose waves around her shoulders, still damp from a recent shower. The subtle fragrance of her soap mingled with her natural scent, making his fangs ache.

"Kane." His name on her lips sounded like a question. Her honey-brown eyes widened slightly, a hint of wariness flickering behind them.

Through the bond, he felt her surprise, her nervousness, and beneath it—desire. The same treacherous desire that had driven him to her door.

"I..." Kane's mind raced, searching for a legitimate reason to be at her door. "I wanted to remind you about tomorrow's arrangements." The excuse felt flimsy even to his own ears. "The car will be ready at one o'clock to take us to Grove Gardens. To see your family."

Serenity's expression brightened, her lips curving into a smile that sent warmth through him—genuine warmth, not the calculated satisfaction of successful manipulation.

"Thank you for arranging it," she said, leaning against the doorframe. A droplet of water slid from her damp curls down her neck, slowly traveling down her bare shoulder. Kane forced his gaze away, his fingers curling into fists at his sides to keep from reaching out to trace its path.

"How long will I get to stay with them?" she asked, her voice soft with anticipation.

The hallway suddenly felt too narrow, the air between them charged. Kane maintained a careful distance, fighting the urge to step closer.

"Nox has carved out a window of two to three hours," Kane replied, noting how her shoulders relaxed slightly at this news.

Her gratitude seemed genuine, a fact that only complicated things. Kane's awareness of her betrayal warred with the undeniable pull he felt toward her.

"That should be enough," she said, shifting her weight. The movement caused her dress to ripple across her curves. "I can't wait to see them."

Kane cleared his throat, forcing his attention to remain on her face rather than the way the silk clung to her body.

"Will we be..." she started, then hesitated, tucking a damp curl behind her ear. "Will you stay with me the entire time?"

The question hung between them, layered with meaning. Kane's muscles tensed as he imagined spending hours beside her, watching her with her family, seeing another side of her. It would be torture of the most exquisite kind.

"Yes," he said simply, his voice lower than he intended. "Security protocols."

He felt her reaction through the bond—disappointment or relief, he couldn't tell. His gaze drifted past her into her room, where his eyes caught on familiar pages resting atop her duvet.

The contract.

Pages spread in a neat fan, the Elite agreement lay untouched on her bed, a silver pen still capped beside it. She hadn't signed it.

Serenity followed his gaze, her pulse quickening in that telltale rhythm that made his mouth water. "I haven't signed it..." she said, her voice dropping to just above a whisper. She wet her lips. "Yet."

The word hung between them, laden with possibility.

Kane's control fractured. One moment, he stood rigid in the doorway; the next, he surged forward, closing the distance between them in a single fluid movement. His hands found her face, cradling it as his mouth claimed hers with a hunger that shocked even him.

This is strategic, he told himself, even as genuine desire flooded through him. Make her want this. Make her crave you.

But the lie tasted bitter the moment it formed.

Serenity froze for a heartbeat before melting against him. Her lips parted on a gasp, and Kane deepened the kiss, drowning in her taste—sweeter than he'd imagined through countless forbidden fantasies. Her hands clutched at his shoulders, fingers digging into the fabric of his suit as she pressed closer.

The blood bond flared between them, and Kane cursed silently. The bond amplified everything, flooding him with her surprise, her desire, her guilt—tangling with his own until he couldn't tell where strategy ended and genuine need began.

The silk of her dress whispered beneath his fingers as his hands slid to her waist, pulling her flush against him. His fangs descended unbidden, the sharp points grazing her bottom lip without breaking skin.

Kane backed her into the room, kicking the door closed behind them without breaking the kiss.

A torrent of emotions crashed between them—her desire mingling with his primal hunger. He could feel everything she felt: the heat pooling in her core, the nervous anticipation, the guilty thrill of surrendering to him despite everything that stood between them. His own need for her—raw and achingly real—flowed back through their connection, creating a feedback loop that made his head spin.

Her back hit the wall as he pressed against her. He tasted her gasp, felt her arousal mirroring his own.

"Serenity," he growled against her mouth, his voice barely recognizable to his own ears. "I need to taste you."

She tilted her head, exposing the delicate line of her throat, pulse fluttering beneath her skin. The sight of it sent his hunger spiraling. Kane shook his head, dropping to his knees before her.

"Not there," he rasped, hands sliding up her thighs, bunching the silk of her dress. "Here."

He gazed up at her, waiting. Her eyes half-lidded with desire, Serenity nodded, a small movement that sent fire through his veins. Her fingers threaded through his hair as she lifted one leg, then the other, draping them over his shoulders.

Kane inhaled sharply as he discovered she wore nothing beneath the silk dress. The scent of her arousal hit him like a physical blow, making his fangs lengthen fully. He groaned, his hands gripping her thighs as he leaned forward, dragging his tongue along her slick folds in one long, slow stroke.

"Kane," she gasped, her head falling back against the wall with a soft thud.

The taste of her exploded across his senses—sweeter than any blood he'd ever sampled. He devoured her with single-minded intensity, his tongue circling her sensitive bud before dipping inside her entrance. Her thighs trembled against his cheeks as he worked, alternating between gentle suction and firm strokes.

Her pleasure cascaded through their bond, amplifying his own desire to impossible heights. Kane slipped two fingers inside her, curving them upward to find her most sensitive spot. She writhed against him, her fingers tightening in his hair as he worshipped her with his mouth. Kane suckled her clit between his lips, applying gentle pressure with his fangs without breaking skin.

Serenity's moans grew louder, her hips bucking against his face as he increased his pace. Through their bond, he felt her climbing toward release, her pleasure building in tight, hot waves. He growled against her center, the vibration making her gasp.

"Kane, I'm—" she panted, her thighs shuddering around his head.

He doubled his efforts, his fingers pumping into her as his tongue flicked rapidly over her swollen bud. Her walls clenched around him, and he felt the exact moment she shattered. Serenity cried out, her body convulsing as pleasure crashed through her. Her release flooded his mouth, and Kane lapped at her hungrily, drawing out every tremor of her orgasm until she sagged against the wall.

Kane gathered her limp form in his arms, her weight negligible against his strength. The silk of her dress whispered against his suit as he carried her to the bed, laying her down with uncharacteristic gentleness. Her curls spread across the pillow, her skin glowing in the soft light.

Time seemed suspended as he stood over her, drinking in every detail. The curve of her neck where her pulse still raced. The slight parting of her lips. The way the silk hugged her breasts and hips.

Dangerous, he thought. In ways she couldn't possibly understand.

Serenity pushed herself up on her elbows, her movements languid and sensual. She reached for him, palms sliding up his chest, fingertips tracing the contours of his muscles beneath the fine fabric of his shirt. Kane's breath hitched as her hands moved lower, exploring, claiming. Heat radiated from her touch, burning through layers of clothing to brand his skin.

When her fingers reached his belt, deftly working the buckle, reality crashed through his desire-fogged mind. The surveillance footage flashed behind his eyes—Serenity standing at his desk, going through his computer, stealing information. The rebels' interest in Cavern 47. Her divided loyalties.

The contract. She hasn't signed it yet.

Kane caught her wrists, stilling her movements. The sudden tension in his body made her look up, confusion clouding her features. Her desire still pulsed, but Kane forced himself to focus through the haze of his own need.

"We can't do this," he said, his voice hoarse with restraint. "Not until you sign."

Serenity blinked, her lips parting in surprise. "The contract?"

Kane released her wrists and stepped back, putting necessary distance between them. The scent of her arousal still clung to his lips, making his resolve waver dangerously.

"The agreement exists for a reason," he said, straightening his tie with practiced movements even as his hands shook slightly. "It's protection. For both of us."

Her eyes narrowed, hurt flashing across her features before hardening into reserve. She tugged her dress down over her thighs, the silk settling against her skin with a whisper that seemed to mock him.

"Protection," she repeated, the word hollow. "Or control?"

The question struck him—not because it was unfair, but because it was too accurate. Kane fought to keep his expression neutral as he gestured toward the contract still spread across her bed.

"When you're ready to commit," he said, each word measured, "I'll be waiting."

Without another word, he turned and strode from the room, closing the door behind him with careful restraint that cost him dearly. The hallway felt simultaneously too narrow and endless as he walked away from her, every step a battle against his instinct to return.

He made it to his office by sheer force of will, shutting the door behind him. The silence enveloped him like a shroud. Kane loosened his tie with a savage jerk, his knuckles white with tension. Her taste still lingered on his tongue. The memory of her soft sighs echoed in his ears, tormenting him.

Kane sank into his chair, disheveling the usually impeccable strands of his hair. The bond between them throbbed like an open wound, her confusion and desire still bleeding through despite his attempts to shut it down. He could feel her frustration, her anger, her guilt... and beneath it all, a hurt that mirrored his own.

"Fuck," he growled, slamming his fist against his desk. The force of the blow sent a spiderweb of cracks through the glass surface. Kane stared at the damaged surface, his reflection fractured in the glossy finish.

Just as his thoughts threatened to spiral, Nox walked in.

"Rhyzan called. He just came from talking with Raelinn, Natalia, and Desmond. They're all on high alert. They'll be watching Celearius more closely in the next few days for anything that might serve as a distraction."

"Distraction?" Kane asked, his brows knitting together.

"Yes, he thinks they're going to plan diversion tactics—something to keep you occupied and away from here."

Kane stood and walked over to the window, looking out onto the dark city, his city. "Good. We're so close now. I don't want anything to interfere."

"I also don't want her to get hurt in the process of all this."

"Believe it or not, I don't want to see her hurt either, Nox," Kane's voice was low and heavy with unspoken emotions. He stared out at the glittering cityscape, his reflection in the window a ghostly overlay of conflicted silver-blue eyes. His responsibilities pressed down on him, a constant reminder of the precarious balance he fought to maintain.

Nox stepped closer, his presence a steadying force in the turmoil. "I know you don't, but I also know this betrayal cut deeper than the rest."

Was he that transparent? He pressed his palm against the cool glass. "I'll be fine. I'll do what needs to be done. For our people, for the future we've worked so hard to build."

The unspoken hung heavy in the air between them—the sacrifices they'd made, the secrets they'd kept, the burdens they carried. Kane's gaze drifted back to the window, to the city that depended on him, even as his heart yearned for the one who had betrayed him.

"I understand, but maybe—"

"Keep me informed of any developments." He turned back toward the window so Nox wouldn't see the conflict in his eyes. "And Nox..." Kane's voice was barely audible, a whisper infused with pain. "If it comes down to it, if she truly is a threat to everything we've built... you know what must be done."

There was a heavy silence, then Nox answered. "I understand. You have my word."

As Nox left the room, Kane leaned his forehead against the cool glass, his eyes slipping shut. His desire, her betrayal, and his duty all collided within him, a maelstrom of emotion that threatened to pull him under. But he couldn't afford to break, not now, not when so much hung in the balance.

Sitting back at his desk, he tried to throw himself back into his work, but his thoughts drifted to her. He thought back to Nox's words when he first found out about her betrayal. About how she was doing this for her family.

It's possible she's innocent and caught up in all of this to protect her family. As much as he wanted to believe it, it was her father who'd created the weapon, and who knew what other weapons he might have created.

He was drawn to her. He didn't know if it was the bond amplifying natural attraction, if it was her rare blood calling to him, or if it was simply... her. But he couldn't deny that he wanted her. He craved her.

He would not be blinded. Celearius was his focus. Squashing this rebellion. Not Serenity... the Elite. He would need to keep reminding himself of this every time he was with her.

Because if he didn't, she would be his downfall.

And the terrifying truth was that it didn't terrify him as much as it should.

CHAPTER SIX

Evie stared at both plans for the deadly killing device—the real version and the sabotaged copy she'd spent the past two days creating. They looked nearly identical except for a small change to a number in the formula, which would render the device inactive if used. Making the device incapacitated was easy; what was not easy was the formula itself.

For the formula to function, they would need large amounts of the Elite's blood continuously pumped into the air for weeks, if not months, to take effect truly. Meaning they would have to continuously draw from her in a short period of time, which would eventually kill or severely weaken her.

A cold realization swept through her as she traced the equation. Serenity's father had been developing this before he died. Who else knew these plans existed? Or knew that his daughter had a rare blood type?

Even if she altered the formula to render it harmless, the very existence of these plans would put Serenity in terrible danger. The vampyrs would never believe the daughter of the formula's creator was innocent if this weapon was deployed. With the right scientist, they could easily make these plans harmful again, especially if they had Serenity.

Staring at the formula's blood requirements made it horrifyingly clear—even the sabotaged version would tell the rebels exactly what they needed: an AB negative human. She needed to talk with Kane. There was no way in good conscience she could let Sebastian see these and hand them over to the rebels.

She reached for her comm device, her fingertip just brushing it when the apartment's security system chimed. The soft melodic tone echoed through the apartment, followed by the distinctive sound of Sebastian's footfalls on the wooden entryway. Back early from his shopping trip.

Moving quickly, she placed the plans back into the drawer hidden under her desk and locked it with her thumbprint. The biometric lock pulsed blue, then disappeared, confirming security just as Sebastian called out.

"Evie?"

She pulled up a few Elite files on her computer before calling back. "In my office."

Sebastian appeared in the doorway moments later, his tall frame silhouetted against the hallway light. His arms were laden with glossy shopping bags from Celearius' most exclusive boutiques. His smile, usually so disarming, now seemed different somehow.

"Always working." He crossed to her desk, bending to kiss her.

His lips lingered on hers, tender yet possessive, melting away her tension despite the knowledge she now carried. When he pulled back, his eyes crinkled at the corners with familiar warmth that made her heart ache. How much of him was real and how much was fabrication?

"What's got you so focused?" Sebastian asked, setting his bags down as he perched on the edge of her desk. He gestured toward her screen with casual interest.

Evie forced a smile, grateful for the mundane cover the files provided. "Just reviewing potential Elite-patron matches. Kendra and Erin are looking for another Elite since Dillion disappeared." She scrolled through a profile—a young woman with promising compatibility markers—letting Sebastian see just enough.

"Always the dedicated administrator," he murmured, tracing a finger along her jawline. "You deserve a break. I've brought some things I think you'll love."

"What's all this?" she asked, letting him take her hand and pull her from the chair.

Evie allowed herself to be led from the office as he grabbed the bags. He guided her through the sleek corridor and into their bedroom, gesturing for her to sit on the plush mattress. The silken comforter yielded beneath her weight as Sebastian disappeared into their walk-in closet with his collection of shopping bags.

"I want to surprise you," he called out, his voice slightly muffled by the closet walls.

The rustle of fabric reached her ears as Sebastian changed. Evie traced her fingers over the intricate embroidery of their bedspread while her mind raced with altogether different patterns—disappeared Elites, suspicious meetings, Sebastian's unexplained absences. How many Elites had vanished or been placed with new, more powerful patrons after Sebastian had mentioned they would be better placed there? Seven in the past year alone.

"You wouldn't believe who I ran into at Vermillion's," Sebastian continued, his voice animated with practiced charm. "Councilor Sian's son? The one who always wears those ridiculous ascots? He was there with his father's Elite—what's her name—Lydia? No, Lilith."

Evie made a noncommittal sound of acknowledgement, her attention fractured. A memory surfaced—Sebastian mentioning how Lilith wasn't the best fit for Silvie and would be better with a different patron. She couldn't see anything wrong with the match until Sebastian reminded her that Sian was looking for an Elite.

"And then I stopped by Aurelian's and picked up your watch," Sebastian continued, emerging from the closet in an elegant charcoal suit that hugged his broad shoulders.

"It's beautiful," she replied, trying to focus on the present moment. "The color brings out your eyes."

Sebastian beamed, clearly pleased with her response. "Wait, I have one more."

He disappeared into the closet again, and Evie's suspicions settled more heavily upon her shoulders. The pattern was too methodical to be coincidence. Sebastian's interest in specific Elites, his subtle suggestions about reassignments, the subsequent disappearances—the evidence had been there all along, breadcrumbs she'd deliberately overlooked because the alternative was too painful to contemplate.

"What about this one?" Sebastian emerged in a midnight-blue ensemble that shimmered subtly under the bedroom's soft lighting.

Even now, with suspicion coiling around her heart, she couldn't help but admire how the deep, rich color complemented his complexion.

"I like that one," she said, her voice softer than she intended. "The midnight blue suits you perfectly."

Sebastian's lips curved into a satisfied smile. "I had a feeling you would prefer this one." He smoothed his hands down the front of the jacket. "It happens to complement that sapphire gown you selected for the Elite Ball. We'll make quite the striking pair."

Evie felt a pang at the thought of appearing beside him at the ball, presenting a united front while harboring such devastating secrets between them.

Sebastian disappeared back into the closet, his voice floating out casual and light. "Speaking of the ball, do you know if Kane is planning to bring Serenity? As his official Elite, I mean."

The question seemed innocent enough, but Evie's senses heightened. Why this sudden interest in Kane and Serenity's arrangements?

"I honestly have no idea," she answered, grateful that the truth required no deception. "Kane keeps his personal affairs private, even from me."

Sebastian emerged in his original clothes, the casual elegance of his daily attire a stark contrast to the formal suits he'd been modeling. He ran his hand through his silver-blond hair, tousling it slightly as he studied her expression.

"You know, if Kane isn't planning to bring Serenity as his official Elite, he should reconsider." Sebastian's voice carried a thoughtful lilt. "The social implications would be significant. The Head of the Council publicly acknowledging his Elite? It would strengthen the program's legitimacy in ways nothing else could."

Evie nodded slowly, measuring her response. "You're not wrong. The symbolic power would be... considerable." She traced a pattern on the bedspread, organizing her thoughts. "But Kane will do what Kane wants to do. He always has."

"Even you can't influence him?" Sebastian moved toward her, his footsteps silent against the plush carpet.

"Especially not me," she said with a small smile that didn't quite reach her eyes.

Sebastian closed the distance between them, cupping her face with one hand. His thumb brushed against her cheekbone as he leaned down, pressing his lips to hers, deepening the kiss. His hands slid down to her waist, pulling her closer as his lips trailed from her mouth to her neck. The familiar warmth of his touch ignited her skin, even as her mind remained coolly analytical. Sebastian's fingers worked at the buttons of her blouse, his intentions clear in the quickening of his breath against her collarbone.

Evie placed her hand over his, stilling his movements. "I can't right now," she said, her voice gentle but firm. "I need to finish the patron matches before the end of the day. And the lab is waiting for me to process the new Elite applications."

Sebastian pulled back, disappointment clouding his features. "You work too hard," he murmured, brushing a strand of hair from her face. "The Elite program would crumble without you."

"The program is bigger than any one person," she replied, standing and smoothing her clothing. "But I promise, when I get home tonight..." She let her voice drop to a sultry whisper. "I'll be hungry."

His eyes darkened with anticipation, the momentary frustration vanishing as he traced her lips with his fingertip. "I'll hold you to that promise."

Evie forced a smile, pressing a quick kiss to his cheek before stepping back. "I should go. They're expecting me at the lab."

Sebastian nodded, watching as she gathered her things. "Don't work too late."

Evie paused at the threshold of the bedroom, turning to face him. The sight of him standing there, handsome and familiar in their shared bedroom, sent a wave of grief through her. How many nights had she fallen asleep in his arms, believing herself cherished and protected? How many mornings had she awakened to his smile, thinking their life together was real?

"I'll see you tonight," she said, the words hollow in her chest.

She turned away before he could see the truth in her eyes. Each step down the hallway felt weighted with the knowledge that her lover of eight years was likely using her. Using the Elite program. Using the Elites themselves.

The front door whispered shut behind her. Evie paused in the corridor outside their apartment, pressing her forehead against the cool wall as reality crashed over her. She'd built a life with Sebastian—shared her dreams, ambitions, even this elegant home with its sweeping view of Celearius. Now the foundation was cracking beneath her feet.

For now, she would maintain the illusion, play the role of devoted partner while she uncovered the full extent of his treachery. Their relationship was already over, shattered by his deception. All that remained was the painful task of untangling their lives while keeping him unaware of her suspicions.

But before she could concern herself with that, she had to talk with Kane. Their plan would endanger Serenity, and as much as he might resent his Elite at the moment, she knew that beneath that resentment lay a man who cared deeply for her.

She just hoped that, when this was over, he would finally get his happy ending.

Because hers was already gone.

CHAPTER SEVEN

SERENITY

Serenity's stomach was in knots, and she couldn't decipher the reason why.

They were currently in the car heading to Grove Gardens, and Kane hadn't spoken one word to her today. He barely even looked at her. Not even a good morning, and it was slowly killing her.

The sleek car glided past the imposing structures of the Silver District, their gleaming facades reflecting the afternoon light in sharp, blinding bursts. She turned her gaze to the window, watching the wealth of vampyr society parade by in stark contrast to where they were headed.

Her fingers unconsciously traced her lower lip, memory flooding her senses—Kane's mouth on hers yesterday, hungry and demanding, then the shocking moment when he'd pulled away, leaving her shaking. After he'd left, she'd lain awake for hours, her body aching with a need that refused to subside. She'd tried to satisfy the hunger herself, fingers searching desperately in the darkness, but the release had been hollow, a poor substitute for what she truly craved.

This morning, the contract sat on her nightstand, its black text stark against crisp white paper. She'd hovered her pen above the signature line three separate times, unable to complete the motion. Signing meant reducing whatever sparked between them to clinical terms—blood exchange, physical contact parameters, payment schedules. It shouldn't bother her, but it did.

There was no future for them anyway, she reminded herself. And yet she couldn't bring herself to sign.

She glanced over at him.

His face was obscured by the file he'd been reading since they'd gotten into the car. That strange awareness between them hummed quietly beneath her skin, present but muted—as if he'd deliberately closed himself off from it. She could barely sense him through it this morning, just a whisper that told her he was there, alive, breathing. But nothing more. The absence felt deliberate, like a door firmly shut.

Last night, after she'd finally succumbed to sleep, she'd dreamed of him... of his touch. He'd gazed at her with such hunger it had scared and excited her, especially when his fangs grazed her neck. She'd wanted them to sink into her.

She looked away, not wanting to think about that dream anymore before her foolish heart got her into trouble. She just needed to concentrate on getting herself and her family through this visit alive.

This morning, she'd been able to call her mom and Beth to let them know she was coming to see them and that she'd be bringing her patron. Her mother told her she already knew since they were searching the place as part of protocol. She'd asked Nox about it, and he told her it was because Kane was visiting with her and it was just standard protocol. She'd gotten a message from Beth an hour ago saying they were in the clear, which gave her some relief.

They were approaching the first checkpoint. The car slowed as the guards scrambled to make themselves busy as the gate opened, and they drove right through without stopping into the Quartz District.

Her finger hovered over the window button as they passed through the lively streets, people moving to and from work rather than leisurely strolling like the evening they'd come here for dinner.

Suddenly, the glass went down, letting in the fresh air. Immediately, she closed her eyes and inhaled deeply, hoping to catch a whiff of the sea breeze. She could feel his eyes on her through the connection—suddenly warmer, more present—but she didn't care as she took another breath, catching a hint of salt on the breeze. It was the balm to her soul.

She took one more breath, really sucking in the salty air, imagining the warm sand beneath her feet and feeling the mists from the crashing waves as they hit the shore. The sun beaming down on her, and the sound of the seagulls as they flew overhead.

She sighed, then opened her eyes to see that they were passing into Easton. She could still feel his gaze on her, but she refused to look his way. With determined vigor, she would get through today.

The various bungalows and small storefronts always reminded her of what a typical human neighborhood would look like, with its fake green grass and white picket fences. The black-and-grey clinical building caught her eye as they turned the corner. It was the only building that felt out of place in the human district. It was also the place that had changed her life, to think it was only a few weeks ago that she'd walked through its steely doors.

His eyes continued to watch her even as they finally crossed into her district, Grove Gardens. A vast difference from Easton. No green grass or white picket fences here. Only rundown shops and dilapidated houses that needed more than a paint job and the patchwork supplies the so-called government claimed to provide.

Anger sparked within her as they passed by the faded brick building with the broken glass windows and every other letter missing from the faded blue sign. She gazed out the window at the neighborhood... her neighborhood. Then she turned and met silver-blue eyes.

"May I ask you a question?" she said, finally breaking the silence. "And will you answer me honestly?"

"Yes. What is it you want to ask me?" he asked softly, closing his folder and placing it to the side.

She took a minute to gather her thoughts as he stared into her eyes. Then she took a breath before she spoke. "Why hasn't the government done anything about cleaning up and restoring Grove Gardens?"

She thought he wasn't going to answer her, especially when he turned away from her glare, but he surprised her when he spoke.

"It is not my responsibility to look after the human districts."

Not his responsibility? She wasn't understanding. "You are the Head of the Council. Why would the human districts not be part of your responsibility?"

He turned to look at her. "I am... but I must leave the humans to run their own districts. Unfortunately, your Councilor has chosen to let your district decline."

"And you think that is okay?"

"No, I do not. But if I take any more control, then Celearius will never succeed."

"And you think it is succeeding now?"

She didn't know whether he would answer the question because they had arrived. She didn't even realize they were in front of her house until Nox opened the door.

"We are here."

As much as she wanted to get out and go to her mother and sister, she found that she couldn't pull her eyes away from his. She wanted to hear his answer.

"No."

She sighed. Then nodded with understanding before she got out of the car. As soon as she approached the steps, the front door opened, and Beth ran out straight into her arms.

"Serenity!"

"Beth." She hugged her tightly, not realizing how much she'd missed her sister in these past weeks. She pulled back to look at her. Beth had gained some weight and had a healthy glow. The medicine was working, and they were putting the money to good use. "Look at you! Have you grown at least an inch?"

"Yes! We went to the big grocery store in Grove Hills, and now the house is full of food. Mom even bought me a chocolate bar. I tried to save some for you, but I couldn't help it. It was so good."

"I'm sure if you're good, Mom will buy you more."

"Only if you promise to keep your room clean."

Serenity looked to see her mom in the doorway. She also had gained healthy weight and had a glow about her. Serenity walked toward her as she stepped from the doorway and hugged her tight.

"Baby, how are you?" her mom asked, pushing her back so she could get a good look at her. "You look good. Have they been treating you well?" she said, lowering her voice.

"Yes," she said, turning to look back at Kane, catching the look of appreciation in his eyes before she turned back to her mother. "Let me introduce you to them."

"Is it safe?" her mother asked, concerned, as her eyes moved to Beth.

That was a good question. Were they safe? She was tempted to look back at him again, but instead she looked her mother in the eye and said, very loudly, "Of course we are. Let me introduce you to them."

She grabbed her mother's and her sister's hands, then led them down the steps.

Her mother's hand trembled as they stepped in front of Kane and Nox. Kane stared down at them, his face unreadable as he looked over both her mother and sister.

"It is a pleasure to meet you, Mrs. Wright. I am Nox, and this menacing fellow is my driver," he said, grinning.

Both Kane and Serenity glanced at Nox before looking at each other. Then Serenity couldn't help the laughter that burst from her mouth. Kane smirked.

Her mother stopped trembling and glanced at her strangely.

"Actually, this imbecile is my driver, and I am Kane. Your daughter is my Elite." Kane held out his hand toward her mom. She hesitated, then reached out her hand to shake it.

"It is nice to meet you, Kane. Thank you for taking good care of my daughter."

"It is you whom I need to thank for having such an incredible daughter." His smirk turned into a smile, which made her mother smile back.

Through the connection, Serenity felt a warmth bloom—genuine, not calculated. It surprised her. He meant it.

"I made some lunch. It's not much since Serenity is the cook, but I thought I would put something together in case you were hungry. Wait, do you eat food?" She looked shocked as soon as the question left her mouth, but Nox answered right away.

"I love a good home-cooked meal. We're so grateful to have Serenity, and we apologize for taking her away, but don't think we'll give her up now with all the delicious food she cooks for us." Then he stooped to Beth's level. "How about we go inside and grab some food before it gets cold? Then you can show me where your mom hides the treats?"

"We made brownies, but Mom says I have to eat some veggies first."

"I think I can convince her to make an exception this time," he smiled, then winked at Serenity's mom. He held out his arm for Beth to take. She gleefully took it, and they walked toward the house together. He whispered something to her that made her laugh out loud as they walked through the threshold.

"Shall we go in as well?" Kane gestured.

"Can I have a moment with my mother?"

He simply nodded and headed into the house. Once she was sure he was inside, she turned to her mother.

"What happened during the search?"

"Nothing. They came mid-morning. There were six of them. They quickly and quietly searched the house. Whatever they moved, they put back." She placed her hand on Serenity's cheek. "Babe, they didn't find anything."

"And the shed?"

"We hid everything under the house. We're okay. Let's just enjoy this."

"I know. I just worry." Serenity wanted to ask her mom if she knew about her father and his dealings with the rebellion, but she couldn't risk Kane overhearing. Also, they simply didn't have time.

She would enjoy this visit as much as possible, and hopefully, on the next visit, she'd be able to really talk to her. "Come on, let's go in before Nox and Beth eat all the dessert."

Her mother laughed—a real, genuine sound that made Serenity's heart lift—and together they walked toward the house where she could hear Beth's delighted giggles echoing from inside.

For now, just for these few hours, she would let herself be happy.

CHAPTER EIGHT

KANE

It was strange being in such a setting again. To sit at a table with people filled with laughter and joy. It had been a long time since he had done something like this. Just sitting, talking, and enjoying each other's company.

Beth seemed to enjoy telling childhood stories about Serenity—like the time she fought off a fearsome rabbit in the garden with a large carrot, or how she almost died trying to save a baby bird off the top of the shed, only for it to fly away as soon as she got near it.

Kane couldn't help the feeling of mirth that swelled within him. The feeling was unsettling but not unwelcome.

He enjoyed seeing her laugh. He liked how her smile lit up her entire face.

Serenity stood and began clearing off the table.

Kane rose from his seat, picking up his own plate and reaching for another. "Allow me to help." His voice was low, intimate in the warm atmosphere of the dining room.

"That's not necessary," Serenity protested, but her smile betrayed her pleasure at the gesture.

"I insist." Their fingers brushed as he took another dish, sending a current of electricity up his arms that settled somewhere beneath his ribcage.

Kane followed her through the swinging door into the modest kitchen, watching her move with practiced efficiency. The space was small but immaculate, forcing them into closer proximity than the formal dining room had allowed. He could detect the subtle notes of her scent here—vanilla and an undertone he recognized as distinctly hers.

Serenity placed her stack of dishes into the sink, the glass clinking softly against the metal basin. She turned and took his load, adding them to the growing pile.

"Are you enjoying yourself?" Kane asked, leaning against the counter. The domestic scene felt surreal—centuries of existence, and here he stood in a human kitchen, watching a woman wash dishes as if they were any normal couple.

"Yes, I am," she whispered, tucking a wayward curl behind her ear. "Thank you for this... for everything. Not just helping with clearing the dishes, but... coming here. Meeting Beth. It means more than you know."

Kane stepped closer, drawn by the vulnerability in her honey-brown eyes. The kitchen suddenly felt impossibly small, electricity charging the air between them. His gaze dropped to her lips, soft and slightly parted. The steady rhythm of her heartbeat quickened, a symphony only he could hear.

"Serenity," he murmured, her name a caress on his tongue.

She tilted her face upward, eyes fluttering closed. The distance between them narrowed to mere inches, the heat of her breath mingling with his. Kane's hand moved of its own accord, fingers brushing the delicate line of her jaw.

The kitchen door swung open with a creak.

"Yes! Time for brownies. I will help," her sister, Beth, said excitedly as she walked into the kitchen.

Serenity jerked backward, colliding with the edge of the sink.

"I heard there is ice cream," Nox chimed in as he walked in behind her, looking at both Kane and Serenity in that maddeningly knowing way.

"Serenity! You know he likes the same ice cream as me," Beth continued, her eyes bright with excitement. "Chocolate fudge brownie, right?"

A flood of warmth pulsed through Kane's chest, quickly replaced by a cold current of unease. The moment with Serenity had passed, leaving him unbalanced. He straightened his shoulders, retreating behind the familiar shield of formality.

"You'll have to excuse me," Kane said, his voice regaining its customary reserve. "I should check in with your mother."

He didn't look at Serenity as he stepped away, couldn't trust himself to maintain his composure if he caught the disappointment—or worse, relief—that might be written across her features. The kitchen suddenly felt stifling.

This is strategic, he reminded himself even as his chest ached. Keep her wanting more. Keep her off-balance.

But the lie tasted bitter.

Kane slipped through the swinging door, the cool air of the dining room washing over him like a balm. Elizabeth Wright sat alone at the table, her weathered hands wrapped around a mug of tea, steam curling into the air between them. She looked up as he approached, her eyes—so like her daughter's—appraising him with quiet intelligence.

As he sat back down, her heart began to beat faster.

"There is no need to be afraid. I have no intention of harming you or your family."

"I do not trust you. You may have gained my daughter's trust, but you are a stranger to me. Vampyr or human, I do not know you."

"That I can understand. Hopefully, in time, I won't be such a stranger, and just as your daughter has learned to trust me, so will you."

"Only time and your actions will tell. What would make me feel better about this is if you promise always to keep my daughter safe—even if it is from yourself."

As much as he wanted to promise that, he couldn't, because he knew he couldn't do that. But he needed to tell her something to appease her.

"Your daughter has a rare blood type, and as much as I want to promise to keep her safe, I cannot. What I can promise is to keep her safe from other Vampyr who intend to harm her, and to keep her alive as long as it is within my power. But that is all I can promise you."

The words were true, but incomplete. He couldn't promise to protect Serenity from himself—from the way he was using her, from the trap he'd woven around her, from the blood bond that tied them together in ways neither of them understood.

"Will she ever be able to come home?"

"She is now registered within the system. The safest place for her is by my side."

Kane watched as tears threatened to spill from her eyes, but as soon as she heard them at the door, she took a deep breath and forced a smile.

"I think Nox may have overdone it with the ice cream on top of the brownies," Serenity said, placing a small bowl with two scoops of ice cream in front of him. The brownie seemed to be hidden somewhere beneath it.

"Everyone deserves two scoops. Besides, I told Beth here that I would personally replace it," Nox said.

She took her seat next to him, and a small moan escaped her lips as she pulled the spoon from her mouth. "Okay, you're right. Two scoops."

Kane noted that they needed to buy ice cream for the apartment.

He took a bite of his own ice cream and realized they would have to buy two cartons. He had forgotten how delicious this icy treat was.

His comm device buzzed. He pulled it out of his suit jacket to check the caller ID.

Rhyzan.

"Excuse me, I need to take this."

Kane stood and walked into the living room, which offered him little privacy.

"You can use my bedroom. It is the door to the right," Beth yelled from behind him. He turned and nodded toward her before entering the door to the right.

"Yes?" he answered.

"They hacked the system again."

He closed the door. He could not risk being overheard, especially here.

"Do you know what they were searching for?"

"Yes, it's definitely a prisoner and the location of this place."

"So it's confirmed they are trying to get a prisoner?"

"Yes, possibly more than one. I let them think they found a backdoor, so they will most likely be back in the system within the next 2-3 hours. Kane, I plan to let them in."

"Good. Does Evie have the plans ready?"

"We actually need to talk about that. She wants to meet with us before she hands over anything. I am actually heading to her now."

"What's wrong?"

"She won't tell me over the phone."

"I will head to her, too."

"Wait, aren't you still at the Elite's house?"

"Yes."

"I will see you soon."

Kane clicked off. They were getting closer and closer to finding them. It was possible he wouldn't need the Elite at all. Then he could end this rebellion and still be able to keep her... not that he should keep her. He pinched the bridge of his nose in frustration at his chaotic thoughts when it came to the Elite.

He placed his device back into his jacket and was about to leave when a picture caught his eye. It was such a simple picture of her, an older man—her father—and a younger Beth. They were sitting on the front porch of this house, laughing. The picture only looked to be a few years old, and the man in the middle was their father, Richard Wright.

Recognition flickered at the edges of his memory, but he couldn't exactly pinpoint it. He pulled out his device and took a picture to send to Rhy. It was then that he noticed the various seashells and oceanic decor scattered around the dresser. He turned to find a collage of cut pictures of the beach and ocean on the wall. This must have been her room before Beth's, or they'd shared it, noticing only that the left side of the room held the sea life decor. He hadn't seen any in her room at home... possibly because she wasn't expecting to stay.

A knock sounded on the door before Nox stepped in, closing the door. "Is everything good?"

"Can you arrange a trip to the beach?" he asked suddenly. It shouldn't be on his mind, but seeing those seashells, that collage of cut pictures—evidence of dreams she'd had to abandon—affected him in ways he didn't want to examine. He wanted to give her the ocean. Not as manipulation. Not as a strategy. Simply because she wanted it, and he found himself wanting to give her anything that would make her smile the way she'd smiled at her sister.

Nox raised an eyebrow in question until his eyes grazed over the sea decor. "Of course, she will love it."

"They hacked the system in the Cavern."

"Not surprised. Your ice cream is melting."

"I have to go. Evie needs to talk about the plans."

"Fine. Come before they think we are plotting their deaths."

Kane smirked, knowing Nox was right, then followed him back to the table.

Serenity glanced at him and gave him a small smile, and he returned it. He visibly saw the tension leave her shoulders. Did she think he would share a meal with her family before killing them? Did she honestly think him so cruel? If he were going to keep her suspicions away, he would have to do a better job at gaining her trust. Starting now.

"Unfortunately, I have to leave."

Sadness crept into her face before she masked it.

"But I will not cut your visit short. Nox will stay here with you until you're ready to come back," he said.

"I will call Rhyzan to come pick you up," Nox said, walking back into the living area as he pulled out his comm device.

"It was a pleasure meeting you all."

"He will be here in about five minutes," Nox said as he sat down, dug back into his brownie sundae, and jumped into conversation with Beth about what games she liked to play.

"I will walk you out," Serenity said, surprising Kane as he walked toward the door.

She followed him out onto her dilapidated front porch. The wood creaked as she moved to walk down the steps, not feeling safe enough to stand on it for more than a few seconds.

"Thank you," she said from the steps. He turned to meet her amber eyes full of gratitude at his level.

"My goal is for this to work."

Her eyes widened for a second before she looked away.

"Please enjoy your time with your family."

Kane turned to see Rhy's sleek black car silently pulling in front of her house. He nodded toward her, but as he was about to walk away, she surprised him by wrapping her arms around his neck. It took him seconds to realize that she was hugging him. It had been so long since he had experienced this kind of affection that it took his brain a moment to process.

When his arms finally moved to return the embrace, the motion felt both foreign and achingly natural. She fit against him perfectly, warm and alive and trusting. She shouldn't trust me, he thought desperately. But his arms tightened around her anyway, just for a moment, before she pulled away.

"I just want to let you know that I really appreciate this." She squeezed tight once more, then pulled away, heading back into the house.

Kane watched her walk inside before he got into the car.

"They found the medicine stashed under the house," Rhy said as soon as they drove off. "I told them not to touch it, but they did take pictures of all that they found."

Rhy pulled out his device and handed it to him. He quickly scanned the pictures, not surprised by anything he found, since her father was a doctor. Everything in the pictures looked to be homemade herbal remedies.

He just wished they'd found more substantial materials so he would know if the weapon had been made or was in the process of being made.

"There were a lot of herbal medicines, but nothing too advanced. Though now I can see why she became an Elite. They were running low on insulin and asthma medicine."

Hearing that gave him hope that she was only a part of this for her family. When had he started hoping for her innocence? When had he stopped seeing her as merely a tactical asset and started... what? Caring?

They continued in silence as Rhy drove them to his office. He tried to keep the Elite off his mind, but failed. He was grateful when they pulled into the garage.

"Evie is waiting in your office for us," Rhy informed him as they stepped into the elevator.

As soon as they stepped off, Kaelen had a Syn ready for him. He didn't want to drink it, but until he could feed again, he needed sustenance. He snatched the bottle and proceeded into his office, where Evie waited for them.

"Evie, what is so important?"

"The weapon plans should be destroyed," Evie said, her voice tight with restrained emotion. She paced the length of his desk, her elegant fingers worrying at the silk scarf around her throat.

Kane lowered himself into his chair and placed the untouched Syn on his desk. "Explain."

"If the rebels get their hands on those blueprints, they'll come for her." Evie stopped pacing and planted her palms on his desk, leaning forward. Her auburn hair caught the light, those distinctive highlights shimmering under the office lighting. "They'll hunt Serenity down like an animal."

Rhyzan moved to the window, his reflection ghostlike in the darkened glass. "We already knew she was in danger due to her blood type. That's why we matched her with Kane."

"This is different," Evie insisted. "The weapon requires more than just a drop of her blood type. It needs significant quantities. Constantly. The way the device is designed..." She straightened, running a hand through her hair. "The toxin within the device would need to be administered into the air over months for it to be effective. The amount needed for one disbursement for one month would be at least one pint of her blood."

"They won't let her go until every last one of us is dead," Rhy concluded.

The implications sank into Kane's consciousness like stones dropping through dark water. "She would be kept like cattle," Kane muttered, his jaw clenching.

"If she resists," Evie said, her voice dropping to a whisper, "they would keep her captive."

The thought of Serenity—bright, fierce Serenity—trapped in some rebel facility, tubes snaking from her veins, her life force slowly draining away... His fingers tightened around the edge of the desk until the wood creaked in protest.

"The worst part I fear," Evie continued, "the weapon is designed to be constantly recharged with fresh blood. One pint to activate, but the blueprints indicate they would have to refresh it weekly with new blood to keep it potent and at its strongest."

Kane's jaw clenched so hard he felt a muscle spasm. "That would kill her within months."

"More like weeks," Rhyzan corrected. "The human body can't replenish blood that quickly. They'd be draining her faster than her body could produce new cells."

Rage surged through him, his vision blurring at the edges.

"If rebels get these plans," Evie continued, "they'll realize what they have in her. And if our side discovers these plans exist..." She hesitated, her eyes meeting Kane's with unmistakable dread. "The Council would sanction her immediate termination. They couldn't risk her falling into rebel hands."

"And if any vampyrs discover these plans exist," Evie added, her voice dropping even lower, "Serenity will never be safe again. Not from the rebels, not from the Council, not from anyone. Both sides will hunt her until the day she dies."

Kane closed his eyes, struggling to contain the storm raging within him. His hands unclenched from the desk, leaving small indentations in the polished wood. The silence in the room stretched, broken only by the soft mechanical hum of the building's climate system. When he finally opened his eyes, the silver-blue had dimmed to a steely gray.

"Destroy them," he said, his voice like granite. "Every trace. Every schematic. Every notation."

The strategic part of his mind screamed that they were giving up leverage, losing a valuable weapon. But the part of him that had felt Serenity's trust, that had seen her joy at her sister's health, that had held her grateful embrace—that part didn't care about strategy. She would be safe. Nothing else mattered.

Evie's shoulders sagged with visible relief. "I'll handle it personally."

"Good," Kane said. "Make certain no copies exist."

Rhyzan stepped away from the window, his verdant eyes gleaming with calculation. "We should still proceed with the original plan. Let Sebastian find whispers of the weapon's existence and the connection to her. Chloe can confirm that such plans exist without mentioning the blood type."

"A half-truth," Kane agreed. "Sebastian will believe he's found exactly what the rebellion needs, and we'll let him believe he's succeeding. It will draw out more rebel operatives."

"There's something else," Evie said, interrupting his thoughts. She reached into her pocket and withdrew a small data drive. "I've been analyzing the blood samples from the Elite candidates, and Serenity's isn't just rare—it's unique. The molecular structure has properties I've never seen before."

Kane took the drive, turning it over in his palm. "Explain."

"Her blood contains compounds that shouldn't be possible. It's as if..." Evie hesitated, choosing her words carefully. "It's as if it evolved to adapt to vampyric biology."

Rhyzan moved closer, his interest piqued. "You're saying her blood is naturally weaponized?"

"No, but it can be. Looking at the chemicals used to make the toxin, her blood adapted itself to the chemical used, which weaponized it," Evie explained.

"Not quite understanding, Evie. What does that have to do with anything?" Rhyzan asked.

"If her blood were combined with the right vampyr blood, it could contain the building blocks to create something new, possibly."

"Like a new species?" Kane asked.

"Possibly, or something else entirely. I am still not sure—it would take years of research and experimenting to conclude anything."

"What would happen if she were given vampyr blood?" Rhy asked, and Kane glared daggers at him behind Evie's back.

"If she were ever to be given vampyr blood, she would most likely have an intense reaction depending on who gave her blood, and I would have to study her blood to see how it changes. Why?" Evie lifted her head from the screen to look at Rhy.

"Nothing. Just curious."

She turned to look at Kane. "You haven't given her your blood? Not even a drop."

Kane schooled his face and lied. "No."

If he told her about the blood, she would ask why he gave it to her, then she would rightfully try to murder him. He wasn't up for it tonight.

"Good."

"I should go," Rhyzan said suddenly, pushing away from the desk. "Chloe will need updates on this development, and we still need to finalize preparations for Cavern 47. If they're planning an attack, we need to be ready."

Kane nodded, grateful for Rhyzan's efficiency. "Keep me informed of any changes."

"Always do," Rhyzan replied, slipping out the door with barely a sound.

The office fell quiet. Kane studied Evie, noting the dark circles under her eyes as she closed the files and removed the data drive.

"There's more," Evie said, breaking the silence.

Kane raised an eyebrow. "More troubling news?"

"Not exactly." She perched on the edge of his desk, crossing her ankles. "Sebastian asked me if Serenity would be attending the Elite Ball next week."

The Elite Ball. Kane had almost forgotten about the annual event—a lavish affair where vampyrs and their Elite mingled in a display of unity and prosperity—a political necessity.

"Did he mention why?" Kane asked, his voice carefully neutral.

"Only that he thought it would be... advantageous for her to attend." Evie's fingers traced an idle pattern on the edge of his desk. "He seemed particularly interested in whether you would be escorting her."

Kane hadn't considered bringing Serenity to such a public event. The Elite Ball was a spectacle of vampyric power and influence—a dangerous place for someone with her unique blood and rebel connections. Yet if Sebastian was asking...

"I wasn't planning on it," he admitted, reaching for the untouched Syn. The synthetic blood was cold against his lips, metallic and lifeless. "But since Sebastian is showing interest, I'll have to change my approach. They could be planning an attack or worse. I'll need to increase security for the event."

Evie nodded, her auburn hair catching the light as she moved. "I thought as much. Should I tell him you'll be bringing her?"

"Yes. Let's see what he does with the information."

A moment passed.

"Speaking of Sebastian," Kane said, setting the synthetic blood aside, "how have things been between the two of you lately?"

Evie's posture stiffened almost imperceptibly. "Fine." She busied herself by hopping off his desk and putting the data drive back in her pocket, not meeting his gaze. "He doesn't suspect anything."

An unspoken truth lingered between them—whatever troubled her about Sebastian remained unsaid. But pressing the issue would only make her retreat further.

"I see," he said simply.

"I should go. I need to destroy the plans and plant some seeds." She paused at the door. "Kane... be careful. With Serenity, I mean. This game we're playing has always been dangerous, but now..."

"I know," he said quietly.

After she left, Kane remained at his desk, his thoughts churning like a gathering storm. The office felt suddenly hollow, the silence pressing in on him from all sides. He reached for the Syn but set it aside again without drinking.

The lie sat heavily with him. He'd given her his blood, created the bond that now pulsed between them like a living thing. A bond that made every deception harder, every manipulation more painful. A bond that let him feel her emotions even as he tried to use them against her.

He hadn't known when he'd bitten her and given her his blood that a bond would form—blood bonds were vampyric myth, ancient lore whispered about but never confirmed. Even now, he wasn't entirely certain what it meant, what it would become. But he didn't regret it. Not when it let him sense her joy, her fear, her trust. Not when it connected them in ways that transcended the physical.

What he hadn't anticipated was how it would complicate everything. How feeling her trust flowing through that connection while he plotted her exploitation would tear him apart. How every lie would taste bitter on his tongue because he could sense her belief in him through the bond. How every strategic move would feel like betrayal because he experienced her genuine affection as if it were his own.

The bond wasn't supposed to exist. But now that it did, Kane couldn't imagine being without it—even as it destroyed his ability to use her the way he needed to.

He'd told himself the family visit, the beach trip he'd just arranged, even ordering the destruction of the weapon plans—all necessary moves to gain her trust, to keep her compliant, to make her useful. But sitting alone in his office, Kane couldn't maintain the pretense anymore.

He reached for the Syn again, grimacing at its lifeless taste.

The bond pulsed with a warmth that felt suspiciously like longing, and Kane forced himself to ignore it.

He had work to do. A rebellion to crush. A city to protect.

Serenity Wright was a means to an end. She had to be.

CHAPTER NINE

Serenity

Serenity woke to a room bathed in silver dawn light, her mind still tangled in yesterday's memories—her mother's fragile smile, Beth's hopeful eyes, and promises she wasn't sure she could keep. They didn't come home until well into the evening, Nox letting her stay later than intended, using the excuse of teaching her sister how to play an old card game. She was internally grateful to him for giving her extra time with her family.

It was still strange leaving them, but there was nothing she could do. Though a small part of her wished she could have seen Jax, her best friend who'd stopped speaking to her after she'd entered the Elite Program. She'd dreamt of him last night—of their last night under the stars, how she'd wished things would have turned out differently between them. Then her dreams turned chaotic. Sebastian's voice whispering in her ear about Cavern 47, mingling with Kane's low rumble as he'd walked her through the Elite contract terms. The two worlds pulling her apart.

Turning her head, she looked at the contract lying on her nightstand. All it would take was a simple signature, and she would be in his arms again.

With a frustrated groan, she pushed back the silken sheets and swung her legs over the side of the bed. The cool wooden floor sent a shock through her bare feet, grounding her in reality.

What was she doing? Playing both sides in a war she barely understood. Spying for the rebels while contemplating signing herself completely over to Kane. The man who'd offered her protection, whose touch still burned on her skin—and yet she was betraying him, stealing information about Cavern 47 right under his nose.

The resistance would get their information either way. At least this way, she could protect her family and... have something for herself. Something real with Kane, even if it was built on lies and only for a little while.

Her fingers trembled as she picked up the pen. One signature and she would belong to him—officially, legally, intimately.

"Damn it all," she whispered, and before she could talk herself out of it, she scrawled her signature across the bottom line with a single, fluid motion.

Serenity Wright.

She stared at those two words as the ink dried. The moment felt irrevocable, transforming from mere signature into something she couldn't take back.

The bond between them—the one she'd felt since their first intimate encounter—seemed to pulse with warmth, as if acknowledging what she'd done.

"It's done," she murmured. "No turning back now."

She folded the contract carefully, sliding it back into its envelope. Time to face the consequences of her choice.

As she walked through the quiet hallway, the envelope clutched in her hand like both shield and confession, she expected to find Nox waiting in the kitchen with his usual sardonic smile. Instead she found Kane. He stood at the counter with his back to her, his broad shoulders taut beneath his shirt. The morning light caught in his dark hair, turning the edges almost blue-black. He turned slowly, those piercing silver-blue eyes finding hers immediately before dropping to the envelope in her hand.

The kitchen fell silent except for the quiet hum of the refrigerator. Serenity's throat tightened as Kane set down his glass with deliberate care.

"You've made your decision." His voice was low, not quite a question, his gaze fixed on the envelope.

Serenity stepped forward, extending the envelope toward him.

"Yes." The single word fell from her lips, heavy with finality.

Kane took the envelope, his fingers brushing hers in a touch that sent electricity racing up her arm. An emotion flooded through her that she couldn't quite name—relief? Hope? It wasn't hers, she realized with a start. It was his, bleeding through whatever this was between them.

He didn't open it immediately, just studied her face with an intensity that made her skin flush.

"Are you certain?" His expression remained guarded, but his eyes flickered with hope.

"Yes, I'm certain," she whispered.

Kane's eyes searched hers, piercing through her defenses as if he could see the lies beneath her certainty. His gaze lingered on her lips, then flicked back to her eyes with an intensity that made her breath catch. The contract envelope dangled forgotten from his fingertips as he stepped closer, close enough that she could feel the heat radiating from his body.

"Serenity..." His voice was rough, almost reverent.

He leaned forward with agonizing slowness, giving her every chance to pull away. Instead, she tilted her chin upward, meeting him halfway. When his lips finally touched hers, the gentleness surprised her. It wasn't the demanding kiss she'd expected, but tender, questioning—a stark contrast to the commanding presence he usually projected.

Her eyes fluttered closed as his free hand came up to cradle her cheek, his thumb tracing her jawline. The kiss deepened, and Serenity felt herself melting into him, her hands finding purchase against his chest where his heart thundered beneath her fingertips.

Her deception pressed against her chest, nearly choking her. She pulled back slightly, her lips still tingling from his kiss.

"Kane—" How could she tell him? That while she'd signed his contract with one hand, she was betraying him with the other? That she could sense his genuine emotions—and they didn't match what Sebastian had told her about Kane?

"There's something I want to show you," he said, his voice low and intimate. He tucked a damp curl behind her ear, his fingertips lingering against her skin.

Suspicion curled through her stomach. Was this a trap? Had he somehow discovered her betrayal? She studied his face, searching for signs of deception, but found only an unusual vulnerability in those silver-blue eyes.

"What is it?" she asked, unable to keep the wariness from her voice.

Kane extended his hand to her, palm up. "Trust me."

Those two words hung between them, weighted with irony she was certain he couldn't comprehend.

Serenity hesitated, then placed her hand in his. His palm was warm, fingers curling around hers with gentle pressure that anchored her to the moment.

Kane led her across the kitchen, past the gleaming countertops, to a door she hadn't noticed before. It was nestled in the corner, unassuming and almost hidden behind the large stainless steel refrigerator. He produced a small key from his pocket, the metal catching the morning light as he unlocked it.

The door swung open to reveal a narrow hallway with polished wood floors that absorbed their footsteps. Three identical doors lined the left wall, their dark metal surfaces unmarked except for one, which had a small peephole.

"Nox's place of residence," Kane said, nodding toward the first door as they passed. His thumb traced absent circles against her skin. "He prefers his privacy, though he's rarely far."

The second door loomed before them, and Kane slowed. "Emergency exit. Leads to a secure staircase that will take you all the way to the lobby."

They continued to the third door at the hallway's end. Kane paused, his expression softening with a vulnerability that made her heart ache.

"This is... a place I've only shown certain people." He pushed open the door, revealing a few steps and another door beyond.

Serenity climbed the steps behind him, her curiosity momentarily overwhelming her guilt.

Kane pushed open the final door, and brilliant sunlight flooded in, momentarily blinding Serenity. She blinked against the sudden brightness, raising her hand to shield her eyes as he gently guided her forward onto what felt like solid stone beneath her bare feet.

"Watch your step," he murmured, his fingers tightening protectively around hers as she crossed the threshold.

As her vision adjusted, Serenity gasped. They stood on a sprawling rooftop garden that stretched across the entire building, an impossible oasis floating above the city. Vibrant blooms in every imaginable hue spilled from ornate planters. Trellises heavy with climbing roses created living archways between sections of the garden, while fruit trees in ceramic pots dotted the perimeter, their branches swaying gently in the morning breeze.

"Kane, this is..." Words failed her as she took another step forward, overwhelmed by the symphony of color and life surrounding them.

A warm breeze swept across the rooftop, carrying with it the unmistakable tang of salt. Serenity closed her eyes, inhaling deeply. The scent of the sea mingled with the garden's floral perfume. She let the salty air fill her lungs, savoring the unexpected connection to the outside world.

"You can see the ocean from here on clear days," Kane said, his voice softer than she'd ever heard it. "Just there, beyond the eastern edge of the city."

Serenity opened her eyes, following his gaze to where the horizon shimmered with a distant blue line.

Kane's hand slipped from hers as he moved to a stone bench nestled between two flowering cherry trees and a cluster of lavender plants. He sat, shoulders slightly hunched, fingers trailing over a carved inscription she couldn't quite make out.

"I built this after the Devastation," Kane said softly, his voice carrying a weight she hadn't heard before. "Becca, my wife... she had a garden of her own. She spent most of her days there until she died."

The pain in his voice was unmistakable. This wasn't the cold, calculating vampyr the rebellion had described. This was a man who'd loved and lost and built a garden to remember.

She moved to sit next to him. Kane stared out over the verdant expanse, his profile etched with an ancient grief. The morning light softened his features, revealing the man beneath the powerful vampyr facade.

"At first, I told myself I created it to help the environment recover," he continued, his fingers finding hers, entwining them. "The radiation had destroyed so much. But over time..." His voice trailed off. "It became my sanctuary. My quiet, peaceful oasis from everything below."

They sat together, shoulders almost touching. Kane's thumb traced absent patterns against her skin, his eyes distant with memories.

"Now I understand why she preferred her garden to anywhere else." A ghost of a smile touched his lips. "There's a certain magic to this place. Something healing." Kane reached out to a nearby rosebush, his fingers gentle as he plucked a delicate white bloom with blush-pink edges. He turned to Serenity, his expression unguarded in a way she'd never seen before.

"Here," he said softly, tucking the flower behind her ear, his fingers lingering against her temple. "Beautiful."

The simple gesture stole her breath. His touch sent shivers cascading down her spine, the flower's petals impossibly soft against her skin. Their eyes locked, and something blazed to life between them, stronger than she'd ever felt it. She could sense his emotions as clearly as her own—desire, yes, but also something tender and vulnerable that made her chest ache.

Serenity couldn't stop herself. She leaned forward, pressing her lips to his with deliberate slowness. The kiss was different from their others—not desperate or hurried, but intentional, as if she could pour every truth she couldn't speak into this one act.

Kane's hand cupped her face, his thumb tracing the curve of her cheekbone as he returned her kiss with equal tenderness. The garden around them seemed to fade away, leaving only this moment, this feeling that transcended words, transcended the lies between them.

And for the first time since signing that contract, Serenity knew—whatever happened, whatever the rebellion demanded, whatever secrets lay between them—she'd made the right choice.

She was exactly where she was meant to be.

CHAPTER TEN

KANE

The moment Serenity's lips touched his, every carefully constructed wall Kane had built over centuries crumbled to dust.

He'd told himself he was prepared for this. That showing her the garden was strategic—creating emotional intimacy to ensure her loyalty. But the instant she kissed him—gentle, deliberate, achingly tender—Kane knew he'd been lying to himself.

I'm lost, he thought as his hand moved to cradle her face. I've been lost since the moment I tasted her blood and discovered this impossible bond between us.

Her lips were soft against his, moving with an intention that stole his breath. The blood bond flared to life, sensations cascading between them like a current finding ground. Desire, guilt, desperate hope—he couldn't tell where her emotions ended and his began.

The kiss deepened, and Kane's tongue slid against hers with delicate precision. Something shifted in her—a dam breaking, desire flooding through her system and washing away hesitation. Her hands moved to frame his face, fingertips tracing the sharp angles of his jaw. A groan rumbled in Kane's chest, unbidden, genuine.

Her scent—jasmine and rose—surrounded him as she pressed closer. The kiss turned hungry, desperate. When her teeth grazed his lower lip, a primal feeling awakened. A growl vibrated deep in his throat.

She rose from the bench without breaking the kiss, moving to straddle him. Kane's hands gripped her hips automatically, steadying her as she settled against him. The hard length of him pressed against her core, and her pleasure spiked—a feedback loop of sensation that nearly undid him.

"Kane," she whispered against his mouth, her voice thick with need. "I want you."

Four words. Four simple words that shattered what remained of his control.

In one fluid motion, Kane stood, lifting her as if she weighed nothing. He carried her across the garden, her legs wrapped around his waist, his mouth never leaving hers. When her back met the cool stone wall, he pressed her against it, his body covering hers.

He pulled back slightly, his breath coming in ragged pants that matched her own. Their foreheads touched, noses brushing, and Kane searched her face with desperate intensity.

"Tell me what you want," he whispered, though he already knew. Her desire was as clear as his own, amplified between them along that invisible thread that bound them together.

Heat bloomed across her skin. "You," she breathed against his lips. "I want you."

Something cracked in Kane. The carefully constructed mask he wore, the strategic distance he maintained—it all fractured under those words and the genuine emotion bleeding across their connection.

"You undo me, Serenity." His voice broke on her name, raw emotion he couldn't contain spilling through. "Every moment with you tears down walls I've built over lifetimes."

She cradled his face between her palms, and Kane registered the slight tremor in his own jaw. "Then let them fall," she whispered against his lips.

And God help him, he did.

His mouth claimed hers with newfound urgency. One hand braced against the wall, the other sliding beneath her tank top, pushing the fabric upward. She raised her arms, allowing him to pull it over her head. The garment fluttered to the ground, forgotten.

Kane's gaze turned molten as it traveled over her exposed breasts. "Perfect," he breathed—and her pleasure at the compliment spiked between them, desire climbing higher.

He lowered his head, taking one peaked nipple into his mouth. Her gasp echoed in the garden—he experienced her pleasure as his own. Every touch he gave, he received reflected back, amplified, until Kane couldn't think, could only feel.

His fangs ached with the need to bite, to claim, to bind her to him in every way possible.

When he pressed her harder against the wall, one hand sliding between their bodies to trace the damp fabric between her thighs, anticipation surged across the connection.

"So wet for me already," he murmured against her throat—and sensed her response to his words, the way they affected her.

Her pleasure fed his, which fed hers, creating an endless cycle that threatened to consume them both.

When he finally freed himself and positioned himself at her entrance, Kane's eyes locked with hers. Trust, desire, fear, hope—all of it crashed between them at once.

"Mine," he growled and thrust forward.

The sensation of being inside her while experiencing her pleasure nearly destroyed him. Kane stilled, giving her a moment to adjust to his size, but really giving himself time to regain some semblance of control.

He began to move, the doubled sensation threatening to undo him completely. His own pleasure and hers, intertwined until he couldn't separate them.

His lips traced a path from her collarbone to her throat. His fangs grazed her pulse point—a question.

Without hesitation, she tilted her head to the side, offering herself to him.

The trust in that gesture broke something fundamental in him.

His fangs sank into her flesh with exquisite precision. Her blood flooded his mouth—ambrosia, impossibly sweet—and her pleasure spiked impossibly higher. The sensation of feeding from her while buried deep inside her, while experiencing every ounce of her ecstasy, nearly sent him over the edge immediately.

When her orgasm built and crested, when she shattered around him, Kane experienced it as if it were his own release.

He roared her name as his own climax overtook him, spilling himself deep inside her while her blood sang on his tongue and her emotions crashed like a tidal wave.

Mine, the bond seemed to pulse. Ours. Real.

With careful movements, Kane lowered her to the ground, his arms supporting her trembling legs.

"I'm sorry," he murmured against her temple, pressing gentle kisses along her hairline. "I shouldn't have taken your blood without asking properly."

She traced her fingers over the marks on her neck, a strange sense of pride in her expression. "Don't apologize. I wanted it." She met his gaze, unflinching. "I wanted all of it."

Instead of responding, he gathered her in his arms and carried her to a patch of lush grass nestled between flowering shrubs. He laid her down gently, his body covering hers like a shield. Sunlight dappled through cherry blossoms overhead, casting them in shadow and light.

"Are you cold?" he murmured, his fingertips tracing patterns on her bare shoulder.

She shook her head, nestling closer into his warmth. The grass tickled her back, but she welcomed the sensation—another reminder that this moment was real. Kane shifted to lie beside her, one arm cradling her against him while his other hand played idly with a curl that had fallen across her forehead.

They lay together in comfortable silence, the garden around them humming with life. Bees drifted lazily between blooms, their gentle buzzing a soothing backdrop to the distant sounds of the city below. The sea breeze caressed their skin, carrying the tang of salt and promise.

"Tell me something about you that I don't know," Serenity murmured, her fingertips following the contours of an old scar that curved beneath his collarbone.

Kane's chest rose and fell with a deep breath. "I used to paint," he said after a moment, his voice quiet. "Landscapes mostly. I haven't picked up a brush in a very long time."

"Why did you stop?"

His hand found hers, thumb tracing her knuckles. "When my wife died, it felt frivolous. I threw myself into work instead—into building Celearius."

"You should try again," she said softly, trailing her fingers across his chest. The sun warmed her bare skin, making her drowsy with contentment despite the weight of their conversation.

Kane's fingers traced idle patterns on her shoulder, his touch gentle but possessive. "Tell me about your family," he said, his voice a low rumble that vibrated through him. "I'm sorry I had to leave."

"But I am glad I got to spend more time with them. It was wonderful to see Beth. I feel like she has grown so much, and it's only been a few weeks." A genuine smile curved her lips. "You know she is the smartest one in her class. But she can be a little feisty."

"I can see where she gets it from," Kane chuckled, the sound rumbling in his chest. "I definitely see the family resemblance."

They fell into easy conversation, lying tangled together on the soft grass. Kane found himself telling her about watching Celearius rise from the ashes of the Devastation, about the first building he'd commissioned, and how he'd insisted on preserving the green spaces that remained.

Kane sensed the exact moment she slipped into sleep—her consciousness fading to gentle dreams of gardens and ocean breezes. He should move. Should return to the work waiting for him below.

Instead, he lay there holding her, experiencing her steady heartbeat, her trust flowing like a river between them.

Her dream shifted—she was dreaming of him, and the affection bleeding across their connection made his chest ache.

I can't keep pretending, Kane thought, staring at the woman sleeping peacefully in his arms. Not to myself. Not anymore.

Serenity stirred in her sleep, contentment radiating from her like warmth.

As exhaustion finally began pulling him under, Kane allowed himself one moment of truth:

He didn't want to let her go.

And that made him more dangerous to her than any rebel ever would be.

CHAPTER ELEVEN

SERENITY

When awareness returned, Serenity felt herself being lifted, cradled against a solid chest. She stirred slightly, recognizing Kane's scent as he carried her from the garden. The sudden shift from sunlight to shadow as they entered the penthouse barely registered in her drowsy state. Through half-lidded eyes, she glimpsed the stairs passing by, then heard a distinct beep as Kane carried her through his bedroom door.

The mattress dipped beneath her weight as he laid her on cool sheets. She curled into their silken embrace, a contented sigh escaping her lips. The soft click of the door closing followed, and Serenity drifted deeper into slumber, cocooned in the lingering scent that permeated the bedding.

Hours later—or perhaps only minutes, she couldn't tell—warm hands skimmed her sides, rousing her from dreams filled with rooftop gardens and ocean breezes. Her eyelids fluttered open to find Kane's face hovering over hers, illuminated by the setting sun streaming through floor-to-ceiling windows. The golden light painted him in amber and shadow, softening the sharp angles of his face.

"I couldn't stay away," he whispered, his voice rough with want. "Not when you're in my bed, looking like that."

His lips found hers before she could respond, the kiss gentle but insistent, drawing her fully into wakefulness. This was different from the desperate passion in the garden—slower, more deliberate, as if they had all the time in the world.

"I need you," he whispered, voice ragged with desire as his lips found the sensitive spot behind her ear. "Again."

Serenity's body responded instantly, arching into his touch as sleep fell away like shed silk. His hands traced the curves of her body with reverent precision, as though memorizing every inch of her skin. That awareness between them hummed to life, pulling taut with renewed hunger.

She gasped as his fingers found her center, already slick with want. Every sensation amplified—his desire feeding hers, hers stoking his, until the room felt thick with need.

"Kane," she breathed, reaching for him.

He moved over her, positioning himself between her thighs with deliberate slowness. This time when he entered her, it was with agonizing care, his eyes never leaving hers. Where the garden had been wild and urgent, this was worship. Every movement deliberate. Every touch reverent.

"You're mine now," he murmured against her lips, the intensity of his gaze making her breath catch. "Tell me you understand that."

The possessiveness in his voice should have frightened her. Instead, it sent heat pooling low in her belly. "Yours," she whispered back, the word escaping before she could stop it.

His eyes seemed to glow in the dim light of the bedroom as he moved within her, each thrust more deliberate than the last. Their bodies moved in perfect rhythm, the friction between them building to an exquisite crescendo.

When release finally came, it crashed over Serenity in waves that seemed to go on forever, Kane following moments later, his forehead pressed against hers as he shuddered above her. His name fell from her lips like a prayer.

They collapsed together, limbs entwined, her head nestled against the solid warmth of his chest as their breathing gradually slowed. Kane's fingers traced lazily along her spine, drawing invisible patterns that made her shiver.

"I should let you rest," he murmured against her hair, though his arms tightened around her, contradicting his words.

"I'm not tired anymore," she said, surprising herself with the truth of it. Despite the day's exertions, she felt energized, alive in a way she hadn't in months.

Kane chuckled, the sound rumbling through his chest. "Good. Because I'm not ready to let you go yet."

They lay in comfortable silence, the room growing darker as the sun continued its descent. Serenity's fingers found the scar she'd traced earlier in the garden, following its path across his collarbone.

"How did you get this?" she asked softly.

Kane's hand stilled on her back. "The Great War," he said after a moment. "Silver blade. Those scars don't heal quite the same as others."

"I'm sorry."

"Don't be. It reminds me of what we survived. What we built after." His thumb traced circles on her shoulder blade. "Sometimes scars are proof we endured."

The weight of his words settled between them. Serenity wondered if her own scars—invisible ones carved by poverty and loss and desperate choices—would someday feel like proof of survival rather than shame.

A sharp buzzing sound pierced their peaceful moment, vibrating against the nightstand. Kane's body tensed against hers, the muscles in his shoulders bunching beneath her fingertips. With a reluctant sigh, he reached over, his warmth temporarily leaving her side as he grabbed his comm device.

The blue light illuminated his features in the dimming room, casting shadows that accentuated the sharp angles of his jaw. His expression hardened as he read whatever message appeared on the screen, the vulnerability that had softened his eyes moments before disappearing behind a mask of cool detachment.

"Fuck," he muttered, sitting up fully. The word sounded wrong in his formal voice—evidence that whatever he'd just read was serious.

"What is it?" Serenity asked, pulling the sheet up to cover herself.

"An incident. Nothing you need to worry about." But the tension in his shoulders told a different story. "I have to go."

She watched as he moved through the room with fluid efficiency, muscles rippling beneath tanned skin as he dressed. The tailored black suit transformed him before her eyes—the vulnerable lover becoming once again the powerful vampyr who commanded Celearius. He fastened cufflinks with practiced precision, smoothed his tousled hair, and became untouchable.

Only the faint marks on his throat—where she'd kissed him—betrayed their earlier activities.

Moving back toward the bed, he leaned down, capturing her lips in a kiss that felt different from the others—desperate, almost fearful, as if he were memorizing the taste of her.

"Stay here. Rest." His thumb traced the curve of her cheek, lingering there. "I'll return as soon as I can."

"How long will you be gone?"

"I don't know." Frustration flickered across his face. "A few hours. Maybe longer." He pressed another kiss to her forehead. "Order something to eat and rest."

"I'll be waiting," Serenity whispered, watching him as he moved toward the door.

Kane paused, his silhouette framed in the doorway. For a heartbeat, he seemed about to say something more—his lips parted, his hand gripping the doorframe as if anchoring himself. But then his comm device buzzed again, shattering the moment.

"Sleep, Serenity," he said, and then he was gone, the door clicking shut behind him.

Serenity remained in Kane's bed for several minutes, surrounded by his scent, his warmth still imprinted on the sheets. Her body hummed with lingering pleasure, muscles pleasantly sore from their lovemaking. She traced her fingers over the marks on her neck—his bite from the garden—and something fluttered in her chest.

You're getting too comfortable here, she thought, finally forcing herself to sit up. Too attached.

The silken sheets pooled around her waist as she reached for her discarded clothing. Her tank top was nowhere to be found—probably still in the garden—so she wrapped the sheet around herself and padded barefoot to the door.

The penthouse felt cavernous and empty without Kane's presence. Serenity hurried through the darkening space to her own room, the sheet trailing behind her like a bridal train.

Once safely inside her quarters, she locked the door and leaned against it, finally allowing herself to breathe.

She moved to the bathroom, letting the sheet drop to the floor as she turned on the shower. The water heated quickly, and she stepped under the spray. The bite on her neck stung under the water. Serenity touched it gingerly, felt the twin punctures, and remembered the exquisite pleasure-pain of his fangs sinking into her flesh.

He fed from me while we... The thought sent heat through her despite everything.

She washed quickly, scrubbing away the evidence of their afternoon, then shut off the water and wrapped herself in one of the impossibly soft towels. She dried off, pulled on comfortable clothes—soft leggings and an oversized shirt—and emerged back into the bedroom.

A soft buzz made her freeze.

Her comm device. On the nightstand where she'd left it this morning.

Serenity's heart rate kicked up as she crossed to it.

The screen glowed with a single message from an encrypted number she recognized:

Be ready tomorrow. 2PM. Details to follow.

Sebastian.

Tomorrow. Another mission. More lies. More secrets to keep from the man whose bed she'd just left, whose taste still lingered on her lips, whose mark still throbbed on her throat.

Serenity sank onto the edge of her bed, the comm device in her hands.

Finally, she typed back a single word: Understood.

The message sent with a soft whoosh.

She stared at the screen, then set the device down. Her fingers trembled slightly as she pulled them into her lap. Tomorrow she would find out what Sebastian wanted. Tomorrow she would take another step deeper.

What am I really looking for? she thought. Cavern 47... what am I really doing?

She lay back on the bed, staring at the ceiling.

But tonight, she was alone with the lingering warmth of Kane's touch and the terrible knowledge that she was falling for the man she was supposed to betray.

The silence of her room offered no answers.

CHAPTER TWELVE

KANE

The silver dagger of morning light sliced through the gap in the curtains, but Kane hardly noticed. His focus remained locked on the surveillance feeds sprawled across the monitors, each pixel a potential harbinger of chaos.

"Any movement?" he asked, his voice low and measured despite the tension coiling through his body.

Rhyzan's fingers danced across the keyboard, switching between camera angles with practiced precision. "Nothing yet. The prisoners in the cavern are following their normal routine. Breakfast service completed twenty minutes ago."

Kane inhaled slowly, taking in the familiar scents that permeated his office—leather-bound books, the subtle cologne Rhyzan favored, and the faint metallic tang that always accompanied Sullivan's presence. The room felt smaller than usual with five vampyrs inside, the air thick with anticipation.

Nox paced near the eastern window, his footfalls silent against the plush carpet. "Do you really think they would have her break in at the same time they break them out?"

"The intelligence is solid," Rhyzan confirmed. "My source confirmed the operation is scheduled for today."

"And yet here we wait," Sullivan muttered from his position by the door, arms crossed over his broad chest. He looked as if he'd rather be anywhere else—preferably directly at Cavern 47 to be in the fight.

"We can't know for certain which will occur first," Evie said, breaking her silence. She sat on the edge of the couch, her slender fingers tracing the leather absentmindedly. "The human rebels aren't known for their precision timing."

Kane's jaw tightened. Through the blood bond, he could still feel echoes of Serenity's contentment from their lovemaking, her lingering sense of safety as she'd fallen asleep in his arms. The bond didn't lie about her trust. It made what was coming worse.

"I've added additional security protocols," Rhyzan reported, tapping a monitor showing the penthouse hallway. "If she attempts to access your private files again, we'll know immediately."

Kane nodded, the weight of his centuries pressing down on his shoulders. "And the cavern?"

"They should get right through if they make any attempts," Rhyzan replied, checking his watch. "Chloe has been prepared and thoroughly fed, so she won't be tempted. Her tracker is active."

The monitors flickered quickly. They would have missed it if they weren't watching so intently. "They're in the system."

The screen cast a blue-white glow across Rhy's face as he typed rapidly, pulling up a different feed onto one of the many monitors.

"They've captured the camera to the south," he announced, then he leaned forward. "Movement in the woods." He enlarged the feed.

Four shadowy figures materialized from the southern treeline, their green camouflage blending with the foliage as they slipped between trunks and undergrowth with practiced stealth.

"There," Kane hissed, leaning closer to the monitor, his silver-blue eyes narrowing. "They're heading for—"

"The emergency exit by the lab," Rhyzan finished, their long years of friendship making words almost unnecessary. "The one place our security was minimal."

"Smart," Nox muttered.

"Look to the north," Sullivan's voice cut through the tension as he pointed to another monitor. "Three more, same tactical gear."

Rhyzan's fingers flew across the keyboard, switching feeds to capture the second group. Their movements were coordinated, precise—military training evident in every step they took.

"They're giving themselves two chances at entry," Nox observed, abandoning his pacing to stand behind Rhyzan's chair. "Or they have two targets."

Evie rose from the couch, her voice soft yet penetrating. "Or multiple exits. They could be planning to enter through one point and escape through another."

"Clever," Kane muttered, the word bitter on his tongue. "They planned this carefully."

Rhyzan's fingers blurred across the keyboard, bringing up several more feeds simultaneously. The monitors filled with new angles—subterranean hallways, guard stations, prisoner cells.

"They've taken over five more security feeds," Rhyzan announced, his voice taut with controlled urgency. "The cavern's security team is completely blind to this intrusion. Their monitors are showing looped footage from earlier today."

Sullivan's fist clenched. "You're saying security won't even know they're being infiltrated?"

"Precisely." Rhyzan's eyes reflected the dancing light of the monitors. "This is a stealth extraction. They don't want alarms. They don't want confrontation. They want to be ghosts."

Evie leaned forward. "How are they able to manipulate our feeds so easily? These systems should be impenetrable."

A hint of something—perhaps pride, perhaps amusement—flickered across Rhyzan's face. "I let them in."

"You what?" Sullivan growled.

"I detected their initial probe and created a backdoor," Rhyzan explained, his verdant eyes gleaming with tactical satisfaction. "I've hitched a ride on their code—we're seeing exactly what they're seeing. Every camera they access, every door they unlock."

Kane's gaze snapped to his oldest friend, understanding dawning. "You're letting them think they've succeeded."

"The best trap is the one your prey walks into willingly," Rhyzan confirmed, tapping commands that split the main monitor into multiple feeds. "They believe they're invisible. They have no idea we're watching their every move."

"Smart bastard," Nox murmured, clapping Rhyzan on the shoulder.

On the leftmost screen, the southern tactical team slipped through the emergency exit, their movements fluid and coordinated. Three figures in black tactical gear, faces obscured by masks, communicating through hand signals. The northern team simultaneously breached through a maintenance tunnel, their entry equally silent.

"They're using the shift change to their advantage," Nox murmured.

Kane watched, muscles coiled with restrained violence, as both teams navigated the subterranean corridors. The southern team moved efficiently, ducking into alcoves whenever a vampyr approached. The timing was impeccable, almost perfect. The northern team moved with the same precision, their steps synchronized with the facility's surveillance blind spots.

"They've done their homework," Evie whispered.

"I let them get limited access to the cavern layout when they first got into the system," Rhy informed them. "They studied it well."

A flash of movement caught Kane's eye on the lower monitor. The southern team had encountered a human worker—a maintenance technician in a gray uniform who had rounded the corner at precisely the wrong moment. The lead operative moved with lethal efficiency, pressing a cloth over the man's mouth. The technician's body went limp almost instantly.

"Chemical sedative," Rhyzan noted clinically. "They're avoiding bloodshed where possible."

The northern team had reached a junction in the corridor, splitting into two smaller units. The lead pair continued forward while the second team branched off toward the east wing—directly toward the cell blocks.

"They're heading for Prisoner 16," Sullivan growled, his body tensing as if ready to spring into action.

"They just made contact with Prisoner 16's cell," Rhy announced.

The operatives disabled the electronic lock with practiced efficiency. The lead figure—tall, broad-shouldered—pressed a device against the control panel. Green lights flashed across its surface before the door slid open with a barely audible hiss.

Sullivan's nostrils flared. "Two weeks of questioning, and he never broke. Not once."

On screen, the young man looked up from his cot, dark circles shadowing eyes that still burned with defiance despite his gaunt appearance. The tattoo Sullivan had mentioned was visible now—an intricate serpent design that began at his collarbone and wound upward, disappearing into his hairline.

"Now we know he's either important to them," Kane said, his jaw tight, "or he knows secrets they don't want us to know."

The rebels moved swiftly, helping the prisoner to his feet. Though weakened, the young man's posture straightened with apparent resolve. The southern team was moving toward the cell block now, their objective clearly the same.

"Is Alpha Team on standby?" Kane demanded, his knuckles whitening as he gripped the edge of the desk. "They don't leave that prison if Chloe doesn't come out with them."

Rhyzan nodded sharply. "Ready to move on your command. Less than a minute away from any breach point."

The northern team reached another cell block—this one in the lower security wing. The lead operative consulted a small device before stopping at a particular door. Cell 23-B.

"Is Chloe with him?" Kane asked.

"Yes, she has been with him since last night," Rhyzan confirmed, tapping quickly to enlarge the feed from Cell 23-B on the main monitor. The camera angle captured the entire small space in stark detail. Jax's lanky frame tensed as the door mechanism clicked, his hazel eyes narrowing with wary anticipation. The moment the panel slid open, he moved with surprising agility for someone who'd spent days in captivity, positioning himself protectively in front of Chloe.

"Good," Kane murmured. "He still thinks she's one of them."

With another keystroke, Rhyzan activated the audio feed. The rebel operative's voice came through the speakers, low and urgent.

"Jax Thornton? We're here to extract you. Come with us now."

Jax took a step forward, his hand reaching behind to grasp Chloe's wrist. "I'm not going anywhere without her."

The operative's masked face turned slightly, examining the petite woman cowering convincingly behind Jax. "Orders were for you only."

"She's coming with us." Jax's voice hardened, fingers tightening around Chloe's wrist. "Or I'm staying."

The lead operative shifted, his stance rigid as he glanced at his teammate. "No, just you. That's my orders."

Jax's jaw clenched, his fingers interlacing with Chloe's. "Then I'm not going anywhere. I won't leave her to be tortured or worse." He pulled Chloe closer to his side, his body language defiant despite the dark circles shadowing his eyes. "Either we both go, or neither of us does."

The operative hesitated, then pressed two fingers to his ear. "Eagle One, we have a complication. Target insists on bringing a female prisoner."

His voice dropped to a whisper as he turned away, the words becoming indistinct.

Tense seconds ticked by. Kane watched the feed intently, noting how Chloe's performance was flawless—the slight tremble in her shoulders, the fearful darting of her eyes, the way she clutched at Jax's arm as if he were her only salvation.

"They're actually considering it," Evie murmured, leaning closer to the screen.

The operative nodded once, then turned back to Jax. "We will take you both. Let's go."

The rebels quickly regrouped, merging both teams in the east corridor. Prisoner 16 stumbled slightly, catching himself against the wall as his weakened legs struggled to maintain pace. Jax kept Chloe pressed close to his side, his protective stance never wavering as they followed their rescuers through the labyrinthine hallways.

"They're heading for the northern exit," Rhyzan noted, his fingers flying over the keyboard to track their movement.

The rebels moved efficiently, guiding their charges through service corridors and past the guards. The lead operative checked his device repeatedly, following the path their hacker had cleared—unaware that Rhyzan had deliberately left this route unobstructed.

"Ten seconds to exit," Sullivan muttered, shifting his weight impatiently. "I hate this plan. Too many unknown factors."

"Agreed," Kane said. "But it's the fastest way to find their headquarters and squash this rebellion."

On screen, the extraction team reached the heavy metal door at the northern emergency exit. The second operative in line pressed a small device against the electronic lock. The mechanism clicked, and the door swung open.

The eight rebels, along with their three rescues, slipped through the exit into the crisp morning air. Kane watched them move in formation toward the treeline. Jax kept Chloe tucked protectively against his side, his eyes darting nervously around him.

Then all hell broke loose as soon as they cleared the treeline.

Sirens wailed, red warning lights bathed the compound in crimson, and a mechanical voice blared through speakers: "Security breach detected. Lockdown initiated. All personnel to emergency stations."

On screen, guards scrambled in confusion, weapons drawn as they rushed toward different sectors of the prison, searching for the source of the breach. None looked toward the northern exit where shadows had disappeared into the treeline.

"Our team will track them through the woods," Rhyzan confirmed, eyes never leaving the monitors. "Chloe's tracker is active and transmitting clearly."

Kane nodded, the tension in his shoulders easing fractionally. If everything went according to plan, they would finally locate the rebels' headquarters.

"Shit."

The single word from Nox cut through Kane's thoughts like a blade. He turned, following Nox's gaze to a monitor in the corner of the array—one showing his penthouse.

Serenity was slipping into his office, her movements quick and cautious. She paused at the threshold, glancing over her shoulder before closing the door behind her.

Kane's chest constricted.

He'd known this was coming. Had planned for it. But watching her betray him hours after she'd slept in his arms—the blood bond let him feel her guilt even as she did it anyway.

CHAPTER THIRTEEN

KANE

The betrayal tasted like ash in Kane's mouth as he watched the scene unfold on the monitor.

On the sleek monitor before him, his Elite—Serenity—crept through his office, comm device clutched in her delicate hand, her lips moving in conversation with someone unseen. Kane's jaw clenched. She pushed his chair back and stood in front of his desk, then began accessing his computer system.

The world narrowed. The prison break, the rebels, the tracking—all of it faded to background noise. Kane's entire focus locked on the small figure moving through his private space with cautious determination.

Hours ago, she'd been in his arms. In his bed. He'd felt her trust through the bond, tasted her blood, heard her say his name like a prayer.

Now he watched her betray him in real-time, and the blood bond made him feel every ounce of her guilt as she did it.

"What is she doing?" Sullivan's voice broke the heavy silence of his main office.

Rhyzan abandoned the prison monitor, his verdant eyes narrowing as he focused on Serenity's actions. She listened to whoever was on the phone, then slowly clicked and typed in codes until she reached the computer's interface. A black box popped up. Then she slowly typed in a code one letter at a time.

"What are they trying to get her to access?" Kane kept his voice level despite the storm brewing inside him. Centuries of control were being tested by this slip of a woman who had somehow breached his defenses—both digital and personal.

"They aren't trying to access anything." Rhyzan's voice carried its usual cold precision. "They're trying to extract everything."

Kane's jaw clenched as Serenity placed her comm device on his console.

"Do you have control over what they're taking?" Kane's voice was barely more than a whisper, his eyes never leaving Serenity's face on the screen.

"Of course." Rhyzan's fingers danced across his own keyboard, faint tapping like raindrops against glass. "I'm feeding her exactly what I want them to see."

Kane nodded once, the motion sharp. His chest felt hollowed out, scraped raw. The scent of her—jasmine and rose—lingered in his memory, taunting him with every breath. He'd let her close. Let her past his carefully constructed walls. And for what? To watch her betray him with such calculated precision?

Through the blood bond, he felt her guilt, her anxiety gnawing at her. She hated this. The knowledge should have provided some comfort—proof she wasn't a heartless spy. But the bond didn't lie. She cared for him. And she was still betraying him.

He forced himself to inhale slowly, to push down the feral part of him that wanted to tear through the city and confront her now. The animal instinct to protect what was his warred with the rational leader who knew information was power.

"She's downloading the primary cache now," Rhyzan murmured, the silver flecks in his eyes brightening with concentration. "I've included everything they received in their previous extraction, but I've added a special folder—detailed notes referencing the weapon. Nothing substantial, just enough breadcrumbs."

Kane nodded, unable to form words. He watched as Serenity finished her download, the progress bar filling with excruciating slowness. Each percentage point felt like another betrayal, another crack in the foundation he'd thought unbreakable.

On screen, she removed her device, carefully inputted a code that wiped her digital footprint from the system, and shut everything down quickly. The screen went dark as she pushed his chair back into its exact position, her movements fluid and deliberate. She paused, scanning the room one final time, ensuring nothing was out of place. Then she slipped out the door, closing it behind her.

"She's good for someone with no training," Sullivan remarked, his tone clinical. "Some hesitation, but efficient."

Kane couldn't respond as he tried to calm the rage within him. He'd just watched the woman who had shared his bed again, whose blood sang to him like no other in centuries, violate everything he'd built.

Kane finally tore his gaze from the now-empty monitor, his silver-blue eyes glowing with an intensity that made even Rhyzan pause in his calculations. The centuries-old control that had kept Kane alive through countless wars, rebellions, and betrayals slipped back into place, piece by cold piece, like armor, until his face became an impassive mask.

But beneath the mask, something had cracked. He couldn't use her and protect her. Couldn't manipulate her and care for her. Couldn't keep his strategic distance while the blood bond tied their emotions together.

He'd thought he could have both. He'd been wrong.

"Kane, you have to remember she is being threatened," Evie began, her voice soft but insistent. "Her family—"

"Where are they now?" Kane cut her off, his voice a controlled rumble that belied the chaos inside him.

Rhyzan's comm device chirped softly. He glanced down, eyes narrowing as he scanned the incoming message. A muscle in his jaw ticked once—the only visible reaction to whatever intelligence had arrived.

"They've taken the beach route," he said, looking up at Kane. "My operatives confirm they boarded two vessels waiting in the shallows approximately twenty minutes ago."

His fingers swiped across the screen, bringing up what appeared to be a satellite map of the coastline. "Based on their trajectory and fuel capacity, they're headed to one of two locations—either making a brief stop at Elysium for supplies, or bypassing it entirely to reach RockDune Beach and cross the desert from there."

Kane moved to the windows, staring out at Celearius spread below him like fallen stars. His reflection in the glass showed nothing of the turmoil within—just the perfect, controlled mask of a leader betrayed.

"If they're headed to RockDune..." Sullivan's voice trailed off, his scarred face shifting as his expression darkened. "Then we were right all along. The rebels have been operating from the dead city."

Kane turned just as Rhyzan pulled up a map of Celearius on the screen, and then a bright blinking orange dot appeared, approaching the private island, Elysium.

"We should have eyes on them within the next twenty minutes," Rhy informed him.

"Good. And she was briefed about the weapon design?" Kane asked.

"Yes. She plans to mention it once they settle and let her know she has information in exchange for their help finding her daughter."

"They will ask Sebastian to confirm the plans are real," Evie informed them. "The notes that they found should help, but they may ask your Elite to find out if the plans are real."

"We'll figure it out when we get to that point. Right now, we need to find out who she was on the call with," Kane said.

"Already on it," Rhy said as he stood from the desk, leaving the tracker on the screen. It was currently stopped at Elysium.

"Were you able to find anything else down in those lockers?" Kane moved to sit at his desk as Sullivan helped himself to his whiskey.

"Unfortunately, no, but it looked as though it had been one of their safe locations before the war. It looks as though those plans were only recently hidden down there. From the looks of the container they were in, I'd say it's only been a year or two since they were put down there," Sullivan said between sips.

"Do you believe they know about the weapon?" Kane pondered aloud.

"If they do, Chloe will be able to confirm it. If we find out they already have the weapon, it will then be Chloe's new mission to find and destroy it. As for now, let us wait and see where this Jax can take us. And if Chloe can confirm Prisoner 16's identity."

Kaelen entered the office. "Sir, my apologies for interrupting, but I wanted to let you know Xavier will be bringing Deyja with him to the Elite Ball. She's demanding that we have her preferred stock when she arrives."

"Thank you, Kaelen. I will deal with it."

He nodded as he removed the bottle of Syn from Kane's desk and walked out. They continued to watch the glowing dot on the screen, which still had not moved from the island.

"Rhyzan, did you tell him?" Evie suddenly said.

"Tell me what?" Kane glared at Rhy. He hated being left in the dark about important information.

"No, I haven't, but I was getting to it," Rhy exclaimed.

"Getting to what?"

"The Elite—"

"Serenity and Jax may have a connection," Evie interrupted. Rhy glared at her.

"Which is?"

"Victoria Fruster," Rhyzan said, pulling up a file on the screen. "She works at the clinic. Listed Richard Wright—Serenity's father—as her professional reference."

Kane's eyes narrowed. "Victoria was captured with Jax?"

"Along with Clyde Struguess," Evie confirmed. "Both names Jax mentioned during interrogation. If Serenity's father connected them professionally..."

"Then my Elite's selection may not have been random," Kane finished.

"Was this the woman with Jax when we picked him up?" Kane probed.

"Yes, along with Clyde Struguess. Clyde and Victoria are the contacts Jax mentioned."

"Interesting. Have you confirmed this connection, or is this the only thing connecting them?"

"As of right now, this is the only thing that is connecting them."

So many thoughts were running through his head, but the one thing that stuck out most was whether Serenity had walked into the clinic that day by chance. Was it possible that they planned this whole thing?

The thought should have brought clarity. If Serenity had been deliberately planted, then everything between them was calculated deception. She was an enemy asset, not a conflicted woman caught between loyalty and survival.

It would make everything simpler.

But through the blood bond, Kane knew better. Whatever the rebels had planned, Serenity's emotions were real. Her desire had been genuine. Her guilt was authentic.

The irony wasn't lost on him.

"Let's see if we can find out more and how deep this connection may go."

"They're moving," Sullivan said, finishing his drink, then he looked over at the screen.

The orange dot moved away from the island and was now heading toward RockDune Beach in the north.

"It may take them a few hours to get to their destination. I just hope Chloe doesn't eat anyone before then," Sullivan said.

"They have eyes on them now. They are keeping their distance and will follow them as long as they can," Rhy said, looking up from his device.

"Good."

Kane stared at the blinking orange dot, his jaw tight. Somewhere out there, Chloe was embedded with the rebels. Jax was being led to their headquarters. And Serenity...

He would use her. Had to use her. Because Celearius depended on it.

The question was whether either of them would survive what came next.

CHAPTER FOURTEEN

RHYZAN

Evening shadows had claimed Celearius hours ago, the city settling into its nocturnal rhythm while Rhyzan remained at his post. The orange dot pulsed like a heartbeat against the digital map's darkness, each blink a reminder of how close they were to finding the rebel headquarters. His office remained silent save for the soft hum of computers and the barely perceptible sound of Nox's breathing beside him.

They'd been tracking Chloe's signal since the prison break that morning—watching the rebels move from the beach to the desert, patient as the hours stretched into the night.

"They're following the western approach," Rhyzan murmured, tapping a slender finger against the glass surface of the monitor. "Predictable. The radiation levels are lowest there."

The Dead City—once called Boston—sprawled across the screen in muted grays and blacks, a ghost of civilization swallowed by nuclear fire decades ago. Chloe's signal moved steadily through its outskirts. They were taking the long approach, not surprising.

Nox leaned forward, his cologne—sandalwood and citrus—wafting into Rhyzan's space. "Do we have anyone following them?"

"Not yet." Rhyzan's eyes narrowed. "Let's see where they're headed first."

Watching Nox's profile in the blue-tinted glow of the monitors, Rhyzan felt centuries compress into seconds. How many surveillance operations had they shared together over the centuries? How many nights spent in silent companionship, watching, waiting, protecting?

"You look contemplative," Nox said, not taking his eyes off the screen. "More so than usual."

Rhyzan allowed himself a half-smile. "Just remembering."

"Dangerous territory." Nox's voice carried a hint of amusement.

"Do you ever think about Dauphine?" The question escaped before Rhyzan could contain it, hanging in the air between them like frost.

Nox stilled, his fingers pausing over the keyboard. "1742 or 1896?"

"1896." The year they had been more—the Belle Époque—a beautiful era that had promised so much and delivered heartbreak instead.

"Sometimes." Nox turned then, his dark eyes meeting Rhyzan's. "We were different creatures then."

"Young, by our standards." Rhyzan's attention drifted from the pulsing orange dot. "Impulsive."

"Stubborn," Nox added, a smile playing at the corners of his mouth.

"Stubborn and afraid," Rhyzan said softly, the words barely audible above the electronic hum. "We couldn't reconcile what we wanted with what we thought we needed."

A shadow passed over Nox's features, vulnerability Rhyzan rarely witnessed these days. "Dauphine was beautiful that spring."

"It was." The memory unfurled—absinthe-soaked nights along the Isère, stolen moments in that attic apartment overlooking La Mure, arguments that ended with shattered crystal and weeks of silence.

"We weren't ready," Nox said, his voice carrying a weight that seemed to bend the air between them. "I wasn't ready."

The orange dot continued its steady progress across the screen, but Rhyzan's focus had drifted entirely.

"Do you think we're ready now?" The question escaped before he could contain it.

Nox's eyebrows lifted slightly. "That depends on what you're asking."

Rhyzan studied the planes of Nox's face—was it curiosity that made him look, or longing he refused to name? The angles and shadows cast by the monitor light accentuated the sharp cut of Nox's jaw, the intelligent glint in his eyes. Those eyes that had witnessed Rhyzan's triumphs and failures across centuries.

Rhyzan's chest tightened. Nox had always been his constant—through wars, through upheavals, through the rebuilding of their world. While Kane had been his purpose, Nox had been his anchor.

"I think," Rhyzan said carefully, "that time changes perspective."

Nox shifted closer, his shoulder almost touching Rhyzan's. "And what does your perspective tell you now?"

The air between them crackled with unspoken history. Rhyzan fought against the magnetic pull, the way he always had. But those reasons felt hollow suddenly, like excuses he'd repeated to himself until they'd worn thin.

"That I've been a fool," Rhyzan whispered. The admission cost him something—pride, perhaps, or the carefully constructed walls he'd built between them.

Nox's gaze dropped to Rhyzan's lips, and hunger awakened in Rhyzan. The steady rhythm of his heart accelerated, each beat a silent rebellion against centuries of self-denial.

"Rhyzan." Nox breathed his name like a prayer, closing the distance between them.

Their breath mingled, warm and intimate. Rhyzan's eyelids grew heavy, the weight of wanting something—someone—for so long crushing his defenses. His fingertips brushed against Nox's, an electric current racing up his arm.

Just once, he thought. Just once to remember what it felt like.

The door swung open with a soft click.

Rhyzan jerked backward, the spell broken. Evie stood in the doorway, her auburn hair catching the dim light as she swept into the room with her characteristic elegance. Her eyes darted between them, taking in their proximity, the charged atmosphere. Her expression shifted—understanding, perhaps curiosity—but she said nothing about what she'd walked in on.

Rhyzan cleared his throat, straightening his already impeccable posture. His heart hammered against his ribs, the remnants of whatever had almost happened still pulsing through his veins. He felt exposed, as if centuries of carefully constructed walls had crumbled in an instant, leaving him vulnerable before Evie's perceptive gaze.

"Where are they now?" Evie asked, mercifully focusing on the screen rather than the tension crackling between them.

Before Rhyzan could gather his scattered thoughts to respond, Nox spoke. "They've been moving quickly. They reached RockDune Beach and are now approaching the Dead City from the east."

Rhyzan moved a chair out for her. "They're slowly making their way through the desert and should hit the city line soon. With the city being so vast, it could take hours or days."

"Forget them for a moment." Evie swiveled in her chair so she was facing him. "Kane. Serenity. What are we going to do?"

"Absolutely nothing," Rhyzan told her. "We can't encourage a bond we all know is forbidden by the Elders."

"And when has Kane cared what the Elders say?" she countered.

"I actually agree with Rhy on this, Evie," Nox said.

"What? Just because you two—"

"I think things will fall into place," Nox said.

Rhyzan glanced at Nox, raising a brow, then shook his head, turning back toward the screen.

Evie looked at him like he was crazy. "Explain."

"They've shared blood," Nox said.

"WHAT?"

"Shit." Rhyzan and Nox said in unison.

Evie was on Nox's throat before Rhyzan could even blink. "I knew you were both lying earlier. Spill it now."

"It was days ago... there was an incident," Nox choked out.

Evie turned to look at Rhyzan. "Talk or I break his windpipe."

Rhyzan knew she was serious. He had no choice but to tell her.

"She cut her finger two days after she moved in, and he bit her violently. She was able to get away, but the damage was done when she threw hot oil on him and herself." He took a deep breath and finished, "He didn't want her to be scarred or for you to find out, so he used his blood to heal her."

Evie let go of Nox, then walked over to him. "He did this not knowing if there would be any side effects. Her blood is different from the others. He could have killed her."

"There were side effects," he muttered.

Her eyes widened with anger as she reached to grab him, but he anticipated her and moved out of her reach. He stood on the other side of the room, prepared to go for the window if needed. Evie was dangerous when she was pissed like this. The number one reason they'd hidden it from her.

"What were the side effects?"

"From what I could tell, she was hypersensitive to everything, and the only thing that would calm her was—"

"The touch of him."

"Yes," Rhyzan said, confused. "How'd you know that?"

Evie sighed, releasing her grip on Nox entirely. Her shoulders sagged slightly as she moved to the nearest chair, sinking into it with uncharacteristic heaviness.

"Because I've seen it before," she said, running her fingers through her auburn hair. "Her blood type—it's not just rare, it's... different. I have theories, but I need more research before I can be certain."

Nox rubbed his throat, straightening his collar with meticulous precision. "What kind of theories?"

"The kind that could change everything we understand about human-vampyr biology." Evie's gaze drifted to the monitor where the orange dot continued its steady progress. "Serenity's blood composition has markers I've never seen in other humans. The hypersensitivity you described—it's just the beginning of what could happen if Kane continues to expose himself to her."

Rhyzan watched the interplay of emotions across her face—concern, scientific curiosity, and something deeper that he couldn't quite place.

"We may have a serious problem with Kane and Serenity," she continued. "For the stability of Celearius, we should keep them apart."

"I agree," Rhyzan said, the words tasting like ash in his mouth.

But as the words left his lips, his gaze involuntarily drifted to Nox. If Kane and Serenity were forbidden from exploring whatever connection existed between them, what hope remained for him and Nox?

Nox caught his gaze, understanding passing unspoken between them. That fleeting moment before Evie's arrival suddenly felt like a mirage that would evaporate under the harsh light of their reality.

"We need to focus on the mission," Rhyzan said, turning back to the monitors. The orange dot pulsed steadily. Duty called, as it always had.

Even if it broke him.

CHAPTER FIFTEEN

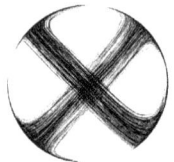

SERENITY

Serenity's skin crawled with the weight of secrets as she paced the vast expanse of her room for the third consecutive morning. The stolen data burned against her thigh through the thin fabric of her pocket—a constant reminder of her betrayal... and guilt.

Three days since she'd stolen files from Kane's office. Three days since she'd last felt his touch. The most she got were glimpses of him disappearing into his office or the elevator closing with him inside. At first, she thought he was avoiding her on purpose. She'd even left her door unlocked, hoping he would join her in the night. Her nerves were frayed and her thoughts scattered. She couldn't eat.

But worse than the fear was the emptiness beside her. The sheets remained cool and undisturbed where his body should have been. His absence had become a physical pain, an ache that settled in her and radiated outward until even her fingertips felt numb with it.

And that strange connection between them—the one she'd felt since their first intimate encounter—had gone cold and distant. Like he'd closed himself off from it deliberately, she could barely sense him through it anymore, just the faintest whisper that told her he was alive, somewhere in the building, but unreachable.

"He's managing the fallout from a prison break," Nox had explained yesterday, his perfect posture betraying nothing as he arranged fresh blood roses in a crystal vase. "Quite messy. Three prisoners escaped from a secured facility."

What Nox hadn't said hung in the air between them. Had Kane seen the footage? Did he know what she'd done? The question festered inside her like an infection.

Last night, she'd lain awake as moonlight crawled across her ceiling, her body aching with exhaustion while her mind raced through darkened corridors of fear and longing. Each time her eyelids had grown heavy, the image of Kane watching surveillance footage of her theft would jolt her back to consciousness, heart pounding like a trapped bird.

"This is ridiculous," she muttered, pressing her palms against her burning eyes. How had she become so dependent on his presence in mere weeks? She'd survived twenty-three years without Kane Draccus. She shouldn't need his body beside her, the steady rhythm of his breathing, the protective curve of his arm around her waist.

Yet she did.

Dawn seeped through the curtains as Serenity made her way to the living area. Her bare feet whispered against the marble floor, each step measured and quiet. Perhaps today would be different. Perhaps today, she would catch more than just his shadow disappearing around a corner.

She positioned herself on the couch facing the main hallway, where she could see anyone coming or going. The minutes crawled by. She traced the cloth pattern on the armrest, cataloging each whorl and stitch. The clock in the corner ticked away seconds that felt like hours. Her nerves stretched taut as piano wire.

A subtle shift in the air was her only warning.

Strong fingers brushed the nape of her neck, sending electric currents cascading down her spine. The connection between them roared to life the instant his fingers made contact, flooding her with warmth after days of cold emptiness. She hadn't heard him approach—hadn't sensed him at all until this moment. His presence paralyzed her, not with fear but with bone-deep yearning.

Serenity closed her eyes, hating how her body betrayed her with its instant response.

"I thought you'd still be asleep," he murmured, his voice a low rumble that vibrated against her skin.

His lips pressed alongside her neck, warm and insistent, leaving a trail of fire in their wake. Serenity's breath hitched, her head tilting instinctively to grant him better access.

"Kane," she whispered, his name a prayer on her lips. "I missed you. I missed your touch so much." The confession tumbled out before she could stop it, raw and honest in the quiet morning air.

He was in front of her in one fluid motion, standing her up as his silver-blue eyes glowed luminous in the pale dawn light. A dangerous and hungry emotion flashed across his features before his mouth claimed hers.

The kiss wasn't gentle. It was possession. His hands slid down her sides, mapping the contours of her body as if committing them to memory. One palm splayed across her lower back, drawing her closer until no space remained between them. The other tangled in her curls, angling her head to deepen the kiss.

She could feel echoes of his desire, his need—emotions that matched her own so perfectly she couldn't tell where hers ended and his began.

Serenity melted against him, her fingers clutching the lapels of his suit. Every sensation intensified—his breath against her lips, the solid wall of his chest beneath her fingertips, the heat radiating through the fabric of his suit. A low moan escaped her as his lips left hers to trace a path along her jawline before settling in the hollow beneath her ear.

"I've missed you too," he murmured against her, his voice rougher than she'd ever heard it.

Her head fell back as his mouth explored the sensitive column of her throat. His teeth grazed her pulse point, not breaking skin but promising something more primal. A shudder ran through her body.

"Kane," she breathed, barely recognizing her own voice. "I thought... I thought you were avoiding me."

His hands slid beneath her sleep shirt, fingers splaying across her bare back, tracing patterns that made her arch against him. When his palms skimmed her ribs, thumbs brushing the undersides of her breasts, Serenity gasped. Time dissolved as each caress became more intoxicating than the last.

His mouth returned to hers, the kiss deep and consuming. She lost herself in it, in him, her body responding with an intensity that threatened to overwhelm her senses. His hands moved lower, fingers tracing the curve of her hips, then skimming along her thighs with deliberate slowness that made her tremble.

The world narrowed to just the two of them—his touch, her gasps, the heat building between them. His fingers brushed along her inner thigh, dangerously close to where she ached for him, before retreating. The teasing pattern continued as his lips traveled from her mouth to her collarbone, each kiss more demanding than the last.

When his hand finally slipped beneath her sleep shorts, Serenity's knees nearly buckled. She clutched his shoulders, grateful for his strength as pleasure coursed through her body.

"Kane," she whispered, her voice thick with need.

His other hand cradled her face, thumb brushing across her lower lip as he watched her reactions with those hypnotic silver-blue eyes. The intensity of his gaze made her feel both vulnerable and powerful.

His fingers moved with deliberate precision, finding the perfect rhythm that made her breath catch and her hips buck against his hand. The pressure built inside her, a coiling tension that wound tighter with each skilled stroke. When his mouth captured hers again, swallowing her moans, Serenity felt herself balancing on the precipice of devastation.

"Let go for me," Kane whispered against her lips, his voice a velvet command.

The tension snapped. Pleasure crashed through her in relentless waves, amplifying everything until she couldn't breathe, couldn't think, could only feel. Her body trembled violently as she clung to him, her face buried against his neck to muffle her cries. Stars exploded behind her closed eyelids as Kane held her steady through her release.

Then suddenly, his warmth was gone. He stepped back, putting space between them while she struggled to remain standing, her legs still quivering from the aftershocks. The abrupt withdrawal left her disoriented, blinking in confusion as Kane straightened his tie with practiced fingers.

"I must go," Kane said, his voice returning to its usual controlled cadence despite the heat still lingering in his gaze. His fingers brushed against her cheek, a fleeting touch that made her lean toward him instinctively. "The Council has been in emergency sessions."

Serenity nodded, trying to compose herself while her body still hummed with pleasure. The contrast between his passionate touch moments ago and his current businesslike demeanor left her dizzy.

"Before I forget," he added, "a seamstress will arrive later to take your measurements and help you pick a gown."

"A gown?" Confusion momentarily overrode the lingering pleasure coursing through her veins.

"For the Elite Ball next week." His expression softened almost imperceptibly. "As Head of the Council, my attendance is required. I'd like you to accompany me."

The Elite Ball. The one Sebastian had mentioned during their outing. Her heart stuttered. Being seen publicly at his side would cement her position and broadcast their connection to everyone in Celearius.

"I... yes. Of course," she managed, tucking a loose curl behind her ear.

Kane nodded once, already stepping away, once again becoming the untouchable Head of the Council.

Before he could turn away, Serenity lunged forward, her fingers closing around his wrist.

"Kane," she whispered, her voice husky with need. "When will you feed again?"

The question hung between them, loaded with implications that transcended mere hunger. His eyes darkened, pupils expanding until only a thin ring of silver-blue remained. The muscles in his jaw ticked as he struggled for control.

He stepped closer, bending to press his lips against hers. The kiss was different this time—restrained yet somehow more intimate, as if he were memorizing the shape of her mouth.

"Soon," he murmured, the single word a promise that sent shivers racing down her spine.

Then he was gone, the elevator doors sliding closed with mechanical precision.

She stood trembling in the empty living room, her body still humming with pleasure while guilt twisted in her stomach. How could she betray someone who made her feel like this? Someone whose touch felt like coming home?

But Beth's face flashed through her mind—healthy, smiling, safe. The rebellion had promised protection for her family. Kane had only promised to keep her alive "as long as it was within his power."

She had no choice. She had to see this through, even if it destroyed her.

She showered, trying to clear her mind, then toweled her hair dry. Three sharp raps at the door announced a visitor.

"Coming!" Serenity called, hastily pulling on a simple dress.

When she opened the door, she found herself face-to-face with a petite woman whose presence seemed to fill the entire doorway despite her small stature. Immaculate box braids were piled atop her head in an intricate crown, and her amber eyes sparked with determination.

"Well, aren't you just a vision," the woman declared, sweeping past Serenity without waiting for an invitation. Her voice carried a melodic lilt that reminded Serenity of her father's old jazz records. "I'm Trina Beaumont, Elite couturier extraordinaire, and honey, we've got work to do."

Nox materialized in the doorway behind her, carrying several garment bags and a smile of apology. "Ms. Beaumont is highly sought after. We're lucky to have her on such short notice." He laid the garment bags across her bed with economical, fastidious movements.

"Lucky doesn't begin to cover it," Trina said, already circling Serenity like a meticulous hawk. "Kane Draccus' new companion showing up at the Elite Ball with anything less than perfection would be sacrilege." Her hands fluttered to Serenity's shoulders, turning her this way and that. "Such beautiful skin tone. We'll need something that complements without overwhelming."

"I really don't need anything extravagant," Serenity protested, feeling suddenly self-conscious under Trina's appraising gaze. "Something simple would be—"

"Simple?" Trina's eyebrows shot toward her hairline. "Honey, there is nothing simple about being on the arm of the most powerful vampyr in Celearius." She unzipped one of the garment bags with dramatic flair. "You'll be the most watched woman in the room. Every Elite, every Council member, every society darling will be dissecting your appearance."

"She's right," Nox said, arranging a few more garments on the nearby chaise with fastidious care. "Your appearance will reflect directly on Kane. More importantly," his voice softened marginally, "he wishes to see you shine."

Heat crept into Serenity's cheeks. "Fine," Serenity conceded, surrendering to Trina's expertise.

The following two hours passed in a blur of fabrics, pins, and Trina's running commentary on each gown's merits. Serenity stood on a small platform, arms extended as Trina pinned and adjusted, occasionally muttering to herself about "proportions" and "highlighting assets."

"This one," Trina declared finally, stepping back to admire her handiwork. "This is the one that will make him forget how to speak."

Serenity caught her reflection in the mirror, and her breath caught. The midnight-blue gown hugged her curves before cascading to the floor in liquid waves. Tiny crystals scattered across the bodice mimicked stars against a night sky, catching light with every breath she took.

"It's perfect," she whispered, hardly recognizing herself.

A distant buzzing sound cut through the moment, drawing both their attention. Nox tilted his head slightly, listening.

"Excuse me, ladies," he said with a slight bow. "I should check who's at the door."

As Nox glided from the room, Serenity carefully touched the fabric, still not fully believing she would be wearing this.

"Let me help you out of that," Trina said, moving behind her to locate the hidden zipper. "Can't risk damaging it before the big night. I'll make a few adjustments, and it should fit you perfectly."

The couturier's nimble fingers made quick work of the fastenings. As the gown slipped from Serenity's shoulders, she hurried into the bathroom to change back into her simple dress, grateful for the moment to collect herself.

"You know," Trina called from the other side of the door, the sound of rustling fabric indicating she was carefully repacking the gown, "when Kane sees you in this, he's going to absolutely devour you." A husky chuckle followed. "In all the best ways, of course."

Serenity's cheeks heated at the memory of Kane's touch just hours earlier. She emerged from the bathroom to find Trina carefully folding the gown back into its protective garment bag. The door opened, and Nox stepped through with Sebastian in tow.

Sebastian's eyebrows shot up when he spotted the garment bags.

"Well, well," Sebastian said, his lips curving into a knowing smile. "I see Kane is finally bringing you into society properly."

Trina snapped her garment case shut with a flourish. "And she'll be the most stunning Elite at the ball, I can guarantee that." Her amber eyes sparkled with professional pride. "He'll be the envy of every vampyr in attendance."

"I'm sure Kane will be quite pleased," Sebastian said, his gaze lingering on Serenity's flushed face. "The Elite Ball is quite the statement. Not every companion receives such... privilege."

Nox gathered the remaining garment bags. "Ms. Beaumont, allow me to escort you out."

"Lovely to meet you, Serenity." Trina clasped her hands with surprising strength. "The gown will be ready two days before the ball. I'll make sure it's delivered."

"Thank you," Serenity managed, still overwhelmed by the entire experience.

Nox guided Trina toward the door with his usual grace. "This way, Ms. Beaumont."

At the threshold, he paused, his voice dropping. "This door stays open when guests are present."

Serenity nodded, understanding.

As Nox's footsteps faded down the hallway, Sebastian moved toward her dresser and started to poke around her things.

"I'm so glad you're going to the ball. I can finally introduce you to more Elites," Sebastian said, looking at her and then at the door, trying to convey a message. He needs to tell her something, but he'll have to do it in code. She played along.

"I hope they're as friendly as you."

"I can't say all that, but they would love to meet you. I told them all about you, especially Dee," Sebastian continued with a meaningful look. "They're looking forward to the present we picked out during shopping. I told him he could get it from you during the ball, so don't forget to bring it."

Serenity's heart stuttered. Sebastian was telling her to deliver the stolen data to Damon at the Elite Ball. She kept her face neutral despite the panic churning inside her.

"Couldn't I give it to you now? So, he doesn't have to wait until then," she asked quietly, pretending to admire one of the jeweled hairpins Trina had left behind. "I have it right here."

Sebastian moved closer, lowering his voice. "The extraction requires your comm device. I don't have what is needed, only he does." He shrugged with practiced casualness. "Besides, I wouldn't see them until the ball anyway, so it wouldn't matter who gave it to them."

Her throat tightened at the thought.

"I understand," she murmured.

Sebastian leaned closer, angling his body away from the door where Nox had disappeared. "I may have found something else," he whispered, barely audible. His eyes darted to the hallway before returning to her. "Information that could change everything—for all of us."

"What do you mean?" she asked, keeping her voice steady despite the storm raging inside her.

Sebastian's fingers drummed a nervous pattern on her dresser. "Nothing certain yet." His voice dropped even lower. "But if what I've seen is true, it could shift the balance between our species forever."

The words settled within her like a stone. What could possibly be significant enough to alter the power dynamics that had ruled their world since the Great Devastation? Her mind raced through possibilities—information about vampyr weakness, technology... a weapon? Whatever it was, Sebastian clearly believed it would change their world.

Sebastian's expression transformed in a blink, the intensity vanishing behind a practiced smile as he clapped his hands together. "Oh! I just had the most brilliant idea. Evie is absolutely magical with makeup—she would never admit it, but she's always wanted a woman Elite to practice on. She would love it!" His voice shifted to a cheerful, casual tone that betrayed nothing of their previous conversation. "You're going to look beautiful. He won't know what to do with you."

Serenity blinked at the sudden shift, momentarily disoriented.

"Makeup? Evie? Never heard those two things together," Nox's cool voice cut through the room as he appeared in the doorway, one eyebrow arched with practiced precision.

"I was just telling her that Evie could help with her makeup for the ball," Sebastian replied smoothly.

"I'll talk to Kane and Evie about it. Good suggestion, though." Nox nodded curtly to Sebastian before turning his attention to Serenity. "I ordered some food since I thought you might be hungry after all the fittings. It should be here soon."

"Thank you," Serenity said. Nox nodded, then retreated, leaving the door open.

Sebastian waited until Nox's footsteps faded before leaning against the dresser with practiced nonchalance. "So, how are you really doing? I heard Kane's been locked away in meetings for days."

Serenity nodded absently as her mind drifted back to Kane's touch that morning, the intensity in his silver-blue eyes as he'd watched her come undone. Her body hummed with the memory.

"...and then the dragons attacked the Council chambers," Sebastian was saying, a knowing smirk spreading across his face.

"What?" Serenity blinked, heat crawling into her cheeks. "Sorry, I was..."

"Thinking about our illustrious Head of Council?" Sebastian finished, his tone teasing but his eyes calculating. "Clearly, you took my advice and seduced him. And it was good."

She opened her mouth to deny it, but she couldn't. "It wasn't on purpose."

"Even if it was, this is good. We want you to get close. The closer you are, the safer you are. I know this is difficult," Sebastian said, his expression softening with something that might have been genuine concern.

Did it make her safer? Because it felt like the game got more dangerous, especially when it came to her heart.

Nox's footsteps echoed in the hallway below, signaling the food's arrival. Sebastian straightened, his mask of casual friendliness sliding back into place.

"I should go," he said, moving toward the door. He paused at the threshold, glancing back. "The ball will be... pivotal. For all of us. Be ready."

Then he was gone, leaving Serenity alone.

She'd made her choice weeks ago when she'd said yes to helping them. She just hadn't realized how much it would cost her.

CHAPTER SIXTEEN

EVIE

The truth was a bullet lodged in Evie's heart, refusing to kill her quickly.

She sat in her darkened office, the blue glow from the security monitor casting shadows across her face as she watched the footage for the fourteenth time. The timestamp read 2:15 PM—five days ago. Sebastian—her Sebastian—moving with practiced efficiency through her private office, his fingers deftly angling her prototype blueprint and then the real one toward his concealed camera. Each movement deliberate. Each betrayal calculated.

Five days. She'd known for five days and said nothing.

Tonight was the Elite Ball. Tonight, he would deliver those plans to the rebellion. And she would have to let it happen.

Evie pressed her fingertips against her temples, where a migraine pulsed with vicious intensity. Eight years of sharing her bed, her home, her secrets—and apparently, her security clearance. The monitor's light reflected off the tears that refused to fall.

Eight years of lies.

The locket at her throat—Sebastian's gift on their fifth anniversary—suddenly felt heavy, constricting. She yanked it off, the delicate chain snapping in her haste. The small oval tumbled onto her desk, the engraved promise facing upward: Forever Yours.

A hollow promise carved in silver.

The evidence before her defied every excuse her heart tried to manu-facture. Sebastian wasn't merely curious. Wasn't just peeking at her work. This was methodical. Professional. The practiced movements of a man who had done this before.

How many times? How many secrets had she unknowingly fed to the rebellion?

She had only caught him this time because she hadn't destroyed the plans. Kane had ordered her to, and she should have obeyed immediately. But she'd kept them—told herself she needed to study them further, to understand the full implications of what Serenity's blood could do. The plans would be safe in her hands, she'd reasoned. She was careful. Cautious.

She'd been a fool.

Her paranoia had finally kicked in, prompting her to activate the secu-rity camera in her home office. Only a handful of trusted people had access to her space. The system had alerted her to a motion detected while she'd been with Rhy and Nox, tracking the rebels' movements toward the Dead City.

She'd watched the footage that night, alone in the darkness, and felt her entire world fracture.

Evie replayed the footage once more, forcing herself to catalog each betrayal. Sebastian lingered over the blueprints for the weapon. He looked confused for a moment as he studied the plans—she guessed he might not completely understand what he had, or that one of them was fake. That small mercy felt like cold comfort.

She should inform Kane.

Evie's fingers hovered over the comm unit. One call to Kane would set everything in motion—Sebastian's immediate detention, interrogation, and... execution. The thought of his body, ashen and still, sent a violent tremor through her hands.

"I can't," she whispered to the empty room.

Her hands trembled as she paused the footage on his face. Even now, even knowing what he'd done, her traitorous heart ached at the sight of him. She remembered the morning he'd brought her coffee in bed just last week, kissed her temple, whispered "I love you" against her skin. Had that been a lie, too? Or had he loved her even while betraying everything she stood for?

Telling Kane meant condemning Sebastian to death. Not telling him meant betraying everything she'd helped build—the fragile peace between humans and vampyr that had cost so many lives.

And then there was Serenity.

The girl was caught in the middle, an unwitting pawn in this deadly chess match. If Sebastian delivered those plans to the Liberation, they would understand what Serenity's blood could do. They would know she was the key to the weapon. They would hunt her down, drain her dry, use her until there was nothing left.

Evie couldn't let that happen. She'd created this disaster by keeping the plans. She had to fix it.

She understood Kane now. Understood the agony of loving someone while watching them betray you. Understood the impossible choice between duty and desire. No wonder he looked haunted every time Serenity entered a room.

When you loved someone who was betraying you, every choice felt like choosing which part of yourself to kill.

Evie closed the footage. The screen went dark, and she was left staring at her own reflection in the black monitor—hollow-eyed, exhausted, broken.

She'd already arranged to have him followed discreetly at the ball. She would watch him hand over the plans, confirm what she already knew in her bones to be true.

And then she would have to decide.

The hardest part would be continuing to pretend that she didn't know. Getting dressed beside him. Letting him fasten the clasp of her necklace.

Smiling at him across the ballroom while her heart shattered with every breath. Watching him destroy everything, including them, and pretending she was blind to it all.

Evie's gaze drifted to the broken locket on her desk, the chain severed, the promise shattered.

Then she would do what she'd always done. Choose duty over her heart. Protect Celearius and Serenity, even if it meant destroying herself in the process.

She picked up the broken locket, running her thumb over the engraved words one final time before dropping it into the waste bin. The soft clink of metal hitting the bottom felt like a door closing.

Evie turned off the monitor and sat alone in the darkness, letting herself break—just for a moment—before she would have to put on her mask and pretend her world wasn't ending.

CHAPTER SEVENTEEN

KANE

Kane checked his watch for the seventh time, the platinum links of the band catching the dim light of his penthouse. Ten minutes until they needed to leave. The Elite Ball waited for no one—not even him.

"She's cutting it close," Nox observed from his position by the elevator, his own formal attire impeccable as always. "Even for a human."

Kane didn't respond. His footfalls were nearly silent against the wood as he crossed to the floor-to-ceiling windows overlooking Celearius. The city sprawled beneath him like a jeweled tapestry, bioluminescent lights pulsing through the arteries of streets and canals. From this height, the division between Inner and Outer City blurred into one harmonious whole—a fiction he sometimes wished were true.

His reflection stared back at him: jaw tight, shoulders rigid beneath his custom-tailored tuxedo. The silver-blue of his eyes had taken on that telltale luminescence that betrayed his agitation. He forced himself to take a measured breath. The scent of Serenity lingered everywhere in the penthouse—that damnable, intoxicating sweetness that saturated his senses, haunted his thoughts, and infiltrated dreams he'd thought long buried.

Five days of maintaining distance while his body screamed to close it.

He'd tried. God, he'd tried to stay away. But she'd sought him out—waiting in the living room at dawn, lingering in the hallway at dusk, her presence a constant temptation he lacked the strength to resist. Each stolen moment had tested his control: a kiss that lasted too long, his mouth at her throat, the taste of her pulse beneath his lips. He'd even fed from her two nights ago, driven by need he could no longer deny.

The makeup artist Evie had arranged—a mousy thing with blonde hair—had darted from Serenity's room thirty minutes ago, offering him only a cursory nod before escaping into the elevator. Yet still no Serenity.

"Perhaps I should check on her," Nox suggested, already moving toward the hallway.

Kane raised a hand. "Wait."

The soft click of a door opening reached his sensitive ears. He turned from the window, his gaze drawn to the hallway entrance like a compass finding north.

Time slowed. His breath caught in his throat.

Serenity emerged like a vision from shadow, the midnight blue of her gown capturing light and scattering it across her form in a thousand glittering points. The dress clung to curves he'd forced himself not to notice, flowing over her hips before cascading to the floor. Her dark skin glowed with an inner radiance, and those silky black curls framed her face in a way that made his fingertips itch to touch them.

Through their bond, he felt her nervousness, her hope that he'd find her beautiful, her uncertainty about the night ahead.

He stood transfixed, unable to form words as she glided toward him, the dress catching light with every step. When she came to stand before him, her honey-brown eyes searched his face, a question in them he couldn't answer. Her mother's herbal soap masked most of her natural scent, but this close, traces of jasmine still enveloped him, clouding his judgment, weakening centuries of carefully constructed walls.

"Kane?" Her voice was soft, uncertain. A tendril of hair fell across her cheek.

He reached forward, brushing it back with fingers that betrayed the slightest tremor. The warmth of her skin burned against his perpetual coolness. A primitive and possessive feeling unfurled within him as he took in the sight of her—radiant, vulnerable, and entirely too tempting.

The pull between them intensified, a magnetic force he'd been fighting since the moment she entered his life. Tonight, with what lay ahead pressing down on them both, he surrendered.

Kane leaned forward, closing the distance between them. His lips met hers with unexpected gentleness, a whisper of contact that sent heat crackling through his veins. Her momentary surprise melted into acceptance as she yielded to him. The kiss deepened, no longer tentative but still achingly gentle. His hand cupped her face, thumb grazing her cheekbone with reverence.

When he finally pulled away, his eyes remained fixed on hers, glowing with an intensity that made her breath catch.

"You are..." Kane paused, struggling to find words that usually came with diplomatic precision. Yet now, standing before this human woman, artifice abandoned him completely. "Exquisitely beautiful."

A flush darkened her cheeks, the rush of blood beneath her skin calling to a primal need within him that he ruthlessly suppressed.

Nox cleared his throat pointedly from the entryway. "I hate to interrupt, but the car is waiting. We need to leave now if we are to arrive in a fashionable manner."

Kane stepped back, offering Serenity his arm with formal precision that belied the storm raging within him. "Shall we?"

She slipped her hand into the crook of his arm, her touch seeping through the expensive fabric of his tuxedo. The contact sent another jolt through him, and Kane clenched his jaw against the sensation.

The elevator descended in silence, the subtle hum of machinery the only sound between them. Kane kept his gaze fixed on the glowing numbers, hyper-aware of Serenity's proximity, of the subtle rise and fall of her chest as she breathed. The confined space amplified her presence, wrapping around him like an invisible chain.

When the doors slid open to reveal the lobby, Nox stepped out first, scanning the area with practiced vigilance before nodding. Kane guided Serenity forward, his hand covering hers where it rested on his arm, a possessive gesture he couldn't quite suppress.

Outside, the gleaming black limousine waited, its engine purring quietly. The driver, a stoic vampyr with eyes that betrayed centuries of service, opened the door with a slight bow. Kane released Serenity's arm, allowing her to slide into the vehicle first.

Inside, he deliberately chose the opposite bench seat, putting as much distance as possible between them. The interior lights cast soft shadows across her face as Kane settled himself firmly on the opposite side. Their knees almost touched in the confined space, and he shifted back, pressing himself against the leather upholstery. The thought of being beside her, feeling her body against his, the whisper of silk against his thigh—it would be too much. His control was already fraying at the edges.

"There are protocols for tonight," Kane said, his voice rougher than he intended. He cleared his throat. "Things you need to understand before we arrive."

Serenity tilted her head, studying him with unsettling perceptiveness. "What kind of protocols?"

"Tonight, you will be formally presented as my Elite." The words hung between them, heavy with implication. "All of Celearius will witness it—the Council members, prominent vampyr families, human dignitaries. It's... ceremonial."

Her brow furrowed slightly. "What exactly does that entail?"

Kane's gaze flickered to the window, watching the glittering cityscape blur past. "When we arrive, we will be announced. You'll need to walk a step behind me, head bowed, until we reach the bottom of the grand staircase."

Serenity's spine stiffened, her eyes widening as the implications sank in. Anger flashed across their bond. "You expect me to what?"

"It's tradition," Kane explained, not meeting her gaze. "A formality that dates back to when Celearius was first established. The Elite walks behind their patron as a symbol of protection—the vampyr leading, watching for threats while the Elite follows in their shadow."

"It sounds like subservience," she said, her voice tight. "Like I'm property."

Kane saw the familiar spark ignite in her eyes—that defiant flame that had drawn him to her from the beginning. Her hands curled into fists on her lap, the fabric of her gown bunching beneath her fingers.

"It's not meant to be demeaning," he tried, though the words sounded hollow even to his own ears. "It's symbolic, part of the ceremony—"

"That treats me as less than you," she finished, jaw set. "I understand perfectly."

The frown that marred her beautiful features twisted something within Kane. Without conscious thought, he slid from his seat, dropping to one knee on the floor of the limousine between them.

He reached for her hand, his fingers hovering uncertainly before gently closing around hers. He could feel her surprise, her confusion warring with lingering anger.

"Serenity." Her name fell from his lips like a prayer. "I know how this appears, and I wouldn't ask it of you if there were any other way. The ceremony is simply part of tradition, something even I cannot break."

Her fingers remained stiff beneath his, but she didn't withdraw.

"There are consequences for breaking this tradition, especially tonight, with dignitaries from other cities watching." Kane's voice dropped lower, a rumble that barely carried over the purr of the engine. "I swear to you, I will make this up to you."

Her expression shifted—not quite forgiveness, but understanding began to soften the hard edges of her frown.

"Fine," she said finally. "I will follow your tradition."

Relief flooded through him.

The limousine glided to a stop before Kane could return to his seat. Through the tinted windows, the Grand Hall loomed—a majestic structure of white stone and soaring spires illuminated against the night sky. The grand entrance blazed with light, and silhouettes of arriving guests moved in an elegant procession up the sweeping marble stairs.

Kane released her hand reluctantly and shifted back to his seat. He leaned forward, his voice dropping to an urgent whisper.

"One more thing, Serenity." His eyes searched hers. "Your safety tonight is paramount. Your mother's herbal soap has helped mask your distinctive scent, but you must still exercise caution."

"I know, Kane. I understand what my blood can do to a vampyr," she said, and they both remembered the night he'd lost control and how she'd only survived due to her quick thinking.

"Good, because tonight there are guests here—vampyr with less... restraint, especially those from the other cities." His thumb traced a small circle on the back of her hand, the gesture unconscious yet intimate. "If you injure yourself, even slightly, the scent of your blood could trigger instincts that are difficult to control."

"No need to sugar-coat it. I know that I wouldn't survive if I spilled a drop of blood in there tonight."

Kane's gaze hardened. "Precisely why you need to exercise caution, especially around the rulers of Kregan. They'll want to meet you." His voice dropped lower, a whisper only meant for her. "When we meet them—Deyja and Xavier—don't maintain eye contact for too long. Their customs differ from ours. Extended eye contact can be interpreted as an invitation."

A flicker of apprehension crossed Serenity's features. "Is there anything else I should know?"

"Trust my lead. Stay close or within sight of Nox or me." His fingers brushed against hers, the briefest touch. "We should go."

The door opened, cool night air rushing in to displace the warmth of their shared space. Serenity accepted his hand, allowing him to guide her from the vehicle onto the cobblestone drive.

The Grand Hall loomed before them, its marble facade bathed in amber light. Massive columns stretched skyward, framing an entrance adorned with intricate carvings of ancient battles between humans and vampyr. History written in stone, sanitized and glorified.

"Remember," he murmured, his breath cool against her ear. "A step behind."

As they entered and approached the top of the staircase, the orchestra's final note hung suspended in the air before dissolving into silence. The sudden quiet rippled through the assembly like a stone dropped in still water, conversation halting as hundreds of eyes—most glowing with the telltale luminescence of vampyr, others merely human—turned toward them.

A liveried herald stepped forward, his voice resonating through the hall with practiced precision.

"Kane Draccus, Head of the Human and Vampyr Council, Commander of Celearius," the herald announced, his voice echoing through the cavernous hall, "and his Elite, Miss Serenity Wright."

A collective murmur rippled through the crowd, a sound Kane had no difficulty interpreting. Curiosity. Speculation. Hunger. His jaw tightened. The protective instinct that had been building since Serenity entered his life surged with unexpected force.

She remembered his instruction perfectly, keeping her head bowed and staying a step behind as they began their descent.

Kane felt the weight of every gaze as they descended the stairs. The marble beneath his polished shoes might as well have been a gauntlet, each step bringing them closer to the assembled power of Celearius. He maintained a careful mask of indifference, though his senses remained hyper-alert to any potential threat to Serenity.

As they reached the bottom, Kane acknowledged several Council members with measured nods. General McGraff inclined his silver head with respectful deference. Elise's crimson lips curved in a smile that didn't reach her calculating eyes. Across the room, he caught sight of Evie near the northern colonnade, her posture perfect as always, but something in her eyes seemed... hollow. She was watching someone—Sebastian, Kane realized—with an intensity that made his instincts prickle.

But there was no time to investigate. The orchestra resumed, strings and woodwinds weaving a haunting melody that floated above the gathering like mist.

The crowd began to disperse, returning to their conversations and champagne flutes filled with blood-infused spirits.

Kane turned to Serenity, who still kept her gaze lowered as instructed. He reached out, his fingers gentle beneath her chin as he tilted her face upward. The soft light caught the gold flecks in her eyes, and his chest tightened.

The urge to claim her mouth again, to taste that sweetness that haunted his dreams, nearly overwhelmed him. Instead, he held her gaze, letting his gratitude flow between them in silent communion.

"Thank you for honoring our tradition," Kane murmured, his fingers lingering a moment longer than necessary against her skin.

The ceremony was complete. They had successfully navigated the first test.

Now the real danger began.

CHAPTER EIGHTEEN

KANE

Movement at the edge of his peripheral vision drew his attention. Two figures approached with deliberate grace, their gaits synchronized in the practiced manner of long-time companions. Kane tensed imperceptibly. The rulers of Kregan had arrived.

Deyja moved like liquid silk, her light caramel skin luminous under the chandeliers. The dark magenta of her hair cascaded in elegant waves past her shoulders, adorned with jewels that caught the light with every step. Beside her, Xavier cut an imposing figure, his dark skin a perfect canvas for the midnight blue formal wear that complemented his twisted locs and meticulously groomed beard.

Kane straightened, placing a protective hand at the small of Serenity's back as he turned to face them. The subtle pressure of his fingers conveyed a silent warning: be cautious. Through the blood bond, he felt Serenity's apprehension sharpen into awareness.

"Kane Draccus," Deyja purred, her voice melodic as she extended her hand. "The years between our meetings grow too long."

"Deyja, Xavier." Kane clasped her offered hand briefly before acknowledging Xavier. "Welcome. I trust your journey to Celearius was pleasant?"

Xavier's eyes remained vigilant even as he offered a cordial smile. "Uneventful, thankfully. We can only hope for the same when returning home."

The underlying message wasn't lost on Kane. Tensions between cities had been growing, making travel increasingly precarious, even for rulers of Xavier and Deyja's stature.

Deyja, however, paid little attention to the exchange. Her gaze had fixed on Serenity with undisguised interest, her nostrils flaring subtly as she inhaled. Kane's muscles tensed as he recognized the predatory gleam in Deyja's eyes, every protective instinct roaring to life.

"She's exquisite," Deyja murmured, circling closer to Serenity. "Such rare beauty." Her fingertips hovered inches from Serenity's face, not quite touching but invasive nonetheless. "Might I have a taste, Kane? Just the smallest sample?"

The request sent ice through Kane's veins. Before he could formulate a response that wouldn't trigger a diplomatic incident, Xavier stepped forward, his imposing presence creating a barrier between Deyja and Serenity.

"Deyja," he chided, his deep voice carrying just enough authority to command attention without creating a scene. "You know Kane has never shared his Elite. Especially one as..." his eyes flickered over Serenity, "precious as this one clearly is."

Relief washed through Kane, though his expression remained impassive. He caught Xavier's gaze and communicated his gratitude with the slightest inclination of his head.

"Indeed," Kane said, his voice smooth despite the tension coiled within him. "Please, enjoy the festivities. The vintage from one of our provinces is particularly exceptional this evening."

Deyja's lips curved into a smile that didn't reach her eyes. "Another time, perhaps," she murmured, her gaze lingering on Serenity before she allowed Xavier to guide her away.

Kane exhaled slowly, his hand still firmly at Serenity's back. The pressure of his fingers increased slightly as he spotted General McGraff making his way toward them, cutting through the crowd with military precision. The aging general's weathered face was set with purpose, and the last thing Kane needed was a detailed discussion of security protocols with Serenity standing vulnerable at his side.

Without hesitation, Kane turned to Serenity, extending his hand. "Would you honor me with a dance?"

Surprise flickered across her features, but she placed her hand in his without question. Kane guided her onto the dance floor with fluid grace. The orchestra shifted into a slow waltz, the melody weaving through the air like silk.

As he swept her into his arms, Kane was struck by how perfectly she fit against him. Her warmth seeped through the fabric of his tuxedo, chasing away the perpetual chill that had been his companion for centuries. The feedback loop was intoxicating—his desire feeding hers, hers amplifying his until the ballroom faded to nothing.

The herbal soap masked most of her natural scent, but this close, traces of jasmine still broke through, wrapping around him like an invitation he desperately wanted to accept.

"I didn't know you danced," Serenity murmured, her eyes studying his face with curious intensity.

Kane's lips curved into a rare smile. "There was a time when I danced at every court in Europe." He guided her through a perfect turn, their bodies moving in harmony. "Though it has been... some time since I've had a partner worthy of the effort."

The slight widening of her eyes sent a ripple of satisfaction through him. He hadn't intended to flirt, but the pleasure of her surprise was too satisfying to regret. He pulled her closer, his hand splayed across her back, feeling the subtle movement of muscle beneath silk.

When was the last time he had held someone like this? Three decades? Four? The years blurred together in endless meetings and diplomatic functions, but this moment crystallized with perfect clarity.

"I find that hard to believe," Serenity said, her lips curving into a smile that made his chest tighten. "A powerful vampyr like you must have danced with countless partners over the centuries."

Kane guided her through another turn. "Partners, yes. But few worth remembering." His voice dropped lower, meant only for her. "None who felt like this."

The slight catch in her breath was audible only to his enhanced hearing, but the flush that crept across her cheeks was visible for all to see. Kane found himself transfixed by the rising color, the quickening of her pulse beneath the delicate skin of her throat. He wanted to press his lips there, to feel her life beating against him.

"You're staring," she whispered, her eyes never leaving his.

"I find it difficult to look anywhere else," Kane admitted, surprised by his own honesty. The words slipped past his careful defenses before he could stop them.

The music swelled around them as they moved together. Kane couldn't remember the last time he'd felt this connected to another being, this aware of every subtle shift in expression, every quickened heartbeat. Serenity's eyes held his, unguarded in this moment of shared intimacy.

"Thank you," he said softly, the words meant only for her. "For earlier. The ceremony. I know it wasn't... easy for you."

Serenity's lips pressed together briefly. "I hated it," she admitted, her voice low but firm. "Walking behind you like that, head bowed—it felt wrong." Her fingers tightened almost imperceptibly on his shoulder. "But I understand why it had to happen. Your position, the traditions..."

Kane pulled her a fraction closer, his thumb brushing against the silk at her waist. "I intend to make it up to you."

"Oh?" A single eyebrow arched, curiosity sparking in her eyes. "And how exactly do you plan to do that?"

"I have something in mind," he said, guiding her through another turn that sent her dress swirling around her ankles. "A pleasant surprise."

"I can't wait," Serenity whispered, her eyes sparkling with genuine anticipation.

The simple phrase sent an unexpected thrill through Kane's body. How long had it been since anyone had looked forward to something he'd planned? Decades, perhaps centuries. Most beings—human and vampyr alike—approached him with calculation, fear, or naked ambition. Never this unguarded delight that transformed Serenity's features into pure joy.

Kane drew her closer, propriety be damned. The music swelled around them as they continued to move. Her body moved in perfect synchronicity with his, as if they'd danced together for centuries rather than minutes. The silk of her gown whispered against his trousers.

"You dance beautifully," he murmured, allowing himself a moment of indulgence.

"My mother taught me," Serenity replied, her voice softening with memory. "Before she got sick. She said every woman should know how to dance, even if just in her own kitchen." Her eyes softened. "We'd push the furniture against the walls and dance until we were laughing too hard to continue."

The image of a younger Serenity dancing with her mother sent an unexpected pang through Kane's chest. Such simple joy, such fleeting human happiness—things he'd long since forgotten in his centuries of existence.

"She taught you well," he said, guiding her through another turn, then drawing her back against him.

For one suspended moment, the crowded ballroom faded away. The weight of responsibilities, the dangers lurking in the shadows—all of it receded until there was only Serenity in his arms, warm and alive and looking at him as if he were more than the cold, calculating leader he'd become.

Their connection blazed bright and clear—no lies, no manipulation, just this. Just them.

"Kane."

The familiar voice shattered the moment. Kane stiffened, his jaw clenching as he reluctantly turned his head to find Nox standing at the edge of the dance floor, his expression carefully neutral. But Kane recognized the subtle tension in his stance.

"What is it?" Kane asked, his hand still resting at Serenity's waist.

Nox stepped closer, his voice lowering. "General McGraff requests a meeting. Immediately. His exact words were 'of dire importance.'"

Kane suppressed a curse. The music continued around them, the other dancers oblivious to the cold dread and pure annoyance pooling in his stomach. Leaving Serenity alone was unthinkable, especially after Deyja's predatory interest. Yet McGraff wouldn't use such language unless the matter truly demanded his attention.

"I need you to stay with Nox while I handle this," Kane murmured, reluctant to release her.

Before Serenity could respond, a smooth voice cut through the moment.

"I believe this is where I cut in."

Sebastian materialized beside them, resplendent in a charcoal tuxedo that emphasized his lean physique. His blonde hair was styled to perfection, and his smile carried that effortless charm that had always grated on Kane's nerves.

Every instinct screamed at him to refuse, to keep Serenity in his arms where she belonged, where he could feel her and know she was safe.

Let him take her, his strategic mind tried to insist. You need to meet with McGraff. This is good. It maintains the illusion that she means nothing more than any other Elite.

But watching Sebastian extend his hand toward Serenity made Kane want to tear the ballroom apart.

There was no strategy anymore. No careful manipulation. No maintaining distance while using her position to his advantage.

There was only her, and the visceral need to keep every other male away from what was his.

Kane's jaw clenched as Serenity placed her hand in Sebastian's. He forced himself to step away, every muscle in his body protesting the movement. Then he watched as Sebastian swept her into the dance.

The bond stretched thin with distance, her emotions becoming muted whispers rather than clear notes. Kane hated it. Hated not feeling her clearly, not knowing if Sebastian said something that upset her, not being able to sense if she needed him.

The bond had become both his greatest weakness and his only comfort. Without it, he felt blind.

Kane's fingers curled into his palm, nails digging into flesh as he watched Sebastian guide Serenity through the steps. The sight twisted something primal inside him.

"Keep your eyes on her," Kane growled to Nox, his voice low enough that only vampyr hearing could detect it. "Don't let her out of your sight."

Nox inclined his head slightly. "We will both have eyes on her."

"If he tries anything, you have my full permission to separate his head from his shoulders," Kane replied, only half-joking.

"I am sure Evie would not approve, but I'll take it under advisement," Nox said dryly.

Kane tore his gaze away from the dancing pair with considerable effort. As he moved through the crowd, human and vampyr parted before him like water. He caught one last glimpse of Evie across the room, still watching Sebastian with that hollow, haunted expression.

Something was wrong there. Very wrong.

But McGraff was waiting, and Kane had no time to investigate. He could only hope that whatever the general needed to discuss was actually of dire importance.

Because if it wasn't, Kane might actually make good on his threat to Nox about separated heads and shoulders.

CHAPTER NINETEEN

SERENITY

The music faded, and a new song started as Serenity's midnight blue gown swirled around her ankles. Sebastian guided her across the ballroom floor, his hand resting lightly at the small of her back. Her heart still hammered at the ghost of Kane's touch lingering on her skin. The confession that had nearly spilled from her lips now sat like lead in her stomach.

Through the strange connection between them, she could feel him moving away—the warmth dimming with distance until it became a cold, hollow ache. He was being pulled somewhere, torn away from her, and the separation made her feel exposed, vulnerable.

"You look absolutely stunning tonight, Serenity," Sebastian murmured, his voice pleasant and measured. His movements were graceful, practiced, as they navigated between the glittering couples.

She forced a smile. "Thank you."

When they were several yards from where Nox stood watching the crowd with predatory attention, Sebastian leaned closer, his lips nearly brushing her ear. "Damon is here. By the bar with his patron, Elise."

Adrenaline shot through her veins. She kept her expression neutral even as her pulse quickened. "Good."

"Don't look directly at him," Sebastian cautioned. "Elise will notice. Look at the bartender instead."

Serenity nodded minutely, allowing Sebastian to twirl her in a direction that gave her a clear view of the sleek marble bar. The polished surface gleamed under amber lights, casting everyone in a golden glow. Serenity studied the bartender, a tall human with meticulously styled hair who moved with practiced efficiency, mixing blood-infused cocktails with a theatrical flourish.

In her peripheral vision, she caught sight of Damon. His midnight black hair contrasted sharply with vibrant emerald eyes that seemed to glow even from this distance. He raised his crystal glass to his lips, taking a measured sip while his patron, Elise—a statuesque vampyr with copper hair—laughed at something another patron had said.

Sebastian's fingers pressed against her waist, a subtle signal. "There's an Elite-only lounge beyond the eastern corridor," he murmured. "Private bathrooms, sitting areas. We'll meet Damon there in a few moments."

Serenity's throat tightened. "How exactly?"

"Once this song ends, tell Nox you need to freshen up." His voice was barely audible beneath the music. "I'll offer to escort you—standard protocol for Elites at formal events."

The final notes of the music faded into silence. Serenity's eyes swept across the crowded ballroom, searching for Kane's imposing figure among the sea of elegant vampyr and their companions. He was nowhere to be seen. A strange mixture of relief and disappointment twisted in her.

Kane felt thin and distant now, muted by whatever was occupying his attention. She couldn't sense him clearly, couldn't tell what was happening or if he'd even noticed her dancing with Sebastian.

Sebastian guided her through the throng of dancers toward Nox, who stood sentinel in his perfect dark suit, his precise nature matching his suit. His gaze hadn't wavered from them once during the entire dance.

It narrowed slightly as they approached, but his posture remained relaxed. "Finished already?" he asked, his tone neutral.

Serenity nodded.

"You're a wonderful dancer," Sebastian said, his voice smooth as polished marble. "Now I see why Kane danced with you for so long."

A flush crept up Serenity's neck. "Thank you. All this dancing, though..." She pressed her hands to her cheeks, feeling the heat there. "I need to use the restroom, and then I desperately need a drink. My throat feels like sandpaper."

Sebastian's lips curved into an amused smile. "I can help with both, in the precise order."

They shared a laugh that sounded far more carefree than Serenity felt. The weight of her mission—of her betrayal—pressed against her ribcage like a physical thing.

"Sebastian can escort you to the Elite Lounges," Nox said, his eyes flicking between them. "I'll wait outside."

Relief washed through her. "Thank you."

Sebastian offered his arm and guided her away from the dance floor, toward an ornate archway that marked the eastern corridor. Nox trailed silently behind them. The sounds of the ballroom gradually faded as they moved deeper into the building, replaced by the gentle click of her heels against polished marble.

They rounded a corner and nearly collided with Evie, who wore a stunning emerald gown that complemented her pale skin. Her eyes widened with surprise, then narrowed with sharp curiosity.

"Sebastian? Serenity? Where are you two rushing off to?" Her voice was light, but Serenity detected a note of suspicion beneath the sweetness.

"Restrooms," Nox answered from behind them. "Elite Lounge."

Evie's perfect smile never wavered, but something flickered in her eyes—calculation, assessment, wariness. Her gaze lingered on Sebastian for a moment too long, studying him with an intensity that made Serenity's skin prickle.

"Sebastian, darling," Evie said, her voice carrying a strange undercurrent. "Meet me by the bar when you're done."

"Of course," Sebastian replied with practiced ease.

Evie's eyes held his for another heartbeat before she stepped aside, allowing them to pass. Serenity could feel her gaze following them down the corridor.

Sebastian led Serenity toward a set of ornate double doors at the end of the corridor. Nox halted at the threshold.

"I'll wait here," he said, positioning himself beside the entrance like a statue come to life.

Sebastian pushed the doors open, revealing a sumptuous lounge bathed in amber light. "Only Elites are allowed inside," he murmured as they crossed the threshold. "It's one of the few places we can speak freely."

The room unfolded before Serenity in a tapestry of luxury and hidden despair. Plush velvet couches lined the walls, occupied by Elites in various states of being. A young woman with auburn hair laughed too loudly at a joke while her hand trembled slightly against her glass. A muscular male Elite leaned casually against the wall, his posture relaxed but his eyes scanning the room with a wariness that betrayed his comfort. Across the lounge, two Elites sat together, their bodies healthy and groomed to perfection, but their gazes vacant—hollowed out from within.

Sebastian guided Serenity past them all, nodding in acknowledgment as several Elites greeted him with varying degrees of enthusiasm. One woman with a delicate silver chain around her wrist raised her hand in greeting, her smile not quite reaching her eyes.

"Sebastian," she called softly. "It's been weeks."

"Mira," he returned with genuine warmth. "How are you holding up?"

"Better than most," she replied, her gaze flicking briefly to Serenity with quiet curiosity before Sebastian steered them onward.

They moved deeper into the lounge, past the main sitting area and down a softly lit corridor lined with doors. Serenity's pulse quickened with each step, the honey-brown of her eyes darkening with apprehension as Sebastian stopped before one of the doors.

The connection with Kane felt even more distant here, muted by walls and distance. She couldn't sense him clearly, couldn't tell if he was still in the ballroom or if he'd noticed her absence. The not-knowing made her hands shake as Sebastian opened the door.

Sebastian pushed open the door and guided Serenity inside with a gentle pressure at her lower back. The room beyond was intimate—a luxurious bedroom with a massive four-poster bed, its center draped in burgundy silk. Crystal sconces cast honeyed light across polished mahogany furniture and thick carpeting that muffled their footsteps.

Serenity froze just past the threshold, her pulse knocking against her throat. Her gaze darted from the bed to the chaise lounge in the corner, to the crystal decanter of amber liquid on the sideboard.

"This is..." she began, unable to finish.

Sebastian closed the door with a soft click. "Private. Secure." His voice remained pleasant, unruffled.

"And a bedroom?"

"Sometimes, when Elites aren't with their patrons, they come here to... have fun," Sebastian explained, his tone matter-of-fact. The corner of his mouth twitched upward. "But that's not why we're here."

Then, as if on cue, there was a soft knock on the door.

Sebastian opened it, revealing Damon's imposing figure. He slipped inside, closing the door with barely a whisper of sound. His emerald eyes flashed with intensity as he surveyed the room before landing on Serenity.

"The comm," he said without preamble, extending his hand toward her.

Serenity fumbled with the tiny silver device nestled in a hidden pocket of her midnight blue gown. Her fingers trembled slightly as she placed it in Damon's palm, the weight of her actions settling like frost across her shoulders.

Damon produced another device from inside his tailored jacket—sleek and compact with a miniature keyboard. He connected her comm to it with a thin, nearly invisible wire and began typing rapidly, his long fingers dancing across the keys. The soft blue glow from the screen cast eerie shadows across the sharp planes of his face.

"How long?" he asked, not looking up from his work.

"Ten minutes, tops. Nox is vigilant tonight," Sebastian replied, moving to stand by the door. He glanced at Serenity, his expression softening slightly. "If anyone asks why you took so long, blame the dress. Those layers make bathroom visits pretty fucking tricky. Plus, you got talking with Mira."

Serenity nodded, her throat too dry for words. The force of what they were doing—what she was doing—pressed against her chest like a vice.

Sebastian turned to Damon, lowering his voice. "I may have found something." His words came faster now, urgent and hushed. "Plans for a weapon—something that could potentially kill or poison vampyr on a mass scale."

Damon's head snapped up, emerald eyes blazing with sudden intensity. "What kind of weapon?" The device in his hands was momentarily forgotten.

"I'm not entirely sure," Sebastian replied, running a hand through his immaculate hair. "The documents were heavily encoded, but I recognized fragments of chemical formulas—compounds that interact specifically with vampyr physiology."

"Did you get copies? Or pictures?" Damon asked sharply, his expression intense as he reached out his free hand.

Sebastian shook his head. "I couldn't get any pictures. The documents were in a secure location with surveillance. Taking photos would have been too risky." Frustration edged his voice. "I had to memorize what I could in the brief window I had access."

Serenity's stomach knotted with tension. Sebastian had access to information that could change the course of the resistance, yet they were still fumbling in the dark. Her anxiety spiked as what they were attempting pressed down on her shoulders, making it difficult to breathe in the close quarters of the bedroom.

A sharp electronic beep cut through the room.

Damon's attention snapped back to the device. "It's done," he said, disconnecting the comm from the larger device and handing it back to Serenity. "Everything on your comm has been copied and cleared. No trace of your communications with us remains."

Serenity slipped the comm back into her hidden pocket, her fingers still trembling slightly. "Am I done?"

Damon paused, his emerald eyes flicking up to meet hers. "I honestly do not know. We need to check these files first." His voice was low and measured. "Then we should be able to give you a definitive answer."

Something cold slithered down Serenity's spine. Not done. Not free. The invisible chains tightened around her wrists, her throat. She didn't know how much longer she could keep up this charade. Every time she was in Kane's arms, the lies... the betrayal killed her.

Damon's eyes flickered to Sebastian. "This weapon you mentioned—I need to know everything. Every compound, every formula fragment, any context you gleaned. If the vampyr are developing something that could shift the balance of power..."

"It wasn't the vampyr," Sebastian interjected, his voice barely audible. "The documents I found were human in origin. Human military research that the vampyr somehow acquired."

The revelation hung in the air between them, dense as smoke. Serenity's mind reeled with the implications. Had humans created a weapon against vampyr? And Kane—the vampyr—had found it?

Damon checked his watch, then nodded curtly, slipping the device back into his jacket. "You both now have a new mission. Find out anything you can about this weapon." He moved toward the door, then paused, glancing back at Serenity. "We will get you out. Just hang on a little longer."

Before Serenity could respond, he was gone.

The door closed behind Damon with a soft click, leaving Serenity alone with Sebastian in the opulent bedroom. The sudden silence pressed against her eardrums, making the sound of her own heartbeat thunderous. She sank onto the edge of the chaise lounge, her midnight blue gown pooling around her like spilled ink.

"A little longer," she repeated, the words hollow in her mouth. "How much longer is 'a little'?"

Sebastian crossed to the sideboard and poured amber liquid from the crystal decanter into two glasses. The gentle clink of glass against glass seemed unnaturally loud in the quiet room.

"Here," he said, offering her one of the glasses. "It helps."

Serenity accepted the drink with trembling fingers, the crystal cool against her skin. The liquor burned a path down her throat, warming her from within even as a chill of uncertainty settled in her bones.

"I don't know what to do anymore," she whispered, staring into the depths of her glass. The amber liquid caught the light, fracturing it into tiny prisms. "Every moment I'm with him, I feel like I'm drowning in lies. And now there's this weapon."

When would it all end?

"Sebastian," Serenity set down her glass with a decisive clink. "Are they really going to get me out? I need the truth."

He didn't answer immediately. The silence stretched between them, taut as a wire. Sebastian's gaze fixed on some distant point beyond her shoulder, his expression unreadable in the honeyed light. When he finally spoke, his voice was measured, careful.

"Yes," he said. "But Serenity, we've never had someone so close to Kane—to his secrets, his vulnerabilities." He leaned forward, the shadows deepening the hollows beneath his cheekbones. "The information you've provided has been invaluable. Lives depend on what we can learn about Cavern 47."

Serenity's throat constricted. "So I'm just... useful." The words tasted bitter on her tongue.

"You're essential," he corrected. "Not expendable. We will get you out."

She wanted to believe him. Needed to. But doubt coiled in her stomach like a serpent, cold and insidious. Her fingers twisted the silky fabric of her gown.

"I want to believe you," Serenity whispered, her honey-brown eyes searching Sebastian's face for any hint of deception. "But how can I trust that when this mission keeps expanding? First Kane's office, then the comms, now this weapon..."

Sebastian's shoulders dropped slightly, a rare crack in his perfect composure. He swirled the remaining liquor in his glass, watching the amber liquid catch the light.

"I understand how difficult this is for you," he said, his voice lower, more intimate than before. "I truly do. This... charade becomes more difficult with each passing day."

She glanced at him, surprised by the raw honesty in his tone.

"We're taught that they're monsters," Sebastian continued, his gaze distant. "That they're predators who see us as nothing more than walking blood bags. That's what I believed when I first joined the resistance." His fingers traced the rim of his glass, the movement hypnotic. "But then you spend time with them. You see them laugh, grieve... love. You witness their kindness, their cruelty—all the contradictions that make them so frustratingly... human."

The words settled between them, heavy with implication. Serenity's chest tightened as unbidden images of Kane flooded her mind—his rare smile, his gentle touch, the vulnerability in his eyes when he'd thanked her for honoring the ceremony.

Sebastian drained his glass in one swift motion, then extended his hand to her with a practiced smile that didn't quite reach his eyes. "We should return. Nox will be getting suspicious."

Serenity nodded, finishing the last of her drink. The alcohol burned pleasantly down her throat, offering temporary warmth against the chill of her reality. She placed her empty glass on the side table and accepted Sebastian's outstretched hand.

They made their way back through the lounge, which now had fewer Elites scattered among the plush furniture. Mira looked up as they passed, offering a small wave that Serenity returned with a tight smile.

As they stepped into the corridor, Serenity immediately spotted Nox, his rigid posture betraying his impatience. His dark eyes narrowed as they approached.

"That took longer than expected," he said, his tone carefully neutral though his gaze was sharp.

Sebastian's laugh was easy, rehearsed. "You know how it is. Serenity met Mira, and they got to talking. It was hard to pull them away."

"Is that so?" Nox's eyes slid to Serenity, assessing.

Serenity's lips parted to respond when the air in the corridor suddenly shifted, growing heavy with a predatory presence. The fine hairs at the nape of her neck stood on end as a tall, statuesque figure materialized at the far end of the hallway.

"So this is where they're keeping all the delicacies," a sultry voice purred, the sound like velvet dragged over broken glass.

CHAPTER TWENTY

SERENITY

Serenity's breath caught in her throat. The woman approaching them moved like liquid shadow, her copper hair cascading down her back in loose waves that caught the amber light. Her caramel skin seemed to glow from within, and her lips—painted the exact shade of freshly spilled blood—curved into a smile that held no warmth.

Deyja. One of the rulers of Kregan.

The bond between her and Kane ignited—his alarm blazing through the distance separating them. But he was too far away.

Nox stepped forward, his posture stiffening as he inclined his head in a respectful but minimal bow. "Deyja. This area is off-limits to vampyr, particularly those without an Elite."

Deyja's lips curved into a smile that never reached her eyes. "Ah, yes, that's what you call your cattle." Her gaze remained fixed on Serenity, nostrils flaring slightly. "Such an... interesting specimen."

The vampyr's scrutiny made Serenity's skin crawl. Each step Deyja took toward her sent electric pulses of fear racing through her body. The air around them seemed to grow colder, thinner.

Nox stepped directly in front of Serenity, his broad shoulders creating a barrier between her and Deyja's hungry gaze. "Perhaps I can escort you back to the main ballroom. There are refreshments—"

"Refreshments?" Deyja laughed, the sound like glass shattering against marble. "You mean that watered-down shit they're serving? No." Her mouth formed a perfect pout. "I'm hungry for richer fare."

The corridor suddenly fell silent. Too silent. Serenity watched as Nox's body went rigid, his spine straightening to an unnatural angle. His fingers spasmed once, twice—then he hit the floor, limbs twitching in uncontrolled spasms.

Fear lanced through her. Through the bond, Kane's answering rage burned—distant but unmistakable. He knew. He was coming.

"Nox!" Serenity's cry echoed off the marble.

Deyja flashed teeth in a smile that promised violence. Then she vanished—copper hair and caramel skin blurring into nothing—leaving only expensive perfume and the iron scent of impending bloodshed.

The doors to the Elite Lounge crashed open.

"No!" Sebastian's voice tore through the silence. He bolted through the entrance, his polished shoes skidding against marble.

Serenity followed. The elegant room had transformed into a nightmare. Screams ricocheted off walls as Elites scattered, their perfect attire disheveled in panic.

In the center of the chaos stood Deyja, magnificent and terrible. She clutched a male Elite against her chest—the one who'd been laughing earlier. Her fangs tore into his throat, and scarlet rivers poured down his neck. His hands clawed weakly at her arms, his strength fading as she drank. His struggles ceased. His arms fell limp.

Deyja released the man. He hit the floor, eyes empty, mouth frozen in a silent scream. Blood pooled beneath him, seeping into the luxurious carpet.

Deyja reappeared behind a female Elite scrambling toward the exit. With one powerful arm, she yanked the woman backward by her elaborate updo.

"Such sweet little things," Deyja purred, licking the woman's throat. "Delicious."

The woman's scream died as Deyja's fangs sank deep. Crimson sprayed across pristine walls, dripping down gold-flecked wallpaper like macabre rain.

Movement flashed in Serenity's peripheral vision. Sebastian lunged toward an overturned barstool, grabbed it, and charged at Deyja from behind. He swung with all his strength, bringing it down across her back with a sickening crack.

The stool splintered into pieces, fragments of wood exploding outward like shrapnel.

Deyja froze mid-feed. Her victim slid from her grasp. She turned slowly, crimson staining her chin, her eyes widening with disbelief before narrowing into slits of pure hatred.

"You dare?" The words slithered from her throat, each syllable dripping with venom.

Deyja's hand closed around Sebastian's throat before he could retreat. His feet left the ground as she lifted him effortlessly, nails digging crescents into his skin. Sebastian clawed at her fingers, oxygen dwindling. Her lips peeled back to reveal fangs still wet with her previous victim's blood, her eyes glowing with malevolent delight.

"A brave little human," she purred, her voice like poisoned silk. "I do enjoy it when my food fights back."

With a flick of her wrist, she spun Sebastian around, yanking his head to the side. His gaze found Serenity's across the room, wide with understanding.

"Run," he mouthed silently.

Deyja's fangs plunged into his throat with savage precision. Sebastian's body convulsed, a strangled cry escaping his lips. The color drained from his collar as his eyes fluttered.

Serenity's world tilted. Sebastian was dying.

No.

Time slowed. Her gaze darted around the room, landing on shattered crystal glasses littering the floor beside an overturned table. Without thinking, Serenity lunged forward, snatching a jagged shard from the debris.

She dragged the crystal across her palm, slicing deep. White-hot pain seared through her hand as crimson bloomed across her skin, dripping between her fingers to the marble floor below.

Kane's reaction blazed through the bond—raw and visceral.

Deyja froze mid-feed, her mouth still latched to Sebastian's throat. The scent of Serenity's blood cut through everything else—different, intoxicating, impossible to ignore. Slowly, Deyja's head turned, nostrils flaring.

Sebastian's body slipped from her grasp, hitting the floor. His chest still rose and fell in shallow movements, but his eyes were unfocused.

"I knew there was a reason Kane was keeping you all to himself," Deyja purred, her voice like velvet stretched over broken glass.

Sebastian's blood painted her lips and chin, dripping onto her elegant dress. Her eyes fixed on Serenity's bleeding palm with naked hunger. Deyja moved toward her, each step measured and deliberate.

"Oh, you're something special, aren't you?" Her voice thickened with desire.

Serenity's muscles locked, her body refusing to obey her desperate command to flee. The crystal shard slipped from her bloodied fingers, shattering against marble with a musical tinkle that seemed obscenely delicate amid the carnage. What had she done? She'd cut herself to distract Deyja from Sebastian, but now those eyes were fixed on her with an intensity that stripped away all pretense of humanity.

"You are mine now," Deyja purred.

Deyja's hand closed around Serenity's wrist in an iron grip. She jerked Serenity forward until they were inches apart, her eyes gleaming with triumph. The scent of copper and roses engulfed her—Deyja's perfume mingling with blood still fresh on her lips.

"Such a waste," Deyja said, lifting Serenity's bleeding palm to her face. "Kane. Keeping this all to himself."

Serenity's heart hammered. Her midnight gown suddenly felt too heavy, too constricting as Deyja's cold breath ghosted across her skin.

Deyja's tongue darted out to trace the ragged cut across Serenity's palm. The contact sent revulsion through her body, but Deyja's grip only tightened, fingernails digging into her flesh.

The moment Serenity's blood touched Deyja's tongue, the vampyr's eyes rolled back in ecstasy, pupils dilating until only a thin ring remained visible. A guttural moan escaped her throat, more animal than human.

"Ambrosia," she breathed.

Deyja ran a cold finger down Serenity's face, tracing her cheekbone with terrifying gentleness. Her nail left a trail of fire in its wake, the sharp edge just barely breaking skin. Serenity's breath caught as Deyja's hand moved lower, hovering at the hollow of her neck. Her smile widened, revealing fangs still slick with Sebastian's blood.

Just as Deyja's fingers reached for Serenity's throat, a large hand clamped around her wrist, stopping it mid-air. Another hand seized her neck from behind, fingers digging into her caramel skin with such force that her flesh dimpled beneath the pressure.

The bond roared to life—white-hot and blazing.

Kane.

Serenity stared as the grip on Deyja's wrist tightened, knuckles white with strain. The hand at her neck squeezed mercilessly, forcing a strangled gasp from Deyja's lips. Her eyes widened in surprise, then narrowed with fury as she was yanked backward with brutal force.

CHAPTER TWENTY-ONE

RHYZAN

The scent of old parchment and polished mahogany couldn't mask the stench of political opportunism wafting from General McGraff. Rhyzan kept his expression impassive as he stood by the leaded glass windows, watching moonlight paint silver across the garden below, where night-blooming jasmine surrendered its petals to darkness. The Elite Ball's distant music filtered through the library's thick walls—a muffled symphony that couldn't quite drown out McGraff's increasingly tedious monologue.

"Scarlet has connections throughout Celearius," McGraff continued, straightening his immaculate uniform. The medals adorning his chest—relics that meant nothing now—clinked softly with each self-important gesture. "Her intelligence network rivals even Rhyzan's."

Rhyzan suppressed a snort. No human network could possibly rival vampyric surveillance perfected over centuries. He shifted his attention to Kane, who sat behind a rosewood desk, one elegant finger tapping an irregular rhythm against its surface. His eyes had glazed over with that particular brand of boredom Rhyzan had witnessed countless times during their long friendship.

"And you believe these... connections... will yield information about the rebels that our own intelligence network cannot?" Kane's voice was smooth as aged whisky.

McGraff puffed his chest. "With all due respect, Draccus, there are whispers in the slums that wouldn't reach vampyr ears. Humans talk to humans."

Kane's finger stilled against the desk, his expression hardening. Moonlight caught in his raven hair, casting silver highlights that matched the coolness in his gaze.

"By slums, I assume you mean the human districts." Kane's voice remained level, but Rhyzan detected the subtle edge beneath. "Your sudden interest is quite curious. Why is that?"

McGraff shifted his weight. "Well, you know I'll be retiring soon—"

"I'll meet with Scarlet," Rhyzan interjected, turning from the window. The general's mouth snapped shut, surprise flickering across his weathered features. "Tomorrow at Waterside Park, near the eastern dock. Sixteen hundred hours."

Kane's eyebrow arched—a flicker of surprise quickly banked behind his usual control.

McGraff's mouth split into a wide grin, relief evident in the sudden relaxation of his shoulders. "I knew you would see the value in this arrangement." He gathered his cap from the side table, the medals catching the lamplight. "I'll inform her immediately. She'll be most pleased."

"I'm sure she will," Rhyzan replied, his voice neutral as winter air.

McGraff offered a crisp nod to Kane. "I'll return to the festivities. You both have a good evening." His boots clicked against the hardwood as he retreated, pulling the heavy library door closed behind him with a soft thud.

Rhyzan counted three heartbeats before Kane spoke.

"What game do you think he's playing?" Kane's voice had shed its diplomatic veneer, now sharp as obsidian. "This reeks of a trap."

Rhyzan traced a finger along the spine of a leather-bound text, feeling the worn binding beneath his fingertip. "Better to spring it under controlled conditions than allow it to catch us unaware." He turned from the bookshelf to face Kane fully. The lamplight caught the silver flecks in his verdant eyes, making them glitter with predatory intent. "If McGraff is working with the rebels—and his timing suggests he might be—then Scarlet could lead us directly to their network. If he's simply incompetent, we lose nothing but an hour."

Kane leaned back in his chair, the weathered wood creaking. His fingers steepled beneath his chin, the signet ring on his right hand gleaming dully in the half-light. "Be careful, Rhyzan. This feels... orchestrated. McGraff has never shown interest in intelligence gathering before. And this Scarlet—I've never heard her name mentioned in any of our reports."

"Precisely why I agreed to meet her." Rhyzan's lips curved into a cold smile that never reached his eyes. "If she's new to the game, she'll be easier to read. If she's experienced and has remained hidden from us, then she's worth meeting regardless."

"Or she could be bait." Kane's voice dropped an octave, resonating with the weight of surviving countless assassination attempts. "The Human Liberation grows bolder, as we already saw with the prison break."

"Speaking of which, any news?"

"Unfortunately, no. They're moving slowly." Kane's expression hardened. "They approached the Dead City's outskirts about two hours ago and have been stationary since—most likely resting for the night. They'll be on the move by morning."

Rhyzan nodded, calculating routes and contingencies with practiced ease. "We should double the patrols along the northern perimeter. Just as a precaution."

"Already done," Kane said, pushing himself up from the desk. The chair scraped against the hardwood floor. "I've also dispatched a team to track their movements without engagement."

"Before you go," Rhyzan said, his voice dropping to a pitch that wouldn't carry beyond the library walls, "I should inform you that Evie knows you shared blood with your Elite."

Kane froze mid-stride, his broad shoulders going taut beneath his impeccably tailored jacket. The temperature in the room seemed to plummet several degrees as he slowly turned, narrowing his eyes to dangerous slits.

"Who?" The single word emerged as a hiss, laced with barely restrained power that made lesser beings tremble.

"It was Nox." Rhyzan maintained his impassive expression, though he noted the pulse of anger that rippled through Kane's formidable frame.

"Nox believed he was helping you," Rhyzan said, his tone softening almost imperceptibly. "Evie expressed concerns that you've grown... unusually attached to your Elite. Nox thought alerting her might help you maintain perspective."

Kane's jaw clenched, the muscle along his temple pulsing with barely contained fury. "Maintain perspective?" The words escaped through gritted teeth. "They presume to know what perspective I need?"

"They worry, Kane." Rhyzan stepped closer, his footfalls silent against the time-worn floorboards. "As do I. I've stood by your side for four hundred years, and never have I seen you willingly share your blood with an Elite. Never have I seen you break your own protocols."

"She was hurt. I couldn't let her suffer."

"Is that what you tell yourself?" Rhyzan's voice remained gentle, probing. "She was hurt, yes. But there were other ways, Kane. Medical salve would have helped her. You chose to give her your blood to heal her."

Kane paced to the window, his reflection fractured in the leaded glass. Behind that exterior, Rhyzan could see the emotions warring—denial battling against something deeper, more primitive.

"She's just an Elite. A means to an end," Kane said, but the words sounded hollow even to Rhyzan's ears. "Nothing more."

"Is she?" Rhyzan's voice remained soft but relentless. "Both Nox and I see how you watch her. We both know what you added to the contract. And you brought her—" He paused, his expression softening. "—you brought her to your rooftop garden, even knowing about her betrayal."

Kane's fists clenched at his sides. "I'm trying to gain her trust."

"Kane, you've never been able to lie to me."

"What would you have me say?" Kane whirled, his composure fracturing. "That—"

Kane's words cut off abruptly. His entire body went rigid, head snapping toward the door like a predator sensing blood. Rhyzan had seen Kane respond to threats before—this was different. This was personal. Visceral. As if Kane had felt the danger rather than heard it.

In the sudden silence, Rhyzan caught it too—the distant, high-pitched shriek that human ears would never detect.

Kane vanished in a blur of movement, the library door slamming against the wall with such force that a leather-bound tome toppled from its shelf.

Rhyzan cursed under his breath, following instantly. The screams grew more distinct now—female, terrified, coming from the eastern corridor. His heightened senses caught the metallic tang of fresh blood cutting through the perfumed air of the ballroom.

The Ball continued largely uninterrupted around him—humans oblivious to the disturbance, their laughter and conversation masking the distant chaos. A few vampyr had turned their heads toward the eastern corridor, nostrils flaring slightly as they caught the scent, but none moved from their positions. Whether from self-preservation or political calculation, they chose to ignore what their senses told them was happening.

Rhyzan slipped between dancers with preternatural grace, following Kane's trail through the crowd. The mingled aromas of champagne, cologne, and warm bodies gave way to something sharper as he approached the eastern corridor—fear, adrenaline, and the unmistakable sweet-copper notes of jasmine and rose with a hint of honeysuckle.

Ambrosia.

A flash of movement caught his eye—Nox rising from the floor outside the Elite Lounge. The normally fastidious vampyr's suit was disheveled, dust marring the perfect black fabric as he staggered upright with a grimace of pain.

"Kane—" Nox gasped, then caught sight of Rhyzan approaching. Without another word, he lunged for the lounge door, throwing it open with such force that the hinges shrieked in protest.

Rhyzan followed instantly, halting at the threshold as the scene inside registered with crystalline clarity.

The lounge's elegant interior had been transformed into a tableau of violence. Kane stood at the center, his massive frame vibrating with barely contained fury as he physically restrained Deyja, whose face was contorted in a rictus of bloodlust. Her lips were stained crimson, fangs fully extended, and her eyes—usually a calculating crimson—had blackened entirely, pupils blown wide with feeding frenzy.

Beyond them, sprawled across an ornate settee, lay the still form of a male Elite, his throat torn open in a gaping wound. No breath stirred his chest, no pulse fluttered beneath his torn skin. Dead. Rhyzan cataloged the fact with clinical detachment even as his gaze swept to Serenity.

She stood frozen, eyes wide with shock, silky black curls in disarray. Blood—her blood—seeped from a deep gash across her palm, its aroma cutting through the chaos like a beacon. The sweet-copper fragrance of Ambrosia that Rhyzan had detected even from the corridor now made terrible sense.

Sebastian lay crumpled near Serenity, his chest rising and falling in shallow, labored breaths. Still alive, but barely.

Movement to his right caught his attention. Nox stood frozen just inside the doorway, jaw clenched tight, tendons straining in his neck as he fought against the primal pull of her blood. His eyes had taken on that telltale glow—hunger warring with iron discipline.

Fuck.

What a goddamn situation they'd gotten themselves into.

CHAPTER TWENTY-TWO

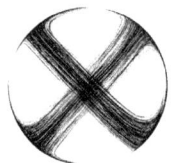

KANE

"Mine. You dare touch her."

Deyja clawed at his fingers, her crimson eyes bulging as Kane tightened his grip. Her skin began to mottle purple, veins protruding beneath his crushing hold. The sweet copper tang of Serenity's blood perfumed the air, calling him like a siren's song. Every muscle in his body screamed with primal need to claim, to taste, to possess.

"You think you can challenge me in my territory?" Kane growled. Centuries of carefully cultivated control threatened to shatter. "You killed an Elite. You injured another. And then—" his voice dropped to a deadly whisper "—you tried to touch what's mine."

In front of him, Serenity's pulse thundered—each frantic beat sending waves of her terror flooding across their bond. The emotion crashed through him, feeding his rage until it became indistinguishable from his own fury. Ambrosia. The rarest blood type, AB-, with notes that sang to him alone. His fangs ached with need.

Across the room, Rhyzan struggled with Nox, whose eyes had gone black with bloodlust. "Control yourself," Rhyzan hissed, but Nox's attention remained fixed on Serenity. Kane heard the scuffle—low hisses, the scrape of expensive shoes against marble—but he couldn't spare the attention, not with Deyja fighting him both physically and mentally to reach her.

Get out of my head! Kane snarled internally as Deyja's presence slithered through his consciousness like an oil slick, seeking purchase in the darkest corners of his mind.

Let me have her, Deyja's thoughts whispered. You smell it too. That blood. Imagine how it would taste flowing over your tongue, coating your throat. Why waste such a delicacy on a weak human who doesn't appreciate what she has?

Kane's vision rimmed with red as his discipline warred against the primal hunger Deyja stoked with her mental invasion. The fragrance of Serenity's blood made his fangs burn.

She's nothing but food, Deyja continued. Livestock. You've grown soft, Draccus.

No, Kane snarled back along their mental link. She's mine. And I will kill anyone—even you—who tries to take what belongs to me.

A soft gasp pulled his attention. Serenity, her face ashen, moved toward Sebastian's crumpled form. She dropped to her knees, reaching toward the unconscious Elite with trembling fingers.

"Don't—" Kane started, but movement across the room fractured his focus. Nox broke free with a violent jerk, shoving Rhyzan backward with a strength born of bloodlust. He lunged toward Serenity, fangs fully extended.

Her fear exploded across their connection, so visceral it nearly drove Kane to his knees.

In that split second of distraction, Kane's grip faltered. Deyja seized her opportunity, twisting with serpentine flexibility and driving her claws into his forearm. Blood—his blood—spattered the pristine marble as she tore through muscle and tendon.

"Nox!" Kane roared, but his friend was beyond reason, drawn inexorably toward the scent of Serenity's blood.

Just as Nox reached for her, Rhyzan tackled him with brutal efficiency. They crashed into a side table, shattering its marble top. Serenity hunched protectively over Sebastian's unconscious form, her eyes wide with terror.

Kane couldn't go to her. Not yet.

Deyja slammed her forehead into his face, cartilage cracking as his nose broke. Pain exploded behind his eyes, but he maintained his grip, spinning her around and driving her into the wall. The stone cracked beneath the impact, dust raining down as Kane pinned her with his full weight. Blood trickled down his face, the metallic taste coating his tongue as he snarled.

"You will not touch her." Each word was a promise etched in granite.

Deyja laughed, the sound manic and frenzied as her eyes darted over his shoulder toward Serenity. "The ambrosia calls, Draccus. Even you can't resist forever."

She twisted violently, claws slashing at his throat. Kane jerked back, feeling the air displace where her talons would have severed his jugular. Every movement was calculated, precise—the product of combat experience perfected over centuries. He caught her wrist mid-strike, bones grinding beneath his grip.

"You forget yourself," he growled, using his superior height to lift her until her feet dangled above the floor. "I am not some fledgling you can overwhelm."

Serenity's pulse echoed in his ears, a frantic percussion keeping time with his own raging desire. He swallowed hard, forcing himself to focus on the immediate threat.

Deyja hissed and twisted in his grasp like a feral creature, no longer the composed, sultry queen of Kregan but something primal and dangerous. Her claws raked across his chest, shredding the expensive fabric of his suit. The pain barely registered through his fury.

"You think you're so much better than the rest of us," she spat, saliva flecking her lips. "Pretending you don't crave her just as desperately."

Kane slammed her against the wall again, plaster crumbling around them. "The difference," he snarled, "is that I have control."

A lie. His control hung by a thread.

Deyja's eyes darted over his shoulder, widening with sudden fear. The presence of another powerful vampyr approached—imposing, furious, ancient as the stones beneath their feet.

Kane barely had time to register the new arrival before Deyja twisted with renewed desperation, her body contorting at an impossible angle as she lunged. Her goal was clear: one final attempt to reach Serenity before she lost her chance.

"Never!" Kane roared, pivoting to intercept her.

But before he could grab her, a blur of motion cut through the room. Xavier, co-ruler of Kregan, materialized between Deyja and Kane, catching his partner mid-lunge with ruthless precision. His fingers wrapped around her throat, the gesture almost tender despite its lethal intent.

"Enough," Xavier commanded, his voice like velvet stretched over steel.

Deyja thrashed in his grip, her eyes wild with bloodlust. "Let me go! Can't you smell it? The ambrosia—"

"I said enough." Xavier's voice never rose, yet the power behind it seemed to shake the foundations of the room.

Suddenly, Deyja's eyes rolled into the back of her head, and she fell unconscious to the floor.

Xavier's gaze shifted to Serenity, measuring her with cool calculation before returning to Kane. "Draccus," Xavier inclined his head, his voice smooth as aged whiskey. "Please accept my deepest apologies for Deyja's... indiscretion. The scent of ambrosia is intoxicating, but her behavior was inexcusable nonetheless."

Kane's jaw clenched so tight he could feel his molars grinding. The casual way Xavier referenced Serenity's blood—as if it were merely a rare vintage rather than the essence of the woman—made his fangs pulse painfully.

Xavier knelt with fluid grace, gathering Deyja's limp form into his arms. Her head lolled against his chest, auburn hair spilling over his sleeve like an oil slick. "We will, of course, accept whatever punishment you deem appropriate for this transgression in your territory."

Behind him, Serenity's pulse fluttered like a trapped bird.

Xavier's words barely registered through the roaring in Kane's ears. His instincts screamed at him to respond to the Kregan ruler, but a more immediate concern demanded his attention. He pivoted sharply, stalking across the room where Rhyzan still struggled with Nox.

His friend's eyes were black pools of hunger, fangs fully extended as he writhed against Rhyzan's iron grip. Every muscle in Nox's body strained toward Serenity.

Kane seized Nox's face between his palms, forcing those obsidian eyes to meet his own. The hunger reflected there was a mirror to the beast clawing inside his own chest—raw, desperate.

"Sleep," Kane commanded, pouring all his authority into that single word. The compulsion flowed from him like a physical force, crashing against Nox's consciousness.

For a heartbeat, Nox resisted, his jaw clenched tight enough to crack teeth. Then his eyes rolled back, lids fluttering closed as his body went limp in Rhyzan's arms.

"Get him out of here," Kane growled. "He'll be useless until he's fed."

The door to the lounge swung open, and Evie's slender form appeared in the threshold. Her nostrils flared instantly, pupils dilating as Serenity's blood hit her. Kane watched the struggle play across her features—the hunger warring with practiced control.

Evie's eyes darted across the room, taking in the carnage with practiced efficiency. Blood spattered the marble, furniture lay in ruins, and the tang of violence hung thick in the air. When her gaze landed on Sebastian's crumpled form, an expression flickered across her face—too complex to name. Relief? Grief? The composure she'd maintained for five days finally cracked.

"Sebastian." His name escaped as barely a whisper.

She pushed past Kane, dropping to her knees beside the injured Elite. Her fingers moved with practiced precision, checking his pulse, assessing the damage. "What happened to him?" The question wasn't directed at anyone in particular; her focus was entirely on the unconscious man before her.

Serenity rose shakily to her feet, blood still seeping from the wound on her hand. "He tried to protect me," she whispered, stepping away to give Evie space.

With monumental effort, Kane tore his gaze from Serenity and turned back to Xavier. The ruler of Kregan still stood with head inclined in respect, Deyja's unconscious form cradled like a fragile treasure. Every survival instinct screamed at Kane to eliminate the threat they represented, but political maneuvering tempered his response.

"You will remain in Celearius," Kane said, his voice a glacial rumble, "until I determine appropriate punishment for this transgression." He straightened to his full height, eyes glowing with barely contained fury. "Return to your assigned accommodation and stay there. Make yoursel ves... discreet." The last word dripped with deadly promise.

Xavier's eyes flickered with perhaps relief that Kane hadn't demanded immediate execution. "Of course, Draccus. Again, I offer my sincerest apologies for this... unfortunate accident." He adjusted his grip on Deyja's limp form, her head lolling against his shoulder. "We will await your judgment."

Then he was gone, moving with that preternatural speed that made even Kane's enhanced vision struggle to track him. The heavy oak doors swung shut behind him with a decisive thud.

Kane inhaled deeply, tasting copper and fear and sweetness that was uniquely Serenity's. The wound on her hand still wept crimson, calling to him with a song he could barely resist.

Finally, Kane forced himself to take a deep, steadying breath. He needed to center himself, to quiet the demands inside him. The air burned in his lungs, thick with the mingled aromas of blood and violence.

He turned to Serenity, his gaze locking with hers across the chaos of the destroyed room. Her honey-brown eyes were wide, pupils dilated with fear and something else—something that made his heart stutter. Recognition. Understanding. She saw the monster beneath his carefully constructed facade again, and she didn't run.

Kane snatched a pristine white handkerchief from his pocket as he crossed to her in measured strides, fighting to keep his movements slow and deliberate. The distance between them felt like an eternity.

When he reached for her injured hand, she flinched—a tiny, involuntary movement that sent a lance of something dangerously close to pain through him. But she didn't pull away when Kane grasped her wrist, delicately turning her palm upward. The laceration carved a crimson line across her skin, blood welling in slow, hypnotic pulses that made his throat constrict with need. He dabbed at the wound with his handkerchief, acutely aware of her quickening pulse, the slight tremor in her fingers.

"Stay still," he murmured, voice rougher than intended. Each gentle press of cloth against her skin required monumental restraint.

Behind them, Evie rose with Sebastian cradled against her, his limp form looking impossibly fragile despite her slender frame. The vampyric strength she normally concealed was on full display as she adjusted her hold.

"I need to get him home," she announced, her voice tight. "He requires immediate attention."

"Will he be alright?" Serenity asked.

"Yes," Evie said as she looked down at Sebastian, whose eyes were closed. "He just needs rest and fluids."

"Take the service corridor," Kane said without looking up from Serenity's hand. "Fewer eyes."

Evie nodded, shifting Sebastian's weight in her arms with effortless grace. The moment she disappeared through the doorway, Rhyzan reappeared, his expression grim as he surveyed the carnage.

"Sullivan is on his way to handle the cleanup," Rhyzan announced, his gaze sweeping over the shattered furniture and blood-spattered marble. "I've secured Nox in the west wing. He'll need to be restrained and fed until the bloodlust passes."

Kane barely acknowledged him, his entire being fixated on the slow seep of crimson between his fingers as he pressed the rapidly staining handkerchief against Serenity's palm.

Before Evie disappeared completely, she paused in the doorway, her eyes meeting Kane's with unexpected intensity. "Kane, you need to heal her wound. Now." The urgency in her voice went beyond mere concern. "Keep these doors closed. The scent will spread and draw others."

As soon as she vanished, Rhyzan closed the doors. Evie was right. If more vampyrs caught Serenity's aroma, there would be bloodshed—his own hands ending the lives of any who dared approach. The thought didn't trouble him. His experience had taught him to do what was necessary without hesitation.

He raised his own hand to his mouth and sank his fangs deep into his palm. The metallic tang of his blood flooded his senses momentarily. He pulled the now-crimson handkerchief away from her wound, revealing the jagged laceration still weeping precious rubies.

"I'm going to heal you," Kane said, his voice a low rumble as he held his bleeding palm above hers. "I'm not certain how your body will respond this time, but I need to get you away from here. Immediately."

Serenity's eyes widened, but she nodded, understanding the gravity of their situation. Despite everything she'd witnessed, she trusted him to keep her safe.

It should have eased the tension.

Instead, it made him want to never let her go.

He positioned his hand above her palm. Crimson drops fell in slow motion, landing with deliberate precision on her wound. The moment his blood touched hers, the bond between them exploded—white-hot and all-consuming. This was more than healing. This was claiming. Binding. Making her irrevocably his in ways she couldn't begin to understand.

The laceration began to close before his eyes, her flesh knitting together with supernatural speed. Kane couldn't tear his gaze away from the sight unfolding beneath his palm.

"We need to leave now." Kane bent and swept her into his arms in a single fluid motion. Her weight settled against him—fragile, mortal. The sensation sent electricity crackling through his veins.

"Close your eyes," he murmured against her hair. "The movement can be... disorienting for humans."

He felt her tense in his arms, then relax as she nodded. Tightening his grip, he cradled her closer, one arm supporting her back while the other hooked beneath her knees.

"Rhyzan," he commanded.

His friend moved instantly to the door, pulling it open with silent efficiency. Kane stepped into the corridor, his enhanced vision cutting through the dim lighting as he moved with preternatural speed. The walls and a few partygoers blurred around them as he navigated the labyrinthine passages of the east side of the mansion, each footfall silent despite his haste.

Serenity's body tensed, her fingers clutching the lapel of his ruined suit.

Kane rounded the final corner, slowing his pace as they approached a nondescript side entrance. Sullivan stood waiting, car keys dangling from his hand.

Kane placed Serenity carefully on her feet before the waiting car, his hands lingering at her waist.

"Are you alright?" His voice emerged as a gravelly whisper, scanning her face for signs of shock or distress.

"I think so." Serenity's voice trembled slightly, but her gaze remained steady, meeting his with that unfathomable courage that both mystified and enthralled him.

Kane reached around her, opening the passenger door of the sleek black sedan. The movement brought him dangerously close. She slipped past him into the vehicle, the brush of her body against his sending electrical currents racing beneath his skin.

Sullivan extended the keys without comment, though Kane caught the subtle tensing in the man's shoulders—the instinctive response of prey recognizing a predator on the edge. Kane took the keys, the metal biting into his palms as he clenched his fist around them.

"You know the protocol. Clean like it never happened. Discreetly inform the patrons of the incident," Kane told him.

"Leave it to me," Sullivan murmured with a curt nod.

Kane slid into the driver's seat, the leather creaking beneath him. The confined space amplified Serenity's presence a hundredfold—jasmine, rose, and copper—calling to the darkest parts of him.

His knuckles whitened around the steering wheel as he fought for focus.

He turned the key with more force than necessary, the engine roaring to life. The vibrations traveled through the chassis, a low rumble that matched the growl building in his chest. He needed to get her away from here—away from prying eyes and hungry fangs.

The tires squealed against the pavement as he accelerated down the private drive, trees blurring into a dark smear beyond the windows. Beside him, Serenity's pulse thundered in his ears.

He needed to get them home before he did something he'd regret. But with every mile, the demands grew louder, his restraint fracturing like ice beneath impossible weight.

He wasn't fighting the monster anymore.

He was fighting the inevitability of surrendering to it completely.

CHAPTER TWENTY-THREE

SERENITY

Serenity's palm ached with phantom pain where the wound had been, her pulse still racing beneath her skin. The memory of glass slicing through flesh replayed behind her eyelids. So much blood. Her blood. Spilled across pristine marble in an offering she hadn't fully understood when she made it.

The sleek black sedan devoured the road beneath them, Kane's knuckles bleached white against the steering wheel. His jaw worked silently, muscles clenching beneath the sharp line of his cheekbone. She stole glances at his profile, carved like granite in the dim glow of the dashboard, unable to look away despite the danger radiating from him in palpable waves.

"That was incredibly foolish," Kane finally broke the silence, his voice a low rumble that barely contained the storm beneath. "Do you understand what you've done?"

Serenity swallowed hard. "I couldn't just watch her hurt Sebastian."

"So you offered yourself instead?" The words emerged as a snarl, eyes flashing in the car's darkness.

She had no answer for him. Not one she could voice aloud, anyway. The truth was too raw. She had known, with inexplicable certainty, he would save her. Even as the glass sliced her palm, even as Deyja's hungry eyes fixed on her blood, some primal part of her had recognized Kane would protect what was his.

Serenity turned away from his intensity, focusing on the passing scenery beyond the tinted window. Elegant homes with manicured lawns slipped by, their windows glowing with warm light. As they accelerated through Waterside Cross, those homes gave way to gleaming buildings that reached toward the night sky.

They were approaching the gate to the Silver District when it happened. The rhythmic sound of Kane's heartbeat suddenly filled her ears—a steady drumbeat that should have been impossible to hear. The engine noise transformed from background hum to thunderous roar, each mechanical component distinguishable in horrifying clarity.

"Kane," Serenity gasped, clutching the dashboard. "It's happening again, like before, after you healed me."

His head snapped toward her. "Tell me exactly what's happening."

"Everything's too loud, too bright." Her voice sounded distorted even to herself. The fabric of her dress suddenly felt like sandpaper. "Your heartbeat—I can hear it. The engine..."

Kane's expression shifted, understanding blazing across his features. Without warning, he wrenched the wheel left, tires screeching as the car veered sharply off their route.

"My blood," he muttered, accelerating through a narrow street. "It's affecting your system again."

Buildings blurred past as Kane pushed the vehicle faster. Serenity's vision sharpened until she could see individual raindrops on the windshield.

"Where are we going?"

"Somewhere isolated," Kane answered. "Away from people."

The car hurtled through neon-lit streets. Each flash of light drove daggers through Serenity's skull. The scent of Kane—sandalwood and bergamot—filled the car, making her mouth water inexplicably.

They veered onto an unpaved road, the sedan bouncing over uneven terrain. Through the windshield, Serenity could make out the skeletal framework of an abandoned construction project looming against the midnight sky.

Kane killed the engine, plunging them into sudden silence. His breathing came in measured increments that told her just how much restraint he was exercising.

"Serenity." The way he said her name—like a prayer and a curse.

His eyes bored into hers, pupils expanded until only a thin ring of silver-blue remained. "Do you trust me?"

"Yes." The word formed on her lips before her mind could analyze it.

The realization struck her with startling clarity. Despite everything—despite the danger, despite the blood and violence—she did trust him.

Kane's expression transformed, hunger unfurling across his features.

"Then run." His voice dropped to a guttural whisper. "Run as fast as you can. Don't look back. If I catch you..." He paused, swallowing hard. "If I catch you, I won't be able to hold back."

Along their bond, she felt his terror—not of hurting her, but of what he'd become if he caught her.

Understanding crashed like lightning. The heightened senses, the hunger in his eyes—this was about her blood calling to him, about the beast he kept chained beneath that sophisticated exterior.

Without hesitation, Serenity flung the car door open. She kicked off her heels, gathering her dress in trembling hands. The construction site loomed before her, a skeletal cathedral of steel and concrete illuminated by moonlight.

Serenity ran.

Her legs carried her faster than she'd ever moved. She veered past shipping containers, their metal surfaces gleaming. The half-constructed building swallowed her as she darted inside. She spotted a concrete stairwell and took the stairs two at a time.

Her heartbeat. Her breathing. If she could hear these sounds with such precision, then Kane could track her through them alone. She forced herself to slow down, placing each foot deliberately as she climbed higher.

On the sixth floor, she eased a metal door open, wincing at the faint squeal of hinges. Beyond lay a mostly enclosed space—walls erected but no windows installed, tarpaulins fluttering at the openings. Moonlight spilled through in silver puddles.

Serenity slipped inside, closing the door behind her. She stood motionless, counting her heartbeats, listening.

A sound from the stairwell—the faintest whisper—shattered her calm. He was coming.

She felt him through their connection—hunger, need, the hunt singing in his blood. And beneath it, affection that made her chest tighten.

Serenity crept across the unfinished floor, dust motes swirling. The space was a maze of half-erected walls and exposed wiring. She darted across debris—pieces of drywall, coils of wire, abandoned tools.

She rounded a corner and found a gaping hole in the floor, a service shaft that plummeted downward. Beside it, a metal ladder descended. With trembling hands, Serenity grasped the cold rungs and climbed down. Her feet landed on concrete below.

A storage closet tucked between support beams caught her attention—door slightly ajar. Serenity darted inside, slipping into the narrow space that smelled of sawdust and metal. She eased the door nearly closed, leaving the thinnest sliver through which to watch. Her pulse thundered as she pressed against rough drywall.

The space enveloped her in shadow. She drew her knees to her chest.

And then—she felt him.

The floor above creaked as he moved with deliberate slowness.

Serenity's breath caught. He was tracking her. And instead of terror, a different sensation bloomed—desire spreading through her veins like wildfire.

She could run again. There was a service door at the far end. She could escape if she truly wanted to.

But she didn't want to.

The truth settled into her bones. She wanted him to find her. Wanted those eyes to fix on her with predatory intent. Wanted those hands to claim what they'd been denied.

Her pulse quickened, but not from fear. Every nerve ending seemed to light up with anticipation.

"I can hear your heartbeat," Kane's voice echoed through the darkness. "I can smell you..."

A shadow passed across the door's opening. Then stillness.

The door ripped open.

Kane filled the doorway, his massive frame blocking all escape. Eyes glowed in the darkness, pupils blown with hunger. His suit jacket and shirt were gone, revealing the sculpted planes of his chest.

"Found you," he rasped, voice barely human.

The bond blazed between them. He was giving her one more chance to refuse him.

Serenity didn't run. Instead, she rose slowly, drawn toward him by a force more powerful than gravity.

"Yes," she whispered. "You found me."

His nostrils flared as he inhaled deeply. His gaze burned through her. The beast that had always lurked beneath Kane's exterior was now fully unleashed.

"Tell me to stop," he rumbled. "Tell me to leave."

But Serenity couldn't form the words. Didn't want to.

"I want you," she whispered. "All of you. Even the parts you're afraid to show."

The last thread of his control broke. In an instant, he crossed the space, his hands gripping her waist with bruising intensity. He lifted her, slamming her back against the wall.

The impact should have hurt—but her hypersensitivity turned harsh sensation into exquisite pleasure.

His mouth claimed hers with savage intensity, teeth scraping her lower lip as his tongue demanded entrance. The metallic tang of blood mingled with the taste of him—dark, intoxicating.

Kane's hands tightened on her waist, fingers digging through the fabric. She arched against him, desperate for more.

"Mine," he snarled against her mouth. "Say it."

"Yours," she gasped. "I'm yours."

Raw hunger flashed in his eyes. With one fluid movement, he gripped the neckline of her dress and tore downward. The fabric rended with a satisfying rip.

The shredded silk slipped down her body, pooling at her feet. Kane's eyes devoured her—predatory, possessive—as his hands followed, rough palms sliding over her curves.

"Beautiful," he rasped, the word vibrating against her skin as his mouth descended to her throat.

His teeth scraped along her pulse point, not quite breaking the skin. The sensation ignited liquid heat. Each touch registered with overwhelming intensity—each callus on his fingertips, each hot exhale, each brush of his chest against her sensitized skin.

Kane's mouth captured hers again, brutal and demanding. His hands gripped her thighs and lifted. She wrapped her legs around his waist, the hard ridge of his arousal pressing against her center.

Kane's hands slid higher, hooking beneath her panties. With one sharp tug, he tore them away. The cool air against her exposed center made Serenity gasp.

"I can smell how much you want me," Kane murmured darkly. One large hand splayed across her back while the other moved between them. His fingers found her slick heat, stroking before plunging inside.

Serenity cried out, inner walls clenching. Kane's thumb found her sensitive bundle of nerves, circling with deliberate pressure that had her writhing.

"Please," she gasped.

Kane's lips curved against her throat. "You want this?"

"Yes," she breathed.

"I've wanted this since I first saw you," he snarled, one hand pinning her wrists above her head while the other worked at his belt. "Dreamed of taking you like this."

The sound of his zipper made her shiver. Every detail registered—the rasp of fabric, the hitch in his breathing.

"Please," she whispered.

Kane's mouth claimed hers again as he freed himself, hot and hard against her thigh. The head of his cock brushed against her entrance.

"So wet for me," he breathed. "So ready."

With a powerful thrust, Kane buried himself inside her. Serenity cried out, back arching as he stretched her. The initial burn transformed into pleasure so intense it bordered on agony.

"Fuck," Kane rasped. "So tight. So perfect."

He withdrew before driving back into her with bruising force. The wall shuddered behind her. Each powerful stroke drove her higher, her shoulders scraping against the rough surface.

His rhythm was relentless, each thrust punctuated by a guttural sound. Serenity's nails dug into his shoulders, breaking skin.

"More," she gasped.

A feral sound rumbled through Kane as he withdrew completely. Before she could protest, he spun her around, pressing her against the wall. The concrete scraped her nipples, pain transformed into sharp pleasure.

His hand gripped the back of her neck while his other hand guided his length back. He drove into her with savage intensity, the new angle allowing him impossibly deeper. Serenity screamed as Kane established a brutal rhythm.

"You feel what you do to me?" he snarled. "What you've always done to me?"

The pressure built inside her, coiling tighter. Her climax crashed through her with devastating force. Serenity screamed as pleasure rippled outward, setting every nerve ending alight.

Kane didn't slow. His fingers dug into her flesh as he pulled her from the wall and sent her sprawling to the floor. The hard stone bit into her knees and palms—but even that registered as pleasure.

Before she could catch her breath, Kane was behind her, dragging her hips upward.

"I'm not done with you yet," he promised.

He entered her again with a single brutal stroke. Her arms gave way, cheek pressed against cool concrete as Kane possessed her with relentless force.

"Kane," she moaned.

His pace increased, flesh meeting flesh echoing through the space. One large hand splayed across her back, pinning her while the other gripped her hip.

His hand slid around her throat, not squeezing but controlling. The pressure created waves of heat as her second climax built.

Kane's rhythm faltered, becoming more erratic. He leaned forward, his chest pressing to her back, his breath hot against her neck. Serenity felt his fangs scrape against her skin.

"Please," she whispered. "Please, Kane."

His snarl vibrated through her as his teeth broke skin.

The twin points of his fangs pierced her neck, and Serenity's world exploded. The bond between them detonated. For an instant, she was him—centuries of loneliness, desperate need crashed through her. And he was her—her terror and trust, her surrender, her... love.

Pain transformed instantly into blinding pleasure. Her second orgasm crashed through her as he continued to move inside her, drinking deeply. Every pull of his mouth matched the rhythm of his thrusts.

Her vision blurred, darkness edging in as her overwhelmed senses overloaded.

Kane snarled against her neck. With one final stroke, he shuddered, his release pulsing hot inside her as he continued to drink. The dual sensation created an intimacy so profound that tears leaked from her eyes.

The pleasure was too much. Her consciousness began to drift as Kane finally, reluctantly, withdrew his fangs. He gently lapped at the puncture wounds, sealing them.

"Serenity," he whispered, his voice hoarse and tender. "My brave Serenity. You're everything."

He gathered her trembling body, wrapping the tattered remains of her dress around her.

"I've got you," Kane murmured, lips brushing her temple. "Rest now."

Her head lolled against his shoulder as he carried her from the building. The moonlight painted silver streaks across his face.

The night air kissed her skin as Kane carried her to the waiting car. Serenity's heightened senses were gradually receding. She felt weightless in his arms.

When they reached the car, he opened the passenger door with one hand. The leather seat felt cool as he lowered her inside.

"Rest," Kane murmured, brushing damp curls from her forehead.

The car started with a gentle purr. Kane's profile was etched in moonlight. Serenity's eyelids grew heavy.

As consciousness began to slip away, she felt his emotions as clearly as her own—his satisfaction, his possessive pride, his... love? The word terrified her, but the truth resonated through their link.

In the haze between wakefulness and sleep, the truth crystallized: she had fallen for him... completely. Not just the sophisticated leader, but the beast beneath—the primal creature who had claimed her so thoroughly tonight.

She belonged to him now, body and blood and heart.

CHAPTER TWENTY-FOUR

Evie

The early morning hours stretched before Evie like an abyss as she stood beside their bed, watching Sebastian's unconscious form. Outside her apartment windows, Silver District remained cloaked in pre-dawn darkness, the city holding its breath between night and morning. The Elite Ball felt like a lifetime ago, though barely six hours had passed since Deyja's attack. Sebastian's usually impeccable appearance was marred by dried blood staining his collar, his breathing shallow but steady. The soft rise and fall of his chest provided the only comfort in this nightmare.

Eight years of waking beside him, sharing her research, building a life together in this sanctuary above the city. And now she knew it had all been built on lies. He'd been feeding information to the rebellion while she'd been too blind—or too in love—to see it.

One call to Kane would end this. But watching Sebastian nearly die tonight, feeling his limp body as she'd carried him to their bed—her traitorous heart refused the logic her mind demanded.

Evie brushed a lock of hair from his forehead, her fingertips lingering against his skin. Cooler than normal—a sign his body was working to heal from significant blood loss. The scent of lavender from her bedside diffuser couldn't quite mask the metallic tang clinging to him.

"What were you thinking?" she whispered, though she knew he couldn't hear her. "Throwing yourself at Deyja like that? Trying to save those Elites?"

Her hand trembled as she pulled it away. He'd been heroic tonight—attacking a vampyr ruler to protect strangers, nearly dying for people he didn't know. How could someone capable of such courage betray everything she believed in?

Evie leaned down and pressed her lips to his forehead, a featherlight touch that felt like goodbye. "Rest," she murmured, her voice cracking on the single word.

When she straightened, her gaze lingered on his face for another moment—memorizing the curve of his jaw, the way his lashes cast shadows on his cheeks, the small scar above his left eyebrow from a childhood accident he'd told her about on their second date. Memorizing him because she didn't know how much longer she'd have before duty demanded she destroy him.

She turned away before the tears could fall.

Her lab called to her—the one place where uncertainties became quantifiable data, where mysteries yielded to methodical inquiry. Where she didn't have to think about the unconscious man in her bed or the impossible choice looming before her.

The private elevator hummed softly as it descended three floors below her penthouse suite. Few knew about her laboratory beneath her apartment building's gleaming facade. Kane had ensured its construction remained confidential, understanding her need for a space where research could flourish without interference or observation.

The doors slid open to reveal her domain—pristine white surfaces gleaming under specialized lighting that mimicked natural sunlight without the harmful UV rays that could damage delicate samples. The air carried the subtle scent of antiseptic, comforting in its clinical familiarity.

Evie moved to her workstation, the glass surface illuminating as it sensed her presence. Her fingers danced across the interface, pulling up files with practiced precision. Serenity's bloodwork appeared first, data cascading across multiple screens in vibrant projections that bathed her face in electric blue.

"Show me what you're hiding," she murmured, zooming in on the cellular structure.

Serenity's blood cells materialized across the screen, their structure unlike anything Evie had seen in centuries of research. The ambrosia—AB negative with that peculiar mutation—possessed cellular markers that defied conventional hematological classification. No wonder it called so powerfully to vampyr senses. No wonder Kane had lost control.

"Computer, display Kane's most recent sample," she commanded.

The visualization shifted, Serenity's cells fading as Kane's blood materialized in deep burgundy. Four hundred years of immortality had refined his cellular structure until it was almost crystalline in its perfection—densely packed with the preternatural proteins that granted vampyrs their strength, longevity, and heightened senses.

Evie's fingertips hovered over the projection, tracing the outline of a particularly unusual protein cluster. "Computer, overlay samples. Kane Draccus baseline and Serenity Wright baseline."

The images merged in a swirl of scarlet and burgundy, Kane's cells appearing almost predatory beside Serenity's—darker, more angular, primitive yet sophisticated. Two opposing forces, never meant to mingle.

Her throat tightened. She knew what came next. Knew what happened when vampyr blood encountered human blood. The violent rejection, the cellular warfare, the inevitable consumption of the weaker by the stronger.

"Now show me the combined sample," she whispered.

The screen flickered, revealing the impossible.

Where the two samples should have battled for dominance, with Kane's vampyric cells consuming and converting Serenity's human ones, an unprecedented reaction had occurred. The cells coexisted, intertwined yet distinct, neither overwhelming the other. Like dancers in perfect synchronization, they moved together without losing their individual identities.

Evie's legs gave out. She sank into her chair, staring at the impossible fusion hovering before her.

"That can't be right," she breathed, but even as she spoke, she knew the data didn't lie. In all her centuries of research, she'd never witnessed anything like this.

She magnified the image further, studying the cellular boundaries where human and vampyr met. The usual rejection response was entirely absent. Instead of destruction, there was harmony—a symbiotic relationship that defied everything she understood about hematological compatibility.

"Computer, analyze the protein structures at the cellular junction."

The visualization zoomed to the molecular level, revealing the intricate dance of proteins at the boundary between the two blood types. Evie leaned closer, her breath fogging the projection slightly as she studied the fusion occurring before her eyes.

Kane and Serenity's blood wasn't just compatible—it was complementary. Two halves of a whole.

A chill ran down her spine as recognition dawned. She'd seen a similar pattern before—not identical, but close enough to trigger alarm bells in her mind. Where?

Her gaze drifted to the locked drawer beneath her work desk.

Evie reached for the biometric scanner hidden beneath the desk's edge. A faint blue light traced the contours of her thumb, followed by a soft click as the drawer unlocked. The metallic scent hit her nostrils before she even saw the blueprints—an acrid, unnatural tang that seemed to cling to the schematics like a warning.

She spread the stolen plans across her desk, their edges curling slightly from repeated handling. She still hadn't been able to destroy them, despite knowing they threatened Serenity's very existence. Scientific curiosity had stopped her each time—or perhaps the nagging sense that these documents contained a puzzle piece she desperately needed.

"Project Hemlock," she murmured, tracing the embossed title with her fingertip.

Sebastian had photographed these in her home office. She'd watched the footage—seen him angle the blueprints toward his hidden camera with practiced efficiency. He'd captured images of both the real plans and the fake ones she'd created as insurance.

God, she hoped the rebellion would use the fakes. Because if they understood what they truly had...

The weapon design was elegant in its brutality: a delivery system for weaponized human blood, specifically engineered to attack vampyr physiology. But it wasn't the weapon itself that had kept her awake night after night—it was the blood modification process detailed in the smaller diagrams.

Evie's gaze lingered on the molecular structures illustrated in the corner of the blueprint. The base component appeared to be ambrosia—blood identical to or possibly extracted from Serenity herself. According to the notes, Serenity's father had reverse-engineered vampyr blood using his daughter's unique cellular markers, creating a formula that would, in theory, cause vampyric cells to attack themselves.

A biological civil war at the cellular level.

But if what she was seeing in Kane and Serenity's combined sample was accurate, the weapon's entire premise was flawed. Their blood didn't fight—it merged. Which meant the weapon wouldn't kill vampyrs as intended.

It would create a different outcome entirely.

Evie pulled up the fake plans she'd created—identical to the real ones except for two crucial alterations in the molecular formula. Only a hematologist would recognize the changes, and even then, they wouldn't know where the mistakes were until they attempted synthesis. The rebellion would waste months, maybe years, chasing a dead end.

Unless they had Serenity's father. Unless he was still alive and could identify the discrepancies.

Her hands shook as she compared the molecular structures in the weapon plans to the fusion occurring in Kane and Serenity's combined sample. The similarities were unmistakable—the same harmonic coexistence, the same complementary protein structures.

"Oh god," she whispered.

The weapon wouldn't destroy vampyrs. If deployed, it would trigger the same fusion she was witnessing in the samples before her. Kane and Serenity's blood had merged because of their unique compatibility, but what if that compatibility could be replicated? What if the weapon didn't kill, but transformed?

Evie's mind raced through the implications. Vampyr exposed to the weaponized ambrosia wouldn't die—their cells would attempt to merge with the human blood, just as Kane's had merged with Serenity's. But without the precise compatibility Kane and Serenity shared, the fusion would be unstable. Unpredictable.

She needed fresh samples from both of them. Needed to test her theory before the rebellion did something catastrophic with incomplete data.

Because if she were right—if their blood truly merged rather than destroyed each other—the weapon wouldn't end the war between humans and vampyrs.

It would create something far more dangerous than either species.

Something neither side could control.

Evie stared at the molecular structures hovering before her. Upstairs, Sebastian slept—traitor and hero both. Somewhere in the city, Kane and

Serenity's blood was creating an impossible fusion. And she was the only one who knew the rebellion's weapon would doom them all.

She reached for her comm device, then stopped. Telling Kane meant confessing everything—and condemning the man she loved.

Outside, dawn broke over Silver District.

CHAPTER TWENTY-FIVE

Rhyzan

The orange dot pulsed on the screen like a tiny digital heartbeat. Mid-morning sunlight streamed through Kane's office windows, the city beyond fully awake and bustling. The Ball felt like a distant nightmare now, though barely twelve hours had passed since its bloodied conclusion. This electronic blip represented their only tangible lead on the escaped prisoners.

The marker's journey through the Dead City played across the display. Hours spent weaving through the city outskirts before vanishing entirely for nearly sixty minutes—a communications blackout that had Sullivan scrambling to recover the signal. When it reappeared, the tracker had somehow migrated to the city center. Since then, movement in a pattern suggesting reconnaissance: west, then north, now holding steady in the midtown district.

A dull ache pressed against his skull. Four hundred years of vigilance had taught the difference between coincidence and conspiracy. This movement pattern reeked of the latter.

His phone buzzed.

Any changes? Sullivan texted.

Negative. Still stationary at the same coordinates.

His phone buzzed again. New message from Kane: On my way.

The timestamp showed an hour had passed since the initial message. The delay was unusual, though not entirely unexpected given last night's events. Easy enough to envision what—or rather who—was keeping Kane occupied.

The door to Kane's office swung open.

"Any developments?" Kane asked, his voice resonating with authority.

Something was different about him. A faint luminescence seemed to emanate from beneath his skin, giving his typically pale complexion an almost vibrant quality. His movements carried a fluid grace lighter than his usual calculated precision.

The bond left its mark. Serenity's blood had affected him more profoundly than he likely realized.

"The tracker remains stationary in the midtown district." A gesture to the pulsing orange dot on the interface. "Been in the same position for three hours now. Sullivan believes they may have reached their base, or a temporary safe house at minimum."

Kane leaned over the screen, his finger tracing the dot's previous path. No hint of the previous night's fury remained in his expression. "Have Sullivan assign one of his men to join the team that routinely patrols the area," he commanded. "We need eyes on the ground, not just digital tracking."

"Baines would be my recommendation—he's passed as human before."

Kane's expression flickered with satisfaction. "How does Chloe plan to communicate her findings?"

"She has a specialized comm device—military grade, untraceable. She'll make contact when she determines it's safe to do so, likely during the night cycles when the rebels are less vigilant. Her primary objectives are locating their headquarters and identifying the leadership structure."

"And if she's discovered?"

"The device has a fail-safe protocol. One press destroys all stored data and transmissions." The thought of Chloe being discovered made his stomach tighten. She was one of their most valuable operatives, and he'd known her for over a century. "She's survived deeper cover operations than this. If anyone can infiltrate their inner circle and pinpoint who's calling the shots, it's her."

Kane's jaw tightened. "I don't like these delays."

"Neither do I, but rushing her would only compromise the operation. She's survived among them for decades before. She knows how to navigate their suspicions."

"Good," Kane said, his silver-blue eyes narrowing slightly. "What of our other... guests? Have Deyja and Xavier remained in their accommodations?"

The morning security briefing with Sullivan had been clear. "They've made no attempts to leave. Only Talia has been permitted to serve them—she's discreet and observant. She reports that Deyja has been unusually subdued."

"Subdued is not a word I'd typically associate with Deyja," Kane murmured, fingers drumming once against the polished desk. "Calculating, perhaps."

Evening light filtered through the windows, casting Kane's face in sharp relief. The faint tension around his eyes was the only visible sign of the weight he carried.

"What are your plans for them?" The question came carefully, neutrally, despite reservations. Deyja was dangerous and unpredictable. The bloodlust she'd displayed at the Ball had been shocking. "The Council will expect a response to such a flagrant violation."

Kane's gaze drifted to the window, where Celearius sprawled beneath them in twilight shadows.

He sighed. "That's the complication. Under normal circumstances, I would bring this directly to the Council. A public trial for a public transgression." His eyes met Rhyzan's, cold calculation evident in their depths. "But doing so risks Deyja revealing Serenity's blood type to the world. Her safety would be compromised. Her blood would become common knowledge."

If the Council learned of Serenity's unique blood composition, she would become a target for every power-hungry vampyr in Celearius. Some would seek to control her, others to drain her dry. Either way, her life as she knew it would end.

"A difficult position. Though Deyja's violation cannot go unpunished."

Kane's expression darkened. "I'm aware. But I need time to consider all angles. Let them stew in their quarters for another day. The anticipation of judgment will be its own form of torment for Deyja." His fingers traced the edge of an antique paperweight on his desk. "By tomorrow, I'll have decided their fate."

"As you wish." The wisdom in Kane's hesitation was clear. As he turned to leave, Kane's voice stopped him.

"Before you go, arrange security clearance to Elysium for tomorrow. For myself and Serenity."

The doorknob felt suddenly cold under his palm. Had he misheard? He turned slowly.

"Elysium?" The private island retreat was reserved for the highest echelon of vampyr society—a sanctuary where even Council members rarely ventured without explicit invitation. "You're taking your Elite to Elysium?"

In four hundred years of friendship, Kane had never taken anyone to Elysium. Not a Council member. Not a trusted advisor. Certainly never an Elite.

And he was taking her there.

More striking still was Kane's casual use of her name. Not "the Elite" or "Miss Wright" but Serenity—intimate, personal.

Kane met his gaze unflinchingly. "Is there a problem?"

"Of course not." The shock coursing through him remained carefully hidden. The request wasn't merely unusual—it was unprecedented. Kane taking an Elite to his personal sanctuary shattered every protocol they'd established over four hundred years. "I'll make the arrangements immediately."

Kane nodded, turning his attention back to the tracker feed as if he hadn't just broken years of carefully maintained boundaries.

"I'm meeting McGraff's agent this afternoon at Waterside Park."

"Take Sullivan with you," Kane said, his gaze still fixed on the screen. "McGraff's sudden interest warrants caution."

"Already arranged. He'll observe from a distance."

Kane nodded, seemingly satisfied. "Keep your comm open. If anything feels wrong—"

"I'll extract immediately. This isn't my first dance with potential informants."

"No, but it might be your most dangerous one." Kane finally looked up. "McGraff's timing is too convenient."

A nod of acknowledgment before slipping through the door, leaving Kane to his surveillance and thoughts of his Elite.

The memory of last night surfaced in the elevator—Nox's eyes black with bloodlust after the Ball's chaos, his normally controlled demeanor shattered by the scent of Serenity's blood. It had taken everything to pull him back from the edge.

What happened afterward had been... unexpected.

The memory of dropping to his knees in Nox's quarters sent heat flooding through him. The taste of Nox still lingered—salt and musk mingling with the metallic undertone that all vampyr carried. Afterward, when Nox had reciprocated with unexpected tenderness, he'd allowed himself a moment of weakness, remaining in those arms longer than wisdom dictated.

He'd slipped away before dawn, leaving Nox sleeping amid rumpled sheets. They hadn't crossed paths since.

What troubled him more—what they'd done, or how much he wanted to do it again?

The elevator chimed as it reached the ground floor, pulling him from his thoughts. More pressing matters demanded attention. The meeting with McGraff's asset, and he needed to arrive early to assess the terrain. The building's marble lobby passed quickly, then the underground garage where his El Camino waited.

Waterside Park stretched before him, a carefully maintained oasis of green amid Celearius' urban sprawl. Afternoon sunlight filtered through ancient oaks, casting dappled shadows across manicured lawns where humans lounged, seemingly carefree despite the tensions simmering beneath the city's surface.

Early by design, a bench with clear sight lines to the eastern dock offered an unobstructed view of the park's main pathways while keeping his back protected by water. Sullivan had positioned himself near the western entrance, nursing a coffee and pretending to read the daily news.

A flash of golden blonde—a human woman approaching with purposeful strides. She wore a sleek navy dress that accentuated her petite frame without sacrificing mobility, paired with modest heels that clicked softly against the pathway's cobblestones. Her posture radiated authority, spine straight as a blade, shoulders squared with confidence that bordered on defiance.

Something about her tugged at memory. A nagging familiarity impossible to place immediately.

"Rhyzan," she greeted, extending a pale hand. Her voice carried a melodic quality, though undercut with steel. "I'm Scarlet. General McGraff said you were expecting me."

"I was indeed. Please, have a seat." He gestured to the space beside him on the bench. Her scent reached him as she settled—peaches with undertones of gunpowder. Curious combination.

"I appreciate your willingness to meet, considering the circumstances," Scarlet said, crossing her legs at the ankle. Her gaze remained alert, constantly scanning their surroundings with the barely perceptible vigilance of someone accustomed to being hunted. "General McGraff speaks highly of your intelligence network."

A thin smile that never touched his eyes. "The General is generous with his compliments when he wants something."

"Direct. I appreciate that." She matched the smile with one equally calculating. "Shall we dispense with the pleasantries then?"

"By all means. What exactly does McGraff hope to gain from this arrangement?"

"Information, naturally. The same thing you want." She extracted a slim data drive from her clutch, holding it between manicured fingers. "This contains dossiers on known Liberation sympathizers within each district."

He took the drive, pocketing it without looking away from her face. "These names will be useful, though the Liberation's growing bolder by the day. Three prisoners escaped from our holding facility four days ago."

"I hadn't heard," Scarlet said, her expression revealing nothing. A slight flutter beneath the pale skin of her throat.

"Few have. We've kept it quiet to avoid causing panic." He leaned back, maintaining an air of casual confidence. "The rebels are becoming increasingly organized. Their tactics suggest military training."

"Concerning," she murmured, her tone carefully neutral.

"Indeed. We've increased security within the Outer City districts. Checkpoints, additional patrols, more surveillance."

Her fingers twitched almost imperceptibly against her knee. "And these escapees—any leads on their whereabouts?"

A pause, as if debating how much to reveal. "They're in Celearius. That we know for certain. Our intelligence suggests they're hiding somewhere within the city limits. Their movements suggest they're receiving assistance from local cells."

A flicker of something passed through her eyes, so quickly it might have been missed.

"I see," she replied, voice steady. "And these dossiers I've provided—they'll help track them down?"

"They're a starting point. I'll begin cross-referencing this information with our existing intelligence and expand from there. McGraff chose well—these connections could prove valuable."

The tension in her shoulders eased slightly.

"I'm glad you find it useful," she said. "General McGraff believes cooperation between our divisions will yield better results than working in isolation."

He reached into his inner pocket and withdrew a sleek black card embossed with silver numbers. "I agree. I'll begin analyzing the information you've provided today. If it proves valuable, I'll contact you with a specific assignment."

Scarlet accepted the card with steady fingers. A faint acceleration of her heartbeat. "How should I reach you if I learn something relevant before then?"

"The card contains an encrypted communication frequency. It will connect directly to my private line."

"I understand," she replied, tucking the card into her clutch with efficient movements. "If there's nothing else..."

"Not at present. Good day, Scarlet."

She nodded once, a crisp professional gesture, before turning and walking away. Her heels clicked a staccato rhythm against the cobblestones, fading as she disappeared around a flowering dogwood.

Three minutes passed before signaling Sullivan with a barely perceptible gesture. Sullivan approached, abandoning his prop newspaper on a nearby bench.

"Let's go." Already moving toward the bright red Chevy El Camino parked at the curb. Sullivan fell into step beside him, his weathered face impassive.

Once behind the wheel, Sullivan turned to him. "What's your assessment?"

Recognition slammed into him, the pieces suddenly clicking into place with crystalline clarity. That face. Those mannerisms. The careful confidence in her movements.

"I know her. She's been seen with Sebastian."

Sullivan's brow furrowed, the network of scars across his face deepening with the expression. "You certain?"

"Absolutely." A catalog of memories unfolded—fragments of surveillance footage, glimpses of social gatherings. "I've seen them together at least three times over the past year—twice at Elite social functions, once at a district charity gala. Always in proximity, though never obviously connected."

"Interesting timing," Sullivan murmured. "And what would Sebastian be doing with McGraff's alleged intelligence asset?"

The real question wasn't just who Scarlet was, but what game she played in this intricate web. His fingers tightened on the steering wheel as he navigated through Celearius' evening traffic, calculating possibilities.

"That is precisely what I intend to find out."

CHAPTER TWENTY-SIX

SERENITY

Warmth and a familiar scent enveloped Serenity like a cocoon, the tangled sheets still carrying Kane's essence—cedar, bergamot, and sandalwood. She burrowed deeper into the plush bedding, reluctant to surrender this moment of peace. The pillow beneath her cheek still held the impression of his head, and she inhaled deeply, letting his scent fill her lungs.

Even with him gone, she felt him—distant but there, focused, working. The awareness hummed beneath her skin.

The mouthwatering aroma of bacon seeped through the bedroom door. Hunger clawed at her insides, reminding her how little she'd eaten at the Elite Ball before everything had spiraled into chaos. Before glass had sliced her palm. Before Deyja's eyes locked on her blood. Before Kane had claimed her with a savagery that made her body ache in the most delicious ways.

Serenity's fingers drifted to her neck, finding the tender spots where Kane's fangs had pierced her flesh. The wounds had healed completely—his blood taking care of that—but phantom sensations lingered, echoes of pleasure so intense it bordered on pain. She closed her eyes, reliving the raw intensity of their connection—how his eyes burned with possession as he claimed her completely.

What they'd shared had been more than physical. It had been transcendent. Every touch, every whispered word of possession, every moment he'd moved inside her had felt like coming home. The way he'd held her afterward, cradling her like a precious treasure despite the savage intensity of their coupling, had shattered the last of her defenses.

She loved him. Completely, irrevocably, terrifyingly.

And he was going to kill her when he discovered the truth.

She pushed the thought aside. First, get her family to safety—Beth, her mother, anyone the rebellion might use against her. Then confess everything.

A soft clatter from the kitchen broke through her reverie. The sound was too precise, too measured to be Kane. She recognized the methodical movements—Nox. Memories from the Elite Ball flooded back. Nox's obsidian eyes fixed on her bleeding palm. The way he'd lunged for her, restrained only by Rhyzan's intervention. His expression had been feral, consumed by bloodlust.

Kane had been right. Cutting her palm had been reckless, dangerous beyond measure. She'd offered her blood in a room full of predators, understanding the consequences only after the glass had sliced through her skin.

Serenity sat up, wincing at the delicious soreness in her muscles. The sheets pooled around her waist, exposing skin marked with evidence of Kane's passion—fingerprints on her hips, tender spots along her collarbone where his mouth had claimed her.

She slipped from bed, her bare feet sinking into plush carpet. Kane's dress shirt hung on the back of a nearby chair, the crisp black fabric a stark contrast against the light wood. Serenity pulled it on, the cotton soft against her tender flesh, the hem falling to mid-thigh. She found his briefs folded neatly in a drawer and slipped them on, rolling the waistband to keep them from sliding down her hips.

The hardwood floor cooled her bare feet as she padded toward the kitchen, hesitating at the threshold. Nox stood with his back to her, his movements precise as he flipped bacon in a cast-iron skillet. Unlike Kane's imposing presence, Nox's frame was leaner, his shoulders less broad beneath his impeccably tailored shirt.

He turned at her approach, a tentative smile softening his usually stern features. The obsidian eyes that had terrified her last night had returned to their normal dark brown, clear, and focused.

"Good morning," he said, his tone carefully modulated, as though testing the waters between them.

"Hi," Serenity replied, crossing her arms over her chest.

"Thought you might be hungry," Nox said, gesturing toward the bacon and eggs sizzling in the pan. The rich aroma intensified.

"Starving, actually," she admitted, sliding onto one of the sleek barstools at the kitchen island. The cool marble surface pressed against her forearms as she leaned forward.

Nox moved with practiced efficiency, plating the food with the same precision he seemed to apply to everything. He set a steaming plate before her—crisp eggs, bacon, and toast—before preparing his own and joining her at the island.

"How are you feeling?" Serenity asked between bites, studying him for any remnant of the feral creature she'd encountered last night.

"Much better," Nox said, his attention flickering briefly to meet hers before returning to his plate. "I wasn't myself. The bloodlust..." He paused, fork suspended midair. "It's rare for me to lose control like that, but you don't understand—you smell like heaven."

"I know." She took another bite of toast.

"Even now. You smell good."

She paused. "Should I—"

"No, I'm fine. I'm not breathing."

"Oh," she said, continuing to chew but watching Nox intently.

"Though what you did at the Ball was incredibly foolish." An edge of frustration crept into his tone as he set down his fork. "Cutting yourself in a mansion full of hungry vampyrs? Do you have any idea what could have happened if Kane hadn't been there?"

Serenity swallowed a bite of egg, averting her attention. "I know. Kane already gave me this lecture last night."

"Did he?" Nox's eyebrow arched, his mouth curving into a knowing smirk. "Based on the marks on your neck and the way his scent has completely overtaken yours, I'd say he did a bit more than lecture you."

Color flooded her cheeks. She fidgeted with the collar of Kane's shirt, suddenly aware of how intimate it must look—wearing his clothes, marked by his passion, sitting in his kitchen.

"He made his point quite clearly," she murmured, focusing intently on cutting a piece of bacon.

Nox's soft chuckle only deepened her blush. "I'm sure he did. Kane has never been one for subtlety when it comes to things—or people—he cares about." His gaze flickered to her neck again, his eyes darkening momentarily before he regained control. "I suppose congratulations are in order. You signed the contract, and you are now sharing his bed."

Serenity choked on her orange juice. She dabbed at her lips with a napkin, buying time to compose herself. "We didn't exactly... I mean, we weren't in his bed when..." She trailed off, mortification washing over her.

"Ah." Nox's lip quirked upward. "Kane always did have a flair for the dramatic."

"How is Sebastian?" she asked, desperate to change the subject. "After what happened at the Ball..."

Nox's expression sobered immediately. "I'm not entirely sure. I meant to check in with Evie after she took him home." He set his fork down, a slight furrow appearing between his brows. "He was unconscious but stable when she left with him."

Serenity pushed her plate away, appetite suddenly diminished.

"Could we go see him?" Serenity asked, worry creasing her brow. "I want to make sure he's alright."

Nox dabbed his mouth with a napkin and nodded. "Of course. Let me finish this, and you go get dressed. Then we can head to Evie's."

"Thank you." Relief loosened the knot in her chest.

Twenty minutes later, Serenity emerged from her bedroom wearing dark jeans and a simple blouse. Her curls were still damp from a hasty shower, but she hadn't wanted to keep Nox waiting.

The drive to Waterside Cross passed in relative silence, both lost in thought. Nox navigated the sleek vehicle through the streets of Silver District with effortless precision, his long fingers tapping the steering wheel. They passed through the gates into Waterside Cross without incident and pulled up in front of the gleaming steel-and-glass building where Evie and Sebastian lived.

Nox parked the car, and they entered the building's airy lobby. As they rode the private elevator upward, Serenity wondered what she would say to Sebastian. How could she explain that she was falling for Kane—that she'd already fallen?

The elevator doors slid open on the penthouse floor. Nox led her down a hallway adorned with abstract paintings that seemed to shift and change as they walked past. He led the way to Evie's door, but as he lifted his hand to knock, the door swung open.

Sebastian stood in the threshold, his normally perfect appearance marred by purplish bruises blooming along his jawline. He wore a loose t-shirt that did little to hide the bandages wrapped around his torso.

"Well, look who's up and about," Nox remarked, eyes narrowing as he assessed Sebastian's condition.

"Takes more than a tussle with a rogue vampyr to keep me down," Sebastian replied with a wince that belied his casual tone. "Just a few bruises and a fractured rib. Nothing that won't heal in a week or so."

"Well, this one was worried," he said, referring to Serenity.

"Not surprised," Sebastian smirked, then said, "Evie's down in her lab. She's been down there most of the morning."

"I'll go see what she's up to. Will you be alright?"

"Yes, I'll be fine."

Nox nodded before turning around and heading back to the elevator.

"Come on in." Sebastian took a step back, opening the door wider. He moved with only the slightest hint of stiffness, though she caught the careful way he avoided twisting.

"How are you feeling?" Sebastian asked, scanning her for injuries as he closed the door.

A laugh bubbled from Serenity's throat, surprising even herself. "Shouldn't I be asking you that question? You're the one who looks like you went three rounds with a freight train."

Sebastian's lips quirked upward. He reached for her hand, turning it over to examine her palm where the glass had sliced through her flesh the night before. The skin was smooth, unmarked—no evidence of the wound that had caused so much chaos.

"Impressive," he murmured, tracing a finger across her healed palm. "A small part of me wishes Evie could do the same. The pain is a bitch." He winced as he shifted his weight.

Sebastian glanced toward the hallway, then lowered his tone. "Come with me. We should talk somewhere more private."

He led her down the corridor, past several closed doors until they reached what appeared to be his bedroom—surprisingly austere compared to the rest of Evie's stylish apartment. A large bed with dark sheets, minimal furniture, a few scattered books, and walls painted a deep charcoal gray.

Sebastian closed the door behind them with a soft click that somehow felt like the sealing of a tomb.

"Evie's security system doesn't monitor private rooms," he explained, gesturing for her to sit on the edge of the immaculately made bed while he remained standing. "We can speak freely here."

Serenity perched on the mattress, her fingers twisting together in her lap. The words she needed to say felt lodged in her throat, heavy and unwieldy.

"I'm glad you're okay," she began, the inadequacy of the statement making her wince. "What you did last night—"

"Was nothing more than what any of us would do," Sebastian cut in, waving away her gratitude. "But that's not why you're here, is it?"

Serenity swallowed hard, her pulse quickening. The words felt trapped in her throat, reluctant to emerge.

"I can't do this anymore," she finally whispered. She forced herself to meet Sebastian's stare. "I need you to get my family to safety—Beth and my mother. And then I'm done with the rebellion."

Sebastian's demeanor remained carefully neutral, though a pained emotion flickered behind his eyes. "Just like that?"

"I won't tell Kane anything that could hurt the movement," she rushed to add, palms sweating as she wiped them against her jeans. "I don't really know anything substantial anyway—not about your operations or leadership. But I need my family safe before I..." She hesitated, the truth catching in her throat.

"Before you what?"

"Before I tell Kane the truth." The admission emerged as barely a whisper. "About everything. About what I've done."

Sebastian studied her for a long moment, understanding dawning across his features, followed by a darker expression.

"You've fallen for him," he said flatly. Not a question—a statement.

She looked away, unable to bear the intensity of his scrutiny. "Yes," she whispered.

"So seduction was never the problem," he said, laughing bitterly. "How long have you been sleeping with him?"

"Since the night I found out Damon was an Elite."

He raised his eyebrows in surprise. "You work quickly."

Serenity's jaw tightened. "It wasn't like that."

"No?" Sebastian's tone hardened, disgust seeping into his words. "Do you actually believe he cares for you? That this is some fairytale romance where the monster learns to love?"

The sudden shift made Serenity flinch. She wrapped her arms around herself, suddenly cold despite the room's comfortable temperature. She felt Kane—distant but present, working in his office. The steady rhythm of his focus was a comfort even as Sebastian's words tried to poison what they'd shared.

"You don't understand—"

"No, you don't understand." Sebastian took a step closer, his blue eyes burning with intensity. "Did you forget what happened at the Ball? How Deyja nearly killed you for a taste of your blood? How Nox—your friendly companion—would have torn your throat out if Rhyzan hadn't stopped him?" His tone dropped lower, more vehement. "That's what they are, Serenity. What Kane is. Predators who see you as food."

Images from the Ball flashed through her mind—blood splattering marble, Deyja's crimson eyes fixed on her bleeding palm, the feral hunger in Nox's look.

But then other memories surfaced—Kane's tenderness afterward, the way he'd cradled her, the reverence in his touch. That warmth contradicted everything Sebastian claimed.

"It's different with Kane," she said, but doubt had already begun to creep in at the edges.

"Different?" Sebastian scoffed. "Because he took you to bed? Because he bit you? Do you think you're special, Serenity? You're just another blood bag to him."

"You're wrong about him." But even as she said it, fear whispered through her thoughts. What if Sebastian was right? What if Kane's passion was nothing more than possession—a predator claiming his prey?

No. She felt his emotions, sensed his care even from across the city. That couldn't be faked. Could it?

Sebastian ran a hand through his silver-blonde hair, frustration evident in the gesture. When he spoke again, his tone had shifted—less confrontational, more calculating. "I found something," he said quietly. "Something that could change everything."

He crossed to a small desk in the corner and pulled open the bottom drawer, extracting a slim comm device. He turned it over in his hands, and Serenity noticed the screen was dark, inactive.

"What is it?" she asked, eyeing the device warily.

"Photos. Blueprints for a weapon that could end this war. I photographed them before the attack at the Ball. I wasn't sure I should hand them over, but after last night, I realized we needed to get this information to the rebellion immediately."

Her blood ran cold. "What kind of weapon?"

"Something that can kill them all," Sebastian said, his eyes gleaming with barely contained fervor. "Not just injure them—actually kill them. Permanently. No regeneration. No recovery."

Her stomach turned. "All of them?"

"Every single vampyr in Celearius, if we deploy it correctly." His fingers tightened around the device. "But we need more information. Technical specifications that I couldn't access."

The implication hung in the air between them. He wanted her to get that information from Kane.

"What exactly does this weapon do?" Serenity asked, though part of her didn't want to know.

Sebastian's fingers tightened around the device, and he hesitated. "I can't go into specifics. Not yet." He glanced toward the door as if someone might be listening. "I'm meeting with Damon and Starr tonight to hand over what I've found so far. They'll know what questions to ask, what information we still need."

"But how does it work? Is it some kind of poison? A virus?" The questions tumbled from her lips before she could stop them.

He slipped the device back into his pocket. "The less you know right now, the safer you are."

Frustration bubbled in Serenity's chest. "Then how am I supposed to help you if I don't even know what you need?"

"By continuing what you've been doing—gathering intelligence from Kane."

"Just like you've been doing with Evie."

Sebastian froze. The muscle in his jaw twitched, but he didn't speak.

"You'd be killing Evie," Serenity pressed, watching him carefully. "The woman you've lived with for—how many years now? You can just easily kill her off?"

An expression flashed across his face—pain, doubt, conflict—before his features hardened into something cold and distant. "Yes," he said, the word hollow. "War demands sacrifices."

Serenity stared at him. This wasn't the Sebastian she thought she knew. The coldness in his stare, the clinical detachment—it terrified her. If he could dismiss Evie's life so easily, what did that mean for Kane? For everyone she'd come to care about?

Kane, working in his office, unaware that people were plotting his death. That she'd been part of that plot, however unwillingly.

She took a deep breath, trying to calm the racing of her heart. Her hands trembled as she clasped them in her lap, focusing on the steady in and out of her breathing until the roaring in her ears subsided.

"Sebastian," she said finally, steadier than she felt. "I told you—I'm done. I'm not gathering any more intelligence. I'm not helping with this weapon." She met his stare directly. "But I need you to promise me."

He raised an eyebrow, waiting.

"My family. Promise me you'll get them out, regardless of what I decide." Her words cracked slightly. "My sister Beth needs her treatments—she can't get them in Celearius. My mother... they're innocent in all this. Please."

Sebastian studied her for a long moment. He ran a hand through his silver-blonde hair again, the gesture seeming more vulnerable than she'd ever seen from him.

"I'll try to convince them," he said finally. "But I can't make any promises. Starr and the others may not—"

"Just try," Serenity interrupted. "Please. They're all I have."

Sebastian nodded slowly, his expression softening. "I'll do what I can."

"Thank you." Serenity rose from the bed, a strange heaviness settling in her. She needed to get out of this room, away from Sebastian's piercing stare and the weight of his expectations.

She slipped out of the bedroom and made her way down the hallway, her footsteps muffled against the plush carpet. Each step away from Sebastian felt like moving through molasses, her thoughts a tangled mess of doubt and fear.

When she reached the living room, she stopped short. Evie and Nox were seated on the plush white sofa, their postures tense as they looked up at her approach. Evie clutched a familiar blood analysis device in her slender hand—the same one they'd used at the clinic when she first signed up to be an Elite.

Serenity's heart slammed against her ribs. Her mouth went dry.

The device. The same type that had malfunctioned during her initial screening, leaving a drop of blood on her arm. The doctor's eyes had gone black with bloodlust in an instant, lunging for her before Kane intervened. She could still remember the terror, the certainty she was about to die, the way Kane had appeared like an avenging angel to tear the doctor away from her.

Every muscle in her body tensed. She took an involuntary step backward, her hip hitting a table.

"There you are," Evie said, her tone carefully neutral. "How are you?"

"I'm... fine," Serenity replied, her pulse quickening as she eyed the blood analysis device in Evie's hand.

"Please, don't look so frightened," Evie said, her manner gentle as she patted the sofa beside her. "I just need another sample from you. I know you've shared blood with Kane. Twice now. I'd like to see if it's affected yours in any way. Purely scientific curiosity."

Nox cleared his throat. "Evie has a... professional interest in the effects of vampyr blood on humans."

Serenity swallowed hard, her attention fixed on the sleek device in Evie's hand. Every instinct screamed at her to run, to make excuses, to do anything but let Evie use that device on her. What if it malfunctioned again? What if the reading raised questions? What if her blood was different now, changed by Kane's?

She felt Kane's steady presence—focused, working, unaware of her panic. She drew strength from that, forcing herself to take a breath.

"Okay," she said, forcing a smile that felt brittle. "Okay."

She crossed the room with measured steps and sank onto the sofa beside Evie, extending her forearm. The cushion dipped beneath her weight, soft and yielding. Too comfortable for the racing of her heart, the cold sweat breaking out along her spine.

Evie's smile was warm as she took Serenity's forearm, her touch gentle but clinical. "This won't hurt a bit. Just a small pinprick."

The cool plastic pressed against her forearm. A tiny sting followed, barely noticeable compared to the thundering panic within her. She held her breath, waiting for the telltale warmth that had spread down her arm the first time, when the device malfunctioned and left that drop of blood exposed.

Nothing happened.

The device worked flawlessly. When Evie pulled it away, there wasn't a trace of blood, to Serenity's overwhelming relief.

Evie nodded and smiled as she examined the readings. "Thank you, Serenity. This is perfect." She turned to Nox, auburn highlights catching the light as she shifted. "Could you remind Kane that I need a blood sample from him as well? The comparative analysis will help me understand the effects better."

"Of course," Nox replied, rising from the sofa with fluid grace. "Ready to go, Serenity?"

Relief washed through her as she stood, grateful for the excuse to leave. "Yes, I'm ready."

The elevator doors closed with a soft hiss, enclosing them in polished steel and silence. Nox studied her from the corner of his eye.

"Everything alright?" he asked, his manner deceptively casual.

"Fine," she lied, forcing her features into what she hoped was a neutral look. "Just worried about Sebastian."

"He'll be fine. Evie will take good care of him," Nox assured her as they got off the elevator.

As they drove back to Silver District, she had to protect Kane. Had to get her family to safety and then tell him everything before it was too late—even if the truth destroyed them both.

CHAPTER
TWENTY-SEVEN

KANE

Kane didn't know what the hell was wrong with him when it came to this Elite... to Serenity. She had gotten under his skin, deep as marrow. Like a virus, or a fever in his blood.

She had invaded every corner of his existence. Not just her fragrance—jasmine and rose with a touch of honeysuckle—but the ghost of her touch, the echo of her laugh, the memory of her warmth pressed against him in the darkness of that half-constructed building.

Even now, he felt her—distant but present, moving through his apartment.

Kane ran his hand through his hair, disheveling the usually immaculate strands. He'd spent the entire day in meetings, unable to focus on a single word spoken by the Council representatives. All he could think about was the curve of her lips, the defiance in her honey-brown eyes, the way her body had melted against his.

A rebel. A spy. A traitor working for the Human Liberation.

He'd known since the moment he'd watched surveillance footage of her breaking into his office, stealing information with practiced efficiency. Every strategic instinct screamed that he should use this knowledge—let her think she was succeeding, feed her false information, trace her contacts back to the rebellion's leadership.

And he had been doing exactly that. Playing the long game. Letting her believe her deception worked while he maneuvered pieces on a chessboard she couldn't see.

Except somewhere along the way, the game had stopped feeling like strategy and started feeling like torture.

Because despite knowing her betrayal, despite understanding she was using him, he'd fallen for her anyway. Completely. Irrevocably. Catastrophically.

"Pathetic," he growled to the empty office, slamming his fist down on the desk. "She's a rebel. The enemy."

But she called to him like a siren's song he had no desire to resist.

Kane couldn't stay in his office another moment. The walls were closing in, memories of her theft mocking him from every corner. He grabbed his keys and stormed out, ignoring the startled glances of his staff.

The drive home was a blur as he weaved through the evening traffic and pedestrians. His hands gripped the steering wheel with unnecessary force, knuckles white against black leather. The Silver District spread before him, its gleaming towers piercing the darkening sky like accusing fingers.

With every mile, she grew clearer in his awareness. She was there. In his space. The knowledge should infuriate him. Instead, anticipation coiled in his gut, urgent and undeniable.

When he finally reached his penthouse building, he barely acknowledged the security guard's deferential nod. The elevator ride felt interminable, each floor passing with glacial slowness as he leaned against the cool metal wall, her nearness thrumming through him.

The soft ping announced his arrival, and as the doors slid open, Kane caught the aroma of clean sweat and expensive cologne. Nox was crossing the foyer, dressed in loose athletic wear, his hair damp from exertion.

"You're back earlier than expected," Nox observed, taking in Kane with clinical precision.

Kane grunted noncommittally, stepping off the elevator.

"Any movement with Chloe?" Nox asked, studying Kane's face with that penetrating stare that always made Kane feel like his second-in-command could see straight through his carefully constructed walls.

Kane's jaw tightened. "The tracking dot has been moving in the same vicinity in the Dead City. But no direct contact yet."

Chloe's continued silence was concerning. She was one of their most reliable operatives—until now. First Serenity's betrayal, and now this. Trust seemed a luxury he could no longer afford.

Nox moved toward the kitchen, rolling his shoulders with the easy grace of a predator. "I'll be in my quarters if you need anything else tonight."

Kane nodded, his thoughts already drifting elsewhere. The penthouse felt too confining, saturated with memories of her—of Serenity moving through these rooms, challenging him, tempting him. He headed toward his office, then paused. The thought of surrounding himself with more work, more problems to solve, made something tighten painfully in his chest.

Instead, his attention traveled up the staircase that led to the upper floor—to her bedroom. His feet carried him forward before his mind fully registered the decision. Perhaps seeing her would provide some clarity, some way to exorcise this obsession that had taken root in his blood.

"She's not up there," Nox called out, his voice cutting through Kane's thoughts.

Kane froze mid-step, one hand gripping the banister. He turned slowly, finding Nox standing at the threshold of his private apartment behind the kitchen. The knowing look in Nox's expression made Kane grimace.

Before Kane could form the question burning on his tongue, Nox tilted his head slightly. "She's on the roof. In the garden."

Nox continued into his apartment, leaving Kane to decide whether he should head to his office and resist the pull or give in.

His heart decided for him, pulling him toward her presence above.

He followed the instinct that drew him to his rooftop garden—a place where he could simply be Kane Draccus. Not a leader, not the Head of the Council, not responsible for an entire city's fragile peace. Just... himself.

His mind still didn't understand why he'd shared this place with her, but his treacherous heart knew all too well.

As he pushed open the heavy door to the roof, the sunset's dying light bathed everything in amber and gold. The aroma of salt from the distant ocean mingled with the earthy perfume of his carefully curated plants. Kane froze.

Serenity knelt among his marigolds, her fingers gently pulling weeds to give them more space to breathe. She hadn't noticed him yet, too absorbed in her task. The fading sunlight caught in her silky black curls, transforming them into a midnight halo. Her profile, etched against the twilight sky, stole his breath.

She hummed softly—some melody he didn't recognize—as she worked. Her movements were precise, practical, and loving at once. She radiated quiet peace as she tended the growing things.

For a moment, he simply watched her. The sight of her here, in his sacred space, touching his plants with such care, should infuriate him. No one came here. Not Council members. Not friends. Not even Rhy.

Yet seeing her here filled some void he'd forgotten existed. Made the garden feel more alive than it had in decades.

Suddenly, her head snapped up. Their eyes locked across the garden, and for one suspended heartbeat, neither moved. Then Serenity scrambled to her feet, soil cascading from her knees as she backed away from the marigold bed.

"I'm so sorry," she blurted, wiping her hands frantically on her jeans. "I shouldn't have touched your garden without asking. I just—" She gestured helplessly at the plants. "It's automatic for me. Back home, we had a small backyard garden. Just a few plants, mostly tomatoes and some herbs, but tending to them always helped me think."

Kane remained motionless, drinking in the sight of her. Dirt smudged her cheek, a single streak of earth that his fingers itched to brush away.

"I love the smell of the ocean air up here," she continued, words tumbling out in a nervous rush.

She kept talking, but Kane barely registered her words. His focus narrowed to the curve of her mouth, the way the dying sunlight caught in her lashes, the smudge of soil across her cheek that made her impossibly more beautiful. His feet carried him forward without conscious command.

Her words faltered as he approached, eyes widening. Her scent filled his lungs—jasmine and soil and something uniquely hers. His heartbeat, normally steady and controlled, thundered against his ribs.

"Kane?" His name on her lips sounded like a question, like a prayer.

He reached her in three more strides, towering over her smaller frame. Time seemed to slow as he lifted his hand, gently brushing his thumb across the soil smudge on her cheek. Her skin burned against his touch, that human warmth he craved beyond reason. Her pulse jumped beneath his fingertips.

Her desire was written in every line of her body, mirroring his own need with devastating precision.

Kane leaned down, giving her time to step back, to turn away, to reject what was happening between them. She didn't move. Her eyes remained fixed on his, pupils dilating as her breath caught. The space between them crackled with electricity, an invisible current drawing him inexorably closer.

Every instinct screamed at him to retreat, to rebuild the walls he'd so carefully constructed. Instead, he surrendered.

Kane captured her lips with his own, the contact igniting a primal hunger within him. Her mouth was impossibly soft, yielding yet demanding as she responded to his touch. The taste of her—sweet like summer berries—flooded his senses, drowning out every rational thought.

She's a rebel spy, his mind whispered. She betrayed you.

But he felt her response—genuine desire, real affection, emotions that couldn't be faked no matter how skilled the deception. The bond didn't lie.

His hands found her waist, drawing her closer until her warmth pressed against the length of him. Each curve of her body fit against his as though explicitly crafted for this purpose. Her fingers tentatively traced up his torso before tangling in his hair, the gentle tug sending electricity racing down his spine.

Kane silenced the warnings with a growl deep in his throat. His hands slid up her back, feeling every curve, every dip, every rise beneath his palms. He devoured her mouth, drinking in her soft sighs like a man dying of thirst.

When she moaned against his lips, the beast inside him snapped. He backed her against the garden wall, lifting her effortlessly so her face was level with his. Her legs wrapped around his waist instinctively, those soft thighs gripping him with surprising strength. The feeling of her pressed against him, warm and pliant yet somehow demanding, made his fangs throb with need.

"Kane," she whispered against his mouth, his name a broken plea that shattered what little restraint remained.

He trailed kisses down her neck, feeling her pulse flutter beneath his lips. The beast within him howled to claim, to mark, to bite—but he resisted, instead grazing the sensitive flesh with his teeth, careful to keep his fangs retracted despite the nearly overwhelming urge to sink them into her skin.

Her pleasure intensified his own need until separation became impossible.

Her fingers tightened in his hair, pulling him closer with unexpected boldness. The sensation sent fire rushing through his veins. He could feel her heart hammering, the sweet nectar of her blood calling to him from just beneath her delicate skin.

Kane growled against her throat, inhaling deeply. His hand slid beneath her shirt, fingers tracing the heated skin of her back. She arched against him, a soft gasp escaping her lips. The sound nearly undid him.

"Push me away. Tell me to stop," he murmured against her collarbone, giving her one last chance to end this madness.

"Don't stop," she whispered, her voice husky with desire. "Take me."

The words flamed a primal hunger within him. Kane spun her around in one fluid motion, pressing her front against the rough stone of the garden wall. His hands slid down her sides, fingers hooking into the waistband of her jeans. He paused, his breath hot against her ear.

"Are you certain?" he rasped, the beast within him straining against the last threads of his control.

"Yes," she breathed, pushing back against him with maddening pressure.

Kane yanked her jeans down in one swift movement, exposing the curve of her ass to the twilight air. His enhanced vision caught every detail—the goosebumps rising on her flesh, the slight tremble in her thighs, the slick evidence of her desire. He freed himself, the cool evening breeze a stark contrast to the heat radiating from his body.

He positioned himself at her entrance, one hand gripping her hip while the other braced against the wall beside her head. He could feel her anticipation, her need, her complete trust in him despite everything. The realization nearly brought him to his knees.

With a single powerful thrust, he buried himself to the hilt. She was tight, hot, perfect—enveloping him completely as a strangled cry escaped her lips. Her inner walls clenched around him, adjusting to his length. He held himself still, giving her body time to adjust.

"You feel..." Kane couldn't finish the sentence, words failing him as pleasure coursed through his veins like liquid fire.

Serenity pushed back against him, a silent plea for movement that shattered his restraint. Kane withdrew almost completely before driving back into her with a force that made the garden wall creak beneath their combined weight. Her gasp transformed into a moan that echoed across the rooftop garden, mingling with the distant sounds of the city below.

He established a relentless rhythm, each thrust deeper than the last. His fingers dug into the soft flesh of her hips, holding her steady as he claimed her body with primal intensity. Their pleasure fed back and forth in an endless loop that threatened to consume him completely.

"Kane," she cried out, breaking around his name. "Please..."

He knew what she needed. His hand slid around her hip, fingers finding the sensitive bundle of nerves between her thighs. The first touch made her body jerk, a shuddering gasp escaping her lips. He circled the sensitive bud with maddening precision, matching the rhythm of his thrusts as he drove into her with increasing urgency.

Her inner walls began to flutter around him, the first telltale signs of her approaching climax. Her pleasure built, cresting, about to break. Kane increased his pace, his fingers working her relentlessly as he bent to whisper against her ear.

"Let go for me," he commanded, his voice a guttural growl that seemed to vibrate through her entire body.

Serenity shattered beneath his touch, her back arching as waves of pleasure crashed through her. Her walls clenched around him with devastating intensity, milking his length as her cries echoed across the garden. The sound of his name on her lips as she came undone pushed him over the edge.

The bond exploded between them as her climax triggered his own. Kane's release hit him with the force of a tidal wave, pleasure exploding through his body as he spilled himself deep inside her. For an instant, their emotions merged completely—her ecstasy became his, his possession became hers, until he couldn't distinguish between them.

His vision blurred, the world narrowing to nothing but the sensation of her body joined with his. A primal growl tore from his throat as he pressed his forehead against her shoulder, his hips stuttering against her as ecstasy crashed over him in relentless waves.

For several heartbeats, they remained locked together, breathing ragged, bodies slick with sweat despite the cool evening breeze. Kane's forehead rested against her shoulder, his arms wrapped around her waist.

Slowly, reluctantly, Kane withdrew from her, taking a step back to create distance between them. The cool evening air rushed between their bodies, a stark reminder of what had just happened. He watched as Serenity adjusted her clothing with trembling fingers, her cheeks flushed with lingering pleasure and perhaps a touch of embarrassment. Kane fastened his own clothes, his movements mechanical while his mind raced.

The silence stretched between them, filled with unspoken questions. Kane cleared his throat.

"You're welcome here anytime," he said, gesturing to the garden around them.

Her face transformed then—not the shy smile he'd seen before, not the guarded one she sometimes wore. This was genuine, unguarded joy that reached her eyes.

Serenity stepped toward him, closing the distance he'd just created. Before he could react, she rose on her tiptoes and pressed her lips against his. The kiss was gentle, almost reverent—so different from the desperate passion they'd just shared, yet somehow more devastating.

Her affection washed over him—real, powerful, undeniable. Not the calculated seduction of a spy, but genuine emotion.

Kane's mind whispered warnings. The Elders would never permit this. She was human. An Elite. Working to destroy everything he'd built. Centuries of vampyr tradition would condemn their union. The Council would see her as nothing more than a tool, a means to an end—or worse, a liability to be eliminated.

But as her lips moved against his, soft and yielding yet somehow commanding, Kane realized with startling clarity that he wanted her to choose him over her mission, over the rebellion, over everything else.

Instead of pushing her away, his arms tightened around her, pulling her closer as if he could somehow absorb her warmth, her life, her essence into his own cold existence.

When he finally broke the kiss, roughness edged his tone. "You shouldn't be up here alone."

Serenity's eyes widened slightly, confusion flickering across her features before understanding dawned. "I'm not alone. I have you," she said, a hint of mischief dancing in her honey-brown eyes.

"You know what I mean," he countered.

"I know. It just helps me think, being up here," she said, taking a step back. Her hand gestured to the garden around them, the plants silhouetted against the darkening sky. "When everything feels so heavy... this place feels like breathing again."

The thought created an unwanted intimacy between them, a shared understanding he couldn't afford.

"You're free to come here anytime," Kane heard himself say, the words escaping before he could reconsider them. "The garden is yours as much as mine now."

Her eyes widened, honey-brown irises catching the last remnants of twilight. The smile that spread across her face made his chest tighten.

"Thank you," Serenity whispered. She stepped back into his arms, letting him fold her against his chest. Her body fit so perfectly against his, warm and solid.

"Thank you for sharing this with me," she whispered against his chest, her voice vibrating through him. "It means more than you know."

She nestled deeper into his embrace, trusting and vulnerable. Her warmth seeped through his clothes, her heartbeat a steady rhythm against him—alive, vital, human.

"Serenity," he whispered, his voice raw with emotion he couldn't suppress. The sound of her name felt like a confession torn from his soul.

She tilted her face up to his, moonlight catching in her eyes. "Yes?"

He traced the curve of her cheek with his thumb, memorizing the texture of her skin and the warmth radiating from her. Her pulse fluttered beneath his fingertips, that precious rhythm of life he'd long ago lost.

"Stay with me tonight," he said, the words emerging as both command and plea.

Her smile bloomed like sunrise. "Yes," she whispered. "Always yes."

Tomorrow he would return to strategy. Tonight, he would simply hold her.

CHAPTER TWENTY-EIGHT

SERENITY

Serenity awoke to the unfamiliar sensation of perfect contentment. Warm and secure in Kane's arms, she lay still, savoring him draped across her body, his chest rising and falling with each breath against her back. Even in sleep, he held her possessively, one muscular arm wrapped around her waist, his legs tangled with hers beneath the silken sheets.

Last night had been... magical. The rooftop garden under twilight, his tenderness afterward as they'd returned to his bed, the way he'd made love to her with an aching gentleness that brought tears to her eyes. The memory still lingered on her skin like a phantom touch.

She felt his peace—deep and rare, a contentment that echoed her own.

She shifted slightly, careful not to disturb him as other memories surfaced. The evening they'd spent together afterward—Kane ordering from Les Reines, the French restaurant where they'd had their first real date. He'd let her request extra dessert without even raising an eyebrow. They'd watched a movie together on his massive leather couch, her head nestled against him while rain pattered against the penthouse windows. His laughter during the ridiculous romantic comedy had vibrated through her, a sound so rare and beautiful she'd committed it to memory.

Serenity shifted carefully, turning to face him without disturbing his sleep. Vampyrs rarely slept deeply, but Kane had been exhausted in ways that transcended physical fatigue.

Her heart swelled as she studied his unguarded face. Sleep softened the hard angles, transforming him from the fearsome Head of the Human Vampyr Council into something almost vulnerable, human. His dark lashes cast shadows against his cheekbones, and his usually perfect hair fell across his forehead in a way that made her fingers itch to brush it back.

How strange that this powerful creature—this ancient, dangerous being who could snap a person's neck without effort—could look so peaceful. So beautiful.

A smile curved her lips as she watched the steady rise and fall of his chest. How many people had seen Kane Draccus like this? Unguarded. At peace.

Suddenly, Kane's hand shot out, capturing her wrist. Before she could gasp, he'd pulled her down against him, his mouth finding hers in a kiss that stole her breath. His lips moved with deliberate precision, coaxing a response she couldn't deny even if she wanted to.

His desire flooded her, along with satisfaction and something deeper—affection that made her heart stutter.

"Thought you could watch me sleep without consequences?" he murmured against her lips.

Her mouth parted under his, surrendering to the heat that immediately sparked between them. Serenity melted against him, her body remembering his contours as if they'd been designed to fit together. His tongue swept against hers, tasting of dark and spice that made her head swim.

"Good morning," she whispered when he finally allowed her to breathe, her voice husky with desire.

Kane's eyes gleamed with satisfaction as he traced her lower lip with his thumb. "You look beautiful in my bed," he murmured, his deep voice rumbling through her where they pressed together. "Like you belong here."

The unexpected tenderness in his words made her pulse quicken. He meant it. Every word.

Before she could respond, a sharp buzz interrupted the moment. Kane growled, reaching for his phone on the nightstand.

Before he could check the notification, a sharp knock echoed through the room. He tilted his head, listening, and a slow smile spread across his face, transforming his features.

"That's for you," he said, anticipation flickering in his silver-blue eyes.

"For me?" Serenity sat up, the sheet pooling around her waist.

"Yes. Go check." He urged her.

Excitement bubbled up in Serenity as she scrambled off the bed, nearly tripping over the tangled sheets in her haste. She snatched Kane's discarded dress shirt from the floor, slipping her arms through the sleeves that hung past her fingertips. The fabric carried his scent—cedar and warm leather—enveloping her as she hastily fastened buttons.

"What is it?" she asked, glancing back at him as she padded toward the door on bare feet.

Kane merely smiled, that rare expression that transformed his entire face. "Go see."

She pulled open the bedroom door, and there on the polished hardwood floor sat a small gift bag in shimmering silver paper, adorned with a delicate blue ribbon. Serenity's breath caught. A gift? For her?

She scooped it up, clutching it to her as she hurried back to the bed, her bare feet silent against the plush carpet. The mattress dipped beneath her as she scrambled back to Kane's side, cross-legged and breathless with anticipation.

"Open it," Kane urged, his voice low and expectant as he sat up against the headboard, sheets pooling at his waist.

Serenity's fingers trembled as she carefully unwrapped the ribbon, savoring the silky texture. She peeked inside the bag and gasped. Reaching in, she pulled out two scraps of sapphire-blue fabric that shimmered like captured ocean waves in the morning light.

"What's this?" She held up the pieces, confused by their small size and strange shape.

Kane's lips quirked upward. "It's a bikini."

"A bikini?" Serenity repeated, turning the garments over in her hands. The fabric felt impossibly smooth, almost liquid against her skin.

"For the beach," Kane explained, his eyes crinkling at the corners. "You mentioned you'd never seen the ocean up close."

The realization hit like a thunderbolt. The beach. The actual ocean. Not just glimpsed from rooftops or seen in movies, but experienced—the sand between her toes, the waves crashing against her legs, the salt spray on her face. Everything she'd dreamed of.

A sound escaped Serenity's throat—a high-pitched squeal of pure delight that surprised even her. She clapped her hand over her mouth, eyes wide with excitement, but couldn't contain the joy bubbling up inside her like champagne.

"The ocean? Really? You're taking me to the actual ocean?" Her words tumbled out in a breathless rush as she clutched the bikini to her chest. "With waves and everything?"

Kane's smile widened. His pleasure at her reaction wrapped around her like a warm embrace.

"When?" Serenity asked, already imagining the feel of sand between her toes, the crash of waves against her skin.

Kane reached for his phone, checking something before turning back to her. "Twenty minutes."

"Twenty minutes?" Serenity scrambled off the bed, nearly tripping over her own feet in her haste. "That's not enough time!"

"Better hurry then," Kane said, his deep voice laced with amusement as she darted toward the door.

Serenity raced down the hallway and up the stairs to her room. Inside, she dumped the contents of the gift bag onto her bed, the shimmering blue fabric catching the morning light. Twenty minutes to get ready for the ocean. Her pulse raced with excitement as she stripped off Kane's shirt.

The bikini bottoms seemed straightforward enough—two holes for the legs, elastic waistband. She stepped into them, sliding the fabric up her thighs. The material hugged her curves perfectly, as if tailored specifically for her body. But when she picked up the top piece, she froze, turning it over in her hands with growing confusion.

Strings dangled from various points of the triangular fabric pieces. Which part went where? How did these tiny scraps of material stay in place? She'd seen bikinis in movies and advertisements, but having never owned one—or even tried one on—she found herself completely baffled.

Serenity attempted to position the triangles over her breasts, holding them in place with one hand while trying to figure out which strings tied where. The fabric slipped, refusing to stay put. After several frustrated attempts, she heard a soft knock at her door.

His amusement reached her before his voice.

"Come in," she called, clutching the blue triangles against her chest.

The door opened, and Kane stood there in dark swim shorts and a loose white cotton shirt, unbuttoned enough to reveal a tantalizing glimpse of his muscled chest.

Serenity turned, a pout forming on her lips as she held up the complicated blue top. "This thing is impossible. There are too many strings."

Kane's eyes crinkled at the corners as he approached. "Turn around. Let me help you."

Her skin prickled with awareness as he moved behind her, his fingers brushing against her bare back. The warmth of his breath caressed her neck as he gathered the strings of the bikini top.

"Hold these against yourself," he murmured, positioning the triangular fabric over her breasts.

Serenity complied, pulse racing as his knuckles grazed her skin. He worked with surprising dexterity, tying the lower strings securely around her ribcage, then the upper ones around her neck. Each touch sent electricity coursing through her veins, his fingertips leaving trails of heat wherever they made contact.

"There," Kane said, his voice dropping to a husky timbre. "Turn around. Let me see you."

Serenity pivoted slowly, suddenly self-conscious under his intense stare. The cool air kissed her exposed skin as Kane's eyes darkened, taking in every inch of her. His silver-blue eyes darkened to stormy seas, hungry and possessive as they traveled from her face down to her toes and back again.

His desire crashed into her—raw, powerful, barely restrained.

"You look..." Kane's voice trailed off, his jaw tightening as he swallowed hard. "You're lucky we're pressed for time. Otherwise, I'd show you exactly how tempting you look in that color."

Serenity bit her lower lip, enjoying the flare of desire in his expression as he tracked the movement.

"There should be a bag at the bottom of your closet," Kane said, visibly restraining himself from reaching for her. "It has everything you'll need—towels, sunscreen, a cover-up."

Serenity crossed the space between them in three quick steps and pressed her lips against his. "Okay," she whispered, breathless with excitement. "I'll be down in five minutes."

Kane's fingers lingered at her waist, reluctance evident in the way his hands tightened briefly before letting her go. "Don't make me come looking for you," he warned, but the corner of his mouth quirked upward, softening the threat.

As soon as the door closed behind him, Serenity hurried to the closet, pulling it open. Her fingers danced over the hanging garments until she found the long, flowing blue dress that had caught her eye before. Perfect for a day at the beach—light enough to slip over her swimsuit, elegant enough to please Kane.

She reached for it, then froze, her hand suspended mid-air as her gaze caught on the shoebox at the back of the shelf. The one farthest to the left. The one containing her mother's gun.

Six silver bullets meant for vampyr hearts.

The weight of that secret pressed against her happiness. But not today. Today was about the ocean, about freedom, about pretending—just for a little while—that her life wasn't impossible.

She found the beach bag exactly where Kane had said it would be—a large woven tote filled with two plush towels, sunscreen, and a wide-brimmed hat like she'd seen ladies wear in movies. She slung it over her shoulder, slipped on a pair of flat sandals, and hurried downstairs.

Kane stood waiting near the elevator, his tall frame silhouetted against the morning light streaming through the windows. The sight of him stole her breath. This man wore loose tan linen pants that hung low on his hips and a white button-down cotton shirt, sleeves rolled up to reveal powerful forearms. His dark hair fell in casual waves rather than its usual slicked-back style.

He looked approachable. Almost human.

"You're staring," Kane said, his lips curving into a smile that transformed his entire face.

Heat rushed to Serenity's cheeks. His eyes sparkled with an unfamiliar lightheartedness, his posture relaxed in a way she'd never witnessed before.

He extended his hand toward her. "Ready?"

She slipped her fingers into his, marveling at how natural it felt. "Ready."

They descended in the elevator, Kane's thumb tracing lazy circles against her skin. When the doors opened, Serenity realized they were in a part of the building she'd never visited before—a grand marble lobby with soaring ceilings and tasteful modern art adorning the walls.

"I've never been through here," she whispered, taking in the opulent space. Crystal chandeliers caught the morning light, scattering rainbow patterns across the polished floor.

"I prefer to use the private entrance," Kane explained, guiding her through the front glass doors.

The gleaming black town car waited at the curb, its polished surface reflecting the morning sunlight. Nox stood beside it, impeccably dressed as always in a tailored black suit that matched the vehicle's sleek exterior. His expression softened when he saw them approaching.

"Good morning," Nox said, his voice carrying genuine warmth.

"Morning, Nox," she replied.

He extended his hand, offering a paper cup that released wisps of fragrant steam. "Chamomile tea with honey. And a blueberry muffin. I thought you might appreciate a light breakfast for the journey."

The unexpected thoughtfulness caught Serenity off guard. "Thank you," she murmured, genuinely touched by the gesture as she accepted both offerings. The warmth of the cup seeped into her palm, comforting and grounding.

Kane's hand pressed lightly against the small of her back as they approached the vehicle. The casual intimacy of his touch sent a pleasant shiver up her spine.

Serenity slid into the plush leather interior of the town car, Kane following closely behind. As he settled next to her, his thigh pressed against hers, solid and warm. The door closed with a soft thud, sealing them in their private world.

"We should reach Elysium in thirty minutes or less," Nox announced as he slipped into the driver's seat. "Traffic permitting."

The car pulled smoothly away from the curb, joining the morning flow of vehicles. Serenity cradled the paper cup between her hands, savoring the delicate floral aroma of chamomile. She took a cautious sip, the honey-sweetened tea warming her from within.

Through the tinted windows, the Silver District unfolded in its morning glory. Towering glass buildings caught the sunlight, transforming ordinary structures into glittering monuments. Well-dressed vampyrs and humans moved with purpose along the immaculate sidewalks, their lives intersecting yet separate.

Kane's arm draped casually around her shoulders, his fingers tracing idle patterns against her skin.

"Hungry?" she asked, breaking off a piece of her muffin and holding it out to him.

Kane leaned forward, his lips parting as he took the morsel directly from her fingers. His teeth grazed her skin, the contact sending a shiver through her. His tongue darted out, capturing a stray crumb from her fingertip with deliberate slowness.

"Delicious," he murmured, his voice a low rumble that vibrated through her.

Serenity swallowed hard and returned to her own breakfast, nibbling at the muffin while gazing out the window. The soft strains of classical music filled the car's interior—something with violins that sounded vaguely familiar, but she couldn't name. The melody wrapped around her like a silk cocoon, enhancing the dreamlike quality of the morning.

Before she knew it, her muffin and tea were gone, and they were approaching the large metal gate that led into Waterside Cross. They barely paused as the gate opened, letting them through.

Kane's comm device vibrated in his pocket, stealing his attention from her. He pulled it out, frowning slightly at whatever message appeared on the screen. His fingers moved quickly, typing a response.

Serenity turned her focus to the window, watching the scenery transform. The imposing high-rises of the city gradually gave way to more modest structures—ranch-style cottages with weathered shingles and colorful doors dotted the landscape. Vegetation grew thicker, more wild.

The car's smooth glide lulled her into a peaceful trance as Kane continued working on his device until they approached another gate—more imposing than the previous, with tall concrete pillars flanking a heavy metal barrier.

This must lead to the beach, she thought, anticipation accelerating her pulse.

Nox rolled down his window. "Good morning. Kane Draccus and his Elite."

The guard nodded respectfully, checking his computer. After a moment, he looked up. "Clearance confirmed. Enjoy your day, sir."

The gate swung open with a soft mechanical hum. As they passed through, all the windows slid down simultaneously, including a panel in the roof Serenity hadn't noticed before. Fresh air rushed into the car, carrying with it an unfamiliar scent—salty, clean, and powerful.

"Stand up," Kane urged, his hand at the small of her back. "Look through the roof."

"I won't let you fall," he promised, his voice soft.

Cautiously, she rose from her seat, Kane's strong hands steadying her waist as she peeked through the roof opening. The gasp that escaped her lips seemed to come from somewhere deep inside her soul.

Blue. Endless, impossible blue stretching as far as her eyes could see. The ocean spread before her like a living, breathing entity, sunlight dancing across its surface in diamond patterns.

Tears welled in Serenity's eyes as she stared, transfixed by the vastness before her. The ocean's enormity overwhelmed her senses—so much larger than she'd imagined from movies or rooftop glimpses.

Overcome with emotion, she dropped back into her seat. In one fluid motion, she flung herself at Kane, arms wrapping around his neck as she pressed her lips to his. She poured every ounce of gratitude, every flutter of joy into that kiss.

"Thank you," she whispered against his mouth between kisses. "Thank you, thank you, thank you."

Kane's arms encircled her waist, pulling her closer as he returned her kiss with surprising tenderness. When they finally broke apart, his eyes had darkened, reflecting an emotion that made her pulse quicken.

Her joy amplified his satisfaction, his pleasure feeding her happiness, until she couldn't distinguish where her emotions ended and his began.

The car continued down a narrow road with the glittering ocean visible on both sides. Serenity pressed her face against the window, drinking in every detail—the way sunlight fractured across the water's surface, the frothy white edges where waves kissed the shoreline, the occasional seabird diving.

When the car finally slowed, pulling into a parking area of crushed shells and sand, Serenity could barely contain herself.

"We're here," Kane said, warmth in his voice at her obvious excitement.

Nox smoothly exited and came around to open their door. As Serenity stepped out, the full sensory experience of the beach overwhelmed her—the briny scent of salt water, the whisper of waves against sand, the caress of ocean breeze. She inhaled deeply, filling her lungs with air that tasted nothing like the recycled atmosphere of Grove Gardens or Silver District.

Kane's hand found the small of her back as he guided her toward a secluded stretch of pristine shoreline where several canopied daybeds stood like elegant sentinels. Each one offered a haven of shade beneath crisp white fabric that billowed gently. Plush lounge chairs surrounded small tables, creating intimate gathering spaces.

"The entire section is ours for the day," Nox announced, his formal demeanor softening. "I'll be at the Beach Shack across the way if you need anything. Just call, and I'll return immediately."

Serenity could barely contain her excitement. "Thank you, Nox."

He gave a slight nod before turning to leave. "Enjoy your day."

The moment Nox's back was turned, Serenity dropped her beach bag onto the nearest daybed and reached for the hem of her dress. In one fluid motion, she pulled it over her head. Her bare feet sank into the warm sand, the sensation so foreign and delightful that a laugh bubbled up from her. Without waiting, she sprinted toward the water's edge.

Just as her toes were about to touch the foaming surf, strong arms wrapped around her waist from behind.

"Wait for me," Kane's deep voice rumbled against her ear.

She turned in his embrace to find him shirtless, his linen pants exchanged for dark swim shorts. Sunlight played across the defined muscles of his chest and shoulders.

"I've waited my whole life for this," she whispered.

"I know," Kane said, his eyes softening. "But I want to experience this with you."

His hand found hers, fingers interlacing as he led her toward the water. The first touch of ocean foam against Serenity's toes made her gasp—cooler than she'd expected, yet somehow perfect. Each gentle wave lapped higher, sending delicious shivers through her.

"It's wonderful," she breathed, mesmerized by the constant motion.

Kane's grip tightened, steadying her as a larger wave rolled in. The salt water kissed her skin, leaving tiny crystals that sparkled in the sunlight.

"Deeper?" he asked.

Serenity nodded eagerly, and together they waded further, the water rising to her waist. Each step brought new sensations—the subtle pull of sand beneath her feet as waves retreated, the buoyancy that made her feel weightless.

"It's better than I imagined," Serenity breathed, turning to face Kane. "So much better."

His joy at her joy wrapped around her heart.

Kane's eyes crinkled. "Watch this," he said, and in one fluid motion, he ducked beneath the surface.

Serenity gasped, spinning as she searched for him. The water's surface remained unbroken until strong hands gripped her waist from behind, lifting her into the air. She squealed with surprise and delight as Kane emerged, water streaming from his dark hair as he held her aloft.

"Kane!" She laughed, gripping his forearms for balance as he spun her in a circle, water spraying around them like diamonds catching sunlight.

When he finally lowered her, Serenity's body slid against his, the water creating delicious friction. Their lips met, salty from ocean spray, as waves rocked them together.

For hours, they played in the ocean. Kane taught her to float on her back, his strong hands supporting her as she stared up at the endless blue sky. They dove beneath waves, chased each other through shallow waters. When her hunger finally pulled them from the water, they feasted on a picnic—succulent fruits, crusty bread, and cheeses that melted on her tongue.

Later, hidden behind a rocky outcropping, Kane took her with the ocean as their witness. Their pleasure intertwined until separation became impossible. Waves hammered against the rocks as he moved within her, the sea's relentless rhythm echoing their fevered lovemaking.

"I love it here," she whispered against his mouth. "I never want to leave."

As the afternoon sun dipped lower, they retreated to one of the canopied daybeds. Serenity stretched out beside Kane, her skin pleasantly warm from hours in the sun, her muscles deliciously tired from swimming.

"I could stay here forever," she murmured, nestling closer. She traced lazy circles on his chest, marveling at the perfection of him.

Kane's fingers combed through her salt-tangled curls. "I'd give that to you if I could," he said, his voice a low rumble.

The steady rhythm of his unnecessary breathing lulled her toward drowsy contentment. The sound of waves crashing created a hypnotic backdrop. For these precious hours, the world seemed impossibly distant.

Until the harsh electronic trill of his comm device shattered the peace.

Kane tensed beneath her, his body transforming from relaxed to alert in a heartbeat. He reached for the device, frowning at the screen.

Alarm surged through him—sharp, cold, immediate. Something was very wrong.

"I need to deal with this," he said, his voice shifting back to that familiar authoritative tone.

Serenity sat up, pulling the loose cover-up around her shoulders as Kane stepped away. She watched his back stiffen as he spoke in low, urgent tones.

Movement caught her eye—Nox approaching rapidly across the sand, his black attire absurdly out of place. Even from a distance, she could see his expression—grim, tight-lipped, his usual calm cracked by something that looked disturbingly like concern.

Kane stood, moving toward him with predatory grace. Their silhouettes stood stark against the horizon. Serenity couldn't hear their conversation, but she saw Kane's shoulders tighten with each word Nox spoke. His face hardened into the mask she knew all too well—jaw clenched, eyes narrowed, mouth pressed into a thin line.

Fury, protectiveness, cold calculation battered against her. Whatever news Nox brought had killed the carefree man who'd played with her in the waves.

Serenity pulled her knees tighter to her, the salt drying on her skin, suddenly feeling uncomfortable. A chill ran through her despite the warmth of the afternoon sun.

Kane nodded once, sharply, then turned back toward her. Each step he took across the sand seemed heavier than the last.

When he reached the daybed, she knew.

"There's been an incident," he said, his voice tight with barely controlled fury. "We have to leave. Now."

Someone had struck at him. At his city. At his people.

And paradise shattered like glass.

CHAPTER TWENTY-NINE

RHYZAN

A rage so hot it scorched his veins burned through Rhyzan as he stood in front of the smoldering ruins of the Grove Hills clinic. Blackened beams jutted from collapsed walls like broken bones, and the acrid stench of melted plastic and charred flesh still hung in the air despite the Outer City firefighters having quelled the flames thirty minutes ago. The red emergency lights of their vehicles pulsed against the darkening sky, illuminating the tear-streaked faces of survivors huddled in thermal blankets.

Almost everyone had escaped—except for two nurses, both vampyr. They'd died pushing humans through windows as the ceiling collapsed, their immortal bodies finally finding an end amidst the inferno.

Two vampyr who'd given their lives to save humans. In the rebellion's narrative, that shouldn't be possible. Heroes didn't exist among monsters. But he'd seen the bodies, heard the survivors' accounts, and it made the destruction feel even more senseless.

They knew it was a bomb placed directly in the file room, destroying Elite records and new applicant information. Positioned where it would do the most damage. Sullivan was already pulling everyone's personnel files from backup servers, cross-referencing access logs. The threat had likely already infiltrated their ranks. They had to continue to tread carefully.

They'd only known something was going to happen because of Chloe. Early this morning, in the pre-dawn hours while the city still slept, they'd received a secure message from her:

Safe. Position secured with cell. Limited trust established. Group preparing for significant action in past 48 hours. Details unclear. Maintain radio silence. Will contact when secure. - C

As significant as this explosion was, there had to be a calculated purpose beyond the devastation. The acrid taste of ash coated his tongue as he surveyed the wreckage. Serenity was with Kane, enjoying a day on Elysium under the sun, far from any offices worth breaking into. What else could the purpose be?

He took out his comm device and called Evie. She picked up on the first ring, her tone crisp and efficient through the chaos around him.

"I already sent more men to all the other clinics within Celearius. They're all being evacuated as we speak so that they can check for any explosives," Evie said before he could even speak, the tension betraying her calm demeanor.

"Good. Where is Sebastian?"

Evie was silent for a moment, the soft hum of laboratory equipment audible in the background. "He's in his room, resting, where he's been for the past two hours."

"I need you to double-check that he hasn't slipped out while you were in the lab."

"I've already checked. I've had eyes on him the whole time," she replied, each word precise as a scalpel.

"Keep your eyes on Sebastian. I don't care if he's sleeping or meditating—if he so much as twitches wrong, I want to know about it." His tone hardened. "And Evie... be careful around him. There's something not right about any of this."

"I know how to handle myself, Rhyzan," she replied with a hint of indignation. "But I'll keep watch. Call me if you learn anything else."

The line went dead just as a firefighter approached, his face streaked with soot, eyes bloodshot from smoke. The human's uniform bore the Outer City insignia, charred at the edges from battling the inferno.

"Sir," the man said, removing his helmet. "We've evacuated all survivors to Mercy General. Twenty-four humans with various degrees of burns and smoke inhalation, plus six vampyr with more severe injuries. They'll recover, though."

The numbers matched what he expected—a small mercy amid the devastation.

"There's something else," the firefighter continued, lowering his voice. "The blood storage was completely empty. Every single vial, every bag—gone. Not destroyed in the fire, but removed. The storage lockers were opened from the inside. No sign of forced entry."

Ice crystallized in his veins. "When did you discover this?"

"Just now, during our final sweep. The blood storage vault is reinforced—designed to withstand fires. The outer door was charred but intact. Inside..." The man shook his head. "Clean as a whistle. Whoever did this knew exactly what they wanted."

"Thank you for bringing this to my attention." He kept his tone level despite the chill spreading through him. "Continue your work. I'll handle this personally."

The firefighter nodded, returning to the smoldering ruins as Rhyzan stepped away, pulling his phone from his pocket. Sullivan answered on the second ring.

"Sullivan, we've got a situation beyond the bombing. The blood stores at Grove Hills have been emptied. Not destroyed. Taken."

Sullivan's curse came through sharp and clear. "How much are we talking?"

"Everything. The entire clinic's supply." He turned away from the ruins, lowering his tone. "And there's more—no forced entry on the vault. This was someone with access or credentials."

"Sebastian?" Sullivan's manner hardened at the name.

"That's my first thought, but Evie swears he's been in his quarters the entire time." His jaw tightened as he glanced back at the destruction. "I don't understand this level of carnage for a blood heist. They could have taken it without the explosion, without the deaths. Unless..."

He paused, the pieces shifting in his mind like a puzzle he couldn't quite solve.

"Unless the blood was secondary," he continued slowly. "Unless this whole thing—the bombing, the theft, the casualties—is designed to force Kane's hand. To make him move in a specific direction."

A heavy silence stretched between them before Sullivan spoke again, his words unnervingly calm. "Unfortunately, Rhyzan, the day is still young. I suspect this is merely the opening act."

"What are you not telling me?"

"This could be a distraction to cover something bigger about to happen," Sullivan replied. "Or it could be bait. Either way, they're controlling the board, and we're reacting exactly as they want us to."

Each possibility more disturbing than the last. If Sullivan was right—if this was all orchestrated to manipulate Kane's movements—then what was the real target?

"Have you updated Kane on the situation?" Sullivan asked.

He stared at the smoldering ruins, the acrid smell of destruction filling his nostrils with each breath. "No. He's at Elysium with his Elite. He's my next call."

"Agreed. Contact me after you speak with him. We need to coordinate our response carefully—if they're trying to control Kane's movements, we need to understand why before we play into their hands."

"Understood."

As soon as the line went dead, he dialed Nox, hating having to interrupt what he knew was Kane's first moment of peace in gods knew how long.

The line rang once. Twice. Three times.

Then Nox's measured tones came through instead of Kane's. "Rhyzan. I assume this is urgent."

"It is." He kept his words clipped, professional, even as guilt gnawed at him. "I need to speak with Kane immediately. There's been an incident."

A pause. Then Nox's reply, quieter now, edged with understanding: "I'll get him."

Muffled sounds on the other end—footsteps across sand, the distant crash of waves, low conversation he couldn't quite make out.

"Rhyzan." Kane's tone came through the line, already hardened back into the voice of the Head of the Human Vampyr Council. Whatever peace he'd found had already fled. "Report."

And just like that, paradise ended.

He began recounting the devastation, knowing that somewhere, whoever had orchestrated this was counting on exactly that.

CHAPTER THIRTY

KANE

The taste of ash filled Kane's mouth—not real, but a ghost of memory from centuries of war and destruction. The bitterness coated his tongue as the town car glided through the streets of Waterside Cross, leaving Elysium's paradise behind with every mile. Each heartbeat pulsed with barely contained fury.

Two vampyrs dead. Protecting humans. And for what?

His phone burned against his palms, the images from the bombing still searing his vision. The Grove Hills clinic—reduced to rubble and smoke, bodies being pulled from the wreckage, human survivors weeping as they clutched at the remnants of vampyr saviors who'd shielded them with immortal bodies that proved, in the end, not immortal enough.

Kane's jaw clenched so tightly he could feel his teeth grinding. He stared resolutely through the window, unable—unwilling—to look at Serenity across from him. The jasmine-and-rose fragrance of her skin, still carrying traces of ocean salt, now felt like a mockery. Only moments ago, that scent had been intoxicating. Now it made his stomach turn.

Her fear bled into him—sharp and acidic, cutting through his rage. She was terrified, though whether of the bombing or of him, he couldn't tell.

His phone buzzed again in his hand.

Rhyzan.

Casualties rising. Third vampyr confirmed dead.

Kane's fingers flew across the screen. Suspects?

Working on it. Explosive signature matched previous HL attacks.

Human Liberation. The rebels. The people Serenity worked for.

His rational mind knew she couldn't have done this. She'd been with him the entire night and day, wrapped in his arms as waves crashed around them. But the network she belonged to—they could have done this. Would have done this.

"Sir?" Nox's tone cut through his spiral of thoughts. Kane's head snapped up, meeting Nox's gaze in the mirror.

"I'll stop at Evie's to drop off Serenity, then cut through the Galway District as Rhy instructed to avoid the main traffic," Nox said, his manner carefully neutral. "The back roads will be faster with all the emergency vehicles heading to Grove Hills."

Kane nodded, grateful for the practical suggestion that would give him space to think. "Fine."

The word came out harsher than he'd intended. He felt Serenity flinch as though he'd struck her, her fingers tightening in her lap.

Perfect. Let Evie deal with her for now. And if Sebastian had recovered enough to talk, perhaps the two of them would reveal something when they thought no one was listening. Deyja's attack at the Elite Ball, now the bombing—the timing felt calculated, orchestrated. He needed to know if they were connected.

Send a surveillance team to Evie's, he typed to Rhyzan. Full audio monitoring.

Kane slipped his phone into his pocket and finally allowed himself to look directly at Serenity. The joy that had illuminated her features at the beach had vanished completely, replaced by a shadow of concern. Her dark lashes swept downward, avoiding his stare. When she looked up, her honey-brown eyes glistened with unshed tears. The sadness there cut through him despite his fury, a sliver of ice piercing the heat of his anger.

Kane forced himself to look away before her emotions could manipulate him further.

The car turned sharply, and Kane's attention snapped to their surroundings. Nox veered onto a side street, taking them past the half-constructed building where Kane had taken her that night after the Ball, where she had been his completely, even if only for those hours.

The memory sliced through Kane's defenses. He remembered the racing of her heart, her uninhibited moans, and the way her body had yielded to his rough touch. How real it had felt. How genuine.

Ahead, a field stretched beside the construction site—once lush but now reduced to patchy, yellowed grass and trampled dirt from construction vehicles. Rolling hills created gentle slopes across the landscape.

"Kane."

Serenity's tone broke through his thoughts, soft yet urgent. He turned toward her, prepared to maintain the cold wall he'd erected between them.

But something in her look made his blood freeze. Her eyes weren't focused on him but past him, out the window, widening with terror.

Pure fear exploded from her—primal, immediate, overwhelming.

Every instinct in Kane's body screamed danger at once. The hairs on his neck stood rigid. A flash of movement in his peripheral vision. The squeal of tires. The acrid scent of burning rubber.

He lunged across the space between them, wrapping his arms around Serenity and pulling her against him. His body moved on pure instinct, centuries of survival hardwired into his reflexes.

Metal shrieked against metal as a massive black SUV rammed into the town car's side with devastating force. Glass exploded inward, showering them with crystalline shards. The impact sent shockwaves through the vehicle, and Kane felt the sickening lurch as they left the pavement.

The world tilted violently. Through the windows, sky and earth traded places in dizzying rotation. The car rolled—once, twice—tumbling down the gentle slope of the field like a child's toy discarded by an angry god.

Kane's muscles strained, holding Serenity against him as they were thrown against doors, ceiling, and seats in rapid succession.

Finally, with a bone-jarring crash, the vehicle slammed to a stop on its side, metal groaning in protest.

Kane's ears rang with a high-pitched whine that gradually gave way to an eerie silence broken only by the tick-tick-tick of cooling metal and the shallow rasp of breathing. Blood trickled down Serenity's temple, her eyes wide and glassy with shock. Jagged glass fragments glittered in her hair like deadly diamonds.

Her pain registered sharp but manageable. No major injuries. Her pulse fluttered visibly at her throat—too fast, but there. Alive.

Relief flooded through him with unexpected intensity.

"Can you move?" Kane demanded, his tone guttural.

She nodded once, a jerky motion. "I-I think so."

"Don't move." He gripped her shoulder. "I need to see what's happening."

Serenity nodded as he shifted carefully, pushing down the window partition to check on Nox. When he looked through, he found the front of the vehicle empty—but the driver's door hung open, torn from its hinges.

Kane glanced out the front windshield. They'd rolled down into the field, landing perhaps thirty yards from the road. The black SUV was nowhere in sight, but tire tracks scarred the grass leading back toward the main street.

Nox must have jumped out during the roll—likely pursuing their attackers on foot. Good. If anyone could track them down, it was Nox.

Beyond the field, a line of trees offered cover. If things went south, they'd need to reach that shelter.

Kane moved back to Serenity, who was leaning against what was now the floor of the car, trying to wipe crimson from her head and leg with trembling fingers.

The scent hit him then—her blood, sweet and potent, flooding his senses. The cuts weren't deep, but each one threatened to push him over the edge. His fangs descended involuntarily, hunger clawing at his throat.

Kane bit into his finger, feeling his fang pierce through flesh. He smeared the dark, viscous blood across her wounds, watching as the skin knitted together beneath his touch. He prayed it would take some time before the effects overwhelmed her system—they needed her clearheaded.

Once her wounds sealed into faint pink lines, he met her gaze. "We need to get out of here. I need to find Nox, see if he was injured."

She nodded, her pupils already dilating slightly—the first sign his blood was affecting her system.

Kane rose in one fluid motion, his fingers wrapping around the door handle above them. With a grunt, he pushed, metal groaning in protest before the door tore free with a screech of twisted hinges, crashing onto the ground in a cloud of dust.

Cautiously, he lifted his head into the open air.

The field stretched before him, tall grass swaying in the breeze. No sign of Nox anywhere—he must still be pursuing the SUV. The construction site loomed to their left, its skeletal framework of steel beams casting long shadows in the afternoon sun.

Too many hiding places. Too much cover for an ambush.

With effortless grace, Kane pulled himself from the wreckage, then reached back for Serenity.

Her warm fingers clasped his forearm, trembling slightly as he hoisted her up until she perched on the car's exposed side. He dropped to the ground with a soft thud and was reaching up to help her down when white-hot agony tore through his shoulder, the impact staggering him.

Serenity's scream tore through the air. "Kane!"

Her terror crashed into him like a physical blow.

His name became a desperate prayer on her lips as another bullet ripped through his back, burrowing deep into muscles and sinew. The distant crack of gunfire finally registered in his ears, followed by the metallic click of a chamber reloading.

Kane pivoted toward the construction site, his preternatural senses pinpointing the shooter's location among the framework of steel beams. The scent of gunpowder hung acrid in the air as he took one determined step forward, only to freeze at the sound of Serenity falling from the vehicle.

He spun back, lunging to catch her before she hit the ground, when another bullet tore through his thigh with surgical precision. The impact drove him to his knees on the rough, debris-strewn ground.

Silver.

The realization came with the distinctive burn spreading through his veins like liquid fire, his immortal flesh already blackening around the wound. Poison crept outward in dark tendrils beneath his skin, yet his focus remained on Serenity's ashen face. Crimson matted her hair where it had fallen across her forehead, but the bullet had missed her.

Relief flooded his system, momentarily dulling his own agony.

Though his vision was beginning to blur at the edges, Kane scanned the perimeter, catching the telltale glint of a rifle barrel behind a steel beam on the sixth floor. The distance—impossible now with the toxin eating through his system.

Serenity's words cut through the fog of pain. "Kane. Kane, we have to move, or they're going to kill you." Her gaze darted over his shoulder, pupils dilated with fear, before locking on his face. "I don't think they'll shoot me."

Kane's silver-hazed stare met hers, the veins around his eyes darkening to charcoal as the venom spread. Sweat beaded on his pale skin.

Her certainty reached him—desperate, but real. She believed it. And she might be right.

But the thought of a bullet tearing through her soft flesh made his stomach clench.

Gritting his teeth against the searing agony, he pushed himself upright, muscles trembling as his good leg took his weight. The world tilted and swam before him, trees and sky bleeding together like watercolors in rain.

The distant metallic click of a rifle being readied echoed across the field.

Before he could react, Serenity lunged forward, pressing against his much larger frame. The crack of gunfire split the air, followed by the dull thunk of a bullet embedding itself in the car's metal frame inches from where they stood.

His instincts screamed to push her aside, yet his poisoned muscles betrayed him.

Her determination blazed fierce—she would not let him die.

"Move," he growled, but she pressed harder against him, stubborn and terrifyingly mortal.

Rage and gratitude warred within him as he dragged her toward the treeline, his arm locked around her waist. He hated needing her, hated wanting her, hated how her pulse hammered against his skin like a promise he couldn't keep.

When they reached the woods, he collapsed against rough bark, breath ragged. The toxin crawled through his veins like ice-fire, a familiar enemy he'd survived before—but never with someone he couldn't afford to lose watching him fall.

Serenity dropped to her knees in the damp soil before him, her dress darkening where they pressed into the earth.

"Your comm device—where is it?" Her words shook, but her eyes remained steady.

"Right pocket," Kane managed through clenched teeth, the venom creating a metallic taste in his mouth.

Her fingers brushed against his thigh as she reached into his pocket, sending an electric jolt through his weakened nerves. She quickly searched the device, then pressed a button.

"Rhyzan. We need help," she said, her tone beginning to fade in and out. "We were rammed by a car... Kane's been shot... I don't know where Nox is."

A pause as she listened, her free hand unconsciously gripping Kane's arm.

"The bullets—I think they were silver... his veins are turning black." Another pause. "I'm not sure—maybe one or two. Yes, okay. Will that work?... Okay, hurry."

The device beeped as she ended the call. She rose slowly, towering over his slumped form, her shadow falling across his face. In the dappled forest light, her expression shifted between determination and terror, her pupils wide and dark.

Her resolve crystallized—fierce and unwavering. Whatever Rhyzan had told her, she was going to do it.

Kane would have given his immortal soul to read the thoughts flickering behind those eyes before she sank back to her knees, fallen leaves crunching beneath her.

"You need to drink. I know you said it was too soon, but if you don't, you'll die. Rhyzan said this will slow the poison in your system until they can get here."

She tilted her neck and leaned down toward him until he felt her skin pressed against his lips.

Kane recoiled, even as his body screamed for relief. The toxin clawed through him like barbed wire, yet the thought of taking her blood—so soon after last time, risking the effects on her system—made him hesitate.

Serenity pressed her neck against his mouth, pleading. His fangs descended involuntarily, pricking her skin.

The first drop touched his tongue, and shame collided with desperate need.

He growled, trying to turn away, but when her other hand cradled his head, something broke inside him.

Her love poured into him—unconditional, terrifying, real.

Kane surrendered, drinking deeply while hating himself with each swallow. It was too soon to take this much. Her system would be flooded with his essence, the effects amplified beyond what was safe.

But the alternative was death, and she wouldn't allow it.

Slowly, he forced himself to stop—not nearly enough to fully counteract the venom, but enough to give him a fighting chance. He would make it enough. It would be some time before Rhyzan arrived with backup, and he was still weak from the toxin.

But he wouldn't let anything else happen to her.

"We need to keep moving," he said, pushing himself off the tree, knowing there were still rebels nearby. "They'll be coming after us."

Serenity nodded, her expression serious. She was proving to be far more resilient than he'd expected.

Just as Kane pushed against the tree to stand, two shots cracked through the stillness of the forest. Pain exploded in his side, then his chest, the impacts slamming him back against the rough bark. The world tilted sickeningly as he slid down, legs giving way beneath him.

"Kane!" Serenity's scream pierced the air. She lunged forward, throwing her weight over his as he collapsed to the forest floor, pressing against his wounds.

The venom worked with terrifying efficiency now, tendrils of paralysis creeping outward from each bullet wound. His fingers twitched uselessly against the earth. The taste of her blood still lingered on his tongue, a cruel reminder of what he stood to lose.

Boots crunched on fallen leaves, surrounding them in a tightening circle. Six figures materialized from the forest shadows, clad in military-grade fatigues with faces obscured by tactical masks. Their weapons—sleek, modern rifles—trained on him and Serenity with deadly precision.

The paralysis crawled up Kane's limbs, stealing his mobility inch by inch. His muscles locked rigid. He tried to lift his arm, to push Serenity behind him, but his body refused to respond.

The toxin had rendered him utterly helpless.

"Get off him," one of the masked figures barked, reaching for Serenity's shoulder with gloved fingers.

She shrugged violently away from the touch, still draped protectively over Kane's paralyzed form. "Don't touch me!" Her tone cracked with desperation as she pressed herself closer.

Kane's jaw clenched in frustration—the only movement left to him. He couldn't speak, couldn't fight, couldn't protect her.

The masked figure reached for her again, more forcefully this time. "Move, or we shoot him in the head."

"Serenity."

The name hung in the air, spoken with familiarity that made Kane's blood run cold despite the fire racing through him. One of the masked figures stepped forward, lowering the rifle slightly as gloved hands reached up to remove the tactical mask.

The face revealed was young—early twenties—with hazel eyes hardened by life in the Outer City and a jaw set with grim determination. Sandy brown hair fell across his forehead as he stared at Serenity with an expression that mixed relief and regret.

Kane watched through his fading vision as Serenity's body tensed above his. She turned her head slowly, her breath catching with an audible gasp that vibrated through her chest where it pressed against his paralyzed form.

"Jax?"

Her shock, her confusion—but no recognition of betrayal. She knew this person. Cared for him, even.

This was her contact. And from the way the young man's expression softened, their connection ran deeper than a simple alliance.

He was helpless, paralyzed, dying—and her past had just walked out of the shadows to reclaim her.

CHAPTER THIRTY-ONE

"Jax?" The name escaped Serenity's lips as a whisper, her heart stuttering.

Time seemed to slow as she stared at the familiar face among the rebels. Jax—her childhood friend, her confidant, her best friend since they were six years old—stood before her, rifle pointed at Kane.

"Get up, Serenity." Jax's voice was harder than she remembered, stripped of its usual warmth. "We need to move. Now."

Her legs trembled as she slowly rose to her feet, but she planted herself firmly in front of Kane's slumped form. The forest floor shifted beneath her, damp leaves clinging to her knees where her dress had pressed into the dirt. Kane's labored breathing behind her was the only indication he was still conscious.

His pain radiated into her—sharp, burning, relentless.

"What are you doing here?" Her words sounded foreign to her own ears—thin and reedy with shock.

Jax stepped closer, lowering his weapon slightly. "Getting you out, like we planned. Like you wanted." His hazel eyes darted between her and Kane, hardening when they landed on the vampyr. "Step aside, Ren."

The old nickname hit her hard. How many times had she imagined this moment? Being rescued, going home, returning to her family? But now the fantasy tasted like ash in her mouth.

"Put your weapons down," she demanded, glancing at the other masked figures surrounding them. None complied.

Jax's expression hardened. "This isn't negotiable, Ren. We need to leave now."

Serenity's attention snapped back to Kane, and her breath caught. The silver poison had spread visibly through his system, black veins crawling up his face like dark lightning. His silver-blue eyes had dulled to a stormy gray, the skin around them tight with agony. Each labored breath seemed to cost him tremendous effort.

She felt him slipping—the awareness dimming like a candle flame guttering in the wind.

She couldn't leave him like this.

"My family," Serenity gasped, her mind finally catching up through the shock. "Jax, tell me you got my family out first."

Hesitation, guilt—flickered across Jax's face before his expression hardened again. "You were the priority. We'll get them later."

"What?" The word tore from her throat. "No. That wasn't the deal. My family first—always my family first." Her voice rose, panic clawing up her spine. "You have to go back for them now!"

"There is no now," Jax snapped, taking another step toward her. "Your mother and sister are safe where they are for the moment. You're not. The entire city is going to be looking for you in about five minutes."

"I don't care!" Serenity's hands balled into fists at her sides. Heat rushed to her face as rage and betrayal collided inside her. "They promised me! They swore to me they would get them out first!"

"Less than two minutes," one of the masked figures called out, voice muffled behind tactical gear. "We need to move. Just take her."

"Fuck!" Jax growled, patience evaporating as his gaze darted between Kane and the treeline. "We don't have time for this!"

"I'm not leaving him," Serenity said, her voice breaking as she backed up until her legs pressed against Kane's slumped form.

Before Serenity could drop to her knees, Jax lunged forward, grabbing her around the waist. She felt herself being yanked away from Kane, her fingers desperately clawing at the earth to stay near him.

"No!" The scream tore from her throat as she thrashed against Jax's grip. Her nails dug into his forearm, drawing blood, but his hold only tightened. With a grunt, he heaved her over his shoulder. The world tilted sickeningly as blood rushed to her head.

"Let me down!" She pounded her fists against his back, kicking wildly. Her gaze remained fixed on Kane's paralyzed form. His eyes—those beautiful silver-blue eyes now clouded with pain—followed her movements, the only part of him that could still respond.

Jax's arm clamped around her thighs like an iron band, immobilizing her lower body as he turned to face Kane. With his free hand, he raised his weapon, pointing it directly at Kane's head.

"If you don't stop struggling and come with us now, I will put a bullet through his skull," Jax said, his fingers tightening on the trigger. "I swear to God, Ren."

The world stopped. Serenity's breath caught as she stared at the barrel pressed against Kane's temple. The black metal looked obscene against his pale skin, now mapped with dark veins spreading beneath the surface. Her struggling ceased instantly, her body going limp over Jax's shoulder.

"Please," she whispered over the rushing in her ears. "Don't hurt him."

Jax's grip on her thighs loosened slightly. "Are you going to cooperate?"

She nodded, unable to tear her gaze from Kane's face. His eyes—now clouded with pain—locked with hers, conveying a feeling that made her heart splinter. Was it permission? Forgiveness? Or simply goodbye?

His love wrapped around her one final time—fierce, protective, absolute.

"Yes," she managed, her voice cracking. "Just... don't shoot."

Jax lowered his weapon and turned away from Kane's prone form, carrying her into the forest. As branches whipped against her face, Serenity gasped for air that wouldn't come. Kane's image burned in her mind—those blackened veins spreading across his skin, his eyes following her as she was taken from him.

She could still feel him—barely—a faint pulse of life that grew weaker with each yard of distance.

"Kane needs help," she said, her voice breaking. "The silver will kill him."

"That's the point," one of the masked men muttered somewhere ahead.

She twisted on Jax's shoulder, trying to see his face. "Jax, please. You have to go back. He'll die."

"Good." The single word fell from his lips like a stone. "One less bloodsucker in the world."

The cruelty in his tone—from the boy who'd shared his lunch with her when she had none, who'd held her hand at her father's funeral—felt like betrayal. This wasn't the Jax she knew. Or maybe it was, and she'd been blind all along.

After what seemed like an eternity, Jax finally set her down. Before she could react, he grabbed her wrists, yanking them behind her back. Something thin and plastic bit into her skin as he bound her hands together.

"What are you doing?" She twisted against the restraint, the plastic wire cutting deeper.

"Insurance," Jax muttered, his hazel eyes avoiding hers. "Can't risk you running back to him."

Serenity's throat constricted, tears threatening to spill as Jax pulled her forward. Her thoughts remained with Kane, alone in the forest, poison spreading through his veins. Would Rhyzan find him in time?

The awareness had faded to almost nothing now—a thread so thin she could barely sense it.

They trudged through dense underbrush for what felt like hours but was likely only minutes, until the towering wall of Celearius loomed before them. Its imposing concrete structure, normally viewed from within, looked even more formidable from this angle—a stark boundary between worlds.

The group stopped abruptly at what appeared to be an unremarkable patch of ground near the base of the wall. Two of the masked men dropped to their knees, frantically brushing away dirt and debris to reveal a circular metal cover half-buried in the earth.

"Manhole," Jax explained tersely, his grip tightening on her arm. "Old drainage system. Predates the wall."

The men worked quickly. One descended first, disappearing into the darkness. Another grabbed her arm, pulling her forward.

"I'll help you down," Jax said, his voice softer now as he guided her toward the opening.

Serenity peered into the hole, the stench of mildew and stagnant water rising to greet her. Her stomach lurched, but before she could protest, hands pushed at her back, forcing her forward. With her hands bound behind her, she couldn't catch herself as she tumbled through the opening. A strangled cry escaped her lips as she fell, only to be caught roughly by unseen hands below.

"Got her," a gruff voice announced as her feet touched slick concrete.

The dim light filtering through the manhole illuminated a narrow tunnel stretching into darkness. Water trickled somewhere in the distance, the sound echoing against stone walls. Jax dropped down beside her, his landing far more graceful than her own. One by one, the other men followed until only one remained above.

"Thirty minutes," the man above called down before sliding the heavy metal cover back into place with a reverberating clang that sealed them in darkness.

The thread snapped.

Serenity gasped as the awareness severed completely, the sudden absence hitting her like a physical blow. Her knees gave out, but Jax caught her before she could fall.

"What's wrong?" he demanded, concern breaking through his harsh demeanor.

"Nothing," she lied, her voice hollow. But inside, she was screaming. The emptiness where he'd been felt like a wound that would never heal.

A flashlight beam cut through the darkness, revealing damp brick walls coated with decades of slime and mildew. The tunnel stretched before them like the throat of some ancient beast, swallowing light and hope with equal hunger. Serenity stumbled forward as Jax pushed her from behind, her bound wrists making balance nearly impossible on the slick concrete.

"Keep moving," he ordered over the constant drip of water.

The tunnel narrowed as they progressed, forcing them to walk single file. Moisture seeped through her thin dress, chilling her to the bone despite the summer heat that had warmed her skin hours ago at the beach. The perfect day now seemed like a distant dream from another lifetime—a beautiful memory shattered by bullets and betrayal.

Her feet slipped on algae-covered stone, and she would have fallen if not for Jax's hand gripping her arm. His hold tightened, fingers digging into her flesh as he hauled her forward. "Almost there."

They rounded a corner where the tunnel widened into a small chamber. Another metal ladder stretched upward toward a second manhole cover. Dim light filtered through the edges, casting ghostly patterns on the damp walls.

"This is it," one of the masked men whispered, holstering his weapon to climb the ladder. The scrape of metal against metal grated through the chamber as he pushed the cover aside.

Serenity stared upward, the plastic cutting deeper into her wrists as Jax pushed her toward the ladder. "How am I supposed to climb with my hands tied?"

"You're not." Before she could protest, Jax crouched and hoisted her over his shoulder again, her stomach pressed against his collarbone. The sudden motion knocked the breath from her lungs.

Her body bounced against him as he ascended the ladder one-handed, his free arm wrapped around her thighs. Each rung brought them closer to whatever waited above.

As Jax reached the top of the ladder, harsh sunlight blinded Serenity. He hefted her off his shoulder onto a narrow concrete platform that jutted out from the exterior wall. The platform couldn't have been more than six feet wide, barely enough room for their group to stand. Serenity's legs shook beneath her as she regained her balance.

A small motorboat bobbed in the murky water below, tethered to a rusty metal ring embedded in the concrete. The vessel looked old—peeling paint and weathered wood that had seen better decades. One of the masked men climbed down first, steadying the craft as it rocked against the platform's edge.

"Down you go," Jax muttered, placing his hands on her waist.

Before she could protest, he lifted her again and lowered her into the waiting arms below. Without her hands to balance, she stumbled, nearly toppling into the brackish water as the boat tilted precariously under her weight.

"Sit," the man ordered, pushing her toward a bench that ran along the center of the boat. She obeyed, her knees weak from exertion and fear. Jax dropped down beside her, followed by the remaining men. The last one untied the rope, and with a sputtering roar, the engine came to life.

The boat pulled away from the wall, cutting through murky water as Celearius loomed behind them. Serenity stared at the massive structure, its concrete facade stretching toward the sky like a monument to humanity's fear.

Time blurred as the boat skimmed across the water. The late afternoon sun beat down on them, turning the spray into diamonds that mocked her misery. Minutes or hours, she couldn't tell.

She kept reaching for it instinctively—trying to feel Kane, to know if he was still alive. But there was nothing. Just void.

Serenity stared blankly at the water as they passed the pristine shores of Elysium. The island beach where she'd been with Kane just hours ago looked like a mirage in the distance, its white sand gleaming in the fading light.

The boat curved around the island, cutting through the choppy waves with enough force to send spray across her face. The salt water stung her eyes, but she welcomed the distraction. As they passed the docks of Waterside Park, she could see a few guards strolling the docks, oblivious to the drama unfolding on the water.

"Heads down," one of the masked men ordered as they sped past.

Jax's hand pressed against the back of her neck, forcing her to bow her head. Through the curtain of her salt-crusted hair, she could see the shoreline up ahead—wild and untamed, nothing like the manicured beaches of the city.

The boat lurched as it scraped against shore, the jarring impact rattling through Serenity's already aching body. Coarse sand crunched beneath the hull. Strong hands gripped her upper arms, hauling her upright before her feet could find purchase. She stumbled as they dragged her over the side, her bare feet plunging into frigid water that sent shockwaves up her legs.

"Move," someone growled behind her, shoving her forward through ankle-deep water toward the barren shoreline.

The sand burned against her cold, wet feet as they forced her up the beach. Wind whipped her salt-crusted hair across her face, stinging her eyes. Beyond the dunes, partially hidden by scrubby vegetation, sat a rusted tan truck, its paint weathered to match the surrounding landscape. If she hadn't been looking directly at it, she might have missed it entirely.

"In," Jax commanded, yanking open the rear door.

Someone shoved her from behind, sending her sprawling face-first into the truck's filthy cargo area. Without her hands to break her fall, her cheek slammed against the metal floor, sending stars bursting behind her eyes. Before she could recover, a body dropped down beside her, the truck dipping under the added weight.

The door slammed shut, plunging the cargo area into semi-darkness. The only light filtered through a small, dirt-smudged window separating the cab from the cargo hold. Serenity struggled to sit upright, her bound hands making the simple movement a challenge. Her shoulders screamed in protest as she finally managed to prop herself against the metal wall, knees drawn to her chest.

The truck roared to life, lurching forward with enough force to slam her back against the wall. Gravel crunched beneath tires as they accelerated, each bump in the road sending jolts of pain through her already battered body. The smell of rust, oil, and sweat filled her nostrils, making her stomach churn.

Through the dim light, she could make out Jax's profile as he settled on the opposite side of the cargo area. He'd removed his mask, revealing the familiar face that now seemed to belong to a stranger. His hazel eyes studied her with an intensity that made her skin crawl.

She became aware then of something odd—or rather, the absence of something. Kane's blood had healed her cuts after the crash, and she'd drunk from him to save his life. By now, she should be overwhelmed with hypersensitivity, her senses amplified to the point of distraction. But she felt... normal. Tired, aching, traumatized—but not the overwhelming sensory overload she'd experienced before.

Was it because she'd taken less? Or had something changed between them?

"You alright?" Jax finally broke the silence, his voice cutting through the rumble of the truck's engine.

Serenity turned her face away, staring at the rusted metal wall.

"Where are you taking me?" she asked, ignoring his question. Her voice sounded strange to her own ears—raspy from screaming, devoid of its usual warmth. "When are we going to get my family?"

Jax leaned forward, the dim light from the cab's window casting shadows across his features. "We already have them, Ren."

The words took a moment to register. Relief flooded through her so suddenly that her vision blurred. "What? You have them? Mom and Beth? They're safe?"

"They're safe," Jax confirmed, his expression softening slightly. "We got them out this morning, before we came for you."

This morning. While she'd been waking in Kane's arms. While they'd driven to Elysium, played in the ocean, and made love on the sand. Her family had been extracted to safety.

"You lied," she said, the realization settling like lead in her stomach. "Before. You said we'd get them later."

Jax had the grace to look uncomfortable. "I needed you to cooperate. Couldn't risk you fighting us if you thought your family was still in danger."

The manipulation stung, even though the end result was what she'd wanted. "Where are they now?"

Jax shifted, his boots scraping against the metal floor. "Somewhere secure. Outside the walls, away from vampyr reach."

They were safe. The thought should have brought pure relief, but instead it twisted painfully in her chest.

"Why now?" she asked after a moment. "Why did you come for me today? I was supposed to get more information about the weapon plans."

"I'm not sure." Jax's gaze shifted away from hers, fixing on some point beyond her shoulder. "Things changed. Plans accelerated."

The truck hit a bump, jostling them. His answer felt hollow, rehearsed. The Jax she knew couldn't lie to save his life—always rubbing the back of his neck when he tried, a tell she'd called him out on countless times.

And there it was—his hand moving unconsciously toward his neck before he caught himself.

"Were you always part of the rebellion?" she asked, watching his face carefully. "All this time?"

Jax's expression hardened, jaw tightening beneath stubbled skin. "No. But I would have been if they'd come to me sooner."

His answer didn't surprise her. She knew what the vampyrs had taken from him—his parents, his baby sister, all killed in the final days before the treaty. His hatred had always run deep.

They drove for what felt like hours, the sun sinking toward the horizon and painting the sky in shades of orange and pink through the grimy window. Serenity leaned her head against the cool metal wall of the truck, trying to find a position that didn't make her bound wrists scream with pain. The vehicle bounced over increasingly rough terrain, each jolt sending fresh waves of discomfort through her body.

By the time the truck finally slowed, twilight had settled over the landscape. She lifted her head, peering through the small window. Through the gathering darkness, she caught glimpses of a massive rock formation looming ahead—weathered stone jutting from the earth like the spine of some ancient beast.

Levee's.

They were outside Celearius—beyond the walls of Grove Gardens, in the untamed territory where rebellion festered.

The back doors swung open, flooding the space with the last rays of dying sunlight. Serenity squinted against the sudden brightness as rough hands pulled her from the truck. Her legs, stiff from hours of confinement, nearly buckled beneath her.

"I know you have questions. I do too, but Starr and Damon need to see you right now," Jax said. He reached into his pocket and pulled out a knife, cutting the plastic restraints on her wrists.

She rubbed her wrists gratefully, the skin raw and angry where the plastic had bitten into flesh. "Thank you."

He nodded, then gestured toward the familiar rock formation. "Come on."

She followed him to Levee's entrance, where he gave the doorman the passcode. They entered through the familiar path, and Serenity's heart clenched with memories of the last time she'd been here—dancing with Tori, taking shots with Clyde, such a carefree moment.

She followed Jax down the short walkway until they reached the main bar area. It felt eerie being there when the space was empty, even though the smell of sweat and yeasty beer still hung in the air. She looked over to the empty back booth where they'd sat on her last visit. It was only a few weeks ago—crazy how fast time moved.

How much had changed since then. She'd been terrified of Kane, desperate to protect her family, willing to do anything to survive.

Now she'd left him dying in a forest, and the absence of him felt like a piece of her soul had been carved away.

"Are my mom and Beth here?" she asked, her voice cracking.

"No, but they're safe. Come, Starr and Damon need to talk to you."

She followed him as he led her through a door on the left of the bar. Inside, Starr—barely five feet tall—slammed her palm onto plans spread across the table, her blonde hair swinging forward as she leaned in. "We have to confirm, or it's pointless. It's the only way," she hissed.

Across from her, Damon—at least six-four with hair as black as oil—crossed his muscled arms. He opened his mouth to argue when the door creaked. Both heads snapped up.

"Serenity." Starr straightened, authority radiating from her slight frame despite having to tilt her chin to meet Serenity's eyes. "Finally." Her delicate fingers gestured with unmistakable command, and even the towering Damon shifted to make space for her.

"Where are my mom and sister?" Serenity asked, her voice steadier than she expected.

Starr's piercing blue eyes assessed her with clinical precision. "They're safe. We took them to our headquarters in the Dead City early this morning, while you were still sleeping."

While she'd been wrapped in Kane's arms, warm and safe and loved. While they'd been planning their perfect day. Her family had been extracted to freedom.

Guilt should be eating at her, but all she could feel was relief that they were okay—and a bone-deep ache for what she'd lost in exchange.

"I want to see them. Now."

"You will," Starr assured her, but her tone carried command rather than comfort. "But first, we need you to tell us what you know about these."

She gestured to the papers spread across the table.

Serenity stepped forward, her bare feet silent against the stone floor. The plans sprawled across the table in organized chaos—diagrams, equations, and detailed sketches of what appeared to be weapons. Her breath caught as her gaze landed on the second set of plans.

The handwriting—those distinctive sweeping g's and sharp, angular t's—was as familiar to her as her own.

Her father's handwriting.

The world tilted. Her father. The man who'd taught her to read, who'd sung her to sleep, who'd died believing he was protecting her future—his handwriting, here, on plans for a weapon designed to kill every vampyr in Celearius.

Memories flooded her—sitting at his knee while he sketched formulas, the patient way he'd explained scientific principles she was too young to understand, the pride in his eyes when she showed interest in his work.

He'd been working on this. All those late nights in his shed, all those careful notes he'd hidden away. He'd been building a weapon to destroy the species that had enslaved them.

And now that weapon sat before her, waiting.

This is what Sebastian had been trying to tell her. The plans that could change everything were these—a weapon that would produce a chemical compound that would destroy all the vampyrs. Not just in Celearius. Everywhere.

Kane's face flashed in her mind—his laugh at the beach, his tenderness as he'd healed her wounds, the way his eyes had followed her even as poison paralyzed him. The feel of his arms around her, the taste of his kiss.

She glanced at Damon and Starr, their eager eyes fixed on her. They didn't know which blueprint was real, but she did. She could see it in her father's careful notations, in the slight variations between the two sets of plans. One was the original. The other was a fake, even though the handwriting was almost identical.

The knowledge burned in her throat like bile.

Tell them, and end the vampyrs forever. Every single one—the cruel and the kind, the monsters and the protectors. Kane. Nox. Evie. All of them would die.

Stay silent, and betray her own species. Let humans remain enslaved, let the oppression continue, let her father's sacrifice mean nothing.

Serenity stared at the plans, her father's handwriting blurring as tears filled her eyes.

Her hand trembled as she reached toward the plans, her finger hovering over the paper.

Tell them which blueprint was real, and every vampyr would die. Kane. Nox. Evie. All of them. The ones who'd shown her kindness, who'd protected her, who'd made her feel like she mattered. Gone.

Stay silent, and betray her own species. Let humans remain enslaved, let the oppression continue, let children be torn from their families. Let her father's sacrifice—everything he'd worked for, everything he'd died for—mean nothing.

She thought of Kane's face as the poison spread through his veins, the way he'd looked at her even as he fell. The memory of his touch still lingered on her skin, refusing to fade. The way he'd held her on the beach, as if she were something precious rather than property.

But she also thought of Beth's excited chatter about real cookies. Her mother's face, fuller and healthier than it had been in years. The children in Grove Gardens who went to bed hungry. The families ripped apart by the Elite program.

Her finger trembled over the plans.

"Which one?" Starr asked, her voice sharp with anticipation.

And Serenity realized with devastating clarity: there was no right answer.

CHAPTER THIRTY-TWO

RHYZAN

Instincts never lie. That's what centuries of survival had taught Rhyzan, though he'd rarely hated being right as much as he did now.

The antiseptic scent of Mercy General's private wing burned his nostrils as he stood vigil beside Kane's hospital bed, watching the monitors track vital signs that had, mere hours ago, threatened to flatline. Four hours since he'd found his oldest friend paralyzed in the forest, poison spreading through his veins like liquid death. Four hours of surgery, transfusions, and uncertainty.

The harsh fluorescent lighting cast Kane's face in a ghostly pallor, though the unnatural green tinge that had mottled his skin earlier had finally begun to recede.

Fingers tightened around the metal railing of the bed. Six bullets. Six. And not ordinary ammunition—these had been laced with silver nitrate that dispersed directly into the bloodstream upon impact. Designed to kill. Most vampyrs would have died after two such wounds. No ordinary vampyr could have survived that much toxin.

The surgical team had extracted all six bullets, each one custom-made with a hollow core containing the poison. Whoever had designed them knew exactly how to kill a vampyr of Kane's age and power. They'd targeted major muscle groups and organs—shoulder, back, thigh, side, chest. Methodical. Professional. Meant to ensure death.

And yet, here Kane lay—still breathing.

The astounding thing was that Kane had required only a single bag of blood in the transfusion, yet his recovery was progressing at a rate that defied all medical understanding. The monitors tracked the rapid normalization of vitals that should have taken days, not hours. Something wasn't adding up.

"Impossible," he murmured, leaning closer to examine the wounds that were already knitting themselves closed. The blackened veins had receded significantly, leaving only faint gray traces beneath Kane's skin.

Serenity had offered her blood during the attack—he'd instructed her to do so when she'd called in a panic. That might explain some acceleration in healing. But this? This level of regeneration after six silver nitrate bullets would challenge even the oldest of their kind.

Kane's connection to Serenity had clearly deepened beyond what anyone realized. Blood bonds of this magnitude were exceedingly rare, especially formed so quickly. If he was right, their connection ran deep enough to save Kane's life against impossible odds.

He'd sent a message to Evie about an hour ago, curious if she'd observed similar phenomena in her research. The phone vibrated with Evie's reply.

Not surprised. Checking on the clinic bombing Elites. Need to stop by the lab first. Will be there soon.

At least someone was tending to the wounded Elites from the bombing. The attack had been calculated—hitting during scheduled three-month health assessments when several Elites were gathered. Three vampyrs dead protecting humans.

The thought twisted something inside him. Heroes didn't exist in the rebellion's narrative. Monsters didn't sacrifice themselves for those they supposedly oppressed. Yet he'd seen the bodies, heard the survivors' accounts. Two nurses had died pushing humans through windows as the ceiling collapsed.

The gaze returned to Kane's still form. The steady beat of the heart monitor provided the only reassurance that his oldest friend remained tethered to this world. Centuries of unwavering loyalty, and he'd nearly lost him today.

"You stubborn bastard," he murmured, a rare smile ghosting across his lips. "You love her that much."

The door to the room opened with a soft click. Nox stood in the threshold. Their eyes met across the sterile hospital room, and for a moment, neither spoke. The last time they'd been alone together, bloodlust had stripped away Nox's usual control, need overwhelming restraint. Now, composure had returned, though tension lingered in the space between them.

"How is he?" Nox asked, his tone carefully modulated as he stepped into the room.

A slow exhale allowed the familiar presence to settle frayed nerves—the history that lay between them—lovers once, now bound by their shared loyalty to Kane. In moments like these, the boundaries blurred.

"Better than anyone could have expected," came the reply, gesturing toward the monitors. "The toxin has nearly cleared his system. At this rate, he'll be fully recovered in another hour, if not sooner."

Nox approached the bed, his movements carrying that characteristic precision. He studied Kane's sleeping form with clinical detachment, but the subtle tightening of his jaw couldn't be missed as he leaned in to examine the healing wounds.

"I was grazed," Nox said quietly, pulling back the sleeve of his torn suit to reveal a bandaged forearm. "Silver bullet. I tried to pursue the vehicle, but—"

"You did what you could. The fact that you're standing here means you made the right call."

Nox's eyes flashed with gratitude before returning to their usual guarded state. "I should have anticipated the attack. The route was compromised."

The mind sharpened on that detail—the route. Of course. Kane should never have been so exposed near Galway, regardless of the shortcut. There should have been guards in the vicinity, especially so close to the checkpoint. Why hadn't anyone responded?

When he arrived first, tracking Kane's emergency signal, the guards were conspicuously absent. They'd shown up only after medical transport had been called.

A vibration against his hip pulled attention away from Nox. Sullivan's name flashed across the screen.

"Sullivan. Tell me you have something."

"The casings match military-grade ammunition," Sullivan's words came through, crisp and efficient. "Custom modifications for the silver nitrate. Not something you'd find on the street."

The jaw tightened. "Two shooters?"

"Yes. We found positions at the construction site on the sixth and tenth floors. Professional setup. Clear sight lines, planned escape routes." A pause. "And Rhyzan? They left no traces. No fingerprints, no DNA, nothing."

The knot in his stomach tightened. He'd suspected as much when he and Sullivan had combed through the forest after tracking the emergency signal from Kane's comm device. The rebels had vanished like ghosts, taking Serenity with them.

"The vehicle?"

"Black SUV, late model. We found tire tracks but lost the trail at Boundary Road. They must have switched vehicles there." Sullivan paused. "But here's what bothers me—they were waiting. This wasn't opportunistic. They knew Kane would be on that route at that specific time."

A hand pinched the bridge of his nose, organizing thoughts. "And the guards? Why wasn't anyone at the Galway checkpoint when this happened?"

Sullivan's pause stretched uncomfortably long. "That's where it gets interesting. All four guards assigned to that sector called in sick within hours of each other yesterday evening. Replacements were supposedly dispatched, but no one ever showed up."

Ice crystallized in his veins. "Someone coordinated this."

"It gets worse. I pulled the call logs. The sick reports came from different locations, different times—but all within a three-hour window. And the replacement orders? They were filed, then deleted from the system. Someone with administrative access."

Inside help. The conspiracy ran deeper than feared.

"There's more," Sullivan's tone dropped lower. "Four more Elites have disappeared since yesterday: Grace Ellis, Mira Kay, Samuel Waters, and Damon Blackwood."

A chill crept along his spine. "Damon? Elise's Elite?"

"Yes. She's demanding to speak with Kane. Immediately. She's already threatened to go to the Council if she doesn't get answers within the hour."

"Wonderful," Nox muttered from across the room, having clearly overheard.

Processing the information rapidly. Four missing Elites. The clinic bombing. Kane's assassination attempt. All within twenty-four hours. This wasn't random violence—this was a coordinated campaign.

"Tell her we'll make finding her Elite our top priority. I'll have Sullivan set up a secure meeting with her after Kane is stable enough to—"

"Sir?" Sullivan's tone cut through the line, shifting to something unfamiliar—hesitant, almost reluctant.

Instinctively bracing for more bad news. "What is it?"

"General McGraff was found dead an hour ago in his quarters. Single gunshot wound to the back of the head. Execution-style."

A grip tightened on the window frame, knuckles whitening. Mc-Graff—the general to the human military, Councilman of Waterside Park, who'd been coordinating with them. The man who'd supposedly been their ally in military intelligence.

Dead.

Nox's head snapped up, his normally composed features tightening with shock. "You should have led with that," he hissed.

The mind raced through implications. McGraff had been their link to military intelligence, their source for tracking rebel movements. If he were dead—executed, not killed in combat—it meant someone knew about his cooperation, which now made Scarlet a suspect.

"Was it made to look like suicide?"

"No. That's the thing—they didn't try to hide it. They wanted us to know it was murder." Sullivan's reply came grimly. "There's a message, Rhyzan. Written on the wall in his blood. Two words: 'Traitors burn.'"

Eyes closed as the pieces fell into place with sickening clarity. The rebellion knew McGraff had been working with them. They'd executed him as a warning. And if they knew about McGraff...

"Scarlet. Have we heard from her since McGraff's death?"

"No contact. I've tried reaching her on the encrypted line. Nothing."

Either she was dead too, or she's the one who did it. Either way, they no longer had another intelligence asset and connection to the rebels.

"How?" Kane's words emerged as a rasp, freezing both men in place.

Spinning toward the bed, heart lurching. Kane's eyes were open—barely, just thin slits of silver-blue in his pale face. But they were focused, aware, burning with fury despite his weakened state.

"Kane." Crossing the room in three strides, relief and concern warring within. "Don't try to move. You've been shot six times with silver nitrate. You need to—"

"How?" Kane repeated, his tone stronger now despite the rasp. His gaze fixed with laser intensity. "How did they know? The route. The timing. Everything."

Nox moved to the other side of the bed, his hand hovering near Kane's shoulder but not quite touching. "We don't know yet. But all the guards called in sick. Replacements never showed. Someone with inside access."

Kane's jaw clenched, a muscle jumping beneath his skin. "Serenity."

The name fell between them like a grenade.

"We don't know where she is," came the careful response, watching Kane's reaction.

Pain flickered across Kane's face that had nothing to do with his wounds. Through whatever connection existed between them, he must have felt her absence like a severed limb.

"She's alive," Kane said, and it wasn't a question. Somehow, despite the distance, despite the bond's limits, he knew. "They took her. Six masked rebels, military training. Jax... Jax Thornton took her."

A glance exchanged with Nox. The bond between them was stronger than either had realized, if Kane could still sense her after being unconscious for hours.

"Then we find her," the tone hardened with resolve. "And we find everyone responsible for this."

Kane's eyes closed briefly, exhaustion pulling at him despite his vampyric resilience. When they opened again, they burned with cold fury.

"They made a mistake," Kane said softly. "They should have made sure I was dead."

And looking at his oldest friend—wounded, yes, but very much alive and absolutely lethal—it was impossible not to agree.

The rebellion had just left Kane Draccus breathing.

CHAPTER THIRTY-THREE

KANE

The orange dot pulsed on the screen like a dying star. Kane's finger hovered over it, tracing its path through the digital map of the Dead City without actually touching the glass. Twenty-four hours since they'd taken Serenity from him. Twenty-three hours and forty-seven minutes since Rhyzan had found him half-dead from silver poison, bullets still burning through his system.

A full day since he'd last held her. Since he'd felt her warmth, breathed in her scent, heard her voice.

Sullivan cleared his throat from the other side of the desk. "We should move against them now. While we have Chloe's location."

Kane didn't look up. His shoulder and thigh still ached where the silver bullets had torn through muscle and sinew. Serenity's blood had saved his life, but the wounds remained tender, a constant reminder of his failure.

Of what she'd risked to save him.

He'd closed off the connection between them the moment he'd regained consciousness in the hospital. Deliberately. Completely. She couldn't feel him anymore—couldn't sense that he'd survived, couldn't know he was alive and planning. He needed that tactical advantage. If she knew he was coming, she could warn them. Intentionally or not.

But he could still feel her. Faintly, distantly, like an echo of a heartbeat carried on the wind. The connection only flowed one way now—from her to him.

"Kane," Sullivan pressed, leaning forward. "The longer we wait—"

"I know exactly how long we've been waiting," Kane growled, dragging his fingers through his hair. The hollow ache in him was a constant reminder of the distance between them. Of watching her disappear into the forest, carried away by rebels. By her people. By a friend.

Kane leaned back in his chair, the leather creaking under his weight. The office felt cavernous around him, the silence broken only by Sullivan's occasional shuffle where he'd taken up sentinel position an hour ago.

Neither had spoken since Sullivan's curt report on General McGraff's death—the human military leader's body found in his apartment hours after the incident. No signs of break-in or struggle. Either he knew his killer, or it was an assassination. Kane was betting on the former. But who would need McGraff out of the way?

Councilwoman Ruess had already sent three candidates for McGraff's position. Kane had dismissed them all. They needed someone who commanded respect from both sides. Not another warmonger or sycophant. Before announcing McGraff's death, he needed someone in place—whether temporary or permanent—so the humans would not grow restless and add fuel to the rebellion's cause.

But all of that felt like an afterthought compared to the pulsing beacon on screen. Kane's entire being was fixated on that digital marker—Chloe's tracker, yes, but also the rebel headquarters where his instincts screamed Serenity was being held.

The door to his office swung open, admitting Rhyzan and Nox without announcement. Their expressions told him everything before they spoke—something had shifted, and not for the better.

"We've uncovered a pattern," Rhyzan said, closing the door behind him with barely a sound. "The missing Elites—they're not just disappearing. They're being recruited. Which I'd already suspected, but we finally have proof."

Nox stepped forward, his movements precise as always. "Damon Blackwood, Elise's Elite, appears to be deeply involved with the rebellion. We've traced communications between him and several of the missing Elites."

"And you remember the agent McGraff wanted me to meet," Rhyzan said, taking a seat next to Sullivan with a curt nod of acknowledgment.

"Yes." Kane's attention sharpened, finally torn from the pulsing tracker. "You didn't mention her, so I didn't think her significant."

"She wasn't—until I recognized her. I went back through my surveillance and found these." Rhyzan placed two enlarged photos in front of him. One showed a short, petite blonde woman talking with Sebastian outside a store in the Diamond District. The other showed the same woman with a tall, dark-haired man who appeared to be Elise's Elite.

"I'm assuming the blonde woman is McGraff's agent." Kane picked up the photo of Damon and the woman and examined it more closely.

A cold weight settled in his stomach. Sebastian. Close to Serenity. Had she met Starr or Damon?

"Yes, she identified herself as Scarlet, but according to the communications, she may be going by the name Starr," Nox informed him.

"Do you think she killed McGraff?" Kane asked, picking up the other photo with Sebastian.

"As of right now, all avenues point to yes, but honestly, it could be anyone close to him or possibly someone else in the rebellion," Rhyzan said.

Placing the photo down, Kane felt his chest tighten. Sebastian, Serenity, and Damon are all Elites to the Council members. What other Elites were working for the rebels? The infiltration ran deeper than he'd realized.

"Where is Evie?" Kane asked.

"She's still in her lab. I texted her about an hour ago. She said something about running your blood sample from the hospital," Rhyzan told him.

"And before you ask, Sebastian hasn't left the apartment since the explosion," Nox said, pulling out his phone to check his screen. "He just ordered food about twenty minutes ago."

"Giving Sebastian the perfect alibi." Kane couldn't help thinking something wasn't adding up. "Why would Damon leave Elise now? She's had him for almost four years. And the killing of McGraff?"

"My theory?" Rhyzan leaned closer. "The rebellion is about to make their move and pulling all their agents in. And I don't think McGraff was aligned with them—getting the human leader out of the way makes him easier to replace."

"Then we need eyes on Councilmen Hensen and Fulton. I want their movements tracked from here on out," Kane directed toward Nox, who nodded.

"Rhy." Kane already knew Rhyzan wasn't going to like what he was about to ask, but his heart wouldn't settle until he knew. "I need Chloe to confirm if Serenity is within the rebel headquarters."

Both Rhyzan and Nox exchanged a look that spoke volumes. Rhyzan cleared his throat. "Even if she is there... what's the plan? She was working with them, Kane. She was feeding them information."

"I know what she was doing," Kane said, his voice dropping to a dangerous timbre. "I've known since the beginning. What I need is confirmation of her current location. It was the prisoner, Jax, who took her."

Rhyzan's jaw tightened, a muscle flickering beneath his skin. "You mean who she went with."

"No. Took," Kane said flatly. "I was there. I saw her face. That wasn't extraction—that was kidnapping."

The memory burned in his mind—her terror, her desperate attempts to stay with him even as Jax dragged her away. She'd shielded him with her own body. Had begged them not to kill him. Had given him her blood, knowing it would save his life.

Those weren't the actions of someone planning her escape.

"And once you get confirmation, what's the plan?" Rhyzan said in a deadly whisper. "Go in guns blazing? That will get more people killed and condemn Celearius to failure."

"And it could get her killed," Nox added quietly.

"But isn't this what we've been preparing for?" Sullivan said, finally breaking his silence. "For months now, we've been tracking their movements. We know their approximate headquarters location in the Dead City. It's right there, blinking." He jabbed a finger toward the screen. "Why are we waiting? We should mobilize now—quickly and quietly—hit them hard before they realize we're onto them."

"He's right," Kane agreed.

The tension in the room thickened, pressing against Kane's skin like a physical weight. Rhyzan's jaw worked silently, the vampyr's normally unreadable expression cracking around the edges.

"We're not ready for a large-scale attack," Rhyzan said, each word measured and careful. "We don't know their full numbers, their defenses, their contingency plans. Anything could go wrong."

Kane's gaze returned to the screen where the tracker pulsed steadily. The sight of it called to a primal need in him, possessive and desperate.

He needed her back. Every part of him screamed to get her back.

"We go in," Kane decided, his tone final. "Sullivan is right—we've prepared for this. We must do what's best for Celearius. Shutting down the rebellion before they do any more damage is top priority."

Sullivan pushed his chair back and stood, his network of scars catching the light as he moved to the digital map display. "I have an idea that might settle this. One that gives us an advantage without risking a frontal assault."

Kane raised an eyebrow, watching as Sullivan's fingers traced the intricate network of lines beneath the main city grid.

"I've been studying these maps for weeks now, cross-referencing with intel from Chloe, and David, our historical cartographer." Sullivan tapped the screen, enlarging a section of underground tunnels. "The rebels aren't just using buildings in the Dead City—they're utilizing the old subway system and sewer networks to move around undetected."

Kane leaned forward, his interest piqued. He studied the intricate web of tunnels Sullivan had highlighted.

"If we come at them head-on from the south as they'd expect, they'll see us coming from miles away." Sullivan's finger traced a path along the northern edge of the Dead City. "But if we circle around and come in from the north through these access points, we could catch them completely off guard."

"How long would that take?" Kane asked, already calculating the logistics.

Sullivan traced his finger along the northern edge of the map, following a faded line that disappeared into the shadowed areas of the Dead City.

"It would take us a few hours to go around, set up, and then move in. The terrain is rough, but navigable. Our teams could be in position before midnight."

Kane studied the route, mentally calculating distances and potential obstacles. The northern approach made strategic sense—the rebels would be watching the southern routes, expecting a direct assault from Celearius.

"It's not enough," Rhyzan said, stepping closer to the display. "If we only come from one direction, we risk them slipping away through these tunnels." His finger traced additional pathways on the western and eastern edges of the map. "We should deploy teams here and here as well. Create a three-pronged assault."

Kane's attention followed Rhyzan's movements across the glowing display.

"With teams entering simultaneously from multiple points," Rhyzan continued, "we could force them toward Celearius, where the Outer City police could be waiting if necessary. They'd have nowhere to run."

"A pincer movement," Kane murmured, studying the approach. "Force them into a bottleneck."

Sullivan nodded, satisfaction evident in the set of his scarred jaw. "Exactly. We contain rather than scatter. Minimal casualties, maximum efficiency."

The plan unfurled in Kane's mind like a deadly flower. It was elegant in its simplicity yet complex enough to anticipate the rebels' likely countermoves. They would surround them completely, cutting off all escape routes.

"I want our best on this, Rhyzan. Only your most trusted soldiers from Galway District, and pull in the top cadets from the Academy." Kane commanded. "No rookies. No one with questionable loyalties. This operation requires absolute discretion."

His gaze returned to the pulsing beacon on screen. She was there, in the heart of enemy territory. Every instinct in his body screamed to go after her immediately, but the leader in him knew better. Strategy over impulse. Always.

"We move in fifteen hours," Kane announced, his decision final. "That gives us time to position our teams and coordinate with local forces."

Rhyzan straightened, jaw set in determination. "I'll begin preparations immediately."

"Sullivan, contact Lieutenant Jones," Kane ordered, his silver-blue eyes flashing with authority. "Have him ready the Outer City police in Grove Gardens and Easton as a precautionary measure. If any rebels slip through our net, I want them contained before they reach civilian areas."

Sullivan nodded sharply. "Consider it done."

As Sullivan moved toward the door with purposeful strides, Rhyzan followed behind, but Kane's tone cut through the air like a blade.

"Rhyzan, wait."

The vampyr paused, turning with a questioning look.

"Before you go—I need confirmation that Serenity is there." Kane's manner remained steady despite the storm raging inside him. "Have Chloe verify her presence at the rebel headquarters."

Rhyzan's jaw tightened. For a moment, Kane thought he might refuse, might argue the futility of such knowledge. Instead, Rhyzan pulled out his phone, his fingers moving across the screen with precision.

"Done," he said after a moment, slipping the device back into his pocket. "I'll let you know as soon as we have confirmation."

Kane nodded once, the gesture both dismissal and thanks. As the door closed behind Sullivan and Rhyzan, silence settled over the office like a shroud.

Nox remained, his presence a quiet constant as he studied the digital map. The tracker continued its hypnotic pulse, each flicker a reminder that she was out there. Alive. Waiting.

"You'll be coming with us," Kane said, leaving no room for discussion. "Your priority is to get Serenity and her family to safety. At all costs."

Nox's eyebrows rose slightly, the only indication of his surprise. After a moment, his lips curved into a small smile—one of the rare, genuine expressions that transformed his usually stoic features.

"Of course," he replied, inclining his head. "I'll ensure their safe extraction personally."

Kane turned back to the map, tracing the route with his finger. "I want her family brought to Cavern 52 once secured," he said, then paused, vulnerability flickering in his silver-blue eyes. "And Serenity... bring her to me."

The words came out rougher than intended, weighted with everything he couldn't say. He didn't know what he'd do when he saw her again. Didn't know if he'd demand answers or simply pull her into his arms.

Didn't know if the betrayal would matter more than the desperate need to have her back.

All he knew was that he needed her whole, safe, real.

In his arms, where she belonged.

Nox's smile faltered, the expression smoothing into careful neutrality. He simply nodded, the barest incline of his head acknowledging the gravity of Kane's request. Without another word, he turned and left the office, the door closing behind him with a soft click that seemed to echo in the sudden emptiness.

Kane stood alone, all of Celearius pressing down on his shoulders like a physical burden. The tracker continued its pulse on the screen.

He moved to the window, staring out at Celearius spread before him. Lights glimmered against the darkening sky, vampyrs and humans alike going about their evening routines, blissfully unaware of the storm gathering on their horizon.

But all he could think about was her.

She had saved his life—given him her blood when he was dying, shielded him with her fragile human body, begged them not to kill him. The memory of her being torn from his arms burned hotter than any physical wound.

Kane pressed his palm against the cool glass, staring out at the city he'd spent centuries protecting. He'd killed for Celearius. Had sacrificed everything for its survival.

But standing here now, Kane realized with devastating clarity that he would burn it all down if it meant getting her back.

Fifteen hours. Then he'd have his answers.

And gods help anyone who stood in his way.

CHAPTER THIRTY-FOUR

SERENITY

She couldn't do it. She couldn't lie... and she couldn't tell the truth.

Serenity sat in a dimly lit room, facing Starr and Damon. The air was heavy with tension as they questioned her. Hours had passed since Jax had torn her from Kane's side, since she'd watched silver poison spread through his veins. Hours of tunnels and boats and trucks, and now this—an interrogation disguised as concern.

"You've never seen your father working on these plans before? Or maybe lying around?" Damon asked for the second time.

"No, I haven't seen these plans before." Not a full lie. She had seen parts of the weapon formulas in her father's medical journals, but at the time she'd thought they were just drawings. She'd had no idea it was some kind of deadly weapon. Even now, she wasn't completely sure how the weapon worked or what it did.

But she knew which set of plans was real.

She could see it in her father's careful notations, in the slight variations between the two sets of blueprints. One was the original. One was the fake Evie had created.

"Have you heard any whispers about it? Seen it on any screen while you were there?" Starr asked softly. By there, Serenity assumed she meant in Celearius, with Kane.

She could answer this one honestly. "No, the only weapon I've heard mentioned was from Sebastian himself."

Starr and Damon exchanged looks, communicating silently before Damon nodded. Serenity hoped they were satisfied with her answers. Hoped they wouldn't push further, wouldn't force her to make the choice she was desperately avoiding.

Tell them which blueprint was real, and every vampyr would die. Kane. Nox. Evie. All of them.

Stay silent, and her father's sacrifice—her people's freedom—would mean nothing.

She chose silence.

"Thank you, but now we owe you an apology," Starr said, her expression softening as she leaned forward and touched Serenity's hand. "We're sorry about the attack in Waterside Cross. We had to act fast to get you out of there. We're just glad you aren't injured."

"Actually, I was injured," Serenity confessed. "He healed me."

Starr and Damon looked at each other again, then Damon stood, moving over to another table in the corner.

"How many times has Kane healed you?" Damon asked over his shoulder as he reached into an overhead cabinet and took down a black device.

"I'm not sure... I think about twice... no, three times," Serenity admitted.

Damon turned, and Serenity saw he held a hemoptic device. "We need to take a sample of your blood, if that's okay with you?"

Serenity stared at the device, her stomach knotting. The sight sent a familiar trigger of panic through her body. No matter how safe she felt, memories flooded back to that day in the clinic—the doctor's eyes going black with bloodlust, Kane tearing him away from her. She took a deep breath, calming her nerves. She needed answers. And there were no vampyrs here.

"Why do you need my blood?" she asked, steadier than she felt. "And why did you really get me out? I deserve the truth."

Starr sighed, pushing a strand of blonde hair behind her ear. "Kane has a rare gift, even among vampyrs. His ability to heal is... exceptional. And your blood type is equally rare. We need to make sure you're alright after multiple exposures to his blood."

The explanation felt incomplete. Serenity's fingers traced the skin where Kane's blood had healed her wounds. "Evelyn wanted a sample of my blood, too, for the same reason. Everyone seems very interested in what's flowing through my veins, but nobody wants to tell me why."

Damon approached with the device, his expression unreadable. "I'm not surprised Evelyn wanted a sample. She's always been interested in the effects of Kane's blood on humans."

"Sometimes the effects can be..." Damon continued, his tone clinical as he prepared the device. "Unpredictable. But you seem fine."

His blood didn't affect her as much this time. She could hear the rhythm of their heartbeats, but the sound was slowly fading. The hypersensitivity that had overwhelmed her before—the amplified senses, the almost painful awareness—was barely present. She wasn't sure whether to mention the diminished side effects, but instinct told her to keep it to herself.

Serenity eyed the device with apprehension but extended her arm anyway. Damon placed it against her skin and quickly pressed the button. Just as with Evelyn, it was quick and painless. "All set."

"The reason we extracted you when we did," Starr said, moving closer, "is because of what you made possible for us."

Serenity's brow furrowed. "What do you mean?"

"What we mean is," Damon interjected, "because of the information you provided, we were able to get Jon out. And your friend Jax. Thanks to you."

"Retrieve who? Jon? Jax was in Cavern 47?"

"You'll meet Jon later. He's currently resting. But it seems your friend Jax got himself in trouble with the vampyrs due to his hatred toward them." Starr smiled at Serenity. "Lucky for him, he has good friends."

Damon's lips curled into a small smile. "You're a brave woman, Serenity. We're lucky to have you on our side."

Just then, the door creaked open, and Jax stepped into the room. Serenity's heart lurched—half joy, half dread—as she met his familiar gaze. His jaw was set tight, the way it always was when he was holding back words. She wanted to run to him like she would have before, but her feet felt weighted to the floor. The last time they'd actually spoken before he took her, he'd hated her for her betrayal. Now he stood before her, her oldest friend and her harshest judge, and she didn't know whether to embrace him or defend herself.

"Jax, is everything secure still?" Damon asked.

"Yes, no one followed us. Cleeve and Ben hid the truck and the others are near the tunnels, ready to move when you are," Jax informed them, avoiding Serenity's stare.

"Kyle and Ian will lead you back to headquarters," Starr told him. "We have to finish up here, but we want to make sure she's safe."

Jax's jaw tightened, but he nodded without hesitation. "Of course."

Serenity stood to leave, but then Starr handed her a pair of flats. "You'll need these until we can get you proper clothing."

"Thank you," Serenity said, then added, "Especially for getting my family out."

Serenity followed Jax out. He led her to the familiar cave entrance at the back of Levee's, where they would escape when the bar got raided by the Outer City police. As she approached the opening, she couldn't help but look back at the entrance, wondering if she ran, could she get back to him. She wasn't far. Once she passed this threshold, there was no going back. Forward was her family, who she loved dearly. Behind her was him, calling her to come back. Screaming for her to return.

Making one of the hardest choices of her life, she stepped through the opening.

The familiar mushroom-blue glow and quietness of the cave engulfed them. They moved through the cavern until they came to the path that split three ways. Three men waited for them. This time they had removed their masks.

Two of the men were young—not much older than Serenity herself—with the wiry builds and hollow cheeks of those who'd grown up with too little food. The third was older, his face weathered like cracked leather, a jagged scar cutting through his left eyebrow.

"This is Kyle and Ian," Jax said, gesturing to the younger men. "And this is Dean."

Serenity nodded, unable to form words as exhaustion swept through her body. The adrenaline that had sustained her was fading, leaving her hollow and aching.

"We're going back to headquarters. Cleeve and Ben will go back with Starr and Damon," Jax said, his words echoing against the cavern walls.

Dean nodded and turned toward the leftmost tunnel. "This way. Watch your step—the ground gets slippery about halfway through."

Serenity followed Dean as Kyle and Ian fell in behind her and Jax. Her borrowed flats slid against the damp stone as darkness pressed around them, broken only by the narrow beams of flashlights.

They walked through the tunnel she had walked through a thousand times, until the dirt walls turned into smooth stone. Only thing missing was the old rusty lantern. Finally, they reached the makeshift ladder.

Dean and Kyle went up first. They knocked twice, then whistled. Serenity assumed that was the signal for clear, since Jax started heading up the ladder. He held out his hand for her when she reached the opening.

As she climbed out, familiar dust coated the floor, swirling in the air. Light shone brightly through dirty, cracked windows of the abandoned warehouse loft, casting long shadows across concrete.

Debris still littered the floor and all their furniture was in place like they'd never left—even the tattered Cougars banner hung on the wall.

It was just a few weeks ago she'd been here with Jax, Clyde, and Tori. It was the last normal evening she'd had.

Dean led them outside, past all her memories.

"Stay close and stay alert," Dean cautioned them before leading them deeper into the Dead City, the crumbling ruins a stark reminder of past devastation.

Slowly, they began their journey into the city streets, moving quickly and sticking to the shadows until they'd moved about three blocks. They paused when they heard a helicopter overhead, hiding in corners of ruined buildings.

They continued through the streets until they came to an old train station door. The skull and bones symbol was carved into the stone to the left of the door—if she hadn't been looking for it, she would have missed it.

Kyle and Ian led them down the stone steps as Dean took up the rear.

When they came to part of a collapsed platform, Jax helped her down, then took off his coat and offered it to her.

Hesitantly, she took it and put it on. "Thank you," Serenity said, clutching the coat tighter around her shoulders. The fabric still held Jax's warmth and smelled faintly of machine oil and the cheap soap from Grove Gardens—scents that carried her back to simpler times. Before Kane. Before everything changed.

Water dripped somewhere in the darkness, the steady plink-plink echoing through the cavernous space. Rats scurried in the shadows, their tiny claws scratching against debris. The sounds of the Dead City—sounds she'd once known as intimately as her own heartbeat.

"Watch your step here," Jax warned, his words bouncing off the tiled walls.

Ahead, Kyle and Ian moved with practiced efficiency, checking corners before motioning them forward. Dean brought up the rear, his weathered face constantly scanning for threats.

Serenity's thoughts were a whirlwind of emotions—gratitude for Jax's presence, guilt for involving her family, and an underlying tension she struggled to define.

She and Jax fell into step as they walked through the old, dilapidated tunnels with some distance between them and the other men.

"You okay?" Jax's words cut through the silence, drawing her attention.

Serenity offered a small smile, though her heart was racing. "Yeah, just trying to take it all in."

Jax slowed his pace slightly, his gaze fixed on her. "I'm sorry about telling your family. I just didn't know how to take what you did." He rubbed his neck, looking sheepish—almost like her best friend again.

She met his stare, feeling a rush of conflicting emotions. "I know, Jax. And I'm sorry about not telling you. I was just a coward. I didn't want to burden you."

He reached out and gently squeezed her shoulder, his touch grounding her. "No, I get it. I'm an asshole when it comes to the vampyrs. I should have seen what you were trying to do for your family. If I'd realized Clyde's talk about the Human Liberators was real, then we could have come to them instead of you having to endure being with him."

Serenity nodded, also wishing things had been different. "Thank you for understanding."

Jax's lips curved into a faint smile. "It's what friends do, right?"

"Yes. Always."

Jax's hand closed around hers, and she started at the sudden contact.

"How are you feeling?" he murmured, concern etched into his features. "You all right?"

She managed a small, weak smile. "Yeah, just a bit overwhelmed, I guess. This place gives me the creeps."

He squeezed her hand reassuringly. "I know, but we're almost there. Just a few more blocks."

She nodded, then decided to ask the question that sat burning in her mind. "Jax, how did you get involved with the rebe—the Human Liberators?"

Jax's expression grew somber, and Serenity could tell this was not an easy topic for him. "It's a long story. But it started when I got captured in a raid at Levee's. I got drunk and was too slow to get to the escape. Clyde and Tori got captured too, trying to save my stupid ass."

He ran his hands down his face, exasperated, before continuing. "I thought they were going to take my blood and let me go like they did Tori and Clyde, but I was detained for unknown reasons. I was taken to a new location where they tried to torture information from me, but I held strong. I was able to meet Chloe. I can't wait for you to meet her."

Serenity couldn't help but notice the change in Jax's tone when he mentioned Chloe. His words lightened, and his expression took on a warmth she hadn't seen since before she'd joined the Elite program.

"She's incredible, Ren. So brave. The vampyrs took her child—her little girl, only three years old—and they..." His voice dropped lower, redness creeping up his neck. "They forced Chloe to... service the prisoners. To keep them comfortable. To keep them compliant. They told her if she refused, they'd hurt her daughter. She hasn't seen that little girl in months, doesn't even know if she's alive."

Serenity's stomach turned. Sexual exploitation, using a child as leverage. The cruelty of it made her feel sick. But something about the story didn't align with what she'd seen of vampyr society. Kane had spoken often about protecting the vulnerable, about balance. The laws she'd read, the policies she'd observed—none of it suggested this kind of systematic abuse.

"They just... took her child?" she whispered. "And forced her to—"

"That's what they do, Ren. They take what they want." The warmth remained in his tone, buoyed by his obvious affection for this woman.

"We're going to help her get her daughter back. Clyde's already got a plan in motion."

Serenity stared at Jax, her mind struggling to process his words. Using a child as leverage for sexual slavery? The vampyrs she'd known—Kane, Evie, even Rhyzan in his cold efficiency—had never struck her as the type to harm children. Even Nox had spoken of the importance of preserving innocent life.

"Are you sure they took her just to control Chloe?" Serenity asked, her words barely above a whisper. "That doesn't sound like—"

"Like what? The benevolent rulers they pretend to be?" Jax's manner hardened. "Wake up, Ren. They're monsters. They drain us for food and use our children as bargaining chips. Chloe hasn't seen her daughter in months, doesn't even know if she's alive."

The tunnel seemed to narrow around her, the air growing thicker. Her head throbbed, making it difficult to sort through the conflicting narratives. The Kane she knew had shown her kindness, protected her, made love to her with such tender care. But Jax's words painted a different picture entirely.

"Is it true, Jax?" The words tumbled from her lips before she could stop them. "Would the weapon plans they have kill the vampyrs?"

She needed to know.

"Yes." Jax's grip on her hand tightened, his stare blazing with intensity. "They've taken everything from us. Our freedom, our families, our humanity. We're fighting for our survival, Serenity. And sometimes, survival means doing what needs to be done, no matter how hard it is. We can't let them keep doing this to innocent people."

She wasn't sure she fully understood. It wasn't like all the vampyrs were bad. She thought of Nox and how he'd been nothing but kind to her, making her comfortable in Kane's home. And Evelyn had also been considerate, just wanting to make sure her friend was fed and healthy. Even Rhyzan had made sure she was okay. Not all vampyrs were bad, and some were even innocent. She didn't know how she felt about killing innocents for the greater good.

"They've taken everything from us. Our freedom, our families, our humanity. We're fighting for our survival, Serenity. And sometimes, in war, sacrifices have to be made." Jax's grip tightened further, conviction burning in his gaze.

This wasn't the time or place to question their plans. She just wanted to get to her family. She would figure everything else out once she saw them and knew they were safe.

Serenity nodded slowly, understanding his reasoning even if she didn't necessarily agree with it. "Alright," she said softly. "We'll do what we have to do."

Jax looked at her with intense gratitude and pulled her into a tight embrace, burying his face in her hair. "Thank you," he whispered. "I couldn't do this without you."

Serenity wrapped her arms around him, feeling the urgent beat of his heart. She knew they were in for a fight like nothing they'd ever experienced before, but as long as they were together, they could face anything, even if her heart was breaking for every moment of it.

They continued until they came to a collapsed tunnel. Serenity thought he might have taken a wrong turn, but then he lit a lamp hidden near a bench and led them through a red door at the end of the station. The room had a gaping hole that led out into another tunnel. He helped them over the low-bearing wall, and they walked until they reached a large pair of steel doors. Serenity felt a mixture of excitement and trepidation as Dean knocked thrice and shouted, "Freeborn!"

The steel doors groaned open, revealing a vast underground chamber carved from the bedrock itself. The air hung thick with the smell of sweat and gunpowder, illuminated by strings of mismatched industrial lights that cast long shadows across the uneven floor. At least fifty rebels moved through the large, cavernous space—some hunched over maps spread across old liquor barrel-tables, others cleaning weapons or passing around dented metal canteens. In the far corner, a woman demonstrated knife techniques to three teenagers.

Amidst the controlled chaos, Serenity spotted Clyde's towering figure and Tori's copper-red hair gleaming under the harsh industrial lights. Their eyes locked across the chamber, and everything else faded away. Relief flooded through her as Clyde's weathered face broke into a rare grin. He elbowed his way through the throng, Tori darting between bodies with practiced ease. They collided with Serenity in a tangle of limbs, Clyde's muscled arms engulfing both women.

"You're here," Tori whispered against Serenity's shoulder, as if afraid she might disappear.

Serenity hugged them back, feeling comfort wash over her as she reunited with her friends.

"We've been waiting for you," Clyde murmured, his deep rumble against her cheek. "Knew you'd make it back to us."

"I didn't," Serenity admitted, cracking. "I thought I'd never—"

"Beth! Wait!"

The high-pitched call cut through the cavern like a bell, stopping Serenity's heart mid-beat. She turned just as a small figure barreled through the crowd.

"Serenity! Serenity!"

Beth's voice—her sister's voice—slammed into her with more force than any physical impact. She stepped out of Clyde and Tori's embrace, her heart swelling as Beth's small figure darted toward her through the crowded chamber. She dropped to her knees, arms outstretched, and caught her sister in a fierce hug that nearly knocked her backward. Beth's arms wound around her neck, squeezing with surprising strength.

"You're here! You're really here!" Beth sobbed against her shoulder, her small body trembling.

Serenity buried her face in Beth's short curly hair, breathing in the familiar scent of her sister—earthy and clean, like her mother's herbal soap. She felt whole again, holding this precious piece of herself that had been missing for so long.

Over Beth's shoulder, Serenity spotted her mother making her way through the crowd. The sight of her—walking steadily despite her usual limp, face lined but glowing with relief—made Serenity's chest tighten painfully. Her mother's eyes shimmered with unshed tears as she moved closer. Mom looked different—her face fuller, her gaze brighter than it had been in years.

"Serenity." Her mother's words broke on the second syllable as she reached them, her arms opening wide.

Serenity rose from her knees, still clutching Beth against her side, and stepped into her mother's embrace. The familiar scent of home—of safety and childhood—washed over her as her mother's arms encircled both her and Beth. For one perfect moment, the world narrowed to just the three of them, whole and together again.

"How are you feeling, sweetheart?" Her mother pulled back slightly, searching Serenity's face with that penetrating look that had always seen straight through her childhood fibs.

A hundred answers crowded Serenity's throat. The weight of everything—Kane, the rebels, the lies, the truth—pressed against her chest, but she couldn't break down. Not here, surrounded by strangers watching her reunion. She swallowed hard and simply nodded, unable to form words past the knot in her throat.

Her mother's expression softened with understanding. Those familiar lines around her mouth deepened as she gave Serenity's arm a gentle squeeze. "It's okay, sweetheart. You don't need to explain anything now."

The relief of not having to speak, to justify, to explain was almost overwhelming.

Jax approached them, his footsteps echoing against the stone floor.

"I should show you where you can get cleaned up," he said, gentler than before. "There's a shower area, and we've got some clean clothes that should fit you. After that, you can get something to eat and rest."

Beth's fingers tightened around Serenity's, reluctant to let her go.

"I want to come with you," Beth insisted, digging deeper into Serenity's arm.

"We'll catch up," her mother said, placing a gentle hand on Beth's shoulder. "The doctor wants to check Beth's breathing again, and I need to get my medication. We won't be long."

Serenity hesitated, reluctant to let them out of her sight so soon after finding them. "Are you sure? I can wait."

"Go on," her mother urged with a soft smile. "Get cleaned up. You look exhausted, sweetheart."

Serenity nodded, bending to kiss Beth's forehead before following Jax across the cavernous chamber. As they walked, she took in her surroundings more carefully. The rebel headquarters was far larger than she'd initially realized. What had seemed like fifty people was closer to a hundred, maybe more. They moved with purpose through the interconnected tunnels and chambers—some carrying weapons, others hunched over maps or computer terminals that glowed in the dim light.

A movement in the far corner caught Serenity's attention. Her heart stuttered as a familiar silhouette emerged from the shadows. Tall, imposing, with dark hair and piercing eyes that had once looked at her with predatory hunger.

Dex.

The vampyr from the alley—the one who had cornered her that night before Sebastian intervened. Ice flooded her veins. A vampyr. Here. In the rebel headquarters, where they were planning to kill all vampyrs. Her mind reeled with confusion as Dex moved with that fluid grace unique to his kind, speaking with a cluster of rebels as if he belonged there.

Why would the rebellion be working with a vampyr when their weapon would kill them all? Unless he didn't know. Unless they were using him, too. Or unless everything she'd been told was a lie.

"What is it?" Jax asked, following her stare.

Serenity's throat constricted. Should she tell him? Would he even believe her?

"It's nothing," she finally managed, though her heart hammered against her ribs. "Just... seeing all these people. It's overwhelming."

Jax's expression softened with understanding. "Come on," he said, leading her further down, then stopping in front of a green door.

He pushed it open, gesturing for her to enter. "After you."

The room was small but surprisingly clean, with four narrow beds arranged against the walls. A curtained alcove housed a simple shower stall and toilet in the corner. The air smelled faintly of soap and disinfectant—a stark contrast to the earthiness of the main cavern.

A woman sat up in one of the beds, a book open on her lap. She looked up as they entered, her pale green eyes immediately locking onto Serenity with an intensity that made the hairs on the back of her neck stand up. Her soft brown hair fell in waves around her heart-shaped face, and when she smiled, dimples appeared in her cheeks.

"Serenity, this is Chloe," Jax said, softening in a way Serenity had never heard before. "Chloe, this is my best friend I told you about."

Chloe's smile widened as she set her book aside and rose from the bed with fluid grace. "It's so wonderful to meet you finally. Jax has told me so much about you."

Serenity took Chloe's outstretched hand, noting how cool and smooth it felt against her own. Something about the woman's touch sent an uncomfortable shiver up her spine. The way she moved—calculated precision, like every gesture had been choreographed. Whatever it was, Serenity couldn't shake the feeling that something wasn't quite right.

"It's nice to meet you too," she said, withdrawing her hand a little quicker than was strictly polite.

Serenity could see why Jax was captivated. The way his expression softened when he looked at Chloe, how his entire demeanor changed in her presence—it was obvious he was completely smitten.

"You must be exhausted," Chloe observed, sweeping over Serenity's disheveled appearance. "I can't imagine what you've been through."

Serenity nodded, suddenly aware of how her entire body ached.

"There are fresh towels and some clean clothes in that cabinet," Chloe said, pointing to a small metal cabinet in the corner. "Nothing fancy, but they're clean. The shower has hot water, which is a luxury around here."

Jax shifted uncomfortably, darting between the two women. "We'll let you get some rest. I need to check in with Damon anyway, who should be back soon."

"And I should help with dinner preparations," Chloe added, moving toward the door with that same graceful fluidity. "Come find us when you're ready. Or sleep—whatever you need."

The door closed behind them with a soft click, leaving Serenity alone for the first time since being dragged from Kane's side.

The silence pressed against her eardrums, deafening after hours of chaos. Her legs gave out suddenly, and she sank onto the nearest bed. The exhaustion hit her all at once, and as the tears began to flow, Serenity didn't try to stop them. They streamed down her face, hot and relentless, her shoulders shaking with silent sobs. She pressed her fist against her mouth to muffle the sound, not wanting anyone to hear her breaking apart.

Kane. The memory of his touch on the beach, his laughter in the sunlight, the way his eyes had followed her as she was dragged away—it all crashed over her in waves of agony. She would never feel his arms around her again, never see that rare smile that transformed his entire face, never hear his voice dropping to that husky timbre reserved just for her.

"He'll hate me now," she whispered to the empty room, the words tearing at her throat. "He'll think I planned it all."

And why wouldn't he? She'd lied to him repeatedly, hidden her true purpose, betrayed his trust at every turn. Now she'd disappeared during an attack that had left him poisoned and possibly dying. The evidence against her was overwhelming.

Serenity wrapped her arms around herself, trying to hold the pieces together. But the ache in her chest threatened to hollow her out completely.

Suddenly, warmth spread through Serenity's body, starting from her core and radiating outward. The familiar scent of cedar and warm leather filled her nostrils, so powerful and immediate that she spun around, certain Kane stood behind her.

The room was empty.

She pressed her fingers to her lips, the phantom sensation of his kiss lingering there. His scent enveloped her completely—that distinctive blend that was uniquely his. For one breathless moment, she could almost feel his presence.

Was he alive?

Then the sensation faded, dissipating like morning mist under harsh reality.

Serenity closed her eyes, allowing the wave of sadness to wash over her rather than fighting it. When she opened her eyes again, her vision was clearer.

She would protect her family at all costs. That was what mattered.

She pulled herself to her feet, wiped her face, and moved toward the shower. She would clean up. She would eat. She would rest.

And tomorrow, she would figure out what the hell was really going on in this place.

CHAPTER THIRTY-FIVE

KANE

The scent of her lingered in his blood, a whisper of jasmine and defiance.

Kane crouched on the steel beam jutting from the skeletal remains of what had once been a vibrant northern financial district. Wind whipped through his hair as he stared down at the ruins of Dead City, his enhanced vision cutting through the darkness to track movement in the streets below. Forty stories up, the height would have terrified most, but to Kane it offered perfect vantage—a predator's perch.

She was down there. Underground. Moving.

Six hours until dawn. Six hours until his forces moved in and he had her back.

He closed his eyes, letting the connection between them pulse like a second heartbeat. The blood bond had strengthened since she'd saved his life in the forest, her essence flowing into him, creating a tether he hadn't anticipated. When her guard dropped—when sadness overwhelmed her—her mind had opened to him like a flower unfurling its petals. A momentary glimpse, but enough.

Enough to know the truth.

Kane's jaw tightened. She hadn't betrayed him willingly. The realization should have eased the knife-edge of rage that had been his constant companion these past days, but instead, it sharpened to a lethal point. He would find her. He would reclaim her. And those who had dared to touch what was his would suffer for it.

What he would do when he had her back—whether he would kiss her until she surrendered completely or punish her for her involvement with the rebellion, willing or not—remained uncertain. But one thing was clear: she was his. Completely. Irrevocably.

Footsteps approached from behind, nearly silent against the steel beam. Kane didn't turn. Only two people would dare approach him when he was like this.

"How many?" he asked, the wind carrying his words away.

Sullivan stepped into his peripheral vision, his network of scars silver in the moonlight. "About a hundred, give or take. Concentrated mostly in the main hub and northern tunnels."

Kane nodded, calculating the odds. His forces outnumbered them three to one. It wouldn't be a battle—it would be a slaughter if this didn't go smoothly.

"Are all troops in position?" He stood, balancing effortlessly on the narrow beam as Rhyzan approached from the other side. Rhyzan's face was a mask of controlled tension, his eyes reflecting the distant city lights.

"Eastern teams are almost in position," Rhyzan reported quietly. "We're just waiting for Lieutenant Keller's squad to reach their entry point at the old subway terminal. Ten minutes, maybe."

Kane nodded, his gaze never leaving the sprawling ruins below. He could sense her beneath the earth, alive and safe. For now.

"And?" he prompted.

"I've confirmed she's there." Rhyzan's voice dropped even lower. "Chloe met her and has constant eyes on her."

Something tight in Kane's chest loosened fractionally.

"There's more," Rhyzan continued, hesitation edging his normally confident tone. "We may have a larger problem. Chloe overheard a conversation that suggests the rebels may have acquired weapon plans—or something significant."

Kane's head snapped toward Rhyzan, his silver-blue eyes narrowing to dangerous slits. "Explain."

Rhyzan's features tightened. "Chloe intercepted fragments of a conversation between rebel soldiers. They were discussing a chemical weapon that targets vampyr blood. And Serenity's name came up... repeatedly."

Kane's blood turned to ice. The weapon plans. The ones Evie had said she would destroy. But had she? He'd never confirmed with her, had never followed up in the chaos after the attack. If the rebels had acquired those plans...

"Call Evie," Kane's voice cut through the night air, sharp as a blade. His grip on the steel beam tightened until the metal groaned beneath his fingers. "I need confirmation that she destroyed those weapon plans. Now."

As Rhyzan turned away to make the call, Kane added, "Also, have Nox confirm that Sebastian hasn't left Evie's apartment in the last twelve hours."

Rhyzan nodded and moved away, pulling out his phone.

Kane turned his attention back to the ruins below, his enhanced vision picking out movement in the shadows. Rage bubbled beneath his skin. The rebels had always been a threat, but a manageable one. With those plans, they became an existential danger to every vampyr in Celearius.

It also meant she was in more danger than before. The rebels would use her, exploit her blood type, weaponize her against her will. He needed to reach her before they hurt her.

A moment later, Rhyzan returned, his expression grim. "Evie's not answering her phone. I've sent someone to her lab."

Kane's jaw clenched. "And Sebastian?"

"Nox confirms he's still in the apartment. Hasn't left since the attack."

The pieces didn't fit. If Sebastian hadn't left, how would the rebels have gotten the plans? Unless Evie had been compromised. Unless she'd lied about destroying them. Unless—

"Sir." Sullivan's voice cut through his spiraling thoughts. "Lieutenant Keller's squad is in position. All teams are ready on your command."

Kane took a deep breath, forcing his mind to focus. The attack had to be coordinated, precise. They would have one chance to get this right, one chance to extract Serenity and her family safely while crushing the rebellion's headquarters.

"Hold position," Kane ordered, his voice steady despite the storm raging inside him. "We move at dawn. No one acts before then unless I give the order."

Sullivan nodded and moved away to relay the command.

Alone on the beam once more, Kane closed his eyes and reached for the bond. She was there, a constant presence in his awareness. He could feel her confusion, her fear, her desperate need to protect her family.

Hold on, he thought, willing the message across the distance between them even though he knew she couldn't hear him. Just hold on a little longer.

The wind howled around him, carrying the scent of rain and ash. Kane opened his eyes, silver-blue gaze fixed on the ruins below where she waited, unknowing.

The rebellion had made a fatal mistake when they took her.

And gods help them all when dawn finally broke.

CHAPTER THIRTY-SIX

Serenity dreamed of silver-blue eyes and ocean waves, the phantom scent of cedar and leather wrapping around her like a forgotten promise.

She jerked awake on the narrow cot, her heart pounding. The rebel headquarters' dim lighting made it impossible to tell if it was day or night in this underground sanctuary. She pushed herself upright, her muscles protesting every movement.

After a shower and several hours of restless sleep, Serenity felt more human, if not entirely herself. She found her family gathered in what the rebels called the Commons—a cavernous space where mismatched tables and chairs clustered beneath strings of industrial lights. A savory scent filled the air, and her stomach growled embarrassingly.

"There she is," her mother called, waving her over with a smile that erased years from her face.

Beth launched herself from her seat, colliding with Serenity's legs in a fierce hug. "You slept forever! I thought you'd never wake up!"

"I needed it," Serenity admitted, ruffling Beth's hair. "I was completely exhausted."

She slid onto the bench beside her mother, who immediately pushed a steaming bowl toward her. The stew smelled better than anything she'd eaten in days. She pushed away thoughts of the beach and picked up her spoon.

"Eat," her mother urged, the familiar worry lines between her brows softening. "You need more meat on your bones."

Tori and Clyde joined them, carrying their own bowls. Clyde's massive frame made the bench creak as he sat down.

"How are you feeling?" Tori asked, her copper hair pulled back in a practical braid. "You look better after some sleep."

"I'm okay," Serenity lied, spooning the rich stew into her mouth. The vegetables were soft, and the broth was hearty, with unfamiliar spices. "This is good."

"They have real food here," Beth whispered. "Not as good as your cooking though."

Serenity smiled, warmth blooming in her chest at Beth's compliment. "I'll cook for you soon. I promise."

Beth tugged at Serenity's sleeve, her eyes bright with excitement. "You won't believe what happened! Tori and Clyde came in the middle of the night. They scared Mom at first, because she thought something had happened to you."

Serenity glanced at her mother, who nodded confirmation.

"Then they explained what you were doing," her mother said. "And how you just wanted us safe."

Beth bounced in her seat, nearly knocking over her water cup. "They put us in this big truck with blankets and everything. They said we were going somewhere safe where the vampyrs couldn't find us."

"They promised to help Mom get her medicine," Beth continued, her words tumbling out in a rush. "The nice lady—Starr—said they have doctors here who can help. Better than the ones at Grove Gardens!"

Serenity's throat tightened. For so long, she'd worried about her mother and sister's medications, about how they'd survive without the Elite stipend. Now, they were here, safe. It was everything she'd fought for.

"And they let me have a cookie before dinner yesterday," Beth continued, oblivious to Serenity's emotional turmoil. "A real one, with chocolate chunks!"

Serenity swallowed the lump in her throat. "That's amazing, Beth."

Her sister leaned closer, lowering her voice conspiratorially. "Do you think we'll be able to see Nox again? He promised me more ice cream when he visited next time."

The question hit Serenity hard. Her spoon clattered against the bowl as memories flooded back—Nox's gentle smile as he'd handed Beth that massive bowl of ice cream, the way he'd pretended not to notice the chocolate all over her face.

"I—" Serenity's voice caught. How could she explain to her twelve-year-old sister that they were now on opposite sides of a war? That the kind vampyr who'd sneaked her dessert was now their enemy?

"I don't think—" Serenity began again, but a hand on her shoulder saved her from answering.

"Serenity." Starr's voice cut through the conversation, her petite frame somehow commanding attention despite her size. "There's someone who wants to meet you. Now, if you don't mind."

Relief washed through her. She squeezed Beth's hand. "I'll be back soon, okay? Save me some dessert if they have any."

Beth nodded, disappointment flashing across her face before she turned back to her bowl.

Serenity followed Starr across the Commons, weaving between tables of rebels who paused their conversations to stare as they passed. Their gazes prickled against her skin. These people knew who she was—what she'd been. Kane's Elite.

"Is everything okay?" Serenity asked, hurrying to keep up with Starr's brisk pace.

"Someone important wants to thank you personally," Starr replied without slowing. "For your contribution."

Serenity slowed her steps, falling slightly behind Starr. The gratitude she'd been holding inside since waking needed to be expressed before she met whoever waited for them.

"Starr, I..." Her voice caught. "I need to thank you. For getting my family out. For keeping your promise." She swallowed hard. "You have no idea what it means to me."

Starr paused, her blue eyes softening momentarily as she turned to face Serenity. "Your family is safe because of the risks you took. The information you provided made it possible."

"What happens now?" Serenity asked, lowering her voice as a group of men passed them in the narrow corridor. "With everything?"

Starr glanced around before stepping closer, her voice dropping. "Once we determine which set of plans is authentic, we'll begin building the weapon. Your father's designs are... remarkable." Her eyes gleamed with something like reverence. "Once we verify which set is real, production can begin immediately. We estimate deployment within weeks."

"Deployment?" The word caught in Serenity's throat. "You mean... using it?"

"That's what weapons are for," Starr said simply.

Weeks. Kane could be dead in weeks. Nox, who'd been so kind to Beth. Evie. All of them.

Only she knew which plans were real, and telling them would mean their deaths.

"But it's only part of our strategy," Starr continued. "We're continuing to build our numbers, training more fighters every day." She paused, studying Serenity's face. "Which brings me to an important question. Now that your family is safe, are you still willing to help us? To continue working for the cause?"

The question landed like a stone in Serenity's gut. Behind her back, her nails bit into her palms, but she kept her expression carefully neutral.

"Of course," she said, hoping her voice sounded steadier than she felt. "That's why I'm here."

Starr's gaze lingered on her face for a moment longer before she nodded. "Good. We'll need people like you—people who understand how the vampyrs think, how they operate. Your time as Kane's Elite gives you insights most of our people don't have."

"What about Sebastian?" Serenity asked, desperate to shift focus away from herself. "Will he be joining us here too?"

A shadow crossed Starr's face. She glanced around before stepping even closer. "Sebastian has a different mission to accomplish. He's more valuable to us where he is right now."

Serenity nodded slowly, her mind racing. Was Sebastian extracting more Elites from the program? Bringing more people to safety like her family? She pictured his face—that sardonic smile, the knowing look in his eyes when he'd told her about her father's work. He'd risked so much already.

"I'm ready to help however you need me," Serenity said quietly, the lie tasting like ash on her tongue.

Starr smiled, apparently satisfied. "Great. Jon is eager to speak with you. He has questions about your time in Kane's household—information that could prove crucial to our success." She gestured down the corridor. "Come. He's waiting."

They climbed until they reached a door that led into what looked to be an old train station office. Dust motes danced in shafts of light filtering through grimy windows. A lean young man with light brown hair and brown eyes sat at the desk with the two weapon plans spread out before him. The papers looked worn at the edges, as if they'd been handled repeatedly.

He stood when she entered and smiled. The expression didn't reach his eyes.

"Thank you, Starr," he said, his voice surprisingly smooth. "I'll take it from here."

Starr nodded, her blonde hair catching the light as she turned to leave. The door closed behind her with a soft click that echoed in the quiet room.

"Serenity Wright," the young man said, gesturing to the seat in front of the desk. "Please, sit. We have much to discuss."

Serenity took the seat, though she perched on the edge of the chair, ready to bolt if needed.

"Would you like a drink?" He motioned to a crystal decanter filled with amber liquid. "It's genuine whiskey, not the synthetic stuff they serve in the Silver District."

"No, thank you," Serenity said, her fingers curling against her palms.

He shrugged and poured himself a generous measure, the liquid catching the dim light as it splashed into his glass. The scent of alcohol cut through the musty air, sharp and biting.

"I wanted to thank you personally," he said, lifting the glass in a small salute before taking a sip. "For helping to get me out of Cavern 47. I would have died there if not for the information you provided."

Serenity's brow furrowed. "You were in Cavern 47?"

"For over a month." His fingers traced the rim of his glass. "Prisoner 16, they called me. The vampyrs kept me isolated in darkness most of the time—mind games, I believe, before the... interrogations." His jaw tightened briefly before the smooth mask returned. "But thanks to you, I'm free now."

"I didn't know," Serenity said quietly. "The information I passed along—I never knew who it was helping specifically."

"Your father would be proud." Jon took another sip, his eyes never leaving her face. "He spoke of you often, you know. When we worked together."

Serenity's breath caught. "You knew my father?"

"Knew him?" Jon's smile turned genuine for the first time. "Dr. Richard Wright was one of my closest collaborators along with Starr's father, Caleb. We spent years developing the framework for the Human Liberation." He leaned back in his chair. "He never told you?"

"I... I knew he was working on something important. But I thought he was creating medicine for our district." Serenity's throat tightened. "He died before he could tell me more."

"He died a martyr," Jon said, his voice taking on a reverent quality. "Killed by enforcers when they discovered him smuggling medicine to the Outer City. Your father's work—these plans—" he gestured to the papers on his desk, "—they're his legacy. His gift to humanity's freedom."

Serenity's breath caught. "They told me he died of a heart attack."

"They lied to you," Jon said simply, watching her reaction carefully. "To cover up what they'd done. To silence any questions."

The words should have brought clarity. Instead, they churned in her stomach like poison.

Did her mother know the truth? Or had Jon's people known because they were there?

And if enforcers had killed him, why hadn't they come for the rest of the family? Why hadn't they searched their home, questioned her mother, torn apart their lives looking for evidence of rebellion?

Kane's enforcers didn't leave loose ends. She'd learned that much during her time in his household.

"I didn't know," she said quietly, because Jon was still watching her.

"Your father protected you from the truth," Jon continued. "He didn't want you or your mother involved. Didn't want you targeted if something went wrong." He paused. "He made me promise to look after you both if anything happened to him. That's why we brought your family here—to honor that promise."

Something about the way Jon said it felt rehearsed.

"I didn't realize you were so..." Serenity hesitated, searching for the right word.

"Involved?" Jon supplied. "I suppose introductions are in order. My name is Jon Sinclair, and I lead the Human Liberation. Have for the past five years, since Caleb and I came together to stand against the tyranny." He set his glass down, leaning forward with sudden intensity. "Everything you've done—every piece of information you've provided, every risk you've taken—it's all led to this moment."

"I'm sure you have questions," Jon continued, his voice taking on a persuasive quality. "About what we're building here, about what comes next."

Serenity did have questions, though probably not the ones he expected. "How long... how long has my father been working on this weapon? Why now?"

"Years," Jon said, satisfaction creeping into his voice. "Your father began developing the weapon specifications a decade ago. Since then, we've been slowly building our network, recruiting Elites like yourself who see the truth of vampyr oppression, gathering resources, waiting for the right moment." His eyes gleamed. "These plans came back to us for a reason. Our time is now. Within weeks, we could have the weapon operational. And when we deploy it, every vampyr in Celearius—in the world—will fall. Freedom, Serenity. Real freedom for humanity."

"And then what? After the vampyrs are gone?"

"Then we rebuild," Jon said simply. "A society where humans aren't cattle, where children aren't forced into servitude, where families aren't torn apart by the Elite program. The world your father dreamed of." He paused. "But we need people like you to make it happen. People who understand both sides, who've seen the system from the inside."

"That's why Starr asked if I'd continue helping," Serenity said slowly.

"We need you, Serenity." Jon's expression turned serious. "You spent months in Kane Draccus's inner circle. You observed his routines, his security measures, his relationships with other Council members. That intelligence is crucial to ensuring our success."

Warning bells rang in Serenity's mind. She chose her words carefully. "I was his Elite. A blood donor. I didn't exactly sit in on Council meetings."

"But you were there," Jon pressed. "In his home, in his private spaces. You must have observed things—vulnerabilities we could exploit, allies who might be sympathetic to our cause, weaknesses in his security."

"The penthouse was heavily secured. Multiple security systems. I didn't have access to most areas."

"But you had access to him," Jon said, his gaze sharpening. "How did he treat you? What was your relationship like?"

The question felt like a trap. "He was... distant. Professional. I was a food source to him, nothing more."

Jon tilted his head, studying her with unsettling intensity. "Interesting. Because the reports I've received suggest something different. Multiple witnesses saw you dining together, spending time alone, traveling to his private beach." He paused. "One might think you grew... close."

"He was ensuring his investment," Serenity said, hating how defensive she sounded. "Elites are expensive. He wanted to keep me healthy."

"And happy?" Jon's smile didn't reach his eyes. "Tell me, did Kane Draccus ever heal you with his blood?"

How did he know? "Once. After an accident."

"I've heard interesting things about you," Jon said, his fingers drumming against the desk. "Particularly about your blood. The vampyrs have a name for blood types like yours—something rare, something they value highly." He leaned forward. "I believe that's why Kane kept you so close and why your father hid you away so long."

Serenity's throat tightened. "What are you saying?"

"I'm saying your blood made you more valuable than you realized," Jon replied. "More valuable than a typical donor. Your father was researching the properties of your blood. He mentioned that it could help us, but..." His expression darkened. "He died before he could tell me how."

"He never told me."

"How have you been feeling since he healed you?" Jon asked, his tone almost clinical. "Any unusual effects? Enhanced senses? Strange dreams? A... connection to him, perhaps?"

The phantom warmth that had flooded through her in the tunnels flashed through her memory—Kane's presence, so real she could almost feel his hand on her face. "No," she lied. "Nothing like that."

Jon's eyes narrowed slightly. "There are rumors that humans have experienced significant side effects when exposed to vampyr blood. Sometimes the blood creates a... resonance between donor and vampyr. Some call it a connection... a bond."

"The first time he healed me, I had a bad reaction," Serenity said carefully. "But it went away after a few hours. Nothing since."

He studied her for a long moment, then sat back. "I see." His smile returned, though it held a calculating edge. "Well, perhaps you're fortunate. Such bonds can be... inconvenient. They cloud judgment, create attachments that shouldn't exist between prey and predator."

As Jon leaned forward to refill his glass, his collar shifted, revealing a serpent tattoo coiling at the base of his neck. The black ink seemed to ripple against his skin in the dim light, its fanged mouth open as if ready to strike.

"Your father believed you were special, Serenity. Not just because of your blood type, but because of your strength. Your intelligence. Your ability to see what needed to be done and do it, no matter the cost." Jon's voice took on a persuasive quality. "He told me that if anything ever happened to him, I should look after you. Make sure you understood the importance of the work."

"I want to help," Serenity said, because it was expected. "My father died for this cause. I owe it to him to see it through."

"I'm glad to hear it." Jon stood, circling around the desk with deliberate slowness. Each step brought him closer until he stood directly in front of her, too close. "Because we need people we can trust. People who won't let sentiment cloud their judgment. People who understand that sometimes, to achieve freedom, we must make difficult choices."

His eyes bored into hers.

"The weapon your father designed will kill every vampyr," Jon continued, his voice soft but edged with steel. "Every single one. Including any you might have formed... attachments to during your time as an Elite. I need to know that when the time comes, you'll be able to accept that. That you won't let misplaced sympathy interfere with what needs to be done."

Kane's face flashed through her mind—the way he'd looked at her on the beach, the tenderness in his touch. Nox's gentle smile as he'd handed Beth ice cream. Evie's brilliant mind and sharp wit.

"I understand," she said, the words tasting like ash.

Jon smiled, apparently satisfied. "Good. Because your role isn't finished. We still need to verify which set of plans is authentic—your father was clever enough to create a decoy, but we need to know which is which. And we need detailed intelligence about vampyr weaknesses, Council vulnerabilities, anything that might help us exploit the chaos when the weapon deploys." He placed a hand on her shoulder. "Your time in Kane's household makes you invaluable to our success."

"I'll help however I can," Serenity managed, though revulsion coiled in her stomach at his touch.

"I hope you and your family are comfortable here," Jon said, stepping back. "We've tried to make the accommodations as pleasant as possible, given the circumstances."

The unspoken threat was clear.

"The living quarters are fine. Thank you," Serenity said, moving toward the door.

Jon's lips curved upward, but the smile remained cold. "I hope you'll continue to be helpful to us, Serenity. Your father would want you to see this through to the end."

The serpent tattoo seemed to pulse in the dim light. Serenity nodded, not trusting herself to speak. She backed toward the door, her fingers fumbling for the handle behind her.

"We'll speak again soon," Jon promised. "There's much more to discuss. And Serenity?" He waited until she met his gaze. "I meant what I said about trust. In times like these, we need to know who our true allies are. I hope you understand what I'm saying."

The threat beneath the courtesy was unmistakable.

Serenity slipped through the door and hurried down the stairs, heart pounding as her footsteps echoed in the narrow stairwell. She descended as quickly as she dared, putting as much distance between herself and Jon Sinclair as possible.

When she finally reached the bottom, she pressed her back against the cool stone wall, trying to catch her breath. Her hands were shaking.

She could never let Jon know about her connection to Kane. He would use it against her. And he'd invoked her father's memory to ensure her compliance. She knew a snake when she saw one—and Jon was coiled right in front of her, ready to strike.

But how could she live with herself if she helped them? And how could she live with herself if she didn't?

CHAPTER THIRTY-SEVEN

SERENITY

Serenity had just reached the Commons, where her mother was talking with Tori and Clyde was playing with Beth, when the floor beneath her lurched violently.

The explosion hit before the sound registered—a bone-deep concussion that knocked the air from her lungs. Dust and chunks of concrete rained from the ceiling. The fluorescent lights flickered once, twice, three times before plunging half the space into darkness.

No. No, no, no.

A child's wail pierced the sudden silence, followed by a cascade of screams. Serenity's ears rang, a high-pitched whine drowning out everything else as she stumbled against the wall, fingers scraping against rough stone. Twenty feet away through billowing dust, a woman clutched her bleeding forehead while a man beside her shouted words Serenity couldn't make out. The acrid smell of smoke drifted through the air, burning her nostrils with each panicked breath.

"BETH!" The scream tore from Serenity's throat before she could stop it. She couldn't see her sister. Couldn't see her mother. Just chaos and dust and terror.

They found us.

Suddenly, a hand gripped her shoulders, fingers digging into her flesh hard enough to bruise. "Serenity, this way. We need to move." Jax's voice cut through the pandemonium, his face illuminated in flashes by sputtering emergency lights. He grabbed her arm and pulled her toward a narrow passage.

"No!" Serenity wrenched against his grip, her voice cracking with desperation. "We can't—my mom—Beth!" Her eyes darted frantically through the billowing dust and screaming crowd. People ran in every direction, colliding, trampling. A man fell and didn't get up. Blood on the floor. So much blood already.

"Clyde and Tori have them. Look!" Jax pointed through a momentary clearing in the chaos.

Serenity's heart lurched as she spotted them—Clyde's massive form supporting her mother's trembling frame, one arm wrapped protectively around her shoulders. A few steps behind, Tori clutched Beth's small hand, the child's tear-streaked face pale with terror as they pushed through the panicked throng.

Relief flooded through her, so intense it made her knees weak. They're alive.

But the relief lasted only a heartbeat before a second explosion rocked the Commons. Closer this time. The ground buckled beneath her feet, and Serenity went down hard, knees cracking against concrete. Screams intensified. More dust, more smoke, the metallic taste of blood in her mouth where she'd bitten her tongue.

Jax hauled her up, his grip unrelenting. "We have to move NOW!"

They ran, stumbling over debris. The sound of their feet echoed against stone walls, mixing with distant gunfire that grew steadily closer. Each crack made Serenity flinch, expecting the next bullet to find her, to find Beth.

As they rounded a corner, a third explosion sent shockwaves through the passage. The ceiling groaned ominously. Chunks of concrete and rebar crashed down ahead of them, missing Serenity by inches. Jax yanked her backward, then forward again, pulling her through the deadly rain of debris. Metal scraped her shoulder—sharp, burning pain—but she didn't slow.

When the shaking finally stopped, dust hung so thick in the air that Serenity could barely breathe. Each gasp felt like inhaling glass. She coughed, doubled over, lungs screaming. Through streaming eyes, she could barely make out Jax's face inches from hers.

"Through here!" He dragged her toward a jagged opening in the concrete wall, the edges sharp enough to draw blood. Metal rebar scraped across her other shoulder as he pulled her through into a room that reeked of gun oil and metal.

An armory.

Rifles and pistols gleamed on wall racks under harsh fluorescent lights. Jax strode to the nearest rack, yanking down weapons with practiced efficiency.

The moment Clyde stumbled through the doorway, Beth clinging to his leg and her mother's face ashen behind them, Serenity's paralysis broke. She rushed to them, hands shaking as she grabbed Beth, checking her sister for injuries with frantic fingers. No blood. No wounds. Just terror in those wide brown eyes.

"You're okay, you're okay," Serenity whispered, not sure if she was reassuring Beth or herself.

Jax thrust a rifle into Clyde's hands. His thumb clicked the safety off with chilling familiarity.

"You think they found us?" Clyde's voice was steady, but his knuckles whitened around the grip.

"Kane's forces," Jax said grimly, his magazine sliding home with a metallic snap that made Serenity's stomach clench. "Three-pronged attack from what the scouts are reporting. East, west, and south tunnels. They're everywhere. Possibly even the North tunnels."

Kane.

He was alive. Kane was here. Kane... was attacking.

And she didn't know whether to feel relief or terror.

Across the room, Tori lifted two heavy rifles from their mounts. "We need to get them out of here," she said urgently, passing the weapons through the doorway to rebels beyond. "The civilians aren't fighters."

"I need to find Chloe." Jax's voice cracked slightly on her name, the first time Serenity had ever heard him sound uncertain.

"She was heading back to your room when I last saw her," Clyde said, gripping his weapon tighter until tendons stood out on his hands. "About twenty minutes ago."

They pressed themselves against the cold concrete wall as more rebels—faces grim and determined, some barely older than Beth—squeezed through the narrow opening. Their hands grabbed frantically for whatever weapons remained on the racks. The metallic sounds of magazines being loaded and safeties clicking off filled the cramped space.

"Head for the East Tunnels," Jax instructed, though his eyes kept darting toward the corridor he'd need to take. "The passage narrows but eventually leads beyond the city limits. I'll catch up as soon as I find Chloe."

Jax gave one last lingering look at Serenity, something unspoken passing between them—apology, maybe, or goodbye—before he nodded and disappeared into the dust-filled darkness.

"Follow me," Clyde commanded, raising his rifle as he moved toward the doorway.

They followed him deeper into the maze of passages, Tori taking up the rear with her weapon raised, Serenity and her family sandwiched in the middle. A few more rebels joined them as they moved quickly through the underground network—a teenage boy who couldn't be more than sixteen, an older woman with scarred hands, a man missing part of his ear.

The stone walls pressed close on either side, the air thick with dust and fear and the copper smell of blood drifting from somewhere ahead. Distant gunfire echoed through the passages, sometimes close enough to make Serenity's ears ring, sometimes fading to nothing before surging back louder than before.

They rounded a corner and froze.

A group of soldiers emerged from a side passage—six of them, maybe seven, black tactical gear, weapons raised and ready. Not rebels. Kane's forces.

Serenity's body moved on instinct, shoving her mother and sister behind her, using herself as a shield. Her heart hammered so hard she could barely hear over the rush of blood in her ears. Tori and several other armed rebels stepped in front of them, creating a human barrier between the soldiers and the civilians.

"Don't move or we'll shoot!" the lead soldier shouted, his voice distorted by a tactical mask.

Serenity could feel Beth's small body trembling against her back, her mother's ragged breathing. Her own breath came in short, sharp gasps that she couldn't control. Time seemed to slow, everything crystallizing to this single moment—the soldiers' fingers on triggers, the rebels' desperate stance.

Please not Beth. Not Mom.

Then one of the rebels—a tall, lithe woman Serenity had seen around the headquarters but never spoken to—stepped forward from behind them, holding up her hands in surrender. "Don't shoot, please."

The soldiers hesitated, eyes flickering between the woman and the rest of the group.

Serenity held her breath, hope and dread warring in her chest.

But just as she thought they might somehow, impossibly escape this, the woman's hands moved with impossible speed. A weapon appeared from behind her back—Serenity didn't even see where she'd hidden it—and she fired. Three shots, three soldiers down, all headshots, faster than Serenity could blink.

Chaos erupted.

"MOVE!" Clyde roared, shoving them backward into another passage as gunfire exploded through the tunnel. The sound was deafening in the enclosed space, each shot a physical assault. Serenity dragged Beth with her, one arm around her sister's shoulders, the other reaching back for their mother. They stumbled over each other, falling against the wall as bullets sparked off stone behind them.

Through the din, Serenity heard screams. The teenage rebel boy went down clutching his leg. The older woman fired back, her face a mask of fury and fear.

And the tall woman who'd started it all—she moved through the soldiers like death itself.

Too fast.

Too precise.

Too powerful.

Serenity's blood turned to ice as realization crashed over her, stealing what little breath she had left.

The woman wasn't human. She was a vampyr.

A vampyr fighting alongside the rebellion. Helping them. Killing Kane's soldiers to protect rebels.

Dex in the headquarters. Now this woman. Vampyrs working with the rebellion—the same rebellion that had a weapon designed to kill all vampyrs.

They didn't know. They couldn't know. They were being used as disposable soldiers, and when Jon deployed the weapon, they would die along with everyone else.

"MOVE!" Clyde's shout snapped her back to the immediate terror. He shoved them further down the passage, firing controlled bursts back toward the soldiers. Shell casings clattered against stone. The smell of gunpowder choked the air.

More people ran past them—rebels and vampyrs alike, all heading toward the main chamber where the sounds of battle grew louder. Serenity caught glimpses through the chaos: a rebel with half his face burned, a vampyr with silver burns across her arms, someone crying over a body in the corridor.

Serenity tried to keep up with the others while protecting her family, but her legs felt like lead, her lungs burning from the dust and smoke. Beth sobbed against her side, and their mother's face had gone sheet-white, her breathing too fast, too shallow.

They burst into the main chamber and Serenity's forward momentum died.

Chaos. Pure, absolute chaos.

The vast space swarmed with soldiers in black tactical gear, rebels firing from behind overturned tables and makeshift barricades. Bodies sprawled across the floor—so many bodies, some moving weakly, most not moving at all. Blood pooled on concrete. Gunfire cracked from every direction at once. Someone screamed, high and endless, until the sound cut off abruptly.

Clyde dragged them sideways, behind large crates stacked against the wall. Tori crouched beside them, her rifle tracking movements across the chamber. Sweat and dust streaked her face.

"We need to get out of here," Clyde said, his voice strained for the first time. "The only way is back the way we came or through those doors."

They all looked toward the main entrance where more soldiers poured in, black-clad and organized, sweeping through rebels with military precision.

"We can take the North tunnels," Tori suggested, jerking her chin toward a passage on the far side of the chamber.

"We don't know what's down there," Clyde countered. "Could be collapsed. Could be flooded. Could be crawling with more soldiers."

"It's that or we die here," Tori said flatly.

Serenity looked at her mother's terrified face, at Beth shaking so hard her teeth chattered. She couldn't let them die here. Not after everything. Not when they'd finally been reunited.

"Let's take the tunnels," she said, surprised by the steadiness in her own voice.

Clyde nodded once, then gestured to the other rebels with them. "North passage. Stay low. Move fast. Don't stop for anything."

The sprint across the chamber was the longest thirty seconds of Serenity's life.

They ran hunched over, using debris as cover, Clyde leading the way with Tori bringing up the rear. Bullets whined past Serenity's head—she felt the air displacement, heard them crack against stone behind her. Beth stumbled and Serenity hauled her up without breaking stride. Her mother fell behind and one of the rebels—the man with the missing ear—grabbed her arm and pulled her forward.

A bullet caught the teenage boy. He went down hard, blood blooming across his shoulder. Serenity's feet wanted to stop, wanted to help, but Clyde grabbed her collar and dragged her past. "Keep moving!"

They plunged into the North passage and kept running.

The tunnel sloped downward, darker than the others, lit only by emergency strips that cast everything in sickly green. They encountered more soldiers as they fled deeper into the underground network—brief firefights that sent them scrambling down side passages, hiding in alcoves, pressing flat against walls as boots thundered past.

Serenity watched as Clyde and Tori took down attackers with silver knives and bullets, their movements fluid and coordinated. They'd trained for this their entire lives, she realized. While she'd been studying nursing with her father, while Beth had been going to school, these people had been preparing for war.

And now the war had come.

Gunfire and shouting echoed behind them, growing closer then farther, impossible to track. Beth was flagging, could barely run anymore. Their mother wheezed with every breath, her face gray.

Suddenly, footsteps approached from ahead. Clyde signaled everyone to stop, flattening against the wall. Serenity pressed Beth against the stone, covering her sister's mouth with one hand to muffle her frightened breathing. Through gaps in the darkness, she saw shadows moving—three soldiers, maybe four, sweeping through with flashlights.

Clyde leaned close to Serenity, his breath hot against her ear. "We need to move. We can't fight them here—tunnel's too narrow. Side passage, twenty feet back. You run, we'll cover."

Serenity nodded, terror making her mute.

They slipped back down the passage as quietly as desperate people could move. Found the side tunnel—barely more than a crack in the wall. Squeezed through one at a time, the stone scraping skin, catching on clothes. Behind them, shouts as the soldiers realized they'd been bypassed.

Finally—finally—cold air hit her face. Real air, not the thick, dust-choked atmosphere of the tunnels.

They burst into early morning light, and Serenity gasped, filling her lungs with clean air after what felt like hours underground. They'd emerged in a deserted part of the Dead City, surrounded by abandoned buildings, their windows like dead eyes. The distant sound of gunfire and shouting still echoed from below, muffled now but relentless.

"Help me block this!" Clyde was already dragging a metal bar toward the tunnel entrance. Serenity and several rebels helped him pile cinder blocks and debris to barricade the door they'd just come through. It wouldn't hold long, but maybe long enough.

"Serenity!"

Tori's voice, sharp with panic, cut through the relief flooding Serenity's system.

Her heart stopped.

She ran toward the sound, dread pooling in her stomach.

As she turned the corner of the building, she saw her mother's face twisted in pain, Tori pale and trembling beside her.

No. Please no.

"What happened?" Serenity demanded, her voice breaking.

"It's Beth," her mother gasped, the words torn from her throat. "She's been shot."

The world tilted. Time stopped. Everything—the adrenaline, the terror, the desperate flight—crashed down on Serenity at once.

Beth lay crumpled against the building's wall, her small hands pressed against her side where dark crimson seeped between her fingers, staining her shirt. Her face was white as paper, her breathing rapid and shallow—the early signs of shock.

No. Not Beth. Anyone but Beth.

"No." The word tore from Serenity's throat as she dropped to her knees beside her sister, hands already moving. "No, no, no."

Training kicked in—her father's voice echoing in her mind from all those hours spent in his makeshift shed. Assess, stabilize, treat. She'd been studying to be a nurse before he died, had dreamed of working beside him, healing their community.

But not Beth. She was never supposed to have to save Beth.

"Beth, look at me. Look at me, sweetheart." Serenity's hands moved with practiced efficiency despite their trembling. She gently pulled Beth's hands away from the wound, assessing the damage. Left side, upper abdomen. The blood pulsed with each heartbeat—arterial bleeding.

This is bad. So bad.

"I need clean cloth," Serenity snapped at Tori, her voice suddenly steady with purpose even as her mind screamed. "Anything. Now."

Tori fumbled with her jacket, tearing off a sleeve with shaking hands.

Serenity pressed the fabric against Beth's wound, applying direct pressure the way her father had taught her. "Stay with me, Beth. Keep your eyes on me. You're going to be fine."

But Beth's pupils were dilating, her skin growing colder beneath Serenity's touch. The blood—there was so much blood, soaking through the fabric, pooling around Serenity's knees, warm and sticky and wrong.

Why won't it stop?

Her sister's breathing grew more labored, each breath a small, desperate gasp.

Serenity's mind raced through everything she knew. Elevate the legs to combat shock. Maintain pressure on the wound. Keep the airway clear. But none of it would matter—not without proper medical equipment, without sterile supplies, without the medications her father would have had.

Without her father.

The realization hit her like a physical blow. If her father were here, he'd know what to do. He'd have the right tools, the right knowledge. He'd save Beth the way he'd saved countless others in Grove Gardens. But he was gone, and all his training, all his careful lessons, weren't enough for this.

I can't do this. I can't save her. I don't know how.

"Please, Beth. Please stay with me." Serenity's voice cracked as tears blurred her vision. She adjusted her grip, trying to stem the bleeding, but it kept coming. Too much. Too fast.

Beth's lips trembled as she tried to speak, but only a small whimper emerged.

"I've got you. I've got you." Serenity stroked her sister's hair with one blood-soaked hand while maintaining pressure with the other. But even as she said the words, she could see the truth in Beth's dimming eyes. Could feel her sister's heartbeat growing weaker beneath her fingers.

Don't take her. Please. Take me instead.

All her training, all her father's lessons—useless. Inadequate. Not enough to save the person who mattered most.

She needed a hospital. She needed her father. She needed a miracle.

And she had no idea how to save her.

CHAPTER THIRTY-EIGHT

KANE

The scent hit Kane first—blood, gunpowder, and fear—a potent cocktail that hung in the stale tunnel air. He moved silently through the darkness, each step calculated despite the urgency pounding through him. Serenity was here. Close. Her jasmine-rose scent called to him beneath the chaos, a beacon drawing him deeper into the rebel stronghold.

Behind him, Rhyzan's footfalls were nearly imperceptible, a ghost's whisper against concrete. They'd separated from the main assault force ten minutes ago, slipping through the eastern access tunnel while Sullivan led the frontal attack from the west and south.

A figure darted from a side passage—female, vampyr, moving with preternatural speed. She registered their presence a second too late. Rhyzan's blade flashed in the dim emergency lighting, opening her throat in one fluid motion. She crumpled without a sound, dark blood pooling beneath her body.

"Another traitor," Rhyzan murmured, wiping his blade clean. "That's the third vampyr we've encountered."

Kane barely spared the body a glance. The knowledge that his own kind had allied with the rebellion didn't surprise him. They'd suspected as much for a while—this was just proof they were right.

"We need to keep moving." Kane pushed forward, his body coiled with tension.

Serenity's fear pulsed through him like a second heartbeat, growing stronger with each step. The sensation was unlike anything he'd experienced before—her emotions flooding his consciousness as if they were his own, urging him forward with desperate intensity.

"She's close," he growled, more to himself than to Rhyzan.

The tunnel widened abruptly, opening into what must have been an old subway station, now transformed into what the rebels called the Commons. The vast underground space swarmed with bodies—rebels fleeing, fighting, screaming as his forces closed in from multiple entry points. Blood and gunpowder saturated the air, nearly overwhelming Serenity's scent.

His gaze cut through the chaos like a predator tracking prey. East. She had gone East. He knew it with bone-deep certainty.

As he moved to follow that invisible tether, a familiar face caught his attention.

Jon Sinclair.

Kane froze, his muscles locking as recognition hit him. Prisoner 16 moved through the chaos with practiced efficiency, weaving between panicked rebels like a shark through churning waters. The human's face was leaner than Kane remembered from the interrogation files, cheekbones more pronounced, but there was no mistaking those cold, calculating eyes.

Jon wasn't fleeing like the others. He was heading with purpose toward a metal door in the far left corner of the Commons, accompanied by three figures Kane recognized instantly: a petite blonde woman—Scarlet, McGraff's supposed agent—Elise's Elite, Damon, if he wasn't mistaken—along with Jax and Chloe, moving in perfect sync with Jon.

"Go," Rhyzan hissed, seeing the same thing. "I'll secure this area."

Kane didn't wait for further discussion. He launched himself forward, cutting through the frenzied crowd with predatory precision. Human rebels and vampyr soldiers scattered before him, instinctively clearing a path. Blood splattered across him as he moved, some his enemies', some not. He didn't care. Nothing mattered except reaching that door before it closed.

Jon's head snapped up, awareness crystallizing in those calculating eyes. For a heartbeat, their gazes locked across the chaos—predator recognizing predator.

Recognition flickered across Jon's face—not fear, but acknowledgment. The corner of his mouth twitched upward in what might have been the ghost of a smile before he stepped backward through the metal door, his companions following.

The metal door began to swing shut.

Kane lunged forward, shoving a female rebel out of his path with enough force to send her crashing into the wall. His muscles coiled, ready to spring the remaining distance—

A gunshot cracked through the air. Pain exploded in his shoulder, the impact barely slowing his momentum. Another rebel stepped into his path, rifle raised. Kane didn't break stride, simply seized the human by the throat and hurled him aside like a ragdoll.

The door sealed with a metallic clang that somehow cut through the cacophony of battle. Kane reached it in seconds, not bothering with the handle. He channeled centuries of rage, power reverberating through his bones. The door tore from its hinges, crashing inward with a deafening screech.

Kane stepped through the doorway, fangs extended, ready to tear through anything in his path—only to find himself staring at an empty storage room. Metal shelves lined with medical supplies, canned goods, and empty ammunition boxes. The stench of dust and mildew hung in the stale air, but no trace remained of Jon or his companions.

"Fuck," Kane snarled, stalking between the shelves. His enhanced senses detected nothing but abandoned supplies and settling dust. No heartbeats, no breathing, no shuffling footsteps. Just... emptiness.

He slammed his fist into the nearest shelf, sending metal buckling beneath the impact. The shelf toppled with a thunderous crash, cans scattering across concrete like metallic hailstones.

Kane prowled the perimeter, running his hands along the walls, searching for hidden panels or concealed exits. Nothing. The room was sealed except for the doorway he'd entered through. It defied logic. Five people had entered, yet none remained.

He closed his eyes, filtering through the cacophony bombarding his senses—gunfire from the main chamber, screams, the crackle of comm devices, Rhyzan barking orders in the distance. Too much noise, too many distractions.

Beneath the chaos, his connection to Serenity remained—pulling northward now, her fear spiking.

Kane's entire body trembled with conflicting impulses. Jon Sinclair was the rebel leader, and he had just let him get away. Every military instinct demanded he pursue this lead before it grew cold.

But Serenity's fear intensified until it felt like a physical hook embedded in his chest, yanking him toward her.

"Goddammit," he snarled, slamming his fist into the wall. Concrete cracked beneath the impact, dust billowing around his knuckles. Blood dripped between his fingers, the minor wounds already healing as he pulled his hand away.

The choice made itself. Strategy could wait. Jon Sinclair could wait.

Serenity couldn't.

He left the room, chaos still raging in the main chamber as he made his way through and entered the northern tunnels. His nostrils flared, catching wisps of jasmine that didn't belong in these dank passages. He pivoted without hesitation, his fingertips brushing the rough wall as he navigated a sharp turn, moving faster through the darkness than any human could safely move.

As he ventured deeper into the Northern tunnels, he detected a metallic tang in the air—the unmistakable scent of blood. His heart clenched with dread.

Without hesitation, he approached a barricaded door, the wooden planks and stone bricks meant to deter intruders easily giving way to his strength. Bursting onto the desolate streets of the old city, Kane scanned the scene with a sharp, calculating gaze. His soldiers, loyal and ready, surrounded the area, awaiting his orders.

The sound of movement reached his ears, drawing his attention—a cluster of figures huddled against the crumbling brick wall of a nearby building.

And there—

Beth's small body lay sprawled on the ground, her brown hair fanned out like a halo against the concrete, dark liquid pooling beneath her. Serenity crouched beside her, shoulders rigid, fingers trembling as they pressed against her sister's wound.

In that moment, Kane made a choice he'd been avoiding for six hours.

He opened the bond.

The wall he'd built between them crumbled in an instant, and his presence flooded across the connection like a dam breaking. His survival, his determination, his desperate need to reach her—all of it crashed into her awareness with the force of a tidal wave.

He felt the exact moment she registered it. Felt her shock, her disbelief, her sudden overwhelming hope as she realized he was alive. That he was here.

When she looked up, her eyes widened, pupils dilating in the dim light—first shock at seeing him physically before her, then the delayed realization that the warmth flooding through her wasn't imagination. It was real. He was real. Alive. Here.

Her lips parted on a gasp, one hand flying to her chest as if she could feel the bond's presence there, tangible and undeniable after days of silence.

Kane pressed his back against the cold stone, drinking in the sight of her even as he melted into shadow. A lanky male with a jagged scar across his jaw—Clyde—stepped in front of Serenity, hand hovering over the weapon at his hip. A female with shoulder-length copper hair—Tori—flanked her other side, muscles coiled tight as a spring. Their heads swiveled, scanning the darkness as if sensing a predator's gaze.

Kane nodded once. His soldiers materialized from alleys and doorways, boots scraping against pavement as they formed a perfect circle around the rebels. He stepped forward, the sole of his boot crunching on broken glass, and watched as heads snapped toward the sound.

Tori's finger twitched on the trigger as Clyde raised his weapon, but Kane moved like liquid shadow. He seized Tori's wrist, twisting until tendons popped and the gun clattered to the pavement. Clyde fired—a deafening crack that split the night—but Kane was already behind him, fangs bared in a predatory smile. Blood pearled at the rebel's throat where his nails broke skin.

The pair fought with desperate fury—all flailing limbs and panicked breaths—but Kane's movements carried the fluid precision of someone who had been perfecting the art of violence since before their ancestors were born. He caught Clyde's punch mid-air, bones crunching beneath his grip, then slammed him into the brick wall hard enough to leave a spiderweb of cracks in the mortar. Tori lunged with a blade that gleamed dully in the sunlight, but Kane sidestepped, hooked his foot behind her ankle, and sent her sprawling face-first onto the concrete.

His soldiers moved to secure them both as Kane's gaze returned to Serenity.

Her jaw trembled once before she clenched it tight, a muscle flickering beneath her skin. A single tear carved a path down her dirt-smudged cheek, catching the sunlight before she could swipe it away with the back of her bloodied hand.

Along the bond, he felt everything—her terror for Beth, her shock at his survival, her desperate hope warring with crushing guilt. She thought he hated her. Thought he'd come for revenge, not rescue.

And then his attention shifted to Beth, wounded and bleeding. The sight affected him viscerally, stirring a tumultuous mix of emotions. This child—innocent, fragile, dying—represented everything he'd sworn to protect when he'd taken control of Celearius. The irony wasn't lost on him that his own forces had likely fired the shot that brought her down.

"Kane." Serenity's voice was barely a whisper, yet it echoed through the stillness. Through the bond, her desperation crashed into him with physical force.

His gaze remained locked on her, his mind racing with conflicting thoughts. He wanted to save Beth, to spare Serenity from the pain of loss. But he also knew what was at stake—the rebellion, the weapon plans, the traitors in his own ranks.

Nox's voice cut through his turmoil as he appeared from the shadows, moving swiftly toward them. "Beth," he gasped, dropping to his knees beside Serenity.

Kane watched as Nox immediately lifted Beth's shirt, revealing a gunshot wound in the left side of her abdomen. Blood pulsed from the injury in rhythmic spurts that matched her weakening heartbeat. The metallic scent filled his nostrils, but it wasn't the sweet ambrosia of Serenity's blood—this was ordinary, tinged with the acrid smell of fear and the approach of death.

"She needs a hospital," Nox said, his fingers already pressing against the wound to slow the bleeding. "She needs—"

"Please." Serenity's voice cracked, and her anguish nearly drove Kane to his knees. "I know I betrayed you and you hate me, but she's innocent. She never knew anything. She's just a child. Please, Kane. Please."

The desperation in her voice tore at him. Kane knelt beside Beth, assessing the wound with centuries of experience. The edges had already begun to blacken—not silver poisoning, but something equally deadly to humans. Infection was setting in fast, too fast. The bullet must have been contaminated.

He could save her. His blood could heal the wound, purge the infection, and restore her failing body. But doing so would cost him the leverage he desperately needed.

"Sullivan," Rhyzan barked into his comm device, appearing at Kane's side. "I need extraction. Northeast tunnel exit, building with the red door. Medical emergency."

Rhyzan turned to Kane, reading the conflict in his expression. "Enough of this. We're taking them all." The decision was made, his tone clear. Kane's soldiers moved to secure the remaining rebels and ensure compliance.

As Nox carefully lifted Beth into his arms, her small body limp and pale, Kane's gaze flickered to Serenity. Her eyes were wide, honey-brown depths filled with a mixture of fear and desperate hope. He saw her inner struggle along the bond—the battle between loyalty to her cause and love for her sister.

And he saw the deeper truth—one that made his chest tighten despite his anger.

She would give him anything to save Beth. Would tell him any truth, betray any cause, sacrifice any principle. The depth of her love for her family was absolute, unwavering, fierce enough to burn down the world.

Just as his feelings for her were.

The realization settled over him like a weight. He'd known it before, of course. Had felt it in the desperate way she'd shielded him from the silver bullets, heard it in her screams as Jax dragged her away. But seeing it now, feeling it through the open bond—the raw, unconditional devotion she had for those she loved—shifted his perspective entirely.

He wanted that devotion directed at him. Wanted her to choose him with the same fierce certainty she chose her family.

And he would have it. One way or another.

"You want me to save her?" Kane asked, his voice quiet but carrying absolute authority. "Then you tell me everything, Serenity. The rebellion. The weapon plans. Jon Sinclair. Every contact, every meeting, every piece of intelligence you fed them. I want names, locations, strategies. Everything you know."

The words hung in the air, heavy with meaning. He felt her flinch as if he'd struck her.

Her expression crumbled, rage and anguish warring across her features. "You're using her to—"

"I'm using the only leverage I have to get the truth from you," Kane said flatly. "You lied to me for weeks. You spied on me, stole from me, and fed information to terrorists who just tried to kill me. Again." He leaned closer, his tone dropping dangerously. "Did you really think there wouldn't be consequences?"

"I didn't—" Her voice broke. "I never wanted—"

"Then tell me the truth." His gaze held hers, unrelenting. "All of it. Or watch your sister die because you chose to protect the people who shot her."

The cruelty of it twisted his gut, but he forced himself to remain unmoved. This was war. This was survival. This was the price of her deception.

Serenity's hands shook as she looked down at Beth's pale face, then back at Kane. He felt her surrender—the moment her resistance crumbled beneath the weight of her sister's life.

"Okay," she whispered, tears streaming down her face. "Okay. I'll tell you everything. Just please—please save her."

Kane held her gaze for one more heartbeat, then nodded once. He moved to Beth's side, gently pushing Nox's hands away from the wound. The child's breathing was shallow, her heartbeat erratic. Another few minutes and it would be too late.

He bit into his wrist, dark blood welling immediately. Pressing it to Beth's lips, he tilted her head back slightly. "Drink," he commanded softly.

The child's survival instinct took over. Her throat worked weakly as his blood flowed into her mouth. He felt the moment it took effect—her heartbeat strengthening, her breathing deepening. The blackened edges of her wound began to recede, healthy pink tissue replacing the infected flesh.

He'd healed humans before, countless times over centuries. Never once had a bond formed. Those were myths, until Serenity had proven otherwise.

This felt different. Expected. Normal.

Within moments, the bleeding stopped entirely. Beth's eyes fluttered open, confused and disoriented but alive.

"Serenity?" she whispered, her voice small and frightened.

"I'm here, sweetheart." Serenity's voice broke as she reached for her sister. "I'm right here."

Kane pulled his wrist away, the wound already closing. He stood, putting distance between himself and the raw emotion threatening to overwhelm him through the bond.

Nox carefully transferred Beth into Serenity's arms. The child clung to her sister, trembling but whole. Alive. Safe.

For now.

"Sullivan's team is two minutes out," Rhyzan reported. "We have secure transport ready."

Kane nodded, then turned back to Serenity. "You're coming with us. All of you." It wasn't a request.

Her mother, who'd been silent through the entire exchange, pressed against the wall in shock and finally found her voice. "Where are you taking us?"

"Celearius," Kane said. "Where you'll be safe until we've dealt with the rebellion."

"You mean where we'll be your prisoners," Serenity said bitterly, still holding Beth close.

"I mean where your family will be protected," Kane corrected, his tone hard. "The rebellion knows you were compromised. They know you have information. Do you really think Jon Sinclair will just let you walk away?"

He felt her realization—the rebellion would see her as a liability now. A loose end that needed to be permanently tied up.

"You don't have a choice," Kane continued. "Come willingly, or I'll have my soldiers carry you. Either way, you're leaving with me."

The sound of approaching vehicles cut through the night—military transports, their engines rumbling. Sullivan appeared from the shadows, gesturing to his team.

"Sir, we're ready to move."

Kane looked at Serenity one last time. He could feel her fear, her anger, her bone-deep exhaustion. But beneath it all, he felt another emotion—one that made his dead heart ache.

Relief. She was relieved he was alive. Relieved he'd saved Beth. Relieved that despite everything, he was here.

"Let's go," Kane said quietly.

Nox helped Serenity to her feet, Beth still clutched in her arms. Her mother moved to her other side, one hand on Serenity's shoulder. They formed a small, protective unit as soldiers surrounded them.

Clyde and Tori, secured by restraints, were already being loaded into one of the transports. The remaining rebels had either fled or been captured. The battle was over.

Kane had won.

But as he watched Serenity climb into the transport, her honey-brown eyes meeting his one last time before the doors closed, he wondered what, exactly, his victory would cost him.

Because along the bond, he felt her heart breaking.

And despite everything she'd done, despite every lie and betrayal, feeling her pain felt like his own.

The transport pulled away, heading back toward Celearius. Rhyzan appeared at his side as the convoy disappeared into the night.

"We secured the Commons and northern tunnels. Minimal casualties on our side. The rebels either fled or surrendered."

"And Jon Sinclair?" Kane asked, though he already knew the answer.

"Gone. No trace." Rhyzan's jaw tightened. "Along with Jax, Damon, Chloe, and Scarlet."

Kane nodded, unsurprised. "Put out alerts. I want every available resource looking for them."

"Already done." Rhyzan studied him carefully. "You saved the child."

"I did."

"And now she'll tell you everything."

"She will."

"Was it worth it?" Rhyzan asked quietly. "Letting Jon Sinclair escape?"

Kane was silent for a long moment, staring at the empty street where Serenity had been.

"Ask me again when this is over," Kane said finally.

He turned and walked back toward the tunnels. There was work to be done—interrogations to conduct, traitors to root out, a city to secure.

But first, he had to deal with Serenity.

And the truth she'd promised to give him.

Even if it destroyed them both.

CHAPTER THIRTY-NINE

SEBASTIAN

Blood stained Sebastian's hands, invisible but impossible to wash away. He adjusted the focus on his binoculars, the cold metal biting into his skin as he tracked the movement of vampyr troops swarming from the tunnels below. The Dead City sprawled beneath him like an open wound, its abandoned buildings and crumbling infrastructure a testament to humanity's fall from power.

The mountain cave provided the perfect vantage point—secluded enough to remain undetected, yet close enough to observe the unfolding catastrophe. The binoculars' enhanced magnification revealed black-clad soldiers emerging from the underground network that had housed the rebel headquarters for the past three years.

He'd spent those years building his cover, playing his role while secretly working toward... what? Freedom? Justice? Revenge? Sometimes Sebastian himself couldn't remember anymore. The lines had blurred so thoroughly that he no longer knew which side of them he stood on.

A helicopter's metallic shell caught his attention as sunlight transformed the military-grade aircraft into a glittering insect against the blood-orange sky. Sebastian tracked its path through his binoculars as it rose from the

Dead City's broken skyline with predatory grace, hovering briefly before banking sharply toward Celearius.

Sebastian lowered his binoculars. He'd been right to suspect Kane would move in fast, but he hadn't expected him to attack from the South tunnels as well as the East and West. Even had soldiers stationed near the North tunnels. Smart move. Then again, Kane had always been smart. It was one of the things Sebastian had learned to respect about him during his years of service.

Or was it deception?

A scuff of boots against stone froze him mid-thought. Sebastian's muscles tensed, his hand instinctively moving toward the concealed blade at his hip. Three distinct footfalls—one heavy and measured, two lighter but equally deliberate. He turned slowly, keeping his movements casual despite the adrenaline surging through his veins.

Jon Sinclair stood at the cave entrance, silhouetted against the fading daylight, his lean frame casting a long shadow across the stone floor. Starr and Damon flanked him like sentinels, their expressions unreadable in the dim light.

"What the hell happened?" Sebastian asked, keeping his tone steady despite the chaos he'd witnessed through his binoculars. His fingertips brushed against the concealed blade at his hip, a habit born of years living on the edge.

Jon stepped deeper into the space, his face now catching the dim light filtering through cracks in the stone ceiling. Fury etched deep lines around his mouth and eyes, transforming his usually composed features into something harder, more dangerous.

"They found us," Jon said, running a hand through his disheveled hair. "Somehow, Kane found the headquarters. And not just found—he orchestrated a perfect three-pronged attack. East, west, and south tunnels simultaneously. Cut off every escape route we'd established."

Sebastian's stomach twisted. "The evacuation protocol—"

"We barely had time to trigger it," Starr cut in, her petite frame vibrating with barely contained rage as she moved to stand beside Jon. "Half our people were still in the Commons when they breached the main chamber."

Jon paced the small confines of the hideout, boots scraping against stone with each agitated step. "The precision of it... the timing..." He shook his head. "Kane nearly had us." Jon stopped pacing, his face darkening with a mixture of rage and something else—something Sebastian recognized immediately. Respect. "Almost have to admire the bastard's tenacity. His strategic mind..." Jon shook his head, a grim smile twisting his lips. "He anticipated every contingency we'd planned for."

Sebastian nodded, unsurprised by Jon's reluctant admiration. He'd observed both men for years, noting the eerie parallels between them—both possessed that same relentless drive, the same need to dominate any situation, the same refusal to accept defeat. Different sides of the same ruthless coin. It made them formidable enemies, but it also made them dangerously predictable to someone who knew what to look for.

Someone who'd learned to play both sides.

"We lost at least twenty people," Damon added, his voice flat as he leaned against the wall. "Maybe more. Hard to get an accurate count with communications compromised."

Twenty people. Sebastian felt the weight of that number settle in his chest. People he'd known. People who'd trusted the intelligence he'd provided. People who were dead because of choices he'd made—or hadn't made.

His thoughts drifted to McGraff—Jon's father, though few knew that connection. The general wouldn't have abandoned his people. He would have stayed and fought. But McGraff was dead now, found with a bullet in his skull and a message written in his blood. Traitors burn.

Jon had insisted it was Kane's doing. Had used his father's death to rally support, to justify escalation. But Sebastian had seen Jon's face when they'd found the body, had recognized something in those cold, calculating eyes that made him wonder.

After all, Jon had visited his father just hours before the general's death. Had argued that humans couldn't follow two opposing leaders, that Mc-Graff's moderate stance undermined their cause. Sebastian suspected it was about power, not principles. But suspicion wasn't proof, and Sebastian had learned to keep his suspicions to himself.

Sebastian watched Jon carefully, his mind racing through implications. The attack had come sooner than expected. Their intelligence had suggested Kane would wait at least a few days to gather his forces. Either their information was wrong, or they'd underestimated Kane's determination.

His bet was on the latter. Though no one had expected them to breach the headquarters, especially not the way they had. Someone must have provided detailed intelligence—someone who knew the layout, the routines, the weaknesses.

Sebastian pushed the thought away before it could show on his face.

"Starr, Damon," Jon said, breaking the tense silence. "Go check if Jax and Chloe made it to the secondary outpost in the west near the mountains. Then send messages to all our people still in Celearius. Everyone needs to go dark until we regroup."

Starr nodded. "Once the troops have cleared, we'll take some people to see what we can scavenge from the headquarters."

"Good," Jon replied, running a hand over his stubbled jaw. "Hopefully they don't find the silver stash, but I suspect that may be their priority."

As Starr and Damon moved toward the entrance, Jon reached inside his jacket and pulled out a weathered leather tube. Sebastian's breath caught as Jon opened it. A knot formed in his stomach as Jon carefully extracted two large papers. The rebel leader's movements were methodical, almost reverent, as he unrolled the documents and laid them flat against the makeshift rock table in the center of the space.

The plans sprawled across the rough stone surface, edges curling slightly in the humid air. Sebastian stepped closer, studying the intricate diagrams and mathematical formulas that covered the papers. Weapon schematics—complex, deadly, and potentially revolutionary if they worked as designed. Chemical compounds were scrawled in the margins alongside molecular structures.

The plans he'd stolen from Evie's lab. The ones that would end the vampyrs as soon as they figured out which was real.

Or would they? Had he stolen them for Jon, or had he stolen them to keep them from Jon? After the Elite Ball, he was reminded of how deadly the Vampyrs were. He gave them on impulse. In anger.

"Was your scientist able to verify these?" Sebastian asked, tracing a finger along one particularly complex equation without actually touching the fragile paper.

Jon's face hardened. "No. And I didn't get a chance to question Serenity about them, but we need verification." He glanced toward the back of the passage, where darkness swallowed the narrow corridor leading deeper into the mountain. "Is she awake yet?"

Sebastian shook his head. "No, not yet. The sedative was pretty strong."

Relief washed through him at the lie. Or was it regret?

"Let me know as soon as she wakes up," Jon said, folding the plans and sliding them back into the leather tube. "The sooner she's conscious, the faster we can determine which of these plans is genuine. Our other option is likely heading back to Celearius as we speak."

Sebastian nodded, keeping his expression neutral. Had Serenity been the one captured instead of escaping with Kane, she wouldn't have survived Jon's methods of extracting information. The rebel leader's interrogation techniques had grown increasingly brutal as the war escalated—something Sebastian had witnessed firsthand during their time together.

But Serenity was safe with Kane now. Or was she? Safe was a relative term when it came to the Head of the Human Vampyr Council.

"I'll send word immediately," Sebastian promised, careful to maintain eye contact despite the deception. Every second he could buy might make a difference.

But for whom?

Jon's gaze lingered on him a moment too long, assessing, calculating. Then he nodded once before following Starr and Damon toward the entrance. "Don't fail me on this, Sebastian. We're too close to lose now."

The weight of those words settled between Sebastian's shoulders as Jon's footsteps faded into the distance. He waited, counting heartbeats until he was certain Jon had truly departed, then moved toward the back of the space where a narrow passage twisted into darkness.

Sebastian retrieved the battery-powered lantern from its hook on the wall, its pale glow barely illuminating the jagged stone walls as he descended deeper into the mountain's belly.

The passage widened into a small chamber where the air hung stagnant and heavy with the scent of fear and sweat. His footsteps echoed off the stone walls as he approached the metal cage tucked against the far wall. The silver-reinforced bars gleamed dully in the lantern light, creating a ghostly halo around the slumped figure inside.

Sebastian set the lantern down, its light casting long shadows across the uneven floor. He crouched beside the cage, fingers curling around the cool metal bars.

Evie lay curled on her side on a thin pallet within the cage, her auburn hair spilling across the rough blanket like liquid fire. Her elegant features appeared peaceful in sleep, but Sebastian knew better. The silver-reinforced bars would already be affecting her system, weakening her even in unconsciousness. Dark veins had begun to creep up her neck—the first visible signs of silver poisoning.

He took her two days ago. Two days of careful planning, of waiting for the right moment, of executing a capture that couldn't be traced back to anyone. Two days of watching her suffer in this cage while he played his role.

But which role? And for whom?

"Evie," Sebastian whispered, his voice rough with emotion he couldn't quite name. "Baby, we'll get through this. Just hold on a little longer."

She didn't stir. The sedative would keep her under for hours yet. Long enough for Sebastian to figure out his next move.

He reached through the bars, his fingers brushing against her cold cheek. She was dying. Slowly, painfully, the silver leeching the life from her with every passing hour. Jon wanted her alive long enough to verify the plans, but after that...

After that, she was expendable.

Unless Sebastian did something to save her.

But saving her meant betraying Jon. Sebastian had stolen the plans from Evie's lab—plans she'd been working on in secret, plans that could shift the entire balance of power. Plans that could end the war, or escalate it beyond anyone's control.

He'd given those plans to Jon. Or had he? Maybe the plans he'd given Jon were the fakes, and the real ones were still safely hidden in Evie's lab. Or maybe both sets were real, and Evie had created a redundancy. Or maybe both sets were fake, and the real weapon was something else entirely.

Sebastian didn't know anymore.

What he did know was that Evie was dying. That Serenity had escaped with Kane. That Jon had twenty dead rebels to answer for. That McGraff was dead, and his son might be the one who'd killed him.

"I'm sorry," he whispered to Evie's unconscious form. Sorry for stealing from her. Sorry for getting her captured. Sorry for loving her while betraying her. Sorry for everything he'd done and everything he was about to do.

Because he was going to save her. Somehow. Even if it meant destroying himself in the process.

Or maybe he was going to let her die. Let Jon use her to verify the plans, then let the silver finish what the cage had started. Let the rebellion have its weapon, let the vampyrs burn, let the world start over from ashes and blood.

Sebastian stood, his joints protesting after crouching for so long. He picked up the lantern, casting one last look at Evie's pale face before turning back toward the passage.

He had decisions to make. Loyalties to choose.

But first, he needed to figure out which loyalties were his own.

The lantern's light flickered as he climbed back toward the main chamber, shadows dancing across the walls like ghosts of all the choices he'd made and all the ones still waiting to be made.

Behind him, Evie slept on, unaware that her life hung in the balance of a man who no longer knew who he was or what he believed.

And somewhere in Celearius, Kane held Serenity captive, demanding the same truths that Jon wanted from Evie.

The only thing Sebastian knew for certain was that before this was over, he would have to choose.

And that choice would determine everything.

DON'T FORGET!

If Kane and Serenity's story kept you turning pages, if the dark power dynamics of Celearius pulled you deeper into its world, or if you found yourself hoping love could survive betrayal, I would be so grateful if you'd consider leaving a review. Your thoughts help other readers discover **The Elite Series**, and they mean more than I can say to an indie author like me.

MARKED is Book Two in the Elite Series, and the story is far from over. Their journey continues in **DESTINED**, coming **August 2026,** and what lies ahead will test everything they've fought for.

Thank you for reading and stepping into the darkness with me.

Also by Charley Black

The Elite Series
Bound

Marked

Destined – August 2026

Within the Darkness Trilogy
Entwined Within the Darkness

A Dance Within the Darkness

Forever Within the Darkness

Blackwater Chronicles – Standalones
A Symphony of Shadows

A Requiem of Flames – TBA

About the Author

Welcome to the world of **MARKED**, where power, secrets, and desire collide. Writing has been my passion since I was twelve, but this story demanded something deeper. It explores loyalty and betrayal, the burden of impossible choices, and a love that is as dangerous as it is consuming.

I live in Rhode Island with my family, balancing writing, work, and motherhood, while building worlds that exist in the shadows. For me, storytelling is about connection, about pulling readers into a place where trust is fragile, emotions run high, and every choice leaves a mark.

Thank you for stepping into this story. What follows is intense, unpredictable, and impossible to walk away from.

You can connect with me on:
Instagram: @authorcharleyblack
TikTok: @authorcharleyblack
Facebook: @authorcharleyblack
Subscribe to my newsletter:
Website: www.charleyblack.com

www.ingramcontent.com/pod-product-compliance
Lightning Source LLC
Chambersburg PA
CBHW050656290626
47170CB00015B/323